BY
DAWN'S
EARLY
LIGHT

NOVELS BY DAVID HAGBERG
Twister
The Capsule
Last Come the Children
Heartland
Without Honor*
Countdown*
Crossfire*
Critical Mass*
Desert Fire
High Flight*
Assassin*
White House*
Joshua's Hammer*
Eden's Gate⁺
The Kill Zone*
By Dawn's Early Light

WRITING AS SEAN FLANNERY
The Kremlin Conspiracy
Eagles Fly
The Trinity Factor
The Hollow Men
Broken Idols
False Prophets
Gulag
Moscow Crossing
The Zebra Network
Crossed Swords
Counterstrike
Moving Targets
Winner Take All⁺
Kilo Option⁺
Achilles' Heel⁺

*Kirk McGarvey Adventures
⁺Bill Lane Adventures

BY
DAWN'S
EARLY
LIGHT

David Hagberg

A Tom Doherty Associates Book
New York

BY DAWN'S EARLY LIGHT

Copyright © 2003 by David Hagberg

The poems "Annabel Lee," "The City in the Sea," and "To One in Paradise" are from *The Complete Poems of Edgar Allan Poe*, published by Random House.

This book is printed on acid-free paper.

Book design by Jane Adele Regina

A Forge Book
Published by Tom Doherty Associates, LLC
175 Fifth Avenue
New York, NY 10010

www.tor.com

Forge® is a registered trademark of Tom Doherty Associates, LLC.

Library of Congress Cataloging-in-Publication Data

Hagberg, David.
    By dawn's early light / David Hagberg.—1st ed.
      p.   cm.
    "A Tom Doherty Associates Book."
    ISBN: 0-765-30454-6 (alk. paper)
    1. United States. Navy. SEALs—Fiction.   2. Nuclear submarines—Fiction.   3. Bengal, Bay of—Fiction.
    4. Pakistan—Fiction.   5. India—Fiction.   I. Title.

    PS3558.A3227B9 2003
    813'.54—dc21

                                                            2003040017
First Edition: August 2003

Printed in the United States of America

0 9 8 7 6 5 4 3 2 1

This book is for Lorrel

BY
DAWN'S
EARLY
LIGHT

BEGINNINGS

1

0613 LOCAL
BAY OF BENGAL

Even three hundred kilometers offshore from Calcutta, in three thousand meters of water, the sea was stained brown by garbage. The 197-foot oceanographic research ship *Eagle Flyer* made her way slowly to the northeast, roughly parallel to India's east coast, wallowing in the long, oily swells.

Marcella Wallner, a slightly built, plain, almost tomboyish looking blonde, had not been able to sleep despite the air-conditioning in her cabin. The sun was just rising on the horizon and already the outside temperature was one hundred degrees Fahrenehit. But she wasn't tired. She had been out here studying sharks for almost two months with another month to go, and she was still excited. This was exactly what she wanted to be doing, skippering a research vessel, in exactly the right part of the world, the Indian Ocean.

She had sent the night watch below, and sat in the pilot's chair, propping her tiny boat shoes on the compass binnacle. Dawn was her favorite time of the day, when the world was as fresh as it would get; quiet, clean, brand-new like a first love. She chuckled aloud.

Someone came onto the bridge from the research center behind her. She saw his reflection in the window glass. "I thought that I was the only one who couldn't sleep," she said.

"What was so funny?" her chief scientist, Dr. John Simensen, asked. The crew called him Long John because of his tall, lanky frame. Marcella thought he was attractive. They had been sleeping together for the past two weeks.

"I thought maybe I was going crazy. It's going to be hot today, the air stinks, the ocean is like a cesspool out here and I'm loving it."

"You *are* crazy," Simensen said. He kissed the nape of her neck and she shivered. "But the rest of us are crazy too. Any hits on the side-scan overnight?"

"I didn't check." A common belief was that sharks never slept. If that were the case they would be detected by side-scan sonar in roughly the same numbers twenty-four hours a day, unless something else was going on. But it wasn't true. Sharks were just like every other animal; they slept. They even took catnaps—or shark naps.

With their side-scan sonar on, actually there were two units, one on each side of the ship, and recording as they moved slowly through the water. They were searching a swath of ocean a hundred meters on either side of the ship to a depth of one hundred meters. The sharks were easy to pick out by their distinctive shape and characteristic cruising patterns.

But they picked out other objects as well: Japanese fishing floats and nets, waterlogged debris that cruised a few meters beneath the surface, and other marine life. The ocean from just under the surface of the waves to a depth of one hundred meters or more was a very busy place.

The water here was as polluted as any deep ocean spot was in the world, so they were also collecting shark specimens for Mote Marine in Sarasota, Florida. Sharks did not get cancer no matter how terrible their environment was, and no one could figure out why. Maybe they produced a special antibody, maybe it was something genetic, or perhaps in their feeding habits. The answer, if it could be translated into something useful for humans, would win someone the Nobel Prize. At thirty-nine years old and newly divorced, Marcella was happy as a clam to be right in the middle of such an operation, and to be sharing it with an interesting, bright, vibrant man.

She chuckled again.

Simensen started to go back into the research center, but his attention was diverted out the windows to port. "What the hell." He took a pair of binoculars out of the rack and raised them to his eyes.

Marcella sat up and looked to see what had got his attention. The air was hazy. The horizon was an indistinct blur against the ripple-free swells. It took her a moment to pick out the dark, rectangular object jutting out of the water.

"What is it?" she asked.

"It looks like a submarine," Simensen said.

Their first officer, Art Anselmo, stepped through the hatch, a pair of binoculars hanging by a strap around his bull neck, the habitual unlit cigar in his mouth, his khaki shirt already sweat stained at the armpits. "That's exactly what it is. Have they tried to contact us?"

Marcella looked up at the radios. All of them were on and switched to VHE channel 16, or single sideband 2182 kHz, the standard calling and distress frequencies. "No."

"How long have they been out there?" Anselmo demanded. He was agitated.

"I just spotted it," Simensen said. "Who are they?"

"Not one of ours," Anselmo said, studying the submarine's sail. Her deck was still submerged. He was a retired navy chief and he knew that he should know this type of boat, but he couldn't dredge it out of his memory. He'd been an aircraft wrench aboard a carrier, not a CIC punk. But suddenly he did know. It was the Russian boat. A Kilo class.

At that moment an intense, extremely narrow beam of sharp green light shot at an angle from the top of the sail, stabbing the sky like a stationary lightning bolt, then was gone.

"Holy shit," Simensen said. "Was that what I thought it was?"

"If you were thinking laser, you might be right," Anselmo replied. He snatched the SSB handset from the overhead and switched frequencies to the guard channel that the Seventh Fleet had used the last time he was out here eight years ago.

Marcella had never seen him like this in the three years they had worked together. He looked frightened. "What the hell is going on, Art?"

"I don't know for sure. But I think that might be a Russian sub, and it's possible that she fired a laser weapon at something. Maybe a spy plane."

"One of our airplanes?"

Anselmo shrugged. "I don't know."

Marcella stared at the submarine's sail, a sick feeling growing in the pit of her stomach. "If that's true, then it could be we're in the wrong part of the ocean at the wrong time."

"Get us out of here right now, Marcie," Anselmo said, careful to keep his manner controlled. "Best possible speed back to Calcutta. We might be able to outrun the bastard if she tries to chase us. She's not a nuke."

Marcella turned to the ship's controls, switched the autopilot off, jammed the twin throttles full forward to their stops, and hauled the wheel hard to port, the big ship heeling over as she accelerated.

"The sub's about eight or nine hundred yards out, can you angle the port side-scan sonar to see that far?" Anselmo asked the chief scientist.

"I think so," Simensen said. He dragged his eyes away from the warship, glanced at Marcella, and hustled back to the research center.

Anselmo keyed the handset. "Any vessel in the United States Seventh Fleet, this is the research ship *Eagle Flyer*. Any vessel or aircraft of the U.S. Seventh Fleet this is the U.S. documented research vessel *Eagle Flyer*, calling securité, securité, securité." It was the international distress call one step below a Mayday. "We have spotted what appears to be a Kilo class submarine, without numbers or markings, that has just fired what we believe was a laser pulse skyward. Our position is eighteen degrees fifty minutes north; ninety-one degrees thirty minutes east."

The ship came around to a course almost due north. Marcella locked the wheel, grabbed a pair of binoculars, went out to the starboard side, and scanned the horizon off their quarter, spotting the submarine's sail just as it disappeared beneath the surface.

She ducked back inside. "She just submerged, Art."

Anselmo nodded tightly. "Securité, securité, securité, any vessel or aircraft in the U.S. Seventh Fleet, this is the U.S. documented research ship *Eagle Flyer*. Our position is eighteen degrees fifty minutes north; ninety-one degrees thirty minutes east—" He glanced over at the instrument cluster. "We're making twenty-five knots on a course of two niner five degrees."

Simensen skewed the side-scan sonar to its shallowest angle, allowing them to see more than one thousand yards out. He raised the gain on the computer monitor in time to make out the bulk of the submarine, which was heading down. An instant later a small object was ejected from the bow of the sub. It seemed to hover for a second or two before it made a wide sweeping turn and headed directly toward the *Eagle Flyer*.

Simensen reared back so fast that he almost fell on his ass. "Holy shit," he mumbled. He hit the key for scale and when the numbers came up he turned and bounded forward to the bridge. "They just fired a torpedo at us," he shouted.

Marcella turned toward him, her mouth open in disbelief. But Anselmo switched the SSB to the emergency guard frequency. "How long to impact?"

"Maybe thirty seconds."

"Sound the abandon ship alarm," Anselmo ordered Marcella.

"Can't we outrun the torpedo, or get out of its way or something?" she demanded in desperation.

"No," Anselmo said. He keyed the handset. "Mayday, Mayday, Mayday. This is the U.S. documented research vessel *Eagle Flyer*. Position eighteen degrees fifty minutes north; ninety-one degrees thirty minutes east. We have twenty-seven POBs, repeat, twenty-seven POBs. We have just been fired on by an unidentified submarine—"

Marcella looked at Simensen and shook her head. She could not believe that this was happening. They weren't at war with anybody. They were a goddamned research ship looking for sharks.

She reached up and hit the klaxon alarm and then got on the ship's PA. "All hands, all hands, this is the captain. Abandon ship! Abandon ship!" She could hear her amplified voice booming throughout the boat. Goddamn the bastards, it wasn't fair.

Anselmo was calling the Mayday, and he reached up and grabbed a handhold to brace himself.

Marcella did the same, and Simensen braced himself in the doorway.

"All hands, all hands, this is the captain. Abandon ship, abandon—"

A tremendous explosion lifted the stern of the *Eagle Flyer* completely out of the water, driving her bows beneath the surface.

Marcella was flung forward, her body smashed into the control panel and then catapulted through the windshield toward the oily swells. Her last thought before she passed out was to wonder if the red ball she was seeing down a long tunnel was the explosion at the stern of the boat, or the rising sun.

2

1923 EDT
NATIONAL RECONNAISSANCE OFFICE
LANGLEY, VIRGINIA

A dozen pictures-in-picture on the big screen in the pit showed real-time images downlinked from the U.S. constellation of intelligence gathering satellites. The screen's in-motion wallpaper showed a Mercator projection of the earth with the current tracks of all 327 spy birds. One of the pictures had gone blank ten minutes ago, and despite Air Force Tech Sgt. Donald Day's best efforts, he wasn't able to restore the downlink.

A quick diagnostic on the Ku band, as well as a sideband of the 440 MHz channel, indicated that the *Jupiter* satellite was up and functioning on the most basic of levels; she was producing electricity from her solar sails to charge her batteries, though the voltage indicators he was looking at were fluctuating strangely. He didn't think he'd ever seen anything like it. But *Jupiter* was no longer producing product, nor was she responding to any commands from ground control.

Sergeant Day slid to an adjacent console facing the big screen and brought up the Astronomical Database out of NORAD in Cheyenne Mountain. There were no unusual solar flares predicted or observed that would affect the bird. He did a quick diagnostic on three other satellites to make sure he wasn't missing something, perhaps a meteor shower in the region. Two of them were the CIA's KeyHole series, the third was a GOES around twenty-four-thousand miles out in a geosynchronous orbit over the Indian Ocean. All three satellites were functioning with nominal ranges.

Next he dialed up Space Command's database of orbiting junk. Everything larger than an orange from hundreds of space missions that had been left behind either by accident or on purpose was plotted on a continuous basis until their orbits decayed and they burned up in the atmosphere. There was nothing closer than five miles in an orbit thirty miles higher than the *Jupiter.*

Finally he brought up the NRO's own schedule of outages due to maintenance routines in case he had missed the NTO (Notice to Observers) when he had come on duty a couple of hours ago. But the daily log was blank for this satellite.

He slid back to his own console and got on the Autovon link to Col. Tom Leonard, the Jupiter program's night duty mission commander.

"This is Kermit Control. I'm showing a failure of JayBird four at approximately zero-zero-sixteen zulu."

"Stand by," Colonel Leonard said.

Sergeant Day looked up at the big board. This was the third satellite in as many weeks to go bad. Coincidence? He sincerely doubted it. But what the hell was going on?

"I'm showing the same thing," the colonel said. "Rerun your diagnostics, and then pull up the last frame numbers. I want to know what she was looking at the exact moment she stopped transmitting."

"Yes, sir. I'll have that done in the next few minutes."

Colonel Leonard prepared the flash message for the Jupiter program's end users, which included the National Security Agency, the Central Intelligence Agency, the State Department, and the Office of Naval Intelligence.

Five minutes later Sergeant Day phoned back with the confirmation that JayBird four went down at 0013 GMT, at a set of orbital coordinates that put her over the Indian Ocean just as dawn was breaking there. This information along with the last several images taken by the satellite were transmitted to the Jupiter program as updates to the original flash traffic.

Forty-five minutes later Colonel Leonard's red phone from the CIA's Directorate of Operations next door chirped, and he picked it up.

"Jupiter Control."

"For Christ's sake, tell me that it's not happened again, Tom," his friend Preston Luney, who was pulling night duty on the technical means desk in the DO, said. They had gone through the Air Force Academy together, and had served on a half dozen assignments during their careers. Leonard had continued in the air force while Luney had resigned his commission. Ironically they ended up working next door to each other.

"You're seeing what I'm seeing," Leonard said. "That makes number three."

"Well, it's no coincidence. We've got a team on the ground in Pakland depending on that feed. What else can we put in position, and I mean pronto?"

Leonard had anticipated the problem and the request. He had dialed up every satellite that could possibly be swung into position to cover the gap left by the out of commission JayBird. "It's slim pickings, Press. The best we can do is move *Albatross-seven* up there. The satellite was one of the older KH-11 series. "But it'll take at least twenty-four hours, and the angle will be real low."

"Okay, do the best you can," Luney said. "What about the last frame?"

Leonard had the last image that the satellite had produced up on his monitor. "What do you mean?"

"Was that an external event, or was the bird already heading into failure mode?"

The image was normal except for a green spot in the middle of the frame. "We think it was a laser strike from a surface source."

"Shit," Luney said. "I was afraid you were going to say something like that."

3

Interservice Agency chief of internal security for the depot, Col. Gonde Harani, put down the telephone with a surprisingly steady hand despite the decision he had to make. But he had a job to do, a responsibility to Pakistan.

The countdown clock showed T-minus seventeen minutes and a few seconds. At this point a specially modified Fokker 27 transport was at ten thousand meters about two hundred kilometers up range and heading for the drop zone. The weather was right, the American *Jupiter* satellite was blind, and the test was a go.

The television images transmitted from the surface one hundred meters above the control room showed a panoramic view of the desert to the west toward the distant border with Iran, and to the south toward the Sihan Mountain range, which was a dark blue smudge on the horizon. This was the most isolated spot in all of Pakistan; far enough from the Indian border so that there would be no possibility of a misunderstanding, and far enough from Islamabad that there would be no prying eyes until the test was completed.

One hundred twenty-seven handpicked personnel here and at the four front-range observation bunkers were geared up for the drop. Colonel Harani guessed that each of them was either thinking of Allah or was pissing in his pants, or both.

After this morning the entire world would be compelled to look upon Pakistan in a new light. The respect would be so immeasurable that even the new government in Islamabad would be able to do little except go along with the new order of things. Little Pakistan would be feared, especially by her neighbors, especially by India, whose army would never again be a threat.

Even the presidents of the United States and Russia, and the premiers of Great Britain and China, would be forced to concede that the dominant force in this region was Pakistan, not India.

Dar el Islam was an ideal whose time had finally come around again. It wouldn't be like Osama bin Laden's warped version of the teachings of Muhammed, but Islam would rise again to the greatness that it once knew.

But not this morning.

Girding himself for what he had to do, Colonel Harani got to his feet and threaded his way down three tiers of computer and control consoles to the test director's position, manned this morning by Army Chief of Staff Gen. Karas Phalodi. Harani was a short, slender, diffident-looking man, especially next to the general, who at six-three was huge by Pakistani standards.

The general looked up, his broad features fiercely determined. As a young officer he had been captured by an Indian border patrol and had spent four years of unimaginable torture in a POW camp before he was finally repatriated. No one in Pakistan wanted this test to succeed more than General Phalodi.

"What is it, Colonel?" the general demanded.

"We have a problem, sir," Colonel Harani said calmly. Only the fact that he was an officer in Pakistan's all-powerful intelligence service, the ISI, allowed him to get so close. He reached out, uncaged the range safety switch, and flipped it to red before anyone had a chance to realize what he was doing, let alone stop him.

The countdown clock halted at T minus 00:16:23. On the surface a red flare rocketed into the sky. Warning klaxons sounded throughout the test range. Aboard the inbound Fokker, alarms went off in the cockpit, and the drop and firing circuits were locked out. Even if the crew wanted to drop the bomb on target they would not be able to do it.

The aircraft commander throttled back and began a slow turn to the left while maintaining altitude, and radio silence. He was following the operations book to the letter. He involuntarily pissed into his bladder bag.

General Phalodi recovered his composure. He got to his feet as his security people, realizing that something was going on, came running. The general gestured for them to halt, as he looked down at Colonel Harani, his legendary temper just barely in check by sheer dint of will. Even so it was several seconds before he could speak, his features a mask of rage.

"What is our problem, Colonel?" he asked in a precisely measured voice.

"My security people at the southern perimeter bunker detected the presence of a small incursion force."

General Phalodi looked over at the radar consoles, but the chief operator glanced at his scope and shook his head.

"Not by air, General. They are ground troops," Harani said. "Three, possibly more."

"Has this threatening ground force been identified?"

"Not yet, sir."

"Had the test gone as scheduled, wouldn't they have been incinerated?"

"No, sir. They have taken up a position behind some sand dunes. As long as they kept their heads down they would have survived."

"After which time your security people could have rounded them up?"

"Yes, sir," Colonel Harani said, not daring to look away. "But not before they could have transmitted information vital to Pakistan's security to their handlers."

"What information would this be, Colonel?" the general demanded. "The entire world will know very soon that we have developed a thermonuclear device."

"Yes, sir. But only an observer on the ground would realize that we have developed a hydrogen bomb small enough to be carried by an airplane, and therefore possibly by a missile."

"But no communications are possible because of the lingering effects of radiation, is this not a fact?"

"So far as I understand the technology, General. But the Americans may have developed—"

"Who is your second in command?" General Phalodi cut him off.

"Captain Amin."

"Where is he at this moment?"

"With our southern perimeter security forces."

"Very well," General Phalodi said. He pulled out his 9mm Makarov pistol and fired one shot at point-blank range into Colonel Harani's forehead.

The colonel's head snapped back, and he dropped to the concrete floor like a felled ox.

The general holstered his pistol. "Call Captain Amin and tell him that he is now in command of depot security. He is to keep his head down until after the test and then he is to round up whoever is running around out there in the desert."

"Yes, sir," an aide said. He motioned for the general's security people to remove the body, but again General Phalodi waved them off.

"Leave it. Perhaps someone else here needs a reminder of what we are doing."

All eyes were on the general. No one said a thing. No one in Pakistan, not even President Pervez Musharraf, dared cross him. He had the loyalty of the army.

"Recommence the countdown."

0929 GMT
IN THE DESERT SOUTH OF
THE KHARAN DEPOT

Former navy SEAL Lt. Scott Hanson crouched with his CIA insertion team behind a sand dune studying the distant depot through binoculars.

Eight Pakistani soldiers, dressed in ranger desert camos, had been on their trail for the past couple of klicks. They had come on foot, spread out, moving cautiously, their AK-47s at the ready.

Fifteen minutes ago a red flare had shot up into the sky, and just two minutes ago a siren had sounded in the distance.

The ranger commander with captain's pips on his collar tabs raised a hand for them to halt. He turned his head and seemed to be listening to something.

He looked up directly at where Hanson was hiding, stared for a few seconds, then gave the signal for his people to turn back.

They immediately headed for a concrete bunker five hundred meters away.

"What's going on, boss?" Bruce Hauglar asked.

"Looks like they're quitting for now," Hanson said. "I don't like it."

Hauglar and their radioman Don Amatozio climbed up to where Hanson lay, and cautiously looked over the edge at the retreating figures.

"Oh, shit, I was sorta hoping that we'd get to play with them," Hauglar quipped.

In the distance to the north they could see the contrails of a high-flying jet. Amatozio pointed his binoculars toward it.

"Multi-engine," he said. "Could be one of their Fokker transports."

Hanson scanned the depot. Five French-made Alouette III attack helicopters were parked in heavily fortified revetments, the openings facing south. The aircraft were painted in camo patterns. The tie-downs had been removed from their rotors. But there didn't seem to be any personnel around them.

Nor did there seem to be any movement anywhere in the depot except for the rangers heading back on the run.

The Pakistanis were going to test a new weapon system here. Probably a multistage ballistic missile; one that would possibly be fired from an underground silo or bunker.

Hanson and his people had been sent in to find out.

So far they'd been lucky since they'd left Kuwait City five days ago aboard a modified P-3C Orion.

There'd been no real challenges, no threat radar lock ons down the Persian Gulf and out into the Gulf of Oman, because the U.S. navy all but owned these skies.

Then on the farthest loop of her supposed Anti Submarine Warfare training mission, the Orion dropped five packages into the Arabian Sea less than twenty klicks off Gwater Bay on the Pakistan-Iran border before making a 180 back to the barn.

All five chutes were made of RAM7 radar-absorbing material, as were the lightweight black-and-gray coveralls the four CIA special operations officers wore, the covers on the personal equipment pods that dangled five meters beneath each man, and the large canister that rode down on the fifth chute.

Radars from the warships of a half-dozen nations, including the French-made DRBV-20C long-range search radar aboard Iranian vessels; the Russian-made Head Net C Air Surveillance Units aboard Indian ships; and the American-made Spy 1D Phased Array System aboard U.S. ships, along with ground units at Bandar Beheshti, Iran and Jiwani, Pakistan painted the Orion, but no one spotted the units floating to splashdown at 0227, exactly three minutes ahead of schedule.

Five seconds after the big canister hit the water, it automatically opened, splitting into two segments. One inflated into a sophisticated six-man speedboat, the other contained a highly muffled thirty horse-power outboard motor, enough fuel for two hundred kilometers running flat out at thirty-five knots, their surveillance and communications equipment, plus some odds and ends such as C4 Semtex with a variety of fuses, a few Claymores, extra water and emergency rations, and one handheld Stinger missile.

Hanson figured that whatever was going to happen would happen any minute now. Everyone at the depot was under cover, and the rangers coming out to find them had been recalled.

It gave him an itchy feeling between his shoulder blades. Someone or something was taking a bead on him.

For the first time that he could remember he suddenly wanted to be home and not on a mission. He was married and he had two children in Williamsburg. They were the light of his life.

He had an older brother who was the president of the United States, the fact of which was very often the bane of his existance. Getting a job with the CIA after the navy had been all but impossible. And then being assigned to the Company's special operations unit within the Directorate of Operations had just about taken a good word from God himself.

No one wanted the president's brother in harm's way. His value as a hostage would be inestimable. But then Billy Carter had been allowed to practically come and go as he pleased. Even Chelsea Clinton attended college in California and England without too much of a fuss. She had Secret Service bodyguards, but hell, as Hanson explained to his brother, his team would be *his* bodyguards.

In the end it had taken a word from the president himself before Scott was allowed to go to work for the Company. Nobody liked it, least of all the president. But Scott was a strong-willed man.

From the moment he could remember growing up in northern California, his brother had political ambitions. It was the running joke in the family that someday Gerald would be the president.

When it became likely, however, Scott and his family had come under the media microscope. Practically every move they made was scrutinized and analyzed to death. The fact that he had served in the navy as a SEAL was great fodder for shows like *60 Minutes* and *20/20*. And when he'd joined the CIA three months before the election the media went wild.

Which lasted until forty-eight hours after the inauguration when the spotlight on Scott and his family was suddenly switched off.

They had been lucky coming ashore ten klicks east of the Pakistani naval air station at Jiwani five days ago just before dawn. By the time the sun had come up on the first morning, they were already nine kilometers inland, safely across the coastal highway, and well hidden for the day in the scrub.

It was summer, and conditions in the bush were less than ideal: heat, bugs, snakes, warm drinking water, and the occasional Pakistani security patrol. But at thirty-six, Hanson—who was the old man of the group—was, like the others, in superb physical condition.

As soon as it was dark they had moved out, putting another twenty kilometers between themselves and the coast by midnight. Each man carried an eighty-pound load. When they put their packs down their muscles burned and they were soaked with sweat. But they could have continued until dawn if that's what the mission required.

Working only by starlight they unpacked their inflatable paragliders, making certain that the shrouds were in direct untangled line with their harnesses and control lines.

Next, they attached the lightweight titanium folding propellers to the six horsepower backpack-mounted motors and filled the tanks with two quarts of gas, which would allow them to run for four hours before they had to land and refuel.

The glider canopies and shrouds were made of the same RAM7 radar absorbing material as the chutes. The motors were extremely well muffled; the sounds and the exhaust heat were direct skyward. The motors were covered with RAM7 and the propellers were painted with a derivative RAM coating.

The farther inland they got, the sparser the population was and therefore the less chance they had of being heard or spotted. But this near to the coast there were plenty of ears so they were careful.

Hanson dropped back to the base of the depression and unslung his 9mm suppressed Sterling submachine gun. He tested the slide. As he suspected, it was fouled by sand.

Amatozio lowered his binoculars to study what looked to him like a wooden bridge, or maybe even something like a very crude log cabin a long way out on the desert floor. It was possibly twenty-five or thirty klicks away. It had to be huge.

Hauglar turned around to say something to Hanson and Mike

Harvey, who was still having trouble with his leg, when a flash of brilliant light blotted out everything.

Hanson instantly knew what it was.

Amatozio screamed at the same moment that Hauglar flung himself down the side of the sand dune.

"It's a nuke," Hanson shouted.

The back of Hauglar's camo blouse was smoking, and most of the hair on the back of his head was singed off.

Hanson scrambled up the side of the dune, grabbed a handful of Amatozio's pant leg and hauled him down.

A mind-splitting thunderclap burst overhead, making any rational thought totally impossible. A second later the air danced in front of their eyes, the sand jumped as if it was water boiling in a pot on the stove, and the temperature went ballistic so that it was almost impossible to breathe.

Hanson shoved Amatozio facedown into the sand beside Hauglar and Harvey, and the four of them huddled together like helpless animals caught in a raging storm.

5

President of the United States Gerald Hanson awoke from a sound sleep, light coming from the open door to the sitting room. His valet, William Attwood, stood there in his plaid robe and slippers.

"I'm sorry to wake you, Mr. President," he said softly so as not to awaken the president's wife.

"What is it?"

"Mr. Stein is here on urgent business, sir."

"Very well." The president got out of bed; his wife turned over in her sleep. Attwood helped him with his robe and went to get coffee as Hanson walked out to see what problem his chief of staff had brought him. He glanced at the clock. It was a couple of minutes after three.

Hanson was the biggest man to occupy the Oval Office since Clinton. But he wasn't more than average size compared to Brad Stein, who had been a first-string linebacker at Notre Dame all four years. Stein was dressed casually in jeans, a short-sleeve Izod, and boat shoes. He looked like he hadn't slept in a week.

"We have a problem, Mr. President."

"Tell me."

"It's Pakistan, sir. About an hour ago they conducted an above-the-ground test of a nuclear weapon at their Kharan Range."

The president was instantly angry. He could feel his face flushing, his blood pressure rising. "Goddammit. We warned them about the consequences of such a test. What the hell do they think is going to happen now? I got General Musharraf's personal word that there would be no further testing."

"Mr. President, it's worse than that."

"What could be worse than Pakistan testing another atomic bomb?

This time above ground. India will have to do something. I wonder if we can stop them."

"It wasn't an atomic bomb," Stein said.

The president eyed him suspiciously. "What was it then, Brad?"

"According to the CIA, AFTAC classified it as a thermonuclear device. A hydrogen bomb. In the three-megaton range." AFTAC, the Air Force Technical Applications Center at Patrick Air Force Base in Florida, monitored the entire world for indications of nuclear weapons blasts.

President Hanson's knees felt weak for a moment, and his heart fluttered, bile rising in the back of his throat. "God in heaven," he said softly. For a second he didn't know what else to say. But then he focused on his chief of staff. "Who did you get that from?"

"Dr. Tyson called me with the heads-up late last night. But she asked that you not be disturbed until they had something solid." Dr. Carolyn Tyson was director of the CIA.

Now that the second Gulf War was over, China was rattling her sabers again, as were Iran and the PLO. Russia was falling ever more deeply into chaos each day. Sooner or later there would be a revolution and the U.S. would have to stand by to help pick up the pieces and sort out the mess. There were still too many nuclear weapons lying around for us not to interfere. Plus the threat of terrorism was very imminent.

With nuclear parity the India-Pakistan question had been in some sort of a very tense stasis. Although the situation out there was critical, it had not been an impossible one to deal with politically since Afghanistan and Iraq.

Until now.

The blinding of our satellites, especially the *Jupiter*, had been done for only one reason. To keep us in the dark until Pakistan conducted their test.

Not only had crucial and expensive American hardware been damaged, a civilian oceanographic research vessel had been lost with all hands.

Enough was enough.

All along Pakistan had vowed that when it developed a nuclear weapon, the bomb would be an Islamic bomb. All Pakistan's brothers in Allah would have it.

By successfully testing a *thermonuclear* weapon, the stakes had suddenly been increased by an astronomical factor. There were only a few nations that possessed hydrogen bombs. The club was very exclusive and extremely deadly. With the H-bomb Pakistan had suddenly become a world player. No thing or no person in the region would ever be safe again. That included the oil fields, all shipping in the Persian Gulf, the Arabian and Red Seas, and perhaps one-fourth of the population of the entire world.

Combined with Pakistan's government that had been coming apart at the seams ever since it had supported the U.S. over the bin Laden issue, the entire region was on the verge of implosion.

In fact, the world was once again on the brink of nuclear disaster.

"Is Dennis up to speed on this?" Hanson asked. Dennis Nettleton was his national security adviser.

"Yes, sir. He's on his way from Georgetown now."

"As soon as he arrives I want my entire National Security Council convened in the Situation Room." Hanson glanced again at the clock. He'd been dreaming about snorkeling on the Australian Great Barrier Reef. Flying through the fantastically clear water in the middle of millions of brightly colored fish, alone. Absolutely alone. "At five o'clock. I want the lid kept on this until we can work out some sort of a realistic position."

"We'll shuttle them through the tunnel from the Old Executive Building."

"Good. I'm going to get dressed now. Call Dr. Tyson and tell her that I want to see her before the others."

"She's already here, Mr. President," Stein said. "She's waiting outside the Oval Office."

Dr. Carolyn Tyson, the director of the CIA and special adviser to the president on security affairs, held a Ph.D. in international studies. But besides being an academic, she'd served as the first woman navy SEAL. She was one of the rare Washington breed who'd been there, done that.

Carolyn Tyson's appointment had not been among Hanson's first, but hers had certainly been the most contentious. She had almost everything going against her. At forty-three she was the youngest DCI. She was the first woman to hold the post. She was divorced, and as her ex-husband—a navy captain—once said: "Carolyn has a killer instinct, the attitude to go with it, and the mouth to tell everyone to get out of her way."

But she was as brilliant as she was deadly. She had the experience, working first with the Office of Navy Intelligence, then for the National Security Agency as director of special projects, and finally working her way through the ranks within the CIA to become deputy director of operations.

Not one member of the Senate mentioned that she was black, though it was obvious that half the country had expected it to become an issue.

"Very well. Tell her that I'll be down shortly," Hanson said. Stein left and Attwood came in with the president's coffee.

"Are we making an early start of it today, Mr. President?"

"That we are, William. Better pick me something stern to wear. I'm going to have to make some tough decisions."

6

D r. Carolyn Tyson *looked* like a special-warfare operator. Her lines were sturdy. Her hair was cut short for a woman, and she wore very little makeup, though her suits were by Gucci, Ferragamo, or Armani and her shoes were handmade in Italy. She wasn't wealthy, but she'd always been careful with what money she'd earned.

She rose from her chair in the corner as President Hanson came around the corner with Brad Stein and Pam Plummer, his press secretary.

"Good morning, Mr. President," Carolyn Tyson said. She had a pleasant face that wasn't quite beautiful and a million-dollar smile when she was in a good mood.

"Well, the fat's in the fire this time," President Hanson said.

"I'm afraid it's even worse than that," Dr. Tyson replied.

The president glanced at Brad Stein. "I'll be real glad when people around here stop saying that."

Coffee service had already been brought in. Pam served the president. Carolyn Tyson and Stein helped themselves.

"We have an hour and a half before the others start showing up," the president said. "I want to know what the hell is going on and why I wasn't warned about this earlier."

"We didn't know ourselves until it happened," Carolyn Tyson said. "But we suspected that they were going to try something radical at Kharan. We thought maybe it might be a cruise missile, which is why I sent a team over there to look."

"They're at Kharan?"

She nodded. "We've temporarily lost contact with them because of the post-blast atmospherics, but that should clear soon."

"The genie is out of the bottle," Pam muttered. She looked at the president. The thermonuclear genie. The nuclear-countdown clock to Armageddon had just started ticking again and they all knew it.

"Mr. President, Scott is over there. He's the team leader."

The president's eyes narrowed. His lips compressed as if he were biting off a reply. When he spoke it was in carefully measured tones. "My brother is in Pakistan? At Kharan?"

"Yes, sir," Carolyn Tyson said. She did not look away; she held his gaze. "We talked when I became the DCI. Scott was either going to be allowed to do the job he was trained for, the job for which he was hired, or I was going to terminate his employment with the Company. You agreed that it was his decision."

Presidents did not like to be reminded of things they might have said in the past. "What are we doing to get them out of there?"

"Nothing for the moment, Mr. President. Not until we reestablish contact. In all likelihood they're just fine. Surprised, but okay. They're professionals, and Scott is one of the best. He has a good head on his shoulders, and the right training and background for the job. It's why the operations officer picked him for the job and that's why Howard and I both signed off." Howard Nelson was the Agency's deputy director of operations.

The president took a moment to recover his composure. "Very well. Meanwhile New Delhi will want to make a preemptive strike on Islamabad and the Joint Chiefs' headquarters at Chaklala. I can't say as I blame them." Hanson was considered to be the most intensely moral president since Truman. A man's word was his bond. Pakistan and India had agreed to an uneasy truce under what was known as the Malta Declaration, where it had been hammered out two years ago.

But eighteen months ago, one of India's top nuclear scientists had been reported missing when his light plane went down on a flight between his home in Ahamadabad and New Delhi. Neither his body nor any wreckage had been found. There were rumors, however, that Pakistani rangers working a rogue operation had forced the scientist's plane down, killed the crew, and whisked him across the border.

If he was behind the new development, India would be even more rabid to even the score.

"We'll have to convince them not to do it," Carolyn Tyson said.

"Pakistan has never tested a new weapon unless they had others already operational. Even though this test was probably not sanctioned by Islamabad, whoever is running the program is following their established protocol." She looked at the others around the Oval Office. "They've tested one hydrogen bomb in the three-megaton range. City busters, they're called when they're that big. They probably have others. If India were to attack now she would get her nose bloodied. Very badly. The casualties could easily run into the hundreds of thousands. Perhaps the millions. They could even touch off a regional war that China would almost certainly have to get involved with." She looked directly at the president. "So would we."

"What are our options?" a subdued Hanson asked. "Especially considering the possibility that Islamabad may not be in complete control."

"First we need to get our *Jupiter* satellite systems back up and running. Without decent electronic and photographic intelligence we'd be making policy decisions in the blind."

"Is the same group in Pakistan reponsible for the attack on our satellites?"

"Ultimately, though they don't have the laser technology to take out our birds. So one of our primary missions is to find out whose submarine fired the laser and stop them from doing it again."

Hanson's jaw visibly tightened. He was an action president. It ran in the family. "God help the bastards when we find out who they are," he said. "Continue."

"Once we make contact with Scott and his people on the ground, we'll know more, but we'll have to get them out of there. If they're spotted, the Pakistani ISI will stop at nothing to destroy them."

Hanson nodded. "They'll use my brother as a hostage if they realize who he is." Killing foreign hostile submarines and saving American lives, his younger brother's included, was right up his alley.

"Then, based on what we've come up with, you'll have to make the final decision, Mr. President," Carolyn Tyson said. "That will be either convincing Pakistan to take control of its weapons—while at the same time keeping India at bay—or ordering a preemptive strike yourself."

"What would our objective be?"

"Deny them a significant portion of their command structure."

"War," the president said after a long silence.

She nodded. "Yes, sir. It might come down to that. Including sending ground troops."

IN HARM'S WAY

1

0830 LOCAL
OFF BARBERS POINT

The SSN21 *Seawolf* nuclear-powered attack submarine surged away from the west coast of the island of Oahu as if she were impatient to rid herself of the Hawaiian island. An eighteen-foot bow wave curled over her low-slung deck.

She was covered in black anechoic tiles that made her look like an ominous, dark sea monster, which she was. With a full load of fifty Gould Mark-48 ADCAP torpedoes, and Tomahawk antiship and land-attack missiles, she had the capability under the right circumstances and with the National Nuclear Command release authorization to start and finish a world war all by herself.

A whole host of people hated the United States and everything she stood for, but there weren't many who doubted her raw power.

Standing on the cramped bridge atop the sail, Cmdr. Frank Dillon Jr., scanned the waters directly ahead of his boat through a pair of standard issue Steiners. The usual contingent of pleasure boats and inshore fishing vessels had come out to catch their departure.

It was a favorite sport amongst a certain contingent of semi-natives, a lot of them ex-navymen. Longer than a football field and capable of diving to depths of more than eighteen hundred feet, the *Seawolf* was a spectacular thing to see in the wild. Better than whales.

Dillon figured that this was going to be his last cruise as a submarine commanding officer before he was bumped upstairs to boss an entire squadron. At thirty-eight he was a little young for the responsibility that would come with his promotion to 06, but he had the experience.

He'd graduated number seven in the Annapolis class of '84, but he'd come out on top in every other navy school he'd attended. That included the submarine officers basic course (SOBC); submarine officers advanced course (SOAC); prospective executive officers course

(PXO); and the top-gun school for submariners: the grueling six-month prospective command officers course (PCO).

He'd served as an engineering officer in the Sturgeon class *Flying Fish*; chief weapons officer in the LA class *Springfield*; exec aboard the *Key West*, which was another LA class nuclear attack submarine, and finally CO of the *Seawolf.*

At just under six feet, he had sandy hair, a thick mustache, a handsome face, and a lean, well-muscled body of a man who worked out a lot.

He also had an ego. Like just about every other submarine commander. There were less than one hundred nuclear submarines in the U.S. fleet. It was a very elite club. Every CO knew every other CO, and each of them *knew* that he was the best. Everybody on Dillon's boat knew it too. They were the dream team: the Miami Heat, Oakland Raiders, Green Bay Packers, and the New York Yankees all rolled into one.

The boat's motto was: *Hunt it, find it, kill it!* There wasn't a man aboard who doubted that they would be capable of handling whatever was thrown at them, by whoever and wherever.

Directly after Annapolis, when Dillon applied for submarine school, his first hurdle was the interview with the director of naval reactors (DNR), a four-star admiral who answered only to the joint chiefs and to God. Eighteen years ago the DNR was Adm. Mark Morgan, who after the interview told an aide that what most impressed him about young Ensign Dillon was the man's no-nonsense attitude and obvious sincerity.

"Look into that officer's eyes and you'll follow him wherever he leads, because you know that he's telling the rock-bottom truth."

Admiral Morgan, now retired in Madison, Wisconsin, was Dillon's mentor and sometime Dutch uncle.

"Now," Ensign Tony "Teflon" Alvarez said at his shoulder. Alvarez was the *Seawolf*'s navigation officer. He was the only other man in the bridge with the captain and an enlisted lookout, CPO3 Bill Proctor, who was scanning the horizon with binoculars.

Dillon picked up the growler phone. "Conn, this is the captain. Have we crossed the one thousand fathom line?"

"Just now, skipper," his executive officer, Lt. Cmdr. Charles Bateman, responded.

Dillon took a five-dollar bill out of his pocket and handed it to his nav officer, who was grinning ear-to-ear. Alvarez had figured their position by feel. "Not bad, Tony."

"Thank you, sir."

Dillon made one last three-sixty and then picked up the growler phone again. "Sonar, bridge. How's it look?"

"No current subsurface targets, sir. We're clear."

"Very well. Conn, bridge. Prepare to dive."

"Aye, aye, sir," Bateman responded.

"Clear the bridge," Dillon ordered. He started his stopwatch.

The lookout was the first through the hatch down three stories to the control room level, followed by Alvarez.

Dillon remained on the bridge for a few moments. This was the start of a ninety-day patrol. They'd had their leave, now it was time to earn their pay. It would be a long time before they would see the light of day or taste the fresh salt air. He was a submariner to the depth of his soul, but he was leaving behind his twin teenaged daughters and his wife, Jill, whose uterine cancer was in remission, but she had to face it alone.

A snatch of something by Yeats came to mind. Something about getting smarter, but sadder with age. The man knew what he was talking about. He too had been there, done that. Jill had taught him that, along with a lot of other things.

Dillon dropped through the hatch and closed and dogged it, then slid the rest of the way down through the sail. At the bottom he stepped aft into the brightly lit, almost airy control room.

"My hatch is closed and secure," he said. He made a quick sweep of his crew. Everyone was where he should be. Along the starboard side left of the periscope platform were the Lockheed Martin BSY-2 combat data systems consoles that were connected to a network of eighty-three Motorola 68030 processors; the Raytheon Mk. 2 fire control system consoles; and the plotting equipment storage racks.

Behind the Type 21 search periscope and the less powerful but more stealthy Type 5 attack scope were two manual plotting tables. Although the *Seawolf,* like all modern American submarines, was equipped with highly sophisticated inertial guidance systems, course plots were still kept by hand on actual paper charts, despite public announcements to the contrary. Weapons firing solutions were often worked out on paper too, as a backup to the Busy-2 system, and to allow the CO to better visualize what was happening in a four-dimensional world.

A maneuvering submarine, firing an even faster and more maneuverable torpedo at a second submarine that was trying to evade being killed, involved a solution that considered depth, range, bearing, and time to impact. Hard to visualize, even harder to pull off.

Along the port side bulkhead were the electronic navigation consoles and in the forward corner the boat's control station, which was manned by a helmsman and a planesman strapped into bucket seats. Alvarez, also working as diving officer, stood behind them. To his left, the chief of boat (COB), Master Chief Arthur Young, sat at the ballast control panel.

Dillon's XO, Charles Bateman, leaned nonchalantly against the periscope platform rail at the officer of the deck's (OOD's) position, a big grin on his freckled Irishman's face. This too was his last cruise before he was jumped to the PCO course, after which he would get his own boat. He wanted to make this cruise his best. And he'd had twenty bucks riding on Alvarez's navigational skills.

Dillon smiled inwardly, his shoreside problems already fading into that special place when he was underway and engaged in the business of his boat. It didn't get any better than this.

He took off his cap and stowed it in a rack with his binoculars and took Bateman's place.

"What's our status, Tony?" Dillon asked.

Alvarez studied the status board to his left, making sure it was green: All hatches and vents were sealed and all their air tanks were fully pressurized and operational.

"Sir, I have an all-green board," Alvarez replied smartly. "Pressures are normal. We are ready in all respects for dive."

"Very well," Dillon said.

COB Art Young unlocked the controls for each of the ballast tanks.

"Dive the boat," Dillon said. "Make your depth six zero feet."

"Aye, dive the boat, make my depth sixty feet," Alvarez said. He was a product of the Los Angeles barrios, and it was only because the congressman from his district was also a Latino and knew the family that Alvarez made it to the academy. He finished in the middle of his class, but no man wore the dolphins more proudly than he did. It was one thing to cruise a lowrider around the 'hood, it was a quantum leap to cruising a billion-dollar submarine around the ocean.

Dillon nodded to Bateman, who reached up and hit the dive warning. A klaxon sounded throughout the boat.

"Flood main ballast tanks. Ten degrees down angle on the planes," Alvarez ordered.

COB Young opened the valves on the main ballast tanks, allowing water to enter from the sea, giving the boat a slight negative buoyancy. Combined with the forward motion of the boat and the down angle on the planes, the *Seawolf* began to settle. Slowly at first but with a steadily increasing speed.

On the surface the spectator fleet saw the tanks venting high pressure air like a pod of whales blowing their lungs on the surface. Boat horns and air whistles hooted across the water. People applauded. It was the best show in town.

Dillon glanced at the ship's chronometer. "Charlie, message Pearl that we're diving at eighteen-forty-one hours zulu. We're commencing robin redbreast patrol as ordered."

Bateman got on the growler phone to the radio shack forward, and relayed the patrol underway message for transmission.

A red indicator light atop the periscope consoles winked red. "Mastheads are wet," Dillon told his diving officer.

"Aye, sir." Alvarez glanced at the indicator for a visual backup, then looked at his diving panel. "Passing five zero feet."

"Message has been sent and acknowledged, skipper," Bateman reported.

"Very well."

COB Young backed down on the main ballast tanks and started procedures to selectively flood a series of trim tanks that would bring the boat steady and level at sixty feet.

"Ease your angle on the planes," Alvarez ordered.

The planesman pulled back on the aircraft-style yoke and the boat slowed its descent, actually skidding precisely to a stop at a depth of sixty feet.

Dillon looked at his stopwatch and zeroed it. From the moment he'd given the order to prepare to dive until now it had taken six minutes and twenty-five seconds. Not bad for a nonemergency dive. "Good job, Mr. Alvarez," he said. "Check all compartments and all machinery in all respects."

"Aye, Captain." Alvarez passed the order through the boat. All section heads reported back on the integrity to sea and machinery conditions in each of their compartments.

Alvarez turned back to the captain. "All compartments report ready for sea in all respects, sir."

"Very well. Make your course two-seven-zero, increase speed to two-thirds. Prepare for emergency steep angle dive to five hundred feet."

"Aye, sir," Alvarez acknowledged the orders. Their original heading away from Pearl had been on a southeasterly course so as not to reveal to anyone on the surface, including satellites, where they were really going. The steep angle dive was part of a series of maneuvers called angles and dangles to find out if the boat would operate properly under extreme conditions, and that everything was in fact securely stowed.

Dillon turned toward the search periscope when a communications specialist came aft from the radio shack.

"Sir, you have flash traffic," he said. "It came as we were diving." He handed the message flimsy to Dillon.

Z184306ZJUL
TOP SECRET
FM: COMSUBPAC
TO: USS SEAWOLF

///FLASH///

A. SEAWOLF IS ORDERED TO RETURN TO PEARL HARBOR IMMEDIATELY.

B. ALL OTHER MISSIONS AND ORDERS ARE SUPERSEDED.

ADM PUCKETT SENDS

Dillon's first thought was that something had happened to Jill and he was being recalled. But submarines were never turned back from patrols because a crew member's family got sick, not even for a captain. And if the Admiral Puckett who had sent the message was *the* Adm. Joseph Puckett Jr., a member of the joint chiefs, the problem wasn't with Jill.

Something had happened, or was about to happen. Something very important.

He looked up. "Belay that order, Mr. Alvarez," he said. He handed the message flimsy to Bateman.

"Reduce speed to one-third, come right to course three-four-five."

"Aye, reduce speed to one-third, turn right to new course three-four-five," Alvarez repeated. He relayed the orders to the helmsman and dialed back the engine order telegraph for the new speed.

"Prepare to surface the boat." Dillon raised the search periscope and did a quick three-sixty. Most of the specator fleet was starting back. When he popped up behind them they would be in for a big surprise.

The entire crew was momentarily taken aback, but not so much as an eyebrow rose as they complied with the new orders.

The CO was in command of the boat. He knew what he was doing. They trusted him.

2

Admiral on the bridge," the marine sentry announced smartly as CINCPAC Vice Adm. Morris Plan came through the hatch, all five-feet-four inches of him wound up like a coiled spring.

"As you were, gentlemen," he said. He'd been en route from his sea cabin when the general quarters had sounded.

The CVN 72 *Abraham Lincoln*'s executive officer, Cmdr. Frank Valentine, handed the admiral a pair of binoculars. The morning eight hundred miles west of Pearl Harbor was magnificent. Puffy trade-wind clouds scudded down from the northeast in a pale blue sky. The massive nuclear-powered aircraft carrier shouldered the twelve-foot swells with apparent indifference as she made thirty-seven knots on a course of 045, directly into the wind for air operations. An F/A-18A Hornet was suddenly propelled along the deck by the steam catapult and was flung into the air, the boom of her afterburners rattling even the bridge windows.

"Off the starboard bow, sir. About three miles out, low," Commander Valentine said. He had a droopy mustache and hair that was a little too long for the commander in chief of the Pacific Fleet's liking, but he was a cum laude master's graduate of MIT's school of nuclear engineering. The kid was on the fast track for his first command within a year and his first star in less than eight years.

Admiral Plan raised the big Steiners with their motion-damping circuitry and searched for the SH-3H Sea King ASW helicopter that had spotted the Russian submarine. "Where's Chuck?" he demanded.

"Sir, the captain went to the CIC as soon as we found out that the mission was compromised," Valentine said.

Admiral Plan's jaw tightened. "There," he said. The four-man chopper with its distinctive front wheel pants hovered one hundred feet over a spot in the sea where she was keeping a running contact with the Russian nuclear attack submarine she had discovered. "Have we set up a TMA?"

"Yes, sir. CIC had the solution almost immediately."

A TMA, target motion analysis, was a solution to a weapons firing problem. When a target was detected by whatever means—sonar, radar, visual, radio, magnetic anomaly detection (MAD), or by the new blue-green laser system they were testing in secret out here—its position, course, speed, and whatever else could be found out including salinity of the water, currents, and wave heights, were programmed into the computers for a weapons solution. If a weapon connected to the system were to be fired it would find its mark. Missiles, torpedoes, whatever the weapons, they would hit their targets so long as the TMA was continuously kept up to date with the latest information.

"Good, I want a Gertrude in the water, right on top of the sons-abitches, and tell them to get the fuck out of my operational area."

"Admiral, the captain is on it, sir," Commander Valentine said.

The helmsman, talkers, nav officer, and port and starboard lookouts were all suddenly seriously busy with their tasks.

Admiral Plan lowered his binoculars and looked up at Valentine, who towered a full head above him. The bridge aboard American nuclear-powered aircraft carriers always came as a big surprise to first-time visitors. It was small, not much larger than the kitchen in an apartment. Nor was there a spoked wheel controlling the ninety-thousand-ton ship. It was mostly done by computers. The steering wheel was actually smaller than a tea saucer. But to one perched in the central island fifty feet above the flight deck, the view was awesome, as was the obvious power of the ship.

"You're right, Commander," Plan said after a moment. "I'm here simply as an observer. This is the captain's show." He smiled frostily. Admirals do not like to be reminded when they are wrong. But if there was a choice between brains or diplomacy, Plan took brains every time. As CINCPAC he should have been back at Pearl commanding the entire Third and Seventh Fleets, not at sea at the command of a battle group testing the navy's latest top secret ASW toy. But, God, he loved it out here. Observer or not, no one was taking it away from him. Not just yet.

Admiral Plan handed the glasses back to Valentine. "Inform the captain that I'm on my way down to CIC."

"Yes, sir," Valentine said.

"Admiral is off the bridge," the marine sentry said as Plan disappeared through the hatch.

Valentine grabbed the growler phone as he and the others breathed a sigh of relief. Plan's temper was short-fused. "CIC, bridge. Tell the skipper that the admiral is on the way down."

The CIC, combat information center, was the heart of the *Abe's* fighting system. Much larger than the bridge, it was packed bulkhead to bulkhead, deck to overhead with electronic equipment, including the new IBM computer systems that controlled the Mark 29 NATO Sea Sparrow basic point defense missile system (BPDMS) and the 20mm Phalanx close in weapons system (CIWS) cannons. The ship's sensors were controlled from here too, including the SPS-48B, which was a 3D long-range air surveillance radar; the SPS-10F surface search radar; and the SPS-49 2D and SPS-43A air search radars.

Air operations of the ship's twenty-four F-14D Tomcats, twenty-four F/A-18 Hornets, ten A-6E Intruders, and four KA-6D Intruder tankers were directed from here with inputs from the E-2C Hawkeyes, S-3A Vikings, and SH-3H Sea King antisubmarine warfare (ASW) platforms. Inputs from everything in the air were added to data from the *Abe's* battle group of two Aegis cruisers, three guided missile destroyers, and six ASW frigates and destroyers plus four attack submarines.

In total, the *Abe's* fighting force was as deadly as and certainly better run than the entire military forces of most of the world's nations.

It made the CIC a busy place on a calm day, and this morning was anything but calm.

Unlike on the bridge, the admiral's presence was not announced here. There was a muted hum of communications between the air traffic controllers and the pilots in the air. Ninety percent of the *Abe's* aircraft were flying, not only keeping tabs on the one Russian submarine they'd already found, but looking for others, and keeping a safe screen around the *Abe* out to more than one hundred nautical miles. A nuclear aircraft carrier was simply too valuable an asset to lose because of inattention, or adherence to the protocol of rank.

The *Abe*'s commanding officer, Capt. Charles Hurly, stood with the air operations officer, Lt. Cmdr. Harry "Houdini" Hudnut, at a chart table working the problem. Somehow a Russian submarine had gotten inside the battle group's screen, so close to the *Abe*, in fact, that if she had surfaced they could have just about swapped spit wads.

Admiral Plan joined them, and they looked up. "It's your show, Chuck, but what's the story?"

"Just the one sub so far," Hurly said, stabbing a blunt finger on a spot just a few miles east of them. He looked like a serious Drew Carey. "But she's an Akula. The best they've got out here."

"Jesus H. Christ, how in hell did they get so close?" Admiral Plan demanded. They could almost see steam rising off the back of his neck. Like a lot of small men, he had attitude. But Hurly had been the CO of the *Abraham Lincoln* long enough not to be intimidated, not even by three stars. His own first star was in Congress right now.

"I don't know for sure yet, but I have a pretty good hunch," Hurly said. He was angry.

Admiral Plan held back from saying anything, but he fixed the captain with a thousand-yard stare; it was like a mongoose staring down a cobra. They respected each other.

"He was here first," Hurly explained.

"Are you telling me that he was waiting for us?"

"That's what it looks like." Hurly glanced at the chart. "There isn't one chance in a million that he could have gotten through our screens. Vince Howe is driving the *Springfield*. He's on point." The SSN 752 *Springfield* was a Los Angeles class nuclear attack submarine, and Vincent Howe was her CO, among the best in the navy.

"Here we go again," Admiral Plan said. "He knew that we were coming, and he knew exactly where on the ridge that we would be conducting our tests."

"But how?" Hudnut blurted. "Even the people who came out to run Deep Pockets didn't know where we were going until we put to sea. And those who knew where, didn't know why."

Hurly and Plan exchanged a glance. Hudnut had just asked the million-dollar question. ONI, the Office of Naval Intelligence, had been looking for a spy somewhere in the Pentagon for the past two years. His code name was John Galt, the same as the character in Ayn

Rand's novel *Atlas Shrugged,* because everyone wanted to know who the hell he was. He had to be highly placed because he had the inside track on a lot of important projects, like Deep Pockets, to test the next generation submarine detection system. And he had to be very good, because the ONI was no closer to catching him than they had been from the start.

"What do you want to do about the Akula?" Hurly asked.

"We have him boxed in, let's see if we can herd him out of here. In the meantime secure the test."

A communications specialist came over with a message flimsy. "Sir, this is flash traffic from Pearl." He handed it to Captain Hurly.

Z184306ZJUL
TOP SECRET
FM: COMSUBPAC
TO: USS ABRAHAM LINCOLN

///FLASH///

A. ADM MORRIS PLAN IS ORDERED TO RETURN TO PEARL BY FASTEST POSSIBLE MEANS.

B. ALL OTHER MISSIONS AND ORDERS ARE SUPERSEDED.

ADM PUCKETT SENDS

Hurly handed it to the admiral. "This is for you, sir."

Plan read the message, his expression darkening. If Joe Puckett had come to Pearl Harbor in person whatever was happening was big.

Plan looked up. "I need to borrow one of your Tomcats and a driver."

3

1200 LOCAL
PACIFIC FLEET HEADQUARTERS

Many mainlanders believe that Honolulu and Pearl Harbor are on the largest of the Hawaiian islands. It's not true. The state capital and famous navy base are on the much smaller island of Oahu, two hundred miles to the northwest of the big island of Hawaii.

Besides being home to more than 850,000 people, Oahu is also home to dozens of military installations, among them Pearl Harbor Naval Station; Hickham Air Force Base; Aliamanu Military Reservation; Camp Catlin Naval Reservation; Tripler Army Hospital; Camp H.M. Smith Naval Reservation; Puuola Navy Rifle Range; Fort Kamehameha Military Reservation; Fort Shafter; Barbers Point Naval Air Station; Red Hill Naval Reservation; Makua Military Reservation; Dillingham Air Force Base, and many others.

Populated by Polynesians around A.D. 500 and discovered by Europeans in 1778 when the English explorer James Cook landed at Kauai, the islands did not become militarily important to the U.S. until late in the 1920s, when Washington awarded a major dredging contract for Pearl Harbor. A deep-water port for major navy vessels was needed to help protect the vulnerable U.S. mainland.

But it wasn't until December 7, 1941, when Pearl Harbor was attacked by Japanese naval air forces, that the place became famous as well as important.

Careers were made or broken here, Dillon thought as he got out of the navy staff car in front of CINCPAC Headquarters.

He had talked it over with his XO on the way back to port. He had a lot of respect for Charlie Bateman. The man was a steely-eyed submariner of the first rank and was going to make one hell of a CO. There wasn't a man aboard the boat who didn't like the XO, and yet when Bateman had to be a stern disciplinarian or a ruthless driver he didn't hesitate for an instant.

But there was nothing to be read into the message other than what it stated. Dillon was ordered home. If they were taking away his boat they wouldn't have sent a four-star admiral all the way from the Pentagon to do it.

He returned the salutes of the two marine sentries armed and dressed in BDUs at the front doors, unable to tell if he was mostly nervous or curious. A young ensign named Rather met him at the reception desk in the busy lobby.

"Good afternoon, Commander. If you'll follow me, sir."

Dillon fell in behind his escort, who went left down the broad main floor corridor to the elevators at the first intersection. Everyone here wore undress summer whites.

Upstairs on the third floor in admiral territory, they headed to the southeast corner of the building, tall bay windows giving an expansive view of the busy harbor, directly to the office suite of Vice Admiral Morris Plan. The chain of command photographs were mounted on the wall, starting with the president of the United States, the secretaries of defense and navy, chairman of the joint chiefs, all the way down to the commander of Pacific submarine forces (COMSUB-PAC), two-star Admiral Herman Gooding.

The pace wasn't so frenetic up here as it was downstairs; the tones were hushed, most of the doors were closed, and an armed marine sentry in BDUs stood at the door to the CINCPAC's offices.

Dillon had never been to Admiral Plan's office before. The anteroom itself was five times as large as most squadron commanders' entire suites. The floor was covered with thick carpeting. Some Wyeths and a few Indian-southwest desert paintings, the artists of which he didn't recognize, hung on the richly paneled walls. The furniture was out of Buckingham Palace.

The admiral's secretary, a grandmotherly-looking woman with white hair in a bun, and narrow gold-framed glasses on a gold chain, looked up from her computer. Her desk was mammoth. "They're waiting inside for you, Commander," she said, no hint of warmth in her voice. "That will be all, Ensign." If the admiral had iron in his gut she had bar steel for a backbone.

"Thank you, ma'am," Dillon said, suppressing a smile. He knocked once on the admiral's door, girded himself and went in. They might jump his ass about something he'd done, or not done, but they would not criticize *Seawolf* or her crew.

"Here he is," COMSUBPAC Admiral Gooding said, slapping the file he was reading down on the long conference table.

Gooding was boss of all submarine activities in the Pacific. He'd earned the nickname Hermann Göring throughout the fleet because of his World War II Nazi-style shaved haircut. Tall, almost cadaverously thin, with a hawk nose, jutting chin, and Jack Nicholson eyes, he was possibly the ugliest man in the navy. But he was bright, fair, and understanding. Got a problem, take it to Hermann Göring. If he doesn't cut you off at the knees he'll solve it for you. Guaranteed.

He thought Dillon was about the best officer he'd ever worked with. As far as Dillon was concerned the feeling was mutual.

Admiral Plan stood across the table from Gooding, and he gave Dillon a critical once-over, but then nodded. "You made good time, son."

"Thank you, sir."

Seated at the head of the table was four-star Admiral Joseph Puckett Jr., a fiercely determined look on his round, pinkish preacher's face. Under thinning white hair, his pale blue eyes and narrow mouth had fooled many an opponent into believing that he was a pushover: weak and ineffective.

Nothing could have been further from the truth. Puckett's bones were said to be made of pure titanium, and his heart was, in fact, a small nuclear reactor. He regularly devoured other admirals and generals, as well as congressmen and CEOs, and even the occasional president, for breakfast.

He never had a problem with lead, follow, or get out of the way. He knew his place in the chain of command, and when the current chairman of the joint chiefs, Air Force Gen. Joel "Blackcap" Zwemmer, stepped down, Puckett would take his place.

Dillon came to attention and saluted. "Commander Dillon reporting as directed, sir."

Puckett sketched a salute. "Stand down, Dillon, I have a job for you," he said. He was a man of very few words.

"Admiral, I was on the way out on patrol. Robin redbreast off the

China southeast coast. My officers and men are geared for the mission, so I'd just as soon stick it out with them."

"*Seawolf* is out," Admiral Gooding said. "Vince is already en route." He gave Dillon a sharp look. Like shut up already.

"I thought the *Springfield* was with the *Abe*'s battle group, sir."

"The *Springfield*'s been detached. The training mission was scrubbed. The *Abe* is on the way back."

"You got a problem with Commander Howe?" Admiral Plan demanded.

"No, sir. He's a good man."

Vince Howe would be spitting bullets about now, Dillon figured. They'd been rivals since SOBC, with Dillon coming out number one and Howe number two right on his heels. Howe had developed a mild dislike for him that never interfered with their work, but always seemed to be there like a nagging toothache. Taking over the *Seawolf*'s patrol like this was going to chap his ass. Dillon had to suppress another smile. Vince Howe was okay. Number two, but okay.

Admiral Puckett studied Dillon as if he were looking at a curiosity under a microscope. Submarine drivers were a lot like navy jet jocks: egotistical and cocky. The brass tolerated them because it was the pilots and submarine commanders who won wars. "Have you any other objections, commander?"

"No, sir."

Puckett held his stare for a moment longer, then turned and nodded to Gooding. "Brief him."

"Okay, Frank, you're going to have to park your ego outside on this one. You were picked for this mission because you were the best. But when you get back you won't be able to tell anybody about it. Ever. No bragging rights. Vince Howe was told that *Seawolf* developed a mechanical problem, and it's going to stay that way. Clear?"

Dillon groaned inwardly, but he nodded. "Yes, sir."

"We're keeping a tight lid on this because we think it's the only chance we have of saving your life," Gooding explained. "There's a spy somewhere in the Pentagon. Somehow who has access to our sailing orders and mission parameters. Someone who knew what the *Abe*'s mission was. They bumped into an Akula that just happened to be in the neighborhood."

This didn't come as a terribly big surprise to Dillon. Submarine commanders talked to each other. Over the past couple of years there were a number of incidents that seemed to have no rational explanations. Chinese ASW warships just happening to be conducting submarine drills in the Taiwan Strait within hours after an LA sub radioed home with mechanical troubles using SSIX, a satellite link that was impossible to break. Or a pair of long-range Russian Be-12 fixed wing surveillance aircraft showing up off Bear Island in the Barents Sea when an Ohio boomer sub came to a radio depth in response to an ELF message. Incidents like that. There were enough coincidences to make them wonder. This was the explanation. But if it was the one spy, he or she had to be working freelance.

"Your people will remain restricted to the boat. That means no last-minute errands, no phone calls." Gooding glanced at his watch. "We're going to want you out of here ASAP."

"He hasn't been told the mission yet," Admiral Plan said.

Gooding gave Dillon the look. *"Seawolf* is up to the task, Admiral."

He spread out a map of the Eastern Hemisphere from the Arabian Sea and northern regions of the Indian Ocean as far east as the Pacific approaches to Japan, Taiwan, and the Philippines. He stabbed a narrow, bony finger on a spot off India's east coast in the Bay of Bengal.

"About thirty-six hours ago, the *Carl Vinson*'s battle group, on its way up to the Gulf of Oman, picked up a very weak distress signal. The *Vinson* was southeast of the Maldives, at least sixteen hundred miles away, but she managed to pick up enough of the message to make out that a U.S. registered oceanographic research ship, the *Eagle Flyer,* was being attacked by an unknown submarine. They got a position but then the transmission was cut off."

"What happend to the crew? Did they get off?"

"At least three fishing boats responded to the Mayday. They found debris, but no bodies. She must have gone right to the bottom, most of her crew still in their bunks. It was around local dawn."

"Not even one body?" Dillon asked. He was finding it hard to believe the story.

"No," Admiral Puckett said.

"How many were aboard her, sir?"

"Twenty-seven."

"There should have been bodies," Dillon said. "Unless the sub picked them up."

"That's what we're thinking," Puckett said. He motioned for Gooding to continue the briefing.

"There were no markings on the sub, but the person who sent the Mayday thought it was foreign, and probably a diesel boat."

"A Kilo?"

Gooding nodded. "It's possible. Evidently the *Eagle Flyer* stumbled onto something they weren't supposed to see. The sub fired what looked like a green laser beam skyward. That's been confirmed by the NRO. The electronic and optics packages aboard one of their major spy satellites monitoring India's and Pakistan's military activities were knocked out at precisely that moment and from that position."

"We have an independent confirmation that the submarine was not Pakistan's," Puckett said.

"Iranian?" Dillon asked.

"At this point we don't know," Admiral Puckett said. "But a couple of hours later Pakistan conducted an above-ground test of what AFTAC is classifying as a three-megaton thermonuclear device."

Dillon whistled softly. "That's one way of starting a war out there," he said. His wife Jill was a raging liberal, which made for some interesting discussions at the O club. He and Jill were called Beauty and the Beast, with no one willing to admit which one was which. Because of her husband's position she could not join the organizations that she wanted to join, such as the Sierra Club, Greenpeace, or Amnesty International. Instead she kept herself abreast of just about everything that was going on around the world. Elections, revolutions, floods, famines, border wars. Dillon drove attack submarines, and his wife studied the world in order to save it. They were quite the pair, but because of her as well as his own readings and briefings, he knew all about the history behind the struggle between Pakistan and India, and he was not terribly surprised by this news either. He was proud of his wife. She was an independent.

"We want to know whose submarine fired the laser," Admiral Puckett said. "Two other spy satellites have been damaged in the last three weeks. It will stop."

"That boat could be anywhere," Dillon said.

"But we have a timetable," Admiral Gooding said. "We'll know exactly where she'll be and when she'll be there." He pointed to the same spot on the map where the *Eagle Flyer* had been torpedoed. "The space shuttle *Discovery* will be launched on the nineteenth. Two weeks from now. One of her new missions will be to rendezvous with the *Jupiter* and replace her damaged sensors." Gooding looked up. "Over the same spot in the Bay of Bengal."

"And I'll be waiting for her," Dillon said.

"That's the idea, Commander."

4

1400 LOCAL
AT THE DOCK

hat's the story, Captain?" Chuck Bateman asked.

Dillon and Bateman were in the narrow passageway forward of the officer's wardroom, one deck below the control room.

The *Seawolf*'s other twelve officers were already crammed into the wardroom waiting for the CO to explain what was going on. The crew were at their in-port duty stations, in the crew's mess or in their bunks.

"We're heading back out in a few hours with a new assignment. Vince Howe took our patrol."

"Did they give us something good this time?" Bateman asked. With his flaming red hair, freckles, and small-town boyish good looks he could have been a stand-in for an Irish travel poster. Some of the crew called him *Hey, Mikey,* like the little kid in the breakfast cereal ads. Not to his face, of course. He would have cut them off at the knees.

"We're going sub hunting in the Indian Ocean. This time we'll be weapons hot."

A big grin spread across Bateman's face. "All right."

On the way back from the CINCPAC's office, Dillon had thought about the mission and about his crew. Gooding wasn't blowing smoke rings at Admiral Puckett when he promised that *Seawolf* was up to the job. Her crew was the best, and Bateman was the crème de la crème.

Whenever he was given a job, his response was always the same: a big, sloppy Irishman's grin and the two words *all right*. He wanted to run his own boat for one tour, and then retire to become a high school physics teacher back in Boston. But the navy had other plans. He was just too good an officer to lose.

Dillon was torn two ways. He wanted to help his XO, who had become his friend, get what we wanted. Yet he didn't want to lose Chuck to another boat, let alone to civilian status.

This was an important moment in history for him. The right boat, the right crew, and the right mission.

Yeats had written about meeting your fate. Sometimes he played with the poem, changing the words to fit his mood. Jill had taught him that language was plastic, something we could use. Poetry was rare among sub drivers, but for him it was a special and highly refined form of literature, and what subs did was a very special and highly refined form of warfare.

Seawolf was America's newest class of nuclear-powered sub-marines and would remain so until the smaller, lighter Virginia class came into service in the next few years. With a length of 325 feet and a displacement of 8,060 tons submerged, SSN21, the first of her class, was thirty-five feet shorter than Vince Howe's Los Angeles class *Springfield*, yet displaced half again as much.

Equipped with a pressurized water reactor powering two steam turbines, she generated sixty-thousand horsepower. Unlike any other submarine in the U.S. fleet she had no propeller. Instead, *Seawolf* used a pump jet drive, much like Great Britain's Trafalgar class submarines. Her speed submerged was in excess of forty-five knots, and her acceleration was noiseless, vibration free, and nothing short of awesome. There was no propeller cavitation to give them away when they put the pedal to the metal, and along with a range of super-sophisticated accoustical damping techniques she was more like a hole in the water than an actual boat.

All together she was the fastest, most maneuverable, stealthiest, and deepest diving boat in the U.S. fleet. She had better sensors, better computers and battle electronics, and better comms equipment than any other submarine. She had eight thirty-inch torpedo tubes forward for the Mark 48 Mod 4 and ADCAP torpedos as well as a very full complement of Tomahawk and Harpoon missiles and mines.

With even more to come, Dillon thought.

He nodded for Bateman to precede him into the officers' ward-room and they went in. Submarines were too small and cramped, filled with machinery almost everywhere, for the crew to jump to attention every time the captain entered a compartment. But the twelve officers crowded around the long table that was bolted to the deck stiffened slightly, as they looked up in anticipation.

"Good afternoon, gentlemen. We've been pulled off robin redbreast and have been handed a new mission," Dillon said from the head of the table. He didn't sit down. "It's called *urgent suitor.* We're going sub hunting in the Indian Ocean. And we're going in weapons hot. This isn't a drill."

There was a stir, but the wardroom was quiet. Dillon listened for the sounds of his boat, or rather for the absence of noise. Submarines were quiet machines, inside and out. Underway no one shouted, or even raised their voices. The habit carried over in port.

Dillon handed a rolled chart of the Indian Ocean to Bateman. The table was cleared and they spread it out.

"The day before yesterday a Kilo boat came to the surface a couple hundred miles off the coast from Calcutta and fired a laser weapon at one of our spy satellites. In the past few weeks two more of our satellites were fired on and damaged, from the same geographical location."

Dillon pointed to the position on the chart. "An American oceanographic research ship, the *Eagle Flyer,* saw the whole thing and called a sécurité. But the submarine fired on them, and so far as we know there were no survivors among the twenty-seven crew and scientists.

"ONI is just guessing on the type of submarine it was, but I think it's a pretty fair guess. The only nukes we have to worry about are the Chinese and Russians. I was given a fairly high confidence that they had no boats anywhere near there."

The Kilo was a Russian-built diesel electric submarine, and possibly the most successful and widely used sub in the entire world. Like the Russian Kalashnikov assault rifle that three-fourths of all the fighting forces in the world used, the Kilo was a dead simple and exceedingly rugged design. At 230 feet in length, and displacing 3,200 tons submerged, she could make sixteen knots underwater. She carried a crew of around sixty men and officers, and was equipped with six 533mm torpedo tubes and a respectable weapons load. Since she was electric, and therefore had no reactor pumps, she was possibly one of the quietest submarines in the world.

Every submariner had a good deal of respect for the class. In the hands of a good captain and experienced crew Kilos were formidable warships. In addition to HE loaded torpedoes, Kilos were also capable of carrying tube-launched SS-N-15 and SS-N-16 long range nuclear missiles.

"A couple of hours after the satellite was blinded, Pakistan tested another nuclear weapon. This time above ground. The air force believes it was a thermonuclear device."

Their weapons officer, Lt. (jg) Marc "Doctor Death" Jablonski, raised his eyebrows. As far as he was concerned it was only a matter of a few more years before almost every military force in the world went nuclear. When he got out of the navy and finished his Ph.D. in nuclear physics, he wanted to work at Los Alamos on the next generation clean, shock bombs that would kill only people, but leave the environment intact. It would make conventional nukes obsolete.

"The latest satellite that was taken out of service was a *Jupiter* that was put up to monitor both Pakistan's and India's nuclear development programs. We have nothing currently in orbit that can do the same job. Or at least not as good a job. Leaves them a lot of wiggle room.

"In two weeks the space shuttle *Discovery* will be launched. Two days later she'll rendezvous with the *Jupiter* and replace her optics and electronic sensor packages. During at least three orbits on the repair mission, they'll be directly over the same spot in the Indian Ocean where the Kilo fired the laser on three other occasions."

Dillon looked at his officers. Every one of them knew what was coming next, but they wanted to hear their CO give the specific order. He felt ten feet tall.

"Gentlemen, they are not going to fire a laser at our guys aboard the *Discovery,* because we're going to be waiting for them."

"All right," Bateman said.

5

Security on the dock had been super-tight since nightfall. Dillon stood alone on the bridge watching the second of two twenty-one-foot Tomahawk Land Attack Missiles being eased aboard through the weapons loading hatch just in front of the fair water.

The half dozen hard hats crowded around the steeply-angled loading rail were shoreside personnel, experts at weapons-loading procedures.

Most of his crew had no idea what was being loaded, and it would stay that way until they were safely at sea and submerged in a couple more hours. Bateman, Jablonski, Chief Young, and the torpedo room red crew were the only ones in on it.

Bateman came up through the hatch, and looked over the rail. "Number one is secured," he said.

"Good. What's the rumble from the crew, Charlie? Have the section heads been briefed?"

Bateman nodded. "They know we're loading a couple of extra weapons, but they don't know what. I don't think they'd care if they did know. Most of them would think it was cool. Marc does."

Dillon had never kept any essential information from his crew, and especially not his officers, until now. When he'd received his orders he'd glanced over at Admiral Puckett, who looked like an accountant tallying up the ledgers. If the numbers worked out on the plus side, Dillon was in; otherwise he would be relieved of his command on the spot, and someone else would take his place. Another CO, another boat.

The fact of the matter was that only the boomers carried nuclear weapons these days. But he was being asked to load two Tomahawk missiles equipped with the W-80 two-hundred-kiloton nuclear warheads.

The cold war was over; the Russians had gone home to try to straighen out the terrible mess that their economy and government was in. Attack submarines and most surface ships in the U.S. fleet almost never carried nuclear weapons. There was no need for them.

If by chance a nuclear accident happened, or some rogue captain figuring his butt was about to be hung out managed to launch a missile and it detonated on any target anywhere in the world, the U.S. would be in major trouble. If World War III didn't spark off, America's last remaining shred of credibility with the rest of the world would be gone and buried, possibly forever.

Nuclear weapons were nothing more than a deterrent, never meant to be actually used unless all else failed. And the SOP specified *all else*.

> The intention is to give most units a capability to attack land targets and to deter nuclear attack on the U.S. Navy by dispersing a nuclear retaliatory capability throughout the fleet, so that no nuclear attack by any foreign power could destroy the U.S. capability to respond in kind.

Admiral Puckett's argument had been crystal clear to Dillon. Someone in Pakistan arranged to have the U.S. satellites watching over its shoulder put out of commission. They did not care if innocent American civilians were killed. They would not want the shuttle *Discovery*'s crew to fix the satellite. They would try to stop the repair mission. Any interference would be dealt with swiftly and harshly. Pakistan was a nuclear power, and it was controlled by a very unstable military government.

Seawolf was to carry two McDonnell Douglas B/UGM-109 Tomahawk TLAM-N nuclear missiles. If the situation came to it, authorization to release would be sent either by extremely low frequency (ELF) transmission, or via the SSIX high speed satellite submarine communications system.

At that point Pakistan would have been informed that a nuclear armed U.S. submarine was ready to strike. *Seawolf* would be right in the middle of it, with every eye in the world watching.

Dillon watched as the missile disappeared into his boat. It would be slid along torpedo alley through three decks where it would come to rest in its loading rack. The deck openings would be secured and *Seawolf* would be ready to carry out her very clear-cut mission.

Make the rendezvous point. Find the Kilo boat and stop her before she fired at the *Discovery* shuttle repair effort. If possible find out whose navy the submarine belonged to. Report ASAP.

All of that without getting his own boat shot up, and without starting a regional nuclear war that could easily spread to most of the hemisphere.

"Skipper, I don't think that I'd be so enthused about this mission if we were just supposed to go out there and protect one of our spy satellites," Bateman said.

"I know what you mean," Dillon said looking at his XO. The boat and dock were bathed in a harsh violet light that made him uneasy. It was otherworldly. "But our astronauts will be up there. If one of them happened to look down at the wrong time the laser pulse could blind him, maybe even mess up his space suit's life-support system."

"Yeah. And did you take a look at the *Eagle Flyer*'s crew roster? Most of them were scientists, four of them kids, and five of them women."

"I know," Dillon said. Bateman and his wife Kathy had tried for the past four years to have a child without success. Adoption was out of the question because he was gone too much. At least for the moment. In the meantime Kathy's biological clock was counting down. As a result Bateman was a pushover for all women and for any kid under the age of twenty. The younger crew members who knew the score made jokes, but they looked up to him as an older brother, or an uncle.

"They didn't give a damn," Bateman mused.

Dillon watched as the loading gear was lowered back into the boat and the work lights shut off. "As soon as number two is secured and we're put back together, make the boat ready for sea."

"Aye, aye, skipper."

"What about the new crewman we picked up?" Dillon asked.

"Engineer's Mate Bob Crawford. I put his folder on your desk." Bateman took a last look around, then started down the hatch.

"Charlie?"

Bateman looked up. "Sir?"

"They can't do that sort of thing to our people. It's payback time."

A big grin spread across Bateman's face. "All right," he said.

6

Scott Hanson raised his binoculars and studied the barren desert terrain they had crossed in the past thirty-six hours. Looking back, the Kharan drop zone still swirled and seethed in a fantastic dust cloud that would probably last for days. There was little or no wind down there.

The depot seemed so impossibly far away now, and yet so close for all the effort they'd put into getting out of there after the blast.

Now they were being hunted like animals. It was the risk that they'd signed on for when they'd put on the uniforms of the SEALs and the army special forces. But those risks were nothing like the ones they'd taken since becoming civilians. Working for the U.S. military meant that if you were captured you stood a good chance of being treated as a POW. But working for the CIA meant that you were a spy and would be treated as such if captured.

That usually meant torture followed by more torture and then even more torture until your heart finally gave out. Not a pleasant way to die, their instructors at the CIA training facility, the Farm, had warned them.

"So don't get caught."

Hanson was trying just that. Arrive. Look. Listen. Then get the hell out of there without the enemy knowing that you were around. But something had gone wrong.

He was trying to spot a dust plume from one of the Russian-made BTR armored personnel carriers they'd seen back at the depot. But nothing moved now down on the hardpan.

He lowered his binoculars and cocked an ear to listen. But there was nothing. If there was anything in the air it was too far away to hear.

Hauglar, waiting below with Amatozio and Harvey, rocked his hand palm down in the sign of a question. Hanson signaled for him to wait and raised the binoculars again.

That someone was coming was a foregone conclusion. Their position at the depot had been compromised. But he had moved his people south toward the mountains, the same way that they had come in, within a couple of minutes after the blast. It was dangerous, but hanging around posed the greater of the risks. Besides, they had stashed most of their equipment in a narrow hollow at about 8,500 feet. It was equipment they would need not only to make their escape, but to survive.

Hanson did another complete sweep with his binoculars. There was nothing. He breathed a little easier.

It was possible, however unlikely, that the Pakistanis thought they were dead. The military had conducted a test and now the entire world knew that Pakistan had made the leap from small-yield atomic bombs to high-yield thermonuclear weapons. It was an even bigger jump in war technology than from Stone Age axes to fifty-caliber machine guns. An atomic weapon was a popgun compared to a hydrogen bomb.

With luck, Jaybird Four, the *Jupiter* satellite watching India and Pakistan, had picked up the one crucial fact that the seismographs and ionization detectors halfway around the world couldn't have possibly found out: Pakistan's hydrogen bomb was small enough to be dropped from an airplane. Don Amatozio had been looking up range toward the northeast. He had paid the price for doing his job all too well and keeping an eye out for a test tower that wasn't there. The wooden structure he had seen was nothing more than a target. It had been ground zero.

Hanson switched off the binoculars' enhancement circuit and stuffed them into a zippered leg pocket of his camo jumpsuit as he made his way down the hill. He tried to raise as little dust as possible. They still had a couple of hours of daylight left, and he didn't want to advertise their presence. It wasn't the guy you spotted who would give you the most trouble, it was the bastard you *didn't* see.

"We're still in the clear," he said, dropping down beside his banged-up crew. Of the four of them, he was the only one who had escaped any injury.

Bruce Hauglar, from Green Bay, Wisconsin—who they called the linebacker not only because of his hometown, but because of his size—had been flash burned on his back and neck. He was in a lot of pain, but so far he had refused any morphine. He was a lot more functional than the other two. As soon as they had gotten clear, Hanson had lathered Hauglar's burns with ointment and had bandaged them against infection and the extremely excruciating chafe from his uniform and equipment straps.

Amatozio, their radioman, was the worst off. He'd been looking up range when the hydrogen bomb went off at about five thousand feet. His face was burned, but the light and heat had also cooked all the liquid out of his eyeballs, instantly blinding him. His pain was almost beyond endurance. They had given him morphine, but they rode a fine balance: Too little painkiller and he would not be able to function, too much and they would have to carry him.

Tall, lean Mike Harvey, who was a fearless expert with just about every type of explosive known to man, had not been injured in the bomb blast. He had been hurt on the third day out. He'd gone down on his left knee when they'd landed to refuel, felt a sharp pain in his calf and moments later a vicious-looking giant scorpion at least eight inches long scurried off. Within a couple of hours his leg had begun to swell and he'd developed a fever, chills, and nausea. He was still weak, and his leg was still extremely painful and swollen to three times its normal size, but he was recovering.

"How much farther to where we left our gear?" Hauglar asked, gritting his teeth. He was sweating, but not because the heat of the day. In fact, the desert was already cooling off. And he wasn't thinking straight.

"Another eight or ten K," Hanson said. "How are you holding out?"

"I'll manage."

He would have to manage, Hanson thought, or all of them would die out here. Hauglar was helping Amatozio, and Hanson had to practically carry Harvey at times. Another ten kilometers, especially up the steep hills and into the mountains, would take them until midnight, if they were lucky.

"Are we near the hills yet?" Amatozio asked. He sat against a rock, holding his head in his hands. His voice was scratchy.

"We're at the front range," Hanson said.

"Try the satcom again. We might be far enough out from the drop zone for us to get through."

The SSIX-Mini was a high speed burst field transceiver that could talk to the same constellation of satellites that were used to get messages to U.S. submarines. A voice message that might take ten seconds to speak was stored in the transmitter's memory where it was compressed into a one millisecond bundle that was encrypted and then flashed to the satellites. Responses were decrypted and reconstituted inside the receiver and came out sounding like computer-generated voices, which in effect they were.

Hanson took the radio from Amatozio's pack and flipped up the boxy six-inch antenna. The transceiver looked like an old-fashioned cell phone except that it was about half the size of a carton of cigarettes and a lot heavier because of the extended batteries.

He switched on the power and when the ready message came up on the display he keyed the tactical channel stored in its memory.

"March hare, March hare, this is spring wind leader. Say again. March hare, March hare, this is spring wind leader. Acknowledge. Over."

March hare was their mission control on the top floor of the embassy back in Kuwait City.

There was no static from the tiny speaker; no sounds, in fact, that would indicate the unit was operating. Only encrypted messages would be recognized and processed. Everything else was blocked out.

"Try again, Scott," Amatozio said.

"March hare, March hare, this is spring wind leader with red warren. Acknowledge. Over."

Red warren was the name of the mission.

There was no reply. Hanson's gaze strayed to the remnants of the thick haze that still hung over the drop zone. It was slowly drifting to the northeast toward the sparsely inhabited mountains of Afghanistan. The upper-level winds and jet stream would eventually tear it apart and disperse it, though there would be fallout. By now there'd be a lot of international outrage over the test. But communications with their satellites were not going to be possible until sometime later tonight. They would have to get much farther south and much higher into the mountains before they would finally be in the clear.

In the meantime they would have to survive.

Hanson shook his head. "We're still too close to the drop zone."

"I didn't really think that it would work this close, but it was worth a try," Amatozio said. He was obviously in a great deal of pain. His head was completely bandaged, making him look like the invisible man in the old movie.

Hanson figured that he would be able to face just about any kind of a debilitating injury: lose an arm or a leg, or even be paralyzed from the waist down like the *Superman* actor. But he didn't think that he could ever take being blind. He wanted to see his children grow up, walk his daughter down the aisle when she got married, watch sunsets with his wife.

Hauglar and Harvey were looking at him.

"We have two choices," he said, putting his morbid thoughts out of mind. "We either find a hiding spot up in the hills and hold out until we can establish comms with Kuwait City—it would be up to them to get us out—or we make it to our equipment drop."

Hauglar shook his head. "Sorry, Scott, but even if we could stay hidden down here long enough with what little food and water we have, it'd be one hell of a rescue operation this far inland. The Pakis are going to be real alert right now considering that they just gave the finger to the rest of the world."

"You're right, but making it all the way up to where we hid our equipment isn't going to be easy."

"Everybody can give me the rest of their rations and most of their ammunition, and I'll stay here," Amatozio suggested. "I sure as hell can fight a delaying action."

"For Christ's sake, you can't see a thing," Harvey said.

"If I hear somebody coming I can lay down some suppressing fire. Make them think—"

Hanson cut him off. "I'm not leaving anybody behind. Not even someone as ugly as you. We all stay or we all go. It's as simple as that."

"Trying to hide out in the hills isn't going to do us any good," Harvey said. "If I have to climb a mountain backwards on my ass because I can't use my leg, it'd be better than getting captured."

"Agreed," Hauglar said.

Hanson looked over his shoulder toward the mountains that rose like a nearly impenetrable wall above them. If they stayed here their chances of survival were nil. But if they attempted to climb eight or ten klicks up into the rugged mountains in the condition they were in, their chances wouldn't be a whole hell of a lot better. But then a little better was still better than zero.

Hanson stuffed the satcom in his own pack and slung it over his shoulders. "Let's move out, we have a long climb ahead of us."

He reached to give Harvey a hand, but the former army special forces lieutenant got up on his own with a grunt of pain. "I might not do the two-twenty in record time, but I'll manage on my own for awhile."

"Are you sure?"

Harvey nodded. "Might even help get rid of some of the stiffness."

"Does it hurt?"

Harvey managed to laugh. "No more dumbass questions, okay, boss? Let's just get going."

Hauglar grabbed his pack and helped Amatozio to his feet. He gave a nod.

Hanson turned and started back up the arroyo to the crest of the first hill, moving slowly, picking the easiest if not the fastest way up. They would have to conserve their strength now as best they could. By tonight the going would be much steeper, the terrain more rugged, and it would be cold.

The trip up into the mountains with the paragliders had been nerve-racking but exhilarating. These weren't the Himalayas, but until Harvey had taken the scorpion sting they had been feeling pretty good about themselves. Afterwards it had become a matter of desperation: getting over the last snow-covered pass that led down to the desert floor and the Kharan test depot on the other side.

Then, as now, Hanson had made the decision not to leave anyone behind. He had wanted to scrub the mission, but the others, especially Harvey, insisted that they had done the tough part. It would be criminal to turn around and head for home now that they were this close.

But it had been a mistake on Hanson's part. One, he thought, that could very well cost them their lives.

Harvey had slowed them down getting into position at the depot, had slowed their escape and now he and Amatozio were seriously handicapping their retreat back up into the mountains. Of course it was a moot point, because once they got to where they'd stashed their equipment and supplies it would be the end of the line for them anyway.

Hanson reached the top of the hill, took out his binoculars, and again studied the way behind them for any signs of pursuit. But the floor of the desert was clear, and he still couldn't hear anything in the air. Even now, of course, his hearing was affected by the bomb blast. In fact, for the first day and night afterwards none of them could hear a thing. It was only in the past couple of hours that their hearing had started to come back to normal.

Hauglar and Amatozio passed Hanson and started down a narrow defile that descended about twenty meters before the path opened up toward the crest of the next hill.

Harvey came up beside Hanson. "Anything?"

"No, we're still in the clear," Hanson said, pocketing the binoculars. They started after Hauglar and Amatozio.

"What happens when we get there, Scott?" Harvey asked. He kept his voice low.

"Well, for one we should be able to talk to red warren. And we'll have food and water and some heavier firepower."

"Right, and then what?"

"That'll be up to Kuwait City—"

"No, it'll be up to Washington, and you know it. We're too goddamned far inland for any kind of a rescue mission to work. But they'll try it anyway because of who you are. No offense meant, Scott, but a lot of good people could get killed."

"No offense taken," Hanson said. "And you'd never make it with your leg."

"My leg isn't the problem and you know that too. But Don is. We have enough fuel left to at least get us over the pass. From there we could conceivably catch thermals all the way back down to the front range hills. Maybe even as far as Panjgur." He glanced at Hauglar and Amatozio. "But you have to be able to see to fly."

"I was thinking about that too. Maybe we could rig some kind of a tandem harness to connect two of the paragliders together."

"It might work."

"What's your point, Mike?"

"Maybe Don's suggestion wasn't so far off the mark after all. If we can reach the equipment drop, one of us could stay with him while the other two went on to the coast. They'd have twice as much fuel."

"Okay, so two of us make it to the coast, and even to our rendezvous point. Then what?"

"We come back the same way we did before, only this time we bring help and the proper equipment to get Don and whoever draws the lot to stay with him out of here."

"How long would it take?"

Harvey shrugged. "Two days to get out, two or three days to get a rescue mission cobbled together, and two or three to get back in."

"At least a week."

Harvey nodded. "There are lots of places for them to hide up—"

Amatozio heard the helicopters first. He said something to Hauglar, who looked over his shoulder then urgently motioned for Hanson and Harvey to take immediate cover.

At that moment Hanson finally heard the choppers too. He and Harvey scrambled to a pile of boulders that formed a narrow overhang. It wasn't much, but it was better than nothing. Along with their camos and the sun at such a low angle they had a reasonable chance of escaping detection.

"There's more than one," Harvey said.

"Three, maybe four," Hanson replied.

The first camouflaged Alouette III chopper flashed over the ridge about a hundred meters to the east. A second and third topped the hill even farther east, but a fourth thundered directly overhead less than fifty meters up.

7

2100 LOCAL
CHARDAR AIR FORCE BASE TEST FACILITY
NORTHERN PAKISTAN

The British-built Sea King Mk 45 helicopter, its rotors slapping the night air, touched down in front of the blast doors guarding what appeared to be a hardened fighter-interceptor bunker. The military markings on its side had been hastily painted over, replaced by the numbers of a naval air unit at Peshawar.

Ground crewmen hurriedly rushed across the tarmac, and as soon as the chopper's wheels were chocked, the side door was opened. A cadre of elite Pakistan rangers dressed in black night fighter camos and armed with American Colt Commando assault rifles formed a defensive line around the helicopter.

The base was dimly lit in the shutdown mode during which no weapons or systems tests were supposedly being conducted. Only the perimeter was illuminated. The interior of the sprawling base, except for a few barracks and administrative buildings, was mostly in darkness. Nor was there any vehicular traffic or any movement other than around the Sea King.

Nothing to catch the eye of an American satellite, if indeed one of the KH-11s had arrived in the southern sky, as they had been warned might happen.

Still, ISI Maj. Gen. Jamsed Asif thought as he jumped down from the helicopter, it paid to be safe—now of all times. The entire Western world had sharply condemned the test. Even Beijing had temporarily recalled its ambassador. Most ominous, however, was the utter silence from New Delhi. Their spies told them that India's armed forces had been placed on the highest state of alert, and even now troops were massing along the border, especially up around Kashmir. But their analysts at Chaklala predicted that the Indians would not attack immediately, as they rightly should have. Instead they would hesitate because of diplomatic pressures from the West, especially from the United States. And because they were facing thermonuclear weapons.

It was a mistake that would cost them the tactical advantage because of one other vital piece of information that they did not have. That and the fact that the most of the world still believed that Pakistan had allied itself with the U.S.

But nothing could be further from the truth.

General Asif was a slight man, like most Pakistanis, with a soft bronze complexion and black hair. He headed Pakistan's intelligence service and at fifty-four he was as fit as most men half his age. It was a fact of which he was inordinately proud.

He did a quick three-sixty sweep and then nodded to the ranger lieutenant in charge of the security detail.

"Now, now," Lieutenant Kaqqa spoke softly into his lapel mic. Moments later the bunker's blast door rumbled open a couple of meters and then stopped.

"It is clear, sir," General Asif said into the dark interior of the helicopter.

Five-star General Pervez Musharraf, Pakistan's military head of state, came to the open hatch and sniffed the night air, as if he was trying to smell an assassin. Like General Asif, he wore black camos with no insignia of rank. His polished boots were bloused, and he wore a black camo fatigue cap.

He was older than Asif, narrow chest, short bandy legs, and the beginnings of a paunch, but he ignored Asif's hand and jumped down from the helicopter unassisted. Even old fools thinking about setting the world on fire had dignity.

"Where is General Phalodi?" he demanded.

"Sir, the general is inside the bunker," the ranger lieutenant replied. "Shall we move your helicopter under cover?"

"Leave it where it is," General Musharraf ordered.

"Sir, do you wish a detail to go with you?"

"No," Musharraf said, and he started across the tarmac toward the partially opened blast doors.

General Asif fell in beside him. "You're taking an unnecessary risk, General," he said.

General Musharraf hid a smile. "Do you think that one of my rocket scientists will try to shoot me because I am giving him free rein to develop his toys?"

"There could be Indian spies—"

"India would have attacked us by now if they suspected what we were up to," Musharraf replied. He seemed to be supremely confident. "Don't worry, Jamsed, very soon our work will be finished and Pakistan will be secure for the first time in her history." He raised his hand in a fist and shook it once as if he had grasped a deadly snake and was breaking its spine. The gesture had become the symbol for tiny Pakistan breaking the will of the mighty Indian military juggernaut poised along her borders.

A ranger detail met them with a pair of electric carts just inside the entrance. They were whisked through two additional sets of blast doors and down a three-kilometer rock tunnel to the cavernous rocket research group's Chardar development and assembly facility. The complex of offices, living quarters, and a huge assembly hall were hollowed out of the living mountain. It could withstand a direct hit by India's most powerful nuclear weapons.

This was the only truly safe spot in all of Pakistan, and yet everyone walked on tiptoes and spoke in whispered tones. They were playing with the ultimate fire here.

Lying prone on their transportation dollies were five TK7 massive three-stage guided missiles. Their nose cones were detached and were being fitted with copies of the thermonuclear weapon that had been tested two days ago at Kharan Depot. The vast cavern hummed with activity. Strong work lights in the rock ceiling and walls illuminated the space like day. At least two hundred scientists, technicians, engineers, machinists, and air force operators worked on the project around the clock.

General Musharraf had never been here before. After Kharan, however, he felt that he had to see for himself what progress they were making. He was impressed.

"Good evening, sir," General Phalodi said, shambling like a shaggy bear from the glass-enclosed communications center. He brought his heels together and saluted.

Musharraf let him hold the pose for a moment or two, then returned the salute. "I came to see for myself if you are on schedule."

General Phalodi was an old warrior. He didn't flinch. "There are technical problems with the guidance systems. My engineers estimate that it will take six weeks to complete the modifications."

Neither man was kidding the other. Musharraf knew about the delay, and Phalodi knew that he knew. Just as both men knew that the real timetable the engineers had given for the repairs was more like three to four weeks.

This time, however, the game that they had played so many times before was no longer possible. "You have two weeks, Karas. All five rockets must be fitted with their payloads, their guidance systems repaired and programmed, and they must be deployed to their launch sites."

"It is a goal to shoot for, General. Considering the pressure we're under from the U.S. because of the Kharan test. But it is possibly an unrealizable goal."

General Asif wondered if Phalodi was thinking about the ISI colonel he had shot to death two days ago because of a similar delay.

"Nonetheless it must be met," Musharraf said. He glanced at the five missiles. They were basically land-launched versions of the French Aérospatiale M4 submarine-launched ballistic missiles. Thirty-six feet long, more than six feet in diameter, the eighty-thousand-pound missiles could deliver a nuclear payload out to distances in excess of four thousand miles. All of India was reachable.

This was just the first step, Musharraf thought. Each of these missiles could carry one three-megaton thermonuclear warhead. Within three years the warheads would be smaller by a factor of six, allowing the TK7s to carry six multiple independently targeted reentry vehicles (MIRVs). Five missiles could deliver payloads to thirty targets.

Even China did not have the means and certainly not the will to accomplish such a feat, though they were Pakistan's allies.

"You are not aware of the latest intelligence from Washington," Asif told Phalodi. "The Americans will launch a space shuttle to repair the *Jupiter* satellite in less than two weeks. It will be blinded again, of course, but we cannot be sure there will not be a retaliation."

"That is our timetable," Musharraf said. "Within twenty-four hours after the event, we must be ready to launch our second and final test so that we can issue our warning to the criminals in New Delhi."

"The Americans may not give us that much time," Phalodi said.

"All of our submarines and surface ships are accounted for. We have plausible deniability."

"That will not last forever."

"No," General Musharraf agreed. "In two weeks Pakistan must be ready to go to war—thermonuclear war—or at least convince the world that we mean to fight or die."

General Phalodi was one man in Pakistan who knew India's will. He nodded. "The rockets will be ready to fly in two weeks, General. And if India believes we are bluffing, or if the United States will do nothing to control them, we *will* launch an all-out attack."

"It would be suicide," Musharraf said.

Phalodi's thick lips compressed. "Then so be it. I would rather we all be incinerated than to allow one Indian soldier to set foot on Pakistan's soil."

Musharraf raised his hand in a fist and shook it once. It was a deadly game they were playing: the stakes were nothing less than Pakistan's survival versus the containment of India once and for all.

8

1200 LOCAL
JOHNSON SPACE CENTER, HOUSTON

Air Force Lt. Col. Paul Thoreau parked his gunmetal gray Porsche Boxter in the STS 140 mission commander's parking place.

The day was brilliantly hot and brassy. The countryside southeast of Houston was dusty brown. The sun reflected harshly off the silvered windows of the JSC headquarters building. No one moved very fast. It was south Texas high summer.

Thoreau, wearing a NASA blue jumpsuit, had been called over from the neutral buoyancy lab where astronauts in space suits, backed up by rescue divers, worked on simulated extravehicular activities in the huge pool. It was almost the same as working in space, but not quite. Close enough for government work, as most of them thought of it.

Thoreau, who had been pulled from the special action programs at Groom Lake, Nevada—known in the popular press as Area 51—was forty-four, short and slender. As a chief SAPs pilot he had what was considered a super cush job; his work was so secret that even his immediate boss back in Washington couldn't be told what he was doing, or if what he was doing was up to par. It was perfect job security; plus it was something new and exciting every day.

Only one thing could have pulled him away. That was the offer of astronaut training. Four years ago he had made the jump. After three missions, his fourth coming up in less than two weeks, he was never sorry that he had made the switch, even after the *Columbia* disaster.

His only problem, if it could be considered a problem, was that he was every journalist's favorite interview. He held a pair of Ph.Ds in math and physics, he and his wife were competitive ballroom dancers, he was the dashing ace-pilot type, and so far as anyone knew he'd never said a harsh word to anybody at any time for any reason.

He was a little annoyed today, though. The powers that be had changed one of the mission tasks in midstream and now they weren't letting his crew train for it without interruption for what probably would turn out to be nothing more than a heads-up for another photo op.

Upstairs, however, he was conducted to NASA director Robert Bishop's office.

"Thanks for coming over so quickly, Paul," Bishop said, coming around his desk and extending his hand. He had an odd, almost hesitant look on his square, ex-marine commandant's face, as if he were seeing Thoreau under a new light.

They shook hands. "We were suiting up for the NB pool."

"Yes, I know. But this shouldn't take too long." Bishop's secretary was at the door. He motioned for her to close it. "No interruptions, Agnes."

"Yes, sir," she said. She withdrew, closing the door behind her.

"Okay, Paul, the president wants to speak to you."

Thoreau was momentarily confused. "Who?"

"The president of the United States wants to talk to you. Encrypted video link." Bishop turned the computer monitor on his desk so that it and the camera were trainined on Thoreau.

"About what?"

"The mission," Bishop said. He touched *enter*, and the NASA logo was replaced by what appeared to be a live image of the White House.

A few moments later the picture was replaced by a live shot of President Hanson seated at his desk in the Oval Office. It wasn't clear if he was alone or not.

"Colonel Thoreau, I'm sorry to interrupt your training routine. You must be very busy this close to a mission. Especially one that we've changed on you."

"That's okay, Mr. President. But I have to say that your call has come as a surprise, sir."

"I want to talk to you about the satellite repair mission."

"Yes, sir. The NRO's *Jupiter*. We understand the need for secrecy."

"You're going up to replace its electronics and optics packages. You were told that they failed. But that's not quite the whole truth. They were destroyed by a laser strike from an earth-based weapon."

Thoreau took just a moment to digest what he was being told. There weren't many nations that had the technical capability to accomplish such a strike. Russia was chief among them. But that didn't make any sense. "Who did it, sir?"

"We're working on that part. But you need to know that whoever is going on the space walk to make the repairs might be in some danger. Whoever blinded our satellite won't want to see it fixed. We're betting that they'll wait until you're finished, and then shoot it again. We don't think that they'd take the risk of injuring one of you. The repercussions would be nothing less than extremely harsh."

"I understand, sir."

"But the possibility does exist that they'll make a mistake," the president warned. "I want you to understand what you're going up against. And I want to give you the chance to back out."

"How badly do we need that satellite, Mr. President?"

"Very."

"Then we'll go up and fix it, sir. That's what we're being paid to do."

"You'll have help," President Hanson promised. "I can't tell you exactly what kind of help, but you and your crew will not be on your own."

Thoreau grinned. "It's always good to have a backstop, Mr. President. We'll do our best."

"I know you will, Colonel."

1305 EDT
THE WHITE HOUSE

President Hanson broke the connection, then looked over at Brad Stein and Carolyn Tyson, who'd listened off camera.

"He didn't ask the million-dollar question," Stein said.

"Which is?"

"Pakistan is obviously behind the attacks because of the test. They didn't want anybody looking over their shoulders. There's no question about that part. But what do they hope to gain? Where's the payoff for them?" Stein was the president's chief of staff, and he was supposed to have the answers. But he was floundering now and he knew it.

"Continue," the president prompted.

"Even if they had a half-dozen H-bombs, they don't have the means to deliver them. At least I've seen nothing from CIA or NSA to tell us otherwise. India's on the verge of rolling across the border in an all-out offensive. China has jumped into the fray, condemning their allies, and even Putin supposedly had a long talk with Musharraf. Pakistan has the H-bomb, but they can't use it or risk total destruction. They've got themselves into a no-win situation."

"Sorry, Brad, but I can't quite agree," Carolyn Tyson said.

Stein shot her an angry look. "What are they going to do with the damn things?"

"First we have to ask what are *we* going to do about them?" she replied calmly. Stein didn't like or trust her, because he thought that she was after his job. And he knew that she was a lot smarter than he was, and it rankled. Especially in discussions like these in front of the boss.

"What?" Stein demanded.

"Nothing, for now. The situation in Islamabad is too unstable for us to make any kind of overt move. Musharraf and most of their leadership is scattered all over the country at the moment, and they have to be watching for India to launch a preemptive strike any second. Given the right nudge they'd launch their weapons and say the hell with the consequences. That is something we definitely do not want to happen."

"What are you suggesting?" the president asked. "Musharraf refuses to talk to me."

"First we repair the *Jupiter*, which will give us the intelligence we need. And Frank Dillon is the right man to run interference for us. My last mission with the SEALs was aboard the *Flying Fish*. He was aboard. He was pretty young then, but he was a good officer. Knew his stuff."

"The shuttle goes up in two weeks," Stein reminded them unnecessarily.

"We haven't heard from our team on the ground yet, but as soon as we do we'll know more."

"What else is there?" Stein asked. "What else have you come up with that we haven't heard about?"

"Mostly speculation. But what if the bomb wasn't fired from a tower or some other ground installation? What if it was dropped from an airplane? Or delivered by a missile?"

"That would tell us they had the means of delivery," the president said unhappily.

"They still wouldn't dare launch an attack on India," Stein asserted.

Carolyn Tyson shook her head. "They wouldn't have to. Just possessing thermonuclear weapons is enough to elevate them to near-superpower status. Once the situation out there stabilizes vendors would be lined around the block all wanting a piece of the action. Exporting H-bomb technology, for instance, could make them a lot of money." She looked inward for a moment. When she looked up again she seemed to have gathered a new resolve. She liked being the DCI, but she hated the world that she'd inherited to keep an eye on.

"What does the CIA advise?" Hanson asked.

"We need to know if the bomb is portable. We need to know if there are others. We need to know if they have delivery vehicles. We need to know where they're being kept. We're assuming Chardar for now. And then we destroy them. Admiral Puckett agrees."

"I see," the president said after a longish silence.

"There's no other option open to us, Mr. President," she said. "A country like Pakistan simply cannot be allowed to have operational H-bombs."

President Hanson nodded, a troubled expression on his face. "As soon as you hear something, anything from Scott, let me know, please."

Tyson's expression softened. "Certainly, Mr. President."

1330 EDT
THE PENTAGON

The spy known to the FBI and ONI as John Galt backed out of the intercept-decrypt program that linked him with the White House computer system. He closed his laptop's lid and looked out his office window toward the river. The day was warm and hazy.

He did not have complete access to every system within the White House, but he'd been able to dig deep enough to find out at least some of what he wanted to know.

The *Discovery*'s repair mission had not come as a surprise to anyone, least of all Galt. But the president's warning, and promise, that the crew would have help was disturbing.

At the very least his customers had to be warned. Then he would have to find out what kind of help the president was talking about. Galt had not heard a thing, which was unusual for a man in his position.

Something had to be done. And he already had a couple of very good ideas.

He grabbed his cap, left his office and headed to the elevators. He kept seeing the look of calm determination on Lieutenant Colonel Thoreau's face. He smiled to himself.

It was so much better to go up against a confident man. The victory was all the more sweet.

INTO THE TIGER'S LAIR

1

P repare to dive the boat," Dillon said into the growler phone. He did a quick three-sixty, then glanced up at the billion stars overhead. No fanfare this time. Only the lights of a couple of fishing boats far away to the south, and the gleam low on the horizon behind them from Honolulu.

And neither the angels in Heaven above,
Nor the demons down under the sea,
Can ever dissever my soul from the soul
Of the beautiful Annabel Lee.

He'd wanted to call Jill. Wanted it with everything in his heart. He was the commanding officer; it would have been easy. No one would have known he'd broken orders. Only he.

He made another sweep, a shutter closing off that part of his mind, focusing him on the job at hand.

"Clear the bridge," he ordered.

"Aye, aye, skipper," Alvarez said. He disappeared into the boat, followed by the lookout, with Dillon right behind them, dogging the hatch.

His crew was in place when he reached the control room. "My hatch is secure," he said, stowing his cap and binoculars. Exact routines were important aboard a warship, especially a submarine. Their lives depended on doing the same task in exactly the same manner every time.

"Skipper, I have an all-green board," Alvarez announced. "Pressures in the tanks are normal. We are ready in all respects for dive."

"Very well," Dillon said. "Dive the boat. Make your depth sixty feet."

"Aye, aye, dive the boat, make my depth six-zero feet," Alvarez repeated the order.

Bateman sounded the warning klaxon, and as Alvarez went through the steps to dive the boat to periscope depth, Dillon pulled down the growler phone.

"Sonar, conn."

"Sonar, aye."

"How's it look, Ski?"

"No subsea targets, Captain," Chief Sonarman Leonard "Ski" Zimenski, came back. "I have numerous surface vessels to the southeast and northwest. Fishing boats, and one large vessel, inbound to Pearl from the southeast. A container ship."

"Very well, keep a sharp lookout. We could be having company at any time. We've been advised that there's at least one Akula about eight hundred miles west, possibly right on our track."

"Aye, skipper. If he's still around, we'll bag him."

Dillon hung up the phone.

He glanced at the masthead indicators. "Mastheads are wet," he told his diving officer.

"The time is fourteen-twelve Zulu, skipper, shall I message Pearl?" Bateman, his hand on a growler phone, asked.

"Negative," Dillon said. "No message to Pearl."

"Ease your angle on the planes," Alvarez told the planesman, and their rate of descent slowed as the chief of boat balanced the trim tanks. They stopped at sixty feet.

"Check all compartments and all machinery in all respects," Dillon said.

"Aye, Captain," Alvarez responded, and he passed the order to all sections from the forward torpedo compartments to the aft engine room.

Dillon raised the search periscope and made a quick three-sixty sweep, and then a second, much slower sweep. There was a jumble of lights to the southeast, and another off to the northwest. White lights stacked up in vertical columns, and red and green lights on either side. They were fishing boats working the waters west of the Hawaiian islands. He could not make out the lights of the container ship, which was still well below the horizon, and there were no other lights in any direction except for those of Oahu, now far to the east, but the Russians were somewhere out there. He could almost smell them.

He wanted a little time before they made contact. If he couldn't make an end run to avoid the Akula, he wanted at least twenty-four hours to get his crew acclimated. It took that long even for the best to be transformed from a shore-based mob to a smoothly operating team of fighting men.

"All compartments report ready for sea in all respects, skipper," Alvarez reported.

Dillon lowered the periscope, and turned to his control room crew. Bateman and Alvarez were looking at him, waiting for their next orders.

Everyone else was busy at their assigned tasks of keeping the *Seawolf* straight and level at precisely sixty feet. It was a task much like trying to balance an inherently unstable whale on a knife edge while moving through a fluid that was in a constant state of change. Salinity, temperature, and subsea currents all had serious effects on a submarine's trim. The distribution of supplies, food, potable water, sewage, garbage—and even personnel—also had their effects. Their speed through the water and the boat's attitude made a difference. At some combinations the *Seawolf*'s hull form was almost impossible to keep under control. Each time they fired a torpedo, or a tube-launched missile, the boat's trim went through the gyrations of the damned.

Sailing a submarine submerged was like flying a helicopter through Jell-O; it was definitely a full-time job, and definitely *not* a hands-off experience.

"Make your course two-seven-zero. Increase speed to flank. Make your depth six hundred feet."

"Aye, sir. Make my course two-seven-zero degrees, increase my speed to flank, and dive to six-zero-zero feet."

Dillon reached up and braced himself. Bateman did the same at the periscope rail. Everyone else not strapped into their bucket seats braced themselves against something.

Within seconds *Seawolf* heeled sharply to starboard, her bows angled downward at twenty degrees, and she accelerated as if she were a fox with a hot poker suddenly stuck up her ass.

Alvarez was ginning ear-to-ear; he was back in the hood cruisin' chicks in his lowrider, only this was a billion times more cool.

His normally unflappable, mild-mannered XO, Charlie Bateman, who wanted his own boat so that he could hurry up and retire to teach high school math and physics, looked like a kid in a Toys "R" Us store. His eyes were bright, his hair was slicked back like an Irish muskrat's, and he leaned as nonchalantly as he could against the periscope platform rail. "All right," he said softly.

Anyone who had ever experienced the *Seawolf* putting the pedal to the metal while turning and diving, couldn't help from feeling like they had strapped on an F/A-18 Hornet and were being catapulted off the deck of a carrier. The accelerations were awesome.

They hadn't gotten to their angles and dangles first time out before they'd been recalled to Pearl, so this would have to suffice. So far Dillon hadn't heard anything serious crashing inside his boat, though he suspected that there'd be loose clothing, maybe a few books or CDs and a few odds and ends breaking loose here and there. But by the time the next watch came on duty everything would be properly stowed.

His chiefs would see to that.

"Passing one hundred feet," Alvarez said. "Ease left on the helm."

Seawolf's starboard heel began to lessen as the helmsman backed off the rate of turn. Their heading passed west-southwest, and the five digital and one analog compasses in the control room all settled slowly on due west.

"Our new course is two-seven-zero degrees. Passing two hundred feet."

Flank speed submerged was forty-six knots, which was a highly classified figure. But the trick in this maneuver was to maintain that exact speed. With the reactor putting out 110 percent power at straight and level, *Seawolf* could achieve her top speed within less than one mile from a standing start. Diving at a sharp angle, however, could add an extra four or five knots.

Alvarez played a delicate balancing act. *Seawolf* entered a highly unstable zone between forty-eight and fifty knots, in which she was susceptible to pitching downward so violently that recovery was theoretically impossible. The submarine could carry them beyond the crush depth.

Dillon had spent a lot of time thinking about the problem. Under certain combat conditions, when they were trying to outrun an enemy torpedo, for instance, they could end up in such a situation. He had developed a maneuver that worked three times out of five in the model tank. He didn't know if he cared to try it in reality, but it was there.

"Passing three hundred feet," Alvarez reported. He picked up the growler phone at his position, and said something to the engine room officer that Dillon couldn't make out. He probably asked for a specific number of propeller revolutions to maintain flank speed on the way down.

"Passing four hundred feet."

Dillon made his way around the periscope pedestal to the plotting tables, where the assistant navigation officer, Ensign Howard "Buster" Brown, was keeping the dead-reckoning paper plot with the compass readings, speed of advance (SOA) that they took from the boat's external sensors, and a stopwatch. Twice during each six-hour watch, the DR plot was checked against the sub's inertial guidance system's position. Their position was updated when they could get a surface fix as well: satellite, celestial, radio beacon, radar, and visual.

Before they got into the Indian Ocean and up into the Bay of Bengal they would have to thread the needle through the Mariana Islands, south through the Philippines, then Indonesia, the lesser Sunda Islands, and finally the Timor Sea. Land masses, reefs, shallows, sea mounts, and warships from a dozen countries would be in their way. All of it negotiated at flank speed. Their initial plots would have to be right on the money.

Brown, a heavyset young man built like a tree trunk with deep-set dark eyes and close-cropped black hair, was next up for SOAC (submarine officers advanced course). His next billet would be as a section head; probably as chief navigation officer. The man was precise. Which was why Dillon had suggested to Alvarez that Brown start their plot.

"Did you get a reliable fix before we submerged?" Dillon asked.

"Yes, sir. I got a couple of good star shots, two independent satellite fixes, three radar bearings on the island, and I'll do bottom profiling on each leg."

"This will be a tight one, Buster. I don't think I'll be able to get you a surface fix until we're on station. I want you to double-check everybody else's work."

Brown grinned happily. "I'm on it, skipper."

"Passing five hundred feet," Alvarez announced. "Ease your angle on the planes."

Seawolf's depth was taken from her keel amidships. Since her length was in excess of three hundred feet it meant that her bows were already approaching six hundred feet. The boat would have to be leveled out, her ballast tanks adjusted so that she would skid to a stop at precisely six hundred feet.

Alvarez had been aboard less than six months, but already he was a master of the maneuver. He had the touch. He was slick. It's why he was called Teflon.

The boat's extreme nose-down angle leveled off slowly. Alvarez spoke to the engine room again. When he hung up he turned to Dillon. "Skipper, we are at six-zero-zero feet, course steady on two-seven-zero, our speed is flank."

"Well done, Mr. Alvarez," Dillon said. He turned to his XO. "As soon as all sections report normal watch routines, I want all my officers in the wardroom."

"Yes, sir," Bateman said, and Dillon left the control room. "Skipper is off the deck; Brown, you have the conn."

"Aye, aye, sir," Brown responded.

Bateman pulled down the growler phone to start assembling the *Seawolf*'s officers. Frank Dillon was a good man; the very best, in Bateman's opinion. He was usually calm, even cheerful, when they got underway. But this time something was eating at him. Bateman figured that the CO hadn't told them everything yet.

AT DEPTH, on a steady course and speed, there was no sense of motion aboard the *Seawolf*. They could have been in a windowless space in the basement of a very large building. Nor was there any noise. All the machinery within the hull was mounted on noise-damping shock absorbers. Second only to the nuclear reactor itself, *Seawolf*'s noise-abatement equipment and techniques were the most secret things aboard.

Dillon's ten officers assembled in the wardroom looked at him with expectant expressions. The only two officers missing were Brown in the control room and Cunningham in engineering.

As of midnight the crew had gone on the eighteen-hour watch system that was kept aboard all U.S. submarines: six hours on and twelve hours off. Since submarines were so confining, the crews were kept busy. In actual fact there was very little time off to lay around and get bored. During a crewman's twelve hours off he was expected to help with KP; attend classes and study sessions to upgrade his rating; do fire and escape drills; do battle stations missile and torpedo; and, if there was time, sleep.

It was no easier for the officers because they and the chiefs conducted the classes and oversaw the drills.

They lived for action. It was what they had spent months and years training for. *Hunt it, find it, kill it,* were not just words on a plaque. They were etched in bronze in the gut of every man aboard.

Now that they were underway and safely submerged, the skipper had something to say to them. And by the look on his face it was going to be good.

"Gentlemen, I'll make this brief," Dillon began. "There are three items of importance that you were not told back at Pearl. I was ordered to wait until now to finish your briefing for security reasons."

Bateman leaned against the door frame, one eye on Dillon and the other on the corridor and the ladder up one deck to the control room. *Seawolf* was not his boat. Nevertheless, he had a proprietary interest in her and her crew that went beyond that of the usual XO. Dillon had a tight crew, starting at the top.

"The first item of importance to you is comms security. For the duration of this mission there will be no, and I repeat, no communications to or from this boat. That means no updated or changed orders or fresh intelligence; and that also means no familygrams."

During a sixty- to ninety-day mission, every man aboard the boat was allowed to receive a three-hundred character message from a loved one ashore every ten days. Called *familygrams*, the messages were vetted by the squadron commanders at Pearl to make sure they contained nothing disturbing; no Dear Johns, nothing about serious family problems, financial troubles, illnesses. The men aboard a submarine, isolated from the outside world, needed to hear only good things.

Since the messages were so short, everyone had their own abbreviations and personal codes. Entire family sagas were boiled down to a few lines.

S&B BOY 2/3 ALL FINE: DAN BRCS OUT:
SCCR FINAL CHAMPS: HSTN TRIP ON: BGSCRNTV
YR BDAY: CAR OK FALSE ALARM: YR MOM HERE
FOR S&B: DAD GLFNG EVERYDY: BBQ FR SDY'S
ANNV. . . .

Shirley and Ben had a baby boy on February third and everyone was doing fine. Their son Danny had his braces out. The Tigers soccer team won at finals, and as state champs they were going to Houston, Texas in March for the nationals. His wife had bought him a big-screen TV for his birthday, which was yesterday. Their car, which they thought had a problem with the transmission, was okay. But buried in that part of the message were the words *false alarm*. On the way down to the boat for this cruise they had discussed the car's repair problem. He had told his wife to get it fixed immediately, no matter what it cost. They thought that she was pregnant and that she would be needing reliable transportation the closer she got to her due date. But her pregnancy was a *false alarm*. His parents had come out to Honolulu for the birth of Shirley's baby. As expected, his dad went golfing every day. Sandy and Josh, their best friends, were having their eighth anniversary, and his wife threw a backyard BBQ for them . . . and more.

Familygrams were the high points of a crewman's week. Cutting them off would be a hardship.

There were a few raised eyebrows, but no one uttered a word. As the CO said, there were no options this time.

"The second item that you need to know was loaded aboard at

Pearl. The two Tomahawks are TLAMs. Land-attack missiles. And they are nuclear."

Someone whistled softly. Attack submarines very rarely carried nuclear weapons since the end of the cold war. No matter how perfect the fail-safe systems were, something could go wrong. Either the accidental launch of a nuke, or an accidental detonation of one aboard the submarine. It could possibly even happen while the submarine was in a friendly port.

The ramifications would be nothing short of catastrophic for the U.S.

"What are our targets, skipper?" Lieutenant Jablonski, their weapons officer, asked. His expression was unreadable, but he was not unhappy. Dr. Death was on the prowl, this time with the real thing.

"Pakistan's military command headquarters at Chaklala, and Chardar Air Force Base where their nuclear weapons assembly facility is located," Dillon let that sink in. "We'll get authorization to release via ELF. It should be the only comms we receive for the duration."

This was news to Bateman, who immediately understood the implication of their orders. ELF, or extremely low frequency, was a method for communicating with submarines while they were submerged. It was very slow; it took fifteen minutes to send one group of three letters. There was a lot of room for errors and miscommunications.

The president or secretary of state was going to tell the Pakistanis to back off. By developing a thermonuclear device, and by blatantly testing it aboveground, the balance of power between India and Pakistan had undergone a very large change, and the Pakistanis were thumbing their noses at their neighbor.

A war was possible, even likely, now.

The *Seawolf*, armed with nuclear weapons, was being sent out not only to make sure the *Jupiter* satellite and the *Discovery* astronauts fixing it weren't fired at, but to prevent such a war.

Seawolf was going to be used as the ultimate "big stick." The message from Washington to Islamabad would be precise: Deploy your nukes and Pakistan will be subject to immediate nuclear attack.

Dillon caught the look of understanding in his XO's eyes and he nodded. Bateman also understood Dillon's dour mood.

"The last item is the reason behind the tight security at Pearl and the reason for our comms blackout. Our actual mission is known only to a very small handful of people. As far as everyone else is concerned *Seawolf* departed on her normal patrol at robin redbreast." He looked at his people.

"If we get into trouble we're on our own. No one will come to rescue us, because no one will know where we are. The route to our AO was left to my discretion." AO was area of operation. "Our lives might depend on it."

"Not from a Kilo boat, skipper," Bateman said, frowning.

But Dillon looked at him and nodded. "If she had the advantage of knowing that we were coming. And when."

"How?"

"There's a spy in the Pentagon. In the navy, maybe operations, maybe even someone in one of the joint chiefs' offices. If he knew that we were on our way, the advantage would definitely *not* be ours."

2

So when the hell were you going to tell us, Paul?" air force Maj. Susan Wright demanded. "Launch morning?"

She had ridden out this morning with Paul Thoreau to watch *Discovery* moving ponderously toward launchpad B. STS140's mission profile, its *entire* mission profile, had shown up on NASA's special projects Web site this morning. No one knew who'd put it there.

Thoreau stopped the NASA pickup truck at the crawler way intersection to wait for the shuttle to catch up. It was a hundred yards behind and moving slowly.

"I didn't have to tell you anything, because the problem's not going to affect the mission," he said. He got out of the truck and leaned against the fender.

Susan Wright climbed out and stormed around the front of the truck to him. She was a head taller than Thoreau, and was the mission pilot. And she was very good. During a competion between the air force's top fliers and navy fighter pilots at a joint top gun school two years ago she had come out on top. It was the women pilots' turn to stick it to the jocks, and she never let anyone forget that she was the best.

"I'd consider someone shooting at us with a laser weapon is a problem that could put a serious damper on a good day," she said. She'd picked up the nickname Mighty Mouse after *Top Gun*. It was shortened to Mouse, and she hated it, but she never let on.

"They won't be shooting at us, Mouse. It's the satellite they want."

The crawler's tracks crushed the gravel in the broad roadway, making noises like pistol shots over the roar of the diesel engines.

"Not much comfort if they miss and put one through a fuel tank," she argued. Thoreau was watching the oncoming shuttle. He turned to her.

"Look, whoever is doing the shooting is good. They've already blinded three of our satellites by shooting out their optics and electronics packages. That's pinpoint accuracy. They *will* not be gunning for us."

"Unless we happen to get in their way," Mouse Wright said. She glanced over at *Discovery*. "Wouldn't take much of a hole at just the right spot to put us into some serious shit, that's all I'm saying."

She took off her aviator's glasses and put them in one of the zippered pockets in her NASA blue jumpsuit. She was an attractive woman, with short blond hair, and fine features.

The sky was clouding over, but no serious weather was expected for another twenty-four hours. By then *Discovery* would be safely out at the pad, ready for launch in twelve days.

"Do you want to back out?" Thoreau asked. "You have the option. It won't reflect on your NASA record."

She shook her head after a moment. "What about Don and the others?"

"I haven't talked to them yet. I just found out myself this morning. We're still trying to find out how the hell that part of the mission statement got put on the Web. But I'd hazard a guess that Leavenworth might be the next address of whoever the hell did it."

Air force captains Donald Wirtanen and Rodney Conners were payload specialists on this mission. Along with their civilian crew member, Dr. Tom Ellis, they were originally scheduled to deliver a large load of supplies and construction equipment to space station alpha.

Ellis, who was a space medicine and zero-G physiologist, would help implement a long-term nutrition and exercise program for the resident astronauts.

Those missions were still a go. But the *Jupiter* repair mission had top priority. All the way from the Oval Office. And it was that part of the information on the Web site that most baffled Thoreau. There weren't many people who knew.

Thoreau watched the oncoming shuttle in silence for a couple of minutes. The fact of the matter was that he hadn't planned on informing the crew about the laser problem until forty-eight hours before liftoff. At that point they would be isolated from the media.

Bob Bishop had added that stipulation. "I'll back you all the way," he'd said. "But we have to keep this quiet. The fewer who know about the real problem, the better it's going to be for you."

"I'd like to give my crew the same chance to back out that the president gave me," Thoreau had argued.

"That'll be their option right up to T-minus five hours. I can promise you that much."

"That doesn't make any sense, Bob, unless a second crew has been trained."

"There are always replacements standing by, you know that."

"I'm talking about the people trained for the repair mission," Thoreau shot back.

Bishop shrugged. "It's a military problem. If your crew can't or won't handle it, someone else will."

Thoreau had almost backed out then and there, except for one trait of his: it was something he sometimes thought of as a character flaw. It was his superman complex. Truth, justice, and the American way. The president had asked for his help and he had given his word. Nothing could make him back out.

"There'll be an MA briefing, won't there?" Mouse Wright asked. MA was *military aspects*.

"Yeah," Thoreau replied without taking his eyes off *Discovery*. She was beautiful, even clamped to the crawler. Ready to fly.

"When?"

"Soon."

"When?" Mouse insisted.

Thoreau looked at her. "Four o'clock this afternoon."

"Good," she said. "We'll be there. And if someone tries to keep us out I'll withdraw and I think I'll be able to convince the others to do the same."

"Like I said, Mouse, that's your option."

"Goddammit, Paul. I'm not fooling around here. Our lives are at stake. It's tough enough achieving orbit without something going wrong that can kill us. I want to know exactly what we're up against. If you can't trust me—trust your crew—to keep the information secret, then how the hell can you trust us to get you up there?"

Thoreau had imagined this exact conversation, but not for another eleven days. She was correct, of course. And Bishop was just going to have to see it their way. If NASA tried to replace his crew they would have to replace him as well.

He nodded. "You're right, Mouse. But no flash photography or tape recordings."

She grinned. "I read you loud and clear, Colonel."

1600 LOCAL
KSC ADMINISTRATION HEADQUARTERS

A dozen senior military officers and a few civilians were seated around the long conference table in the director's briefing room when Thoreau walked in with his crew.

They took their places across from the mission director, who nodded curtly, and then got up and went to the podium at the head of the room.

"Good afternoon, ladies and gentlemen. My name is Scott Buzby, I am STS one-forty mission director. Let's get the introductions out of the way and then get started. We have a lot of material to go over."

Most of the officers were air force and navy intelligence; several worked for the National Reconnaisance Office, which was run by the air force and which controlled the entire constellation of U.S. spy satellites. The *Jupiter* series was not their newest birds in orbit, but they were important.

The civilians worked for the Central Intelligence Agency and the National Security Agency.

John Galt, seated third from the end by the door, could sense the underlying tension amongst the astronauts. But he knew what the cause was, because he had given it to them.

Putting the *Jupiter* mission repair parameters on NASA's Web site had been fairly easy to do. Just the nudge, he hoped, to get someone to slip up.

The president had promised Colonel Thoreau that STS 140 would get help. Galt wanted to know who was going to help, and in what form that help was going to take.

With any luck, he thought, he'd have the answer to both of those questions before he left this room.

3

Ranger Major Khalid Zafar, aboard the bird squadron lead Alouette, strained against his harness in the open hatch to get a better angle on something he thought he saw on the ground. They had searched for a day and a half now, in ever widening circles from the base without luck. Now that they had reached the foothills their job was one hundred times as difficult as it had been on the open desert. Up here there were hundreds of places for the intruders to hide themselves. They were probably CIA, which meant they were professionals.

"Turn back," he radioed the pilot over his headset. "I think I saw something on the ground."

"Yes, sir," the pilot responded. "Was it the hostiles?"

"No, it was something lying on the ground. At the foot of the hill in the narrow wadi."

The helicopter slid off to the left, its nose dipping as it gathered speed in a tight, gut-roiling turn. Zafar braced himself in the doorway and glanced at the six elite ranger special ops fighters. All of them were tough, highly trained young men who knew how to kill and whose conscience never bothered them. For Allah and for Pakistan, the same as the eighteen rangers in the other three helicopters under his command.

Zafar, who at thirty-seven was too old to advance much further than lieutenant colonel, was almost as tough and almost as fast as the men he commanded. But not quite. And he was proud of them. He hoped that they would never know the true horrors of a war that had come down to a struggle between the religions of Pakistan and the gigantic India. Better not to be captured, because the Indians would not kill you. Instead your life would be made a living hell.

His jaws tightened. He'd been a young sergeant on the same patrol in which General Phalodi as a young officer had been captured by the Indian Army Fifth Division at Kishangarh. Together with fifty of their men, they had endured four years of torture, Zafar never once wavering in his loyalty to Allah, to Pakistan, and to his officers. For all of that he had been given a battlefield commission when they were repatriated, and then had been all but forgotten about.

That did not make Zafar bitter. What rankled most was that he and his men had been assigned out here to provide depot security under the direct command of the ISI. Colonel Harani had been a tough, but reasonable man. Something happened to him, however, and Captain Amin had been promoted. He was one of the most narrow-minded, mean-spirited fundamentalist zealots whom Zafar had ever had the misfortune to serve with.

One day Amin would make general. There could be little doubt of it, because he had the right friends, he said the right things at the right time, he knew how to take orders and blame his failures on others, and he would not let anything stand in the way of his ambition. He was a perfect match for the Butcher, General Phalodi.

They had come all the way around, and the pilot pulled up into a hover fifty meters above the wadi at the base of the hills. Zafar didn't need his binoculars to search for the object that had caught his attention on the first pass.

"There," he told the pilot. "Next to the biggest rock. It's a rucksack."

"Got it," the pilot said after a few moments, and he slid off to the east to come down for a landing twenty-five meters from the spot.

"Unit two, I want a perimeter to the west. Three and four stay aloft, and keep your eyes open."

The unit commanders in each of the other three helicopters acknowledged their orders.

As soon as his helicopter was on the ground, Zafar jumped out, deploying five of his men to guard for a possible ambush from the east and south, while he sent the sixth to check out the rucksack for booby traps.

Zafar let his eyes trace the logical route the rest of the way up the wadi and into the hills. He could almost feel their presence here. They had come this far, stopped to rest, and then had continued. Up into the hills, and into the mountains? Were they actually trying to get to the coast?

Corporal Haddid came back with the pack. "Some nine-millimeter ammunition, two canisters of water, some American MREs, a windbreaker, and these." He held up two pairs of clean white socks and a photograph of a young, good-looking woman in a bathing suit.

"He's a man who likes his comforts," Zafar said. He looked again toward the hills. "Perhaps we should return the socks to him."

"Yes, sir," Corporal Haddid said. "I wonder who the girl is?"

Zafar turned the photograph over. On the back the girl had written a line of Xs and a line of Os, and signed it Rosy. "Evidently a sweetheart," he said.

4

1945 LOCAL
IN THE MOUNTAINS

The desert below them was in darkness, but up here the sun was still low on the horizon and the distant higher peaks were brilliantly lit.

Hanson called a halt, and they all sank down gratefully beneath some trees and gnarly bushes. It was starting to get seriously cold. By the time they reached their cache they would be near the snow line. But they had not heard the helicopters in more than an hour.

"What'd it look like?" Amatozio asked.

"What'd *what* look like?" Hauglar asked.

"The sunset. After an aboveground nuclear explosion it's supposed to be fantastic."

"I don't know. I was too tired to look over my shoulder."

"It wasn't much. I think the winds blew the dust away too fast," Harvey said. In fact the sunset had been extraordinary: blues and brilliant hues of greens and reds and violets. But how did you explain that to someone who would never be able to see again?

Hanson took out the satcom, flipped up the antenna, and turned on the power. When the ready message came up, he keyed the *send* button. "March hare, March hare, this is spring wind with red warren, please acknowledge. Over."

The speaker crackled, then fell silent.

"March hare, this is spring wind. Say again. Over."

". . . hare, your . . . is breaking up. Say . . . condition and . . ."

"March hare, this is spring wind. The package was delivered by airplane. Repeat, the package was delivered by airplane. Do you copy? Over."

". . . March hare, say again your position . . ."

"March hare, this is flash traffic. The package was delivered by airplane. The package was delivered by airplane. Do you copy? Over."

The speaker crackled again, but then fell silent.

Hanson keyed the unit. "March hare, March hare, this is spring wind with red warren. Acknowledge. Over."

There was no response.

"March hare, March hare, this is spring wind, acknowledge. Over."

The unit remained silent.

"Sonofabitch," Amatozio said.

"We'll try again farther up," Hanson said. "It's getting better—"

"Who has my rucksack?" Amatozio asked.

Harvey picked up his own pack from where he'd laid it on the ground, then looked around. "I don't have it. I thought you were carrying it." He looked over at Harvey.

"I don't have it."

"Neither do I," Hanson said. "Did you drop it on the way up?"

Amatozio shook his head. "I don't think so. I had it when we left the depot, I know that much. But after that I don't remember."

"What were you carrying?"

"Rations, water, ammo, socks, a windbreaker; shit like that."

"What else? Anything personal?"

Amatozio shook his head. "No—" Then he stopped. "Shit. It was the picture of Rose. I usually keep it in my coveralls vest pocket. But I was looking at it last night, and put it in my pack instead."

"Anything else?" Hanson asked.

"The comsat radio. But you took it."

That was down on the desert where they had stopped in the arroyo. "How about afterwards, Don? Do you remember picking up your pack?"

"I don't think so. Sorry. I must've left it down there."

"If they found it they know that we're up here," Hanson said, getting stiffly to his feet. "Let's go. We have to get this message home."

5

2110 LOCAL
IN THE FOOTHILLS

Base, this is El Eus'Fuur lead," Major Zafar radioed. "Request that we terminate operations for the night. We can't see much of anything and we're low on fuel again."

"Negative, Major. You will remain on duty until you have the infidels," Captain Amin responded from depot security. "General Phalodi is in total agreement with me that the Americans must not be allowed to escape, or to make it to a position where they can radio a message to their home base. We want them captured tonight. That is a direct order."

"There will be accidents—"

"I don't care if your entire God-accursed command is destroyed in the process. You will bring us those men."

"Not on fumes, Captain."

"We're taking care of that right now, Major Zafar. Stand by," Amin ordered.

Zafar looked up at the pilot, who was studiously looking out the windscreen. They were parked in the wadi at the base of the foothills where they had found the rucksack. The pilot was listening to the radio traffic.

"Fuel and special equipment are being sent to you," Amin came back. He gave a grid reference on the mission map that Zafar and the pilot both checked.

The pilot turned around and held up five fingers.

"We'll be there in five minutes," Zafar radioed back. "What special equipment are you sending?"

"Infrared pods for your helicopters and night-vision units for you and your air crews."

Zafar suppressed a slight smirk. He had requested the FLIR pods and the night-vision goggles last night, and Amin had denied the request. The search was to be conducted in a timely, cost-effective way,

"What are your orders, Captain? Specifically. Do you want the Americans dead, or do you want them captured alive? How we must approach them will be of necessity different depending on your orders."

"I want them alive. I don't care how you do it. Do you understand your orders?"

"Yes, perfectly."

"Then do not fail us, Major."

6

Bruce Hauglar opened one of the personal equipment packs, pulled out a light-brown camo jacket that was lined with warm microfibers and helped Amatozio get it on and zippered up. They had stashed the paragliders, extra rations, and most of the weapons and explosives in a wide, shallow cave that was actually just a depression in the side of the hill with a rock ledge for a overhang.

"Thanks," Amatozio said through chattering teeth. "I guess I was colder than I thought I was." Hauglar was like a big brother to him. They were family. They looked out for each other.

Harvey was checking out the Stinger hand-launched missile while Hanson powered up the satcom with fresh batteries. Hauglar sat Amatozio down on one of the packs and opened a beef stew MRE for him, then walked about ten feet down the path where he started to gather firewood. It was very cold up here and it was going to get much colder before the night was over.

"What are you doing, Bruce?" Hanson shouted down to him.

"I'm going to start a fire," Hauglar said. "It'll be damned cold tonight, and without it we're going to end up in bad shape."

"We're not staying here."

Harvey and Amatozio looked up from what they were doing. Hauglar dropped the couple of pieces of deadfall he'd picked up and came back up the path.

"What the hell are you talking about, Scott? Don's in no shape to continue tonight. Hell, none of us are. One slip and fall and it'd be a disaster."

"But that's the way it's going to be. If we stay here we'll die."

"We haven't heard the choppers all night. The Pakis don't conduct mountain operations in the dark."

"Not unless the stakes are high enough," Hanson said. "But my guess is that they went back to refuel and rig for night ops. They have the Chinese FLIR pods, we know that much. And they sure as hell have night-vision goggles."

"Okay, so we can live without the fire—"

"We're all heat sources, goddammit. We stand out like sore thumbs."

"We need the rest."

"We need to stay alive," Hanson shouted. He glared at the others, his anger boiling over. "I'm not leaving anybody behind. I brought you guys this far, and by Christ I'm going to bring you back."

"Hey, guys," Amatozio said after a beat. "You oughtta try this stew. It's not half bad."

The tension between them was suddenly broken. "We can't stay here. It's suicide," Hanson said. "Anyway, you're right, it's going to get very cold, so the sooner we get over the pass and start back down, the sooner we'll all be warm."

Harvey had the Stinger out. Hauglar glanced over at him. "What about all this shit?"

"We're taking it with us," Hanson said, and he held off Hauglar's immediate objection. "We're going to need it. The Stinger, maybe; the Semtex and Claymores for booby traps; the spare ammunition and food."

"What about the paragliders? That's a lot of extra weight."

"We have about three quarts of gas left for each motor. With that much we can cover a lot of ground once we get over the pass. We'll rig something up so that Don and I can ride in tandem."

Hauglar was finally seeing the wisdom of the orders. He hadn't been thinking completely straight because of his burns and he knew it. When all else fails go with the flow, especially if you trust the boss.

He nodded. "Okay. We can toss a lot of the packaging and combine some of the packs. We should be able to save a few kilos that way. But Don rides with me."

"Good. And I want everybody to get something to eat. Could be our last sit-down meal for a while unless we get lucky."

"What's the plan, Scott?" Harvey asked.

"The closer to the coast we can get the easier it's going to be for someone to come get us," Hanson replied. "Ideally we'll get back to the boat and leave the same way we came in."

No one said a thing. Getting to where they hid the boat and finding it still there was wishful thinking.

"Okay, let's get it together," Hanson said. He keyed the satcom. "March hare, March hare, this is spring wind with red warren. Acknowledge. Over."

"Spring wind, this is March hare. Glad to hear from you guys. What's your situation? Over."

Hanson gave a big sigh of relief. Finally. "March hare, we're heading back to easy rider, but I have flash traffic for you. We witnessed the package. It was dropped from an airplane. Repeat: They dropped the package from an airplane." He pulled a map out of a leg pocket and picked off what he figured were the coordinates of their present position. "We are at reference two three niner seven. Repeat: two three-niner-seven. We have casualties. We need immediate assistance. Acknowledge. Over."

Even accounting for the signal compression delays both ways there was no response.

"Shit." Hanson keyed the satcom again. "March hare, this is spring wind. Do you copy? Over."

There was nothing.

Hauglar and Harvey were watching him, and he didn't want to let his sudden despair show. He gritted his teeth and keyed the satcom again.

"March hare, March hare, this is spring wind. Do you copy? Over."

At that moment they heard the helicopters far below them, but definitely heading their way.

7

Frank Dillon, if anyone had stopped to look in on him in his quarters, appeared to be sound asleep sitting up in his desk chair. Nothing could have been further from the truth. He was in the middle of writing his daily letter to his wife and he was listening to a bit of poetry with her.

Actually, this was supposed to be day three of his original patrol, and according to the schedule they made together before each patrol, at this day and at this hour GMT, he was reading Vachel Lindsay's "The Leaden-Eyed." Jill was reading the same poem at exactly the same time.

It was one of his favorites, so he knew it by heart.

The poem described a people who were the exact opposite of his crew. They were limp, hopeless, leaden-eyed. Jill knew how he felt, and it was why she had directed him to the poem. At first reading, he'd looked up at her and smiled. She knew exactly what it was like for him, being the CO of the *Seawolf*. She had given him a gift, and each time he read this poem, which always came within the first few days of a patrol, he could see her face in its every beautiful detail.

"Captain, this is the conn. We have a positive contact," the OOD reported.

Dillon opened his eyes. Every day at sea he wrote a short letter to Jill. She did the same to him. When he came back from patrol they handed each other their letters, and in that way they knew what the other had done and thought and felt during those days apart.

He reached for the growler phone. "This is the captain. What do we have, Charlie?"

"We've got a Russian sub, about eighty thousand yards out and making a hell of a racket. Ski thinks it's Akula-seven. Makes her the *Brezhnev*."

Dillon glanced at the multifunction display over his desk. They were making forty-seven knots on a course of 270° at a depth of six hundred feet. They'd come something over seven hundred nautical miles from Oahu. "Come to all stop. I want silence in the boat. I'm on my way to sonar. Start a fire control track on the target."

"Aye, skipper."

Lindsay was saying that young people would die like sheep. But not here, not aboard his boat, Dillon thought as he left his stateroom.

"Make a hole," he ordered as he reached the stairs to the upper deck.

Crewmen in the passageway and two on the narrow, steep stairs flattened against the nearest bulkhead as Dillon hurried up one deck where sonar was located just forward of the control room.

The boat's twin turbines were spooling down and his XO was on the 1MC ordering *Seawolf* rigged for silent running.

His sonar officer, Lt. (jg) Chuck Pistole, leaned against a bulkhead just inside the sonar room, one cup of a set of headphones pressed against an ear.

"What's the situation?" Dillon asked.

"Ski picked up the target a couple of minutes ago, skipper. A long way out, maybe eighty thousand yards. But he's sure it's Akula-seven on about the same course we're on."

"We were gaining on him, skipper, but he's pulling away now," Chief Sonarman Zimenski said. He'd been on duty for the last eighteen hours. He often pulled four or even five watches back-to-back, especially at the beginning of their patrols and whenever something interesting started to happen. The long hours didn't seem to bother him. If anything, the more he worked the sharper he became.

Besides, he didn't want to miss anything cool. His all-time favorite character was Jonesy the sonarman in Tom Clancy's *Hunt for Red October*. Ski had modeled his life and career on the fictional character, and he always carried a dog-eared paperback edition of the novel in his back pocket. He could quote most of the book line-by-line. Jonesy never missed a thing.

"Still making a lot of noise?" Dillon asked.

"Yes, sir. He's moving out and he apparently doesn't care who hears him."

"Same course as us?"

"Aye, skipper. Same course and same depth." Zimenski looked over his shoulder, his eyes wide. His dark hair was short-cropped, his face was narrow, his nose large, his chin angular. He looked like the survivor of a Holocaust camp; his cheeks sunken, his uniform fitting him like a scarecrow. "It's like he knew that we'd be here and he was waiting for us to catch up to him. He wanted to make sure we found him."

"If she's the *Brezhnev* that's exactly what I think they're doing," Dillon said. He glanced up at the multi-function display. Their speed was already below twenty knots and dropping fast.

The *Seawolf* was equipped with an updated BQQ 5D sonar suite with its huge bow-mounted passive/active spherical array behind the fiberglass bows and the wide aperture passive flank arrays down the sides of the boat. She was also fitted with the TB-16 and TB-29 surveillance and tactical towed arrays, as well as the BQS 24 active sonar system for close-range work.

No other navy in the world had a better system. And yet all submarines, including the *Seawolf*, were effectively blind directly aft. In their baffles.

As long as the Akula was moving directly away from them, she could not know that she was being followed. But neither could *Seawolf* know if she in turn was being followed if she maintained a steady course.

Dillon stepped back out into the passageway. His XO was at the control room hatch. "Charlie, give me a slow three-sixty to port while we've still got steerage way. Load tubes one and three, come to battle stations torpedo, and stand by to get us out of here."

"Aye, skipper."

Dillon turned back. "We're going to clear our baffles, so look sharp," he told Zimenski.

"Do you think that sierra sixteen is a decoy, Cap'n?" Pistole asked.

"The *Abe Lincoln*'s battle group ran across an Akula out here yesterday. But she was the *V.I. Lenin*. I'd like to know where she is."

Zimenski adjusted his controls as *Seawolf* began her slow turn to port.

"All hands, all hands. Battle stations torpedo. Battle stations torpedo. All sections report."

The 1MC announcement from the conn was muted because *Sea-*

wolf was operating in silent mode. Throughout the boat the crew was quickly and quietly coming to battle stations.

Tubes one and three were being loaded with HE versons of the Mark 48 ADCAP torpedoes, each carrying 650 pounds of PBXN-103 high explosive. The Mark 48s were wire-guided and could seek out and home in on targets out to fifty thousand yards, nearly thirty miles, at speeds of more than sixty knots. The Advanced Capability Mark 48, which was an improvement over the Mod 4s, was smart. It could defeat most enemy electronic and acoustic countermeasures, and could send back targeting data to the *Seawolf* even while she was running. It meant that the Mark 48 ADCAP could be launched and then guided to strike any part of the enemy ship the captain wanted to strike for the maximum effect.

After four minutes *Seawolf* was back on her original course. Zimenski shook his head.

"We're clear, skipper."

Dillon cocked an ear as if he were trying to listen for sounds outside of his boat.

Zimenski suddenly held up a hand. "Wait." He adjusted the gain and a broadband frequency control on his BSY-2 console. The green waterfall display sharpened up. "I have a sound line," he said. "Faint."

The other three technicians manning BSY-2 consoles each took a range of frequencies now that the hunt had begun.

Zimenski keyed his mike. "Conn, sonar. Possible new subsurface contact, designated sierra seventeen. Bearing one-six five, range within two thousand yards and closing slowly."

Dillon donned a headset and listened. At first he couldn't hear much beyond the mush of oceanic background noise. Possibly some biologics a long ways off.

Zimenski made a grease-pencil mark on his screen, which was definitely showing a frequency line now, though an extremely faint one.

Then Dillon had it. Buried in the noise. A rhythmic noise, like a bathroom fan slowly oscillating left, then right, as its blades turned at a constant rate. "It's an air handler of some kind," he said.

"It's an AC fan, skipper," Zimenski agreed. "But the shock absorbers on the motor are going bad. The Viktors and some of the early Mikes have the same problem."

Dillon keyed his headset mike. "Conn, this is the captain. Start a TMA on sierra seventeen. I'm betting she's the other Akula. The *V.I. Lenin*."

"Aye, Cap'n," Bateman responded.

Dillon smiled. "Okay, the *Lenin* went fishing with the *Brezhnev* as bait. Let's see what he does now that he thinks he has us." He gave the sonar crew a nod. "Good job, gentlemen."

8

Sonarman First Rank Gennadi Markin was in trouble.

Each minute that went by in which he didn't report to the captain, he dug an even deeper hole for himself. He was already on the demerit list for failing to detect the American Sea King dipping buoys, which had bracketed them two days ago. Now this.

The other three sonarmen on shift were shooting him sideways glances. They knew enough to stay out of it, to protect their own asses. It was a Russian virtue.

Markin completed the diagnostic on his sonar set, which showed that the equipment was functioning well within its parameters.

Captain Savin was a tough bastard, but he was usually fair and he was always brilliant. He was the smartest man aboard the boat. Everyone had a great deal of respect for him. No one questioned a single order that he gave, no matter how seemingly strange it was at the time.

They had dropped out of sight eight hours ago, even from their sister boat the *Brezhnev*, which had circled around sniffing after their trail.

Then they'd heard the oncoming American submarine, making turns for flank speed, just as the captain had predicted, and almost on the precise course the captain had predicted. The only thing he had gotten wrong was the depth. The *Seawolf* was running at about two hundred meters, instead of the three hundred meters they'd expected.

Brezhnev suddenly got the hell out of there, making a racket as she left. It made Markin wonder if *Brezhnev* had been playing some kind of a trick. First they'd tried to find the *Lenin* without luck, and then when the American submarine had appeared on the acoustic horizon they'd taken off with so much noise that a deaf man could have followed them.

The *Seawolf* passed within one thousand meters of the *Lenin*, which should have turned onto the Americans' course and followed in their baffles.

Markin was supposed to give the go-ahead when the *Seawolf* was safely past.

But the American submarine had simply disappeared four and a half minutes ago.

At first Markin was convinced that he was experiencing an equipment failure. The *Seawolf* was so close that he should have heard something. That was his first mistake, not informing the captain. And then he had compounded his initial error by continuing to look for a phantom electronic problem.

He girded himself, then keyed his headset. "Conn, sonar. Sierra nineteen has disappeared. I believe that he has gone to silent running."

He'd screwed up twice, but there was no reason he couldn't redeem himself by finding the bastard American submarine.

In the control room, Capt. Second Rank Mikhail Savin was at the chart table working the three-sub problem on paper.

His XO, Lieutenant Yuri Sergeyev, was at the weapons control panel on the opposite side of the conn. He answered the sonar call.

"Sonar, conn, this is the *starpom*. What was his last range and bearing?"

Captain Savin looked up and caught Sergeyev's eye. His *starpom* shook his head. The *Seawolf*'s going silent at this moment came as a surprise to him too.

"Range was sixteen hundred meters, bearing one-nine-five."

"Sonar, were there any transients at all? Anything that would help you determine if his aspect was changing, or if he was maintaining his course?"

"Nothing yet, sir. But we're looking."

"Is *Brezhnev* out of range?"

"*Da*, to us. But it's possible Sierra nineteen still has them. Their equipment is . . . very sensitive."

"Keep looking."

"*Da*."

Sergeyev came over to the captain. "The trap was working, but now he knows we're here."

"Or suspects," Savin said. "We're making no noise." Or at least no noise that a *Seawolf*-class submarine was supposed to detect, Savin finished the thought. They'd come through the *Abe Lincoln*'s exercise intact, with only one of them being detected. To this point the intelligence information they were getting from fleet HQ at Vladivostok was spot-on. The *Abraham Lincoln* battle group had been exactly where it was predicted to be, and testing its new laser targeted system, as it was predicted.

The *Seawolf* had come charging out of Pearl Harbor, also as predicted. The trap had been set. The American submarine had approached, then passed, and finally disappeared.

Savin managed a fatalistic smile. Military intelligence was like an opinion. Everybody had something to contribute, but most of the time they didn't know what the hell they were talking about.

"What do you want to do, Captain?" Sergeyev asked. The *Lenin* was said to be the safest place in all of Russia no matter where the boat happened to be, because Savin knew what he was doing.

Savin glanced at the chart. It would have been a nice exercise, to pop up behind an American submarine and go sonar active. Boo! But Vladivostok was taking this exercise more seriously than normal for some reason. They'd come this far, there was no reason not to continue playing the game.

"Make turns for four knots, I want absolutely no pump noises from our reactor. Come left to two-six-zero and maintain our present depth."

Sergeyev, who'd worked his way through four boats, and had given up a command of his own, to serve with Captain Savin, had the utmost respect for the man. But even masters made mistakes. "Sorry to disagree, Captain, but we cannot be certain *Seawolf* has not changed course. We could put ourselves in a collision situation."

Savin nodded. "A good point, Yuri, and a valid one if Sonarman Markin wasn't lying to us." The captain was a small man, less than a meter sixty, and less than seventy kilos. His slight build made his head seem too large for his body. Instead of making him look grotesque, however, his broad forehead and wide-spaced deep blue eyes made him seem infallible.

"Sir?"

Savin turned to the chart where he'd laid out the relative positions of the *Lenin* and the *Seawolf* at ten-minute intervals for the past hour, and the predicted track west. The *Seawolf* had come within one thousand meters of them, directly off their starboard side. He tapped a narrow finger on the chart where the *Seawolf*'s last position had been marked.

"He can't be sixteen hundred meters away on that bearing," Savin said. "It's simple trigonometry. Sonarman Markin lost him, but waited three maybe four minutes to tell us."

"Why?"

Savin shrugged. "He's a good man. We'll find out without ruining him." He smiled again, patiently as a father might with a son. "Four knots, Yuri. Two-six-zero, and quietly."

9

Make turns for two knots, come right to new course three-zero-zero," Dillon ordered his COB.

"Aye, skipper," Master Chief Young responded. "Making my speed two knots, turning starboard to new course three-zero-zero."

The *Seawolf* swung slowly to starboard. Dillon got on the growler phone.

"Sonar, this is the captain. We're making a slow turn to three-zero-zero. I think sierra seventeen will show up in our port quarter. I want to know if there is any aspect change in the target other than from our relative motion."

"Aye, skipper. Stand by," Ski said.

"Our speed is two knots, our course is three-zero-zero," COB Young reported.

"Very well," Dillon said, "Mr. Alvarez, where is the thermocline?"

"Estimate eleven hundred feet, skipper," Teflon responded.

"Chief of boat, I'm going to want a real slow dive to twelve hundred feet. No noise. On my mark."

"Aye, skipper. One-two-zero-zero feet on your mark," Chief Young replied crisply. The captain was going hunting, this time with live fish in tubes one and three. And this was just the beginning of their mission. He had a chance to forget his own complicated life and problems for a while. It didn't get any better than this, in his estimation. He could see that the rest of the control room crew had the same feeling.

"Ski, talk to me," Dillon called back to sonar.

"Don't need the AC blower noises, Captain. Sierra seventeen is now making turns for four knots; I'm counting her prop. She's turned to port. New relative bearing three-two-zero."

Dillon did the math in his head. The *Lenin* had turned to a course of two-six-zero to minimize the danger of colliding with the *Seawolf*, which the *Lenin* thought was still on a course due west. It meant that the *Lenin's* skipper knew that they were here, but not exactly where.

"Stand by," Dillon said. "We'll send sierra seventeen a calling card." He glanced over at Bateman and gave him a nod.

Engineering had brought up a three pound ball peen hammer. Bateman picked it up from the chart table, walked over to the middle of the control room, gave Dillon a big grin, and dropped it to the deck with a tremendous clang.

"Okay, chief, take us down to twelve hundred feet," Dillon said. "But real slow and nice and quiet."

"Yes, sir," Young said. "Two degree down angle on the planes," he ordered. He began slowly adjusting their ballast tanks to a slightly nose-down attitude.

"Has sierra seventeen changed course?" Dillon asked.

"She's coming right, skipper."

"We're going to duck below the thermocline, but it's going to take fifteen or twenty minutes to get there. I want to know the moment sierra seventeen starts down after us."

"Roger that."

"Ski, I want to know if she does anything at all: change course or speed, goes silent, sends up a buoy, opens her outer doors. If she makes so much as a twitch I want to know about it immediately. I'm going to pull a trick on her skipper. But it's not going to work if he knows we've gone deep."

"Yes, sir," Zimenski said. "I'm on it."

"By the way. It was a ball peen hammer."

Zimenski laughed. "We had bets that it was a crescent wrench, skipper."

10

Captain Savin stepped the few paces forward to the sonar compartment. Sonarman Markin was busy with his equipment. A long green line on his display was already fading, but Markin had made a grease-pencil mark.

"What was it?" Savin demanded.

Markin shook his head. He was listening to something in his headphones. "Something heavy. A tool, perhaps. Amidships. Below the sail."

"In the control room?"

"Maybe, Captain. It's hard to tell." Markin made an adjustment to his controls. "The bearing changed to zero-four-zero. Range is now two thousand one hundred meters."

Seawolf had somehow detected them, and had turned right to three hundred degrees. They were trying to sneak off, or perhaps even trying to circle around behind *Lenin*.

But the noise in the control room was as if someone had dropped a heavy tool on the deck. An accident, or a purposeful misdirection?

"Is there anything else?" he asked his chief sonarman.

"No, sir. If he is moving he's being very quiet about it."

"I'm going to put us in his baffles and get in a little closer. Listen with care this time."

Sonarman Markin looked up guiltily, but then nodded. He was being given a second chance. "*Da*, Captain."

Savin went back to the control room. "Yuri, turn right to three-zero-zero."

Sergeyev gave the orders, and *Lenin* eased gently into a right turn, then came back to the captain, who was at the chart table studying the *Seawolf*'s track. "What was the noise, Captain?"

"Someone very clumsy, or very smart dropped something in the control room," Savin said.

Somehow the American boat had detected *Lenin*, or the skipper had been warned, and now he was possibly laying a trap of his own.

The noise had been . . . what? A challenge?

Savin called back to engineering. "This is the captain. Send a pry bar up to the control room on the double."

"Sir?"

"You heard me."

Everyone took a furtive glance at the captain, but no one said a thing. No one would have dreamed of saying anything.

An engineer's mate showed up a minute later with a thick, steel bar of the kind used for prying open stuck hatches.

"Throw it on the deck," Savin ordered.

The young mate was unsure of what he was supposed to do. Everyone heard stories about officers suddenly snapping, going crazy. He glanced at the XO and the others. The XO nodded.

"On the deck, if you please, sailor," Captain Savin said pleasantly.

The mate nodded and tossed the pry bar on the deck. It hit with a tremendous clang that everyone aboard the boat heard.

11

Frank Dillon laughed out loud.

He glanced up at the multifunction display over Zimenski's shoulder as the chief sonarman replayed the sound. They were at seven hundred feet and still heading down.

The noise was sharp. It had to have reverberated throughout the *Lenin*, putting everybody's teeth on edge. And it was definitely not a mistake. The *Lenin*'s CO had sent them a very clear message.

"What was it, Ski, a piece of pipe?" Dillon asked.

"Wasn't hollow, sir. Maybe a crowbar, or a long drift pin, something like that."

"Range and bearing?"

"He's turned to three-zero-zero, still making turns for four knots. Lateral range is two thousand six hundred yards, but he's maintaining his depth."

"He thinks that he's going to run up our tail," Dillon said. He stood in the passageway just outside the sonar room. Bateman had come forward with him to see what the racket aboard the Russian submarine was all about.

"He figures that we found him and set our own trap," Bateman said. "He just told us that he knows all about us."

Dillon smiled. "Or *thinks* he does, Charlie."

They went back to the control room where Dillon called his weapons officer over to the chart table. He plotted the course, speed, and depths of the *Seawolf*, the *Lenin*, and the *Brezhnev*.

"They were out here waiting for us when they got tangled up with the *Abe*'s battle group," Dillon said. "But they stuck around and set a trap for us, which we walked right into. Means they knew we were coming."

"The spy," Lt. (jg) Marc "Doctor Death" Jablonski said.

"Looks like it."

"Well, we can flood tubes one and three. They'll get the message loud and clear," Jablonski said. He flexed his thick arm muscles. He was itching to get into a fight. It was something that his dad, who was a bruiser of a steelworker in Gary, would understand.

"When it's over they'd still know which way they went," Dillon said. "I have a better idea. Oaktree Resource."

"It'd be tight," Jablonski cautioned. "If you think that they know we're up to something they might figure out that we pulled a fast one on them."

"They'll figure that out sooner or later, but it'll give us time to get out of here," Dillon said. "We'll send up two noisemakers: one from the forward three-inch tube and one aft. Set the forward buoy to hover at two hundred fifty feet with a thirty-minute delay. The second one send to the surface on a forty-minute delay."

Jablonski studied the chart for a few moments. "If we do it right now, the buoys will pop up aft of the *Lenin*, in her baffles. She won't hear a thing until they start transmitting."

"Do it."

Bateman grinned. "They're going to have a couple of busy hours sorting things out."

"If they stick around, which I don't think they will," Dillon countered. "They knew that we were heading west, so they might just bug out in that direction hoping to run across us again. So we're going to head south until we're sure that we're clear."

"*If* it works," Jablonski said. He had a basic mistrust of anything that didn't go bang.

"If it doesn't, the navy spent a hell of a lot of money on R and D for nothing," Dillon said.

12

All hell broke loose.

It had been a half hour since they'd heard the noise aboard the American submarine and sent their reply. Savin was starting to get impatient. They had circled in an ever-widening pattern hoping to run up close enough to the *Seawolf* for Markin to snag him. But they'd found nothing.

He was about to step forward into the sonar compartment when a very excited Markin called the control room.

"Conn, sonar, I have many subsea contacts to the west and south-west. Sierra twenty, bearing two-seven-five, range ten thousand meters and closing. Evaluate the contact as a Los Angeles class submarine. Sierra twenty-one, bearing two-eight-zero, range six thousand meters and closing. Evaluate the contact as a second Los Angeles class submarine—"

Savin stepped forward to the sonar compartment and donned a pair of headphones as Markin continued to report to Sergeyev on the conn. The four sonar screens were alive with thick lines indicating solid contacts.

"Sierra twenty-four, bearing two-five-zero, range eleven thousand meters and steady. Evaluate contact as possible *Seawolf* submarine."

"Sierra nineteen?" Savin demanded.

Markin looked up. He was frightened. "I can't tell, Captain. The signal is . . . indistinct."

"At eleven thousand meters?"

"I can't be sure. There's too much turbulence."

Savin could hear it in his headset. It sounded as if half the entire American submarine fleet was bearing down on them. But that was impossible. They'd had no indications; only that of the lone *Seawolf* exactly where he should have been.

Sergeyev was at the control room hatch. "What are your orders, Captain?" he asked.

Markin sat bolt upright, as if his ass had been plugged into an electric outlet. "*Yeb vas*," he swore. "Conn, sonar. I have multiple surface contacts, bearings from two-one-zero to three-zero-zero. Ranges all over the place. Possible carrier group; three destroyers, maybe four. At least five frigates—" He looked over his shoulder at the captain, his eyes wide. "One minute there was nothing, and the next they were there. I think it's the *Abraham Lincoln* battle group."

"That's impossible—"

"Captain, we're running out of room," Sergeyev called urgently.

Savin took off the headphones, set them aside and smiled. He nodded. "Very well. Come right to three-five-zero, make your speed flank and make our depth one hundred meters."

"Why not duck under the thermocline," Sergeyev asked. "They might not hear us."

"I want them to hear us," Savin said. "We've been outmaneuvered. I want them to understand that we are not trying to hide. We are no threat."

13

Quite a racket, sir," Zimenski said. The sophisticated Oaktree Resource computer program filtered out the sonar noises made by the two buoys, leaving behind a relatively quite ocean except for the sounds of the *V.I. Lenin* bugging out to the north at flank speed.

He went back to the control room. "Secure from battle stations. Make your speed flank, course one-eight-zero, depth twelve hundred feet."

The COB repeated the orders.

"Mr. Alvarez, shape us a course that'll get us away from the *Lenin* and *Brezhnev* ASAP. I want to get back to our baseline when we're clear."

"Aye, skipper," Alvarez said.

"XO."

"Yes, Captain."

"Pizza tonight. I want thin and crispy, meat lovers, and lots of it."

"Yes, sir."

14

0005 LOCAL
IN THE MOUNTAINS

Major, I have two, possibly three heat sources above and to our right," the pilot called back. He had never seen any real combat and he was excited.

"Are they man-size?" Zafar demanded.

"They would appear to be—" the pilot said. "Wait. There're definitely three of them, and now perhaps a fourth. They're hidden in the trees, so it's hard to make them out."

"Stay on your present heading as if you haven't seen them," Zafar ordered. "Units two and three, drop behind the rise to the west of the cliff and deploy your people. Unit four, I want you to stand by to the east, a couple of hundred meters below, but remain airborne."

All three unit leaders acknowledged their orders. Two of the Alouettes headed farther up the mountain, while the third peeled off to the east and dropped back.

Zafar gave his rangers the heads-up sign. "We've found them," he shouted over the noise. "I want to take them alive. But I don't want any martyrs."

They nodded their understanding.

Zafar yanked open the door, pulled his Odelf image intensifiers over his eyes and searched the suddenly bright woods for the four American spies. He very much wanted to return to base with four intact prisoners and no casualties of his own.

15

0010 LOCAL
IN THE MOUNTAINS

The two helicopters that had topped the rise above the cache had probably landed and deployed their troops, Hanson figured. There would be no easy escape that way. The nearest chopper had disappeared somewhere to the west; they could hear its rotors in the trees. But the fourth Alouette had taken up station a couple of hundred meters below them at the edge of a narrow clearing.

Hauglar scrambled to where Hanson was crouched behind a tree. "The Claymores and Semtex are in place on either side of the cliff. Don's got the firing switches, so we're going to have to tell him when to do it."

"Good enough," Hanson said. He looked over to where Harvey waited with the Stinger. He was the only one in the group that Hanson could not understand. Harvey was a cold fish; the only thing he seemed to care about were the weapons and the explosives. He never went anywhere, never received letters or phone calls, and never talked about his life outside the service or the CIA. But he was very good at what he did, even if he wasn't Mr. Personality.

"We're not getting out of this one," Hauglar said. He, on the other hand, was their pessimist, while Hanson thought of himself as the realist.

"Probably not. But I think I got through to Kuwait City so they know the situation we're in."

"Maybe Washington can bend a few arms, but it'll probably be too little too late."

Hanson had to smile inwardly. Hope springs eternal, his wife told him from the day they'd met in high school. "I want you and I'm going to get my wish. You want children and I'm going to give them to you."

He stared for a moment at the Alouette hovering below them.

Waiting. For what? He made his decision. "Go over and spot for Mike. I want that chopper bagged right now."

"That's gonna get their attention."

"They're not here to negotiate."

Hauglar scrambled back to Harvey, who immediately got to his feet, shouldered the missile launcher, and aimed it toward the hovering helicopter.

Nothing seemed to happen for several seconds as Harvey switched on the battery, then uncaged the seeker head that locked onto the target.

Hauglar glanced back at Hanson, then tapped Harvey on the ear. "Clear to fire."

The missile was away on a long flash of light, and within a couple of seconds the helicopter exploded with a tremendous boom that hammered off the side of the mountains, spewing flames and white-hot fragments in every direction as the fuselage turned over and fell to the ground.

"The second chopper will be back any minute," Hanson warned. Because of the weight restrictions they had carried only the one Stinger missile for the launch system with no backup.

Hauglar motioned that he was going to spot for Amatozio, leaving Harvey and Hanson with the two LAWs, antitank weapons that weighed less than one-third what a Stinger did. It was a safe bet that their silenced Sterling submachine guns would not take down an Alouette unless they got very lucky. And the LAW rocket was not much better because it was slow enough for an alert helicopter pilot to get out of its way. But for now it was all they had.

They heard the helicopter off to the west, farther up the mountain. It was coming back slowly, the crew cautious now that they'd gotten a taste of what they were up against.

Hanson motioned for Harvey to move off a few meters farther east. They had hastily discussed just this possibility ten minutes ago. They figured that they could down one of the choppers with the Stinger, but the best they could do after that was try for one more.

Hanson would shoot his LAW first. While the pilot was busy evading that missile, Harvey might be able to bag him with the second

LAWs. That's if they were stupid enough to bring a second chopper within range.

After that it would devolve into a firefight on the ground. If they were captured alive there was a good chance that someone would recognize who he was. They wouldn't be taking fingerprints or DNA, but Hanson's face was not unknown on CNN and the other television news networks. When he had joined the CIA a few years ago he had managed to all but drop out of the media's attention for obvious reasons.

But all it would take was one Pakistani soldier with a long memory and a facility for faces for the game to be up.

He'd discussed this at length with his brother, with Dr. Tyson, who was the incoming DCI, and with several Secret Service supervisors whose job it was to keep the president *and* his family alive and out of the hands of their enemies.

No one had been happy about Scott's decision to join the CIA, nor Carolyn Tyson's hiring him. But the president had overridden all the objections.

"All I ask is that you understand your responsibilities. *All* of your responsibilities," his brother had cautioned.

Until this moment the warning had been a moot point.

There was another possibility here, however. A remote chance, one that Hanson didn't even want to think about, that they might get out of this. With two helicopters down, and the troops above them chewed up by the perimeter of Claymores and Semtex mantraps, an end run was just possible.

It would be daylight before the Pakistanis could get anyone else up here. Time enough for them to make it over the pass, and use the paragliders to get a long way down the other side.

Success would depend on none of them sustaining any wounds. The situation was bad enough because of Amatozio's blindness. If they had to carry someone too, using the paragliders would be totally out of the question. He was not leaving anybody behind.

But there was even another possibility. One that was developing in his mind.

The helicopter was farther to the west now, and lower, maybe even below them. Their perimeter was being probed. The Pakistanis couldn't possibly know the size of the force that they were facing. Even if they had spotted all four heat sources, they would have to suspect that there might be others hiding under the overhang, or perhaps farther up or down the mountain. One of their helicopters had been shot out of the sky, so they would be very cautious from now on.

They lost the sounds of the helicopter. Hanson cocked an ear and he heard it again, back to the west, and then it was gone. But the noise hadn't faded in the distance. The rotors had spooled down. The chopper had landed.

The Pakistanis were coming.

16

Major Zafar stood beside his chopper, which had touched down about two hundred meters directly west of where the four Americans had dug in, his stomach sour. He had lost six rangers, a pilot and copilot and a multimillion-rupee helicopter because of his criminal stupidity. He wanted to rush in there with every means at his disposal and crush the bastards; kill them, destroy their infidel, godless bodies; grind them into the dirt.

His six rangers were fanned out about twenty meters into the woods where they had taken up defensive positions. Their safety as well as the ultimate success of the mission was his responsibility, and his alone.

Flames from unit four were still at treetop level. He could smell the burning fuel and plastic. He imagined that he could smell burning flesh.

He took a deep breath to calm himself, then keyed his tactical radio. "Units two and three, say your present positions."

"Command, two. We're one hundred meters above the Americans and west of the cliff."

"Command, three. We're east, about the same distance. What happened, sir?"

Zafar's grip tightened on his 9mm Steyr pistol. "They're somewhat better equipped than we suspected, so watch yourself. We're on the ground two hundred meters west of them, As soon as we're in position we'll begin a diversion. When you hear it, attack them from above. We'll have them boxed in on three sides. If they try to move down the mountain, we'll herd them back to the depot like goats."

"Command, three. Do we still have to take them as prisoners, Major? After what they've done."

"There have been enough casualties. I want them as prisoners, if possible."

"Yes, sir. I understand. 'If possible.'"

It would become increasingly difficult to control them now that their honor was at stake. They still had to return to their duties at the depot where they would face the derision of the ISI troops.

Perhaps bringing back four American bodies would be best.

Despite orders.

Captain Amin's wrath would be bad enough. But Allah could only know what General Phalodi would do to them if they failed. Even President Musharraf had respect for the old warhorse. The Butcher of Punjab.

The Indian army had killed his son. In retaliation, Phalodi had taken thirty-seven Indian army prisoners of war, affixed them with chains to a huge funeral pyre, and burned them alive. Nobody who was there could ever forget the inhuman screams of agony.

That was after the general had himself been held as a prisoner of war.

17

0025 LOCAL
IN THE MOUNTAINS

Hauglar and Amatozio were crouched behind a line of large rocks that were in such a straight row that they could have been placed by hand. Hauglar watched the dark woods above them, while Amatozio held the two detonator transmitters: one for the Semtex they had deployed in half-pound-shaped charges along the perimeter and the other for the eight M18A1 Claymore antipersonnel mines that they had placed ten meters inside the first perimeter. Anything coming at them from above would get severely damaged.

Hanson scrambled over and hit the dirt beside them. "Anything yet?" he demanded.

"I haven't seen a thing, but they're up there, all right," Hauglar said. "I've been hearing noises, maybe about thirty or forty meters out."

"Rats in the attic?" Hanson quipped. They had one chance in a thousand of getting out of this, and he wanted them loose enough to take it.

"Yeah, big rats," Hauglar said.

"What about the first chopper?" Amatozio asked. His bandages were stained and crusty around his eye sockets. He was still in a lot of pain.

"It landed somewhere to the west, I think. I'm assuming that they're heading this way on foot. As soon as they're on top of us, they'll probably start a diversionary attack that will signal the troops above us to come running."

"Why not just pop a few grenades on top of us," Hauglar said. "It'd be easy. Like shooting fish in a barrel."

"Could be they want us alive," Hanson replied. "They're leaving us a back door. Down the mountain."

"Right back to the depot."

"Something like that. So we're going to mostly ignore the diversionary attack, and concentrate on whoever tries to roll down on top of us."

"If they want us to go down, we'll go up," Amatozio said. "Then what?"

"Did I ever tell you guys what my primary rating was in the navy, before I joined the SEALs?" Hanson asked. "Even before I was the president's brother?"

Hauglar shook his head. "No. What was it?"

"Helicopter pilot. If we can take out whoever comes down the mountain, we might be able to climb up to where they parked their helicopters before their pals can figure out what's happening."

Hauglar looked at him to make sure that he was serious. "They have two choppers up there. Could be twenty men. If they hold a few of them back as reserve we wouldn't have a chance in hell."

"We'll never know unless we try."

"Yeah," Amatozio said. "I'm game. Hell, what have I got to lose?"

"We don't have a lot of options, Don."

Hauglar shrugged. "We could surrender."

"Only at the point of a gun," Hanson said. "And we're not there yet. You know damned well what the ISI will do to us if we're taken."

"It's better than being dead. They wouldn't kill you."

"If it comes to that, I hope you're right," Hanson said.

He turned to make sure that Harvey was in position to watch the woods to the west, when three flashes of light followed by three sharp explosions came from that direction. Hanson immediately recognized that they were flash-bang grenades; noisemakers. The diversion had begun. "Okay, this is it."

Harvey fired a couple of short bursts in the general direction of the explosions, and got some sporadic return fire.

Hauglar stood up high enough to see over the rocks and he was immediately shoved back, a bloody crease appearing across the side of his neck, as automatic weapons fire rained down on them from above. He grunted. "Damn!"

"Do the Semtex now!" Hanson shouted.

Amatozio pressed the safety cage-uncage switch; the red ready light came on, and even though he couldn't see the light he hit the *fire* button six times in rapid succession.

Six blossoms of light, followed by six very impressive bangs, followed one after the other forty meters up into the woods. The automatic weapons firing faltered and stopped. Several men screamed. Someone shouted something.

Hauglar got back up. He and Hanson popped over the top of the rocks and emptied their thirty-four round box magazines before dropping back to reload.

A Pakistani ranger yelled something, and seconds later several flash-bang grenades went off harmlessly five or ten meters away.

The firing from the west was intensifying, but there was no time to get over to help Harvey yet. The bulk of the attack was coming down the mountain, just like Hanson figured it would.

He counted to five, raised his Sterling over his head so that it just cleared the top of the rocks, fired a short burst and pulled back.

The return fire was just as heavy as it had been before. If the Semtex had hurt them, they weren't showing it.

"Now!" he shouted to Amatozio, who had the second detonator ready.

This time he had to hit only one button and all eight specially rigged Claymores went off together. The explosions were not very loud, but the mines spewed out a devastating curtain of steel balls that would cut down anything exposed out to a couple of hundred meters.

But there were no screams. No sounds of the wounded or dying. The Pakistanis had either taken cover or had gotten inside the second perimeter already.

Either way it was very big trouble.

Hanson and Hauglar realized at the same instant that the firing from the west had also stopped. They turned around to face the muzzles of four Kalashnikovs, held by four very determined looking men in Pakistani ranger uniforms.

A fifth man, major's pips on his shoulder tabs, night-vision goggles on his face, was speaking into a helmet microphone. Beyond them, Mike Harvey sat on the ground, his hands on top of his head. Two Pakistani rangers pointed assault rifles at him.

Hanson and Hauglar carefully placed their weapons on the ground and held their hands over their heads.

"It's over, Don," Hanson told Amatozio.

"Yes, it certainly is," Zafar said. He shook his head. "Too bad that you are in civilian clothes. You are spies, and you will be treated as such."

18

1650 EDT
NATIONAL RECONNAISSANCE OFFICE, LANGLEY, VA.

DCI Carolyn Tyson, accompanied by her bodyguard, strode through the fourth-floor skyway that connected the Central Intelligence Agency's main building with the annex that housed, among other operations, the NRO. She thought that no matter how much you expected the worst—hell, even prepared for the worst—when it finally did occur it always seemed to catch everyone off guard.

"Good afternoon, Madam Director," the security officer at the end of the skyway said.

"Good afternoon." Tyson signed the roster, left her bodyguard at the security desk and let herself into 401A with her security badge.

The dimly lit room was the skybox above the pit. A couple of leather couches and several easy chairs equipped with built-in telephones faced a floor-to-ceiling one-way window that looked across at the big screen and down at the three tiers of technicians and operators. One of the walls in the skybox contained a dozen built-in television monitors, all blank at the moment.

Brad Cunningham, deputy director of operations, was in deep discussion with the NRO's chief of operations and planning, Col. Thomas "Bear" Branigan. They were sitting in front of the window and they did not look happy.

Cunningham looked as if he had swallowed a football and was trying to choke it back up while catching his breath. His face was red. He always looked that way in a crisis: ready to pass out at any second, but capable of operating on coffee, cigarettes, and adrenaline for amazing periods of time.

Bear Branigan, who'd earned his nickname in Desert Storm because of the way he charged into battle, was thick-shouldered, with ham-hock fists and a broad, impossibly large head that sat squarely on a twenty-three-inch neck. His thick dark hair, bushy eyebrows, and wide, serious eyes gave him the appearance of always being pissed off. His subordinates respected and even liked him. But everybody sharpened up when he charged into a room.

They looked up, and started to get to their feet when Tyson came in, but she waved them back.

"Don't get up. I just want to know what the situation is out there that has you two punching the fire alarm. I'm due to brief the president in about an hour and he's going to want to know what the hell is happening."

"It's not good news, Madam Director," Colonel Branigan said.

"How's our confidence on this one?"

"Eighty-twenty. We could be wrong, but the timing and the position fits—"

"Damn right they do," Cunningham shot back. "They're our guys, all right. And they're either dead or the Pakistanis captured them."

No one had said it aloud, but of the two possibilities, the deaths of all four spring wind field operatives was politically the best one. Tyson sighed to try to settle the butterflies. They were talking about the president's brother. "But that's still not the worst of it," Cunningham said. He was even more shook-up than Tyson had realized.

Branigan's jaw tightened. He had been dead-set against red warren from its inception, preferring instead to rely solely on satellite surveillance. But he had been in on the planning from the get-go, and when JayBird Four had gone offline, he had reluctantly agreed that sending the ground team into Pakistan might always have been the best option. He was a hard charger, but he hated to lose men in the field; even one man down was to him a disaster that could have been prevented.

"What is it?" Tyson asked.

"March hare recorded several partial transmissions from spring wind. Piecing the bits together, we think that Scott and his people got close enough to the depot to actually witness the test. The bomb was dropped from an airplane. A medium transport. Possibly one of their Fokker twenty-seven transports."

Tyson compressed her lips as if she had just tasted something bitter. Bad news on top of bad news.

Colonel Branigan was amazed. "I don't know what the hell their joint chiefs are smoking in Chaklala, but as the kids say, it's gotta be some good shit because those people just thumbed their noses at the entire world. They've all but dared India to make a preemptive strike."

"Are we dead certain about this, Brad?" Tyson asked. The president was going to have another very rough evening.

Cunningham shrugged. "Better odds than Vegas, but we just can't know for sure until we get another transmission."

"Which isn't very likely," Colonel Branigan said. He raised a remote control unit and switched on one of the built-in monitors. The image was very dark, entirely in black and white, the movement almost imperceptible.

It took Tyson a moment to realize that she was seeing a poor quality, very low angle, satellite image of what appeared to be a sparsely populated land mass.

"We're looking at west central Pakistan, the Siahan Mountains south of the Kharan depot. These pictures were downloaded a couple of hours ago from one of the older KH eleven birds that we moved into position when the *Jupiter* went down. The CCD units are not very sophisticated by comparison, and the angle is extremely low."

"That's the city of Panjgur in the lower left corner," Cunningham said. It appeared as a fairly broad area of fuzzy light.

"The operator picked up something unusual in the upper middle of the screen, so he zoomed in," Colonel Branigan said.

The image on the screen tightened. Panjgur disappeared. The charge-coupled device aboard the satellite, which transformed light images from the camera lenses into digital bytes that could be transmitted to the NRO's receiving stations around the world, showed a tiny pinpoint of light that grew and centered on the screen as the cameras were refocused.

"It was a small explosion," Colonel Branigan explained. "Now watch."

Over the next several minutes the images that the KeyHole satellite had picked up needed no explanation. There had been a short, but intense battle in the mountains between a small force, probably less than a half-dozen troops, and a much larger force coming at them from two directions. They could pick out individual small explosions, as well as small arms fire.

"One of the pieces of information that March hare is very clear on, is the position that Hanson reported," Cunningham told Tyson. He looked back at the monitor. "It matches the firefight."

Colonel Branigan turned off the monitor. "We won't have anything back in range now for another three hours."

"They could be anywhere by then," Tyson said.

"Or dead," Cunningham replied, but Tyson disagreed.

"If the ISI is involved, which it almost certainly is, then our people are still alive. They'll be questioned and, depending on how they hold up, they'll either be publically executed so the entire world can watch, or they'll be used as bargaining chips," Tyson said. Her stomach was sour. If anything, the satellite pictures had stiffened her resolve, but she was glad that she wasn't the president.

"We're working on scenarios to get them out of there, ma'am. How far do you want to take them?" Cunningham asked.

"All the way, Brad. We're not leaving our people in Pakistan. None of our people."

19

I want those men out of there, I don't care what it takes," President Hanson said. He was as angry as Tyson had ever seen him. The events of the past twenty-four hours made them all mad. But the president had the power to do something about his anger.

They were gathered in the Oval Office. The DCI had brought over the CIA's Special National Intelligence Estimate and Watch Report on the developing situation in Pakistan. With the president were his National Security Adviser Dennis Nettleton and his chief of staff Brad Stein. They were at a loss for words, but Stein gave voice to his confusion first.

"Mr. President, Scott and his team were sent there to spy," he said. "We can't deny it. So you'll have to call General Musharraf and ask for leniency. Under the circumstances, it's the only thing you can do."

"We don't know that Scott has been identified yet," Carolyn Tyson said.

"Oh, come on, don't be obtuse. You don't have siblings of your own, so you can't understand what it's like for the president."

The man was an insufferable ass. "Mr. President, I think that we need to focus on the main issue at hand: That Pakistan not only conducted an aboveground test of a hydrogen device, but that the weapon was portable enough to be dropped from an airplane."

"We're going to get to that, believe me, Dr. Tyson," the president said precisely. "That, and the fact that the Pakistanis continue to develop sophisticated guided missile systems." He gave Tyson a penetrating look to make his point. "Right now I want to talk about our people. Is there a plan to get them out of there?"

"We're working on scenarios—"

"I don't want scenarios, Carolyn. I want a plan. What are we doing to get them back?"

"I'm sorry, Mr. President, but for now we can do nothing but work out a number of different possibilities for rescue," Tyson said, sticking to her original guns that such an operation would be impossible without hard intelligence. "First, we need to make sure that they were captured alive and not killed in the firefight. We don't have that answer yet. If we can find that out, and then find out where they're being held—it's our best guess that if they're alive the ISI will take them to one of its interrogation centers—then we can go ahead with a firm rescue plan. One that makes sense."

"They could be in Islamabad or even Chaklala or Karachi by now," Stein pointed out. "If that's the case, then getting them out of there might be impossible."

"Carter's people worked out a plan to snatch our hostages out of Tehran."

"Which didn't work, Mr. President." Nettleton interjected.

"Not because of anything the Iranians did," Hanson said. "It was because our aircraft got bogged down in the desert sand. The engines clogged up and there were crashes. Accidents." The president paused a moment. "We *will* get them out of there."

"Once we find out where they're being held, we can work out a plan to free them. Something that won't get the rescuers killed," Tyson said. She was going to have problems with Stein, she could already see it in the way the man was girding himself.

"Getting them out of the country could be an even bigger problem than finding them," Stein said.

"No," Tyson said.

"Beg your pardon, Madam Director?" Stein asked.

Tyson turned to him. "I said, no, Brad. Getting them out of the country will *not* be the biggest problem. Finding out where they're being held will be. We don't have any reliable sources on the ground over there, otherwise we wouldn't have sent the team to watch the test. And considering what they found out for us, we'll pull out all the stops."

"Okay, you tell us: how are we going to do it?"

"By submarine," Tyson said. "Dillon is driving the *Seawolf* out that way right now. We'll send a SEAL team to rendezvous with him. He can drop them ashore, and they can fetch our guys back to the boat and then leave."

"As simple as that?" Stein asked. His dislike was obvious this evening.

"Why no, Brad, almost nothing is as simple as that," Tyson said. "First we'll have to pinpoint exactly where our people are being held. We'll need all the intelligence information we can get on the ISI installation, its location, as well as its layout. Then we'll need to send the *Seawolf*, by stealth, to within a few kilometers of Pakistan's highly patrolled coast, at which time a small team of operators—SEALs— will go ashore. They'll reach the prison by whatever means they can, neutralize as many guards as need be, defeat whatever other security and defensive measures they might encounter, release our four men, and bring them back to the submarine. That, Brad, is not a simple operation."

"Fair enough, Carolyn," the president said. "Do you have a timetable?"

"We've already worked it out with Admiral Puckett's people. The contingency plans are aboard the *Seawolf*, and there's a SEAL team standing by aboard the *Carl Vinson* in the Arabian Sea." She shook her head. Being a SEAL might be dangerous, but it was a lot less contentious than being the DCI.

"There's every chance for a disaster," Stein interjected.

"Yes, there is," she said. She turned to the president. "A political solution, if there is one, would be for the best, Mr. President. Now that we know their H-bomb can be delivered by air the situation is even more critical than we first thought."

"If India gets wind of that fact, we couldn't hold them back from a preemptive strike," Nettleton said. "The whole region would go up in smoke. Along with half the world's oil supplies."

"Then we all have work to do," the president said. "Let's get to it."

20

Dennis Nettleton was on the speakerphone to the embassy of Pakistan on Massachusetts Avenue, just above Sheridan Circle. The president, along with Brad Stein and Carolyn Tyson, listened in, but remained silent.

"The ambassador is in conference, Mr. Nettleton," Saiyed Aly, the ambassador's secretary, said. He was normally an affable man. This evening, however, he was cold to the point of haughtiness.

"Need I remind you, sir, that President Hanson wished to see Ambassador Husain this evening. In fact, he is waiting in the Oval Office at this moment."

"It cannot be helped."

"Considering the gravity of the present situation, we demand that Ambassador Husain acknowledges the president's request."

"You are no longer in position to demand anything from us, Mr. Nettleton. We have long stood by, here in Washington and in New York at the United Nations, listening to this administration and the previous administrations kowtow to the terrorist demands of the Indian government."

Nettleton gave the president a questioning look. It was unprecedented that any ambassador would refuse a summons from the president of the United States. But it was even more extraordinary that an ambassador's secretary would speak in such a harsh, peremptory manner to someone as high ranking as the president's adviser on national security affairs. Nettleton touched the mute button.

"How far should I push him, Mr. President?"

"He wouldn't be talking like that if Husain wasn't right there listening in," the president said. Sandar Abas Husain was the ambassador appointed eighteen months ago by Pakistan's military government. In the last six months Husain had become increasingly aloof, at times even imperious, knowing of course that Pakistan was nearing completion of its thermonuclear weapon.

"What should I say?"

"Brad?" the president asked, turning to his chief of staff.

"I'd say press him. See what he does."

Tyson nodded. "I agree. The only danger is if India finds out that Pakistan's bomb is portable. If Pakistan suspects that the Indians know, then they'll be forced into making an immediate preemptive strike. Go for broke."

The president agreed. "But if India does find out, they'll make a preemptive nuclear strike. It'd come down to a race between them." He nodded for Nettleton to get back to Aly.

Nettleton touched the mute button. "I'm sorry, Mr. Aly, but I thought that you said that the United States government was in no position to demand anything of Pakistan. I must have misheard. But then you are not the ambassador, you are not a diplomat, so we will forgive the lapse for the time being. Pakistan is dangerously close to finding itself in the same untenable position that Iraq found itself in: cut off from the rest of the world, isolated, reviled, economically sanctioned."

"Pakistan will no longer hang her head in shame—"

"Be that as it may, Mr. Aly, the president wishes to speak with Ambassador Husain at the soonest possible moment on an issue of the gravest importance to the continued good relations between Pakistan and the United States."

"The ambassador is in conference, as I have already told you, Mr. Nettleton."

"Pakistan's security is at stake."

"Don't threaten me, sir. Those days are gone forever. Pakistan's sting is much harsher than it has ever been. If we are threatened we will defend ourselves to the fullest limits of our considerable power. Against any enemy, near or far."

When the connection was broken, the president looked at Dr. Tyson. "Do you think they know about Scott?"

She shook her head. "They would have made some reference. Even an oblique one. I think they're stalling for time."

"Why?"

"The million-dollar question, Mr. President."

"One that I need an answer for. And soon."

AMBUSH

1

2000 GMT
SEAWOLF
MID-PACIFIC

The movie tonight was *Contact*, with Jodie Foster.

Dillon unusually took the second hour of the first watch of every other cycle for his turn on the stationary bike in the torpedo room. Captain's privilege. A TV monitor was bracketed to a niche in the bulkhead and the nightly movie started at this hour. *Contact* was one of his favorite films, in part because Jodie Foster could have been Jill's twin sister.

She was sitting on the hood of her car, earphones over her head, her eyes closed as she listened to sounds from space.

The lack of sunlight and exercise were the twin enemies of submariners. Especially since the advent of nuclear power, which made extended underwater cruises possible. They could make freshwater and oxygen from seawater, but for sunlight they had to rely on UV lamps and vitamin D. Since there was nothing else to do aboard a sub except work, sleep, and eat, weight was always a problem. Stashed here and there in the odd corner throughout the boat were exercise machines: the bike in the torpedo room, a treadmill (which Dillon hated) just aft of the baffle behind the sonar dome, and several chin-up bars in engineering, in the crew's mess and in the doorway to the goat locker, which was chiefs' territory.

Dillon did an hour on the bike every other watch, and on the off watches did one thousand sit-ups in his stateroom.

A low-pitched rhythmic noise suddenly started. One pulse. Then two. Then three. Jodie Foster opened her eyes and sat up. She was trying to believe that she was actually hearing the signal she'd been working all of her career as a radio astronomer to hear.

A signal from an intelligent race on another planet.

Dillon loved this part. That precise moment of discovery that took your breath away; when anything and everything was possible. In school he'd been faced with two paths in nuclear physics: pure science or engineering. He'd made his choice, one that he'd never regretted. But he still looked at scientists with a kind of reverence. It was like being a lapsed Catholic who still nodded and mumbled "Hello, Father," when a priest walked by.

Someone rapped on the side of a CO_2 tank with his knuckles. Dillon looked over his shoulder. It was Master Chief Petty Officer Arthur "Mr. T" Young.

Young was the senior enlisted man aboard the *Seawolf,* and therefore was often called upon to be a buffer between the crew and the officers. He was almost always chief of boat starting out on patrol and coming back in. He was also COB whenever they found themselves in a tough situation.

If anyone could be said to uphold navy tradition, it was him. Except that he and the chief engineer Lt. Mario Battaglia were best of friends ashore. The navy usually frowned on fraternization between enlisted men and officers, but no one ever dreamed of breaking up this pair. Without them *Seawolf* would stop functioning as a tightly-run warship. Dillon and his XO gave the direction, but it was duos like Battaglia and Young who provided the glue that held everything together.

"Have you got a minute, Cap'n?" Young asked. He should have been nicknamed Popeye, because he looked like the cartoon character. Short, bowlegged, with thick ham hocks for arms. He and Battaglia, who was a stocky Italian from the Bronx, could have been brothers. But Mr. T. stuck because no one except for the captain knew what the middle initial stood for, and Dillon had promised never to tell a soul.

"Sure thing, Master Chief," Dillon said. He reached over and turned the TV monitor's sound down as Jodie Foster drove at breakneck speed along the desert track beneath the mammoth radio telescopes.

Young came the rest of the way into the cramped corner of the torpedo room and rested a shoulder on a cable-covered bulkhead. He looked worried, which was a switch because he was usually an easy-going man. It was the crew who came to him with their troubles.

"I've got a bit of a problem, skipper. I surely don't know what to do about it, or if there's anything I can do."

"Somebody find out your real name?"

"No, sir, it's not that. It's back ashore."

Dillon frowned. Personal problems were *his* problems because of the effects they could have on the operation of his boat. "Okay, what's the deal?"

Young looked down at his shoes for an uncharacteristic moment or two. When he looked up he seemed sheepish yet determined. "You know my wife, Suze."

"Of course." A couple of times each year Dillon's wife Jill hosted a tea for the ladies of the *Seawolf*. And after each patrol Dillon and his officers and their wives staged a blowout picnic for the entire crew and their wives and sweethearts and kids. Suzanne Young was as well liked among the other enlisted men's wives as Young was with his boys.

"We've been married for twenty-four years, Cap'n. There isn't a thing I wouldn't do for her; climb mountains, walk through fire. Hell, I'd give my life if I thought it would make her happy. But it's not enough."

"I'm all ears, Art, but you're not making sense," Dillon prompted.

"There's another woman," Master Chief Young blurted, and before Dillon could react, he shook his head. "But it's not what you're thinking. She's not some bar girl I picked up somewhere. You know, a one-night stand." He looked away again for a moment. "Her name is Beth Anne Hoding. She's from Newport, originally, but she's living in Honolulu now. She moves to whatever base I'm assigned to. And it's been like that for eighteen years."

Dillon stopped pedaling. For a moment he was struck dumb. He'd intervened in a domestic squabble from time to time, or dealt with a Dear John letter—once even a Dear John letter so cleverly disguised in a familygram that whoever vetted it in Pearl had missed the significance. But he'd never had to deal with anything like this.

"Have you told Mario about this?"

Young shook his head. "No one on earth knows about it except for you, Cap'n."

"Well, you say that it's been going on for eighteen years. What's the problem all of a sudden?" Dillon asked. His question sounded callous to his own ears, but, damnit, what Young had been doing to his wife and to himself and therefore to the boat was wrong.

"Beth Anne has cancer. She's dying. And she has nobody except me."

Jodie Foster was racing through the corridors, and pushing through doors in the main control building, all the while giving frantic instructions via her cell phone.

Dillon shook his head. "I'm sorry, Art. Why didn't you request emergency leave?"

"I wouldn't have gotten it if I'd had the guts to ask, sir. Beth isn't a relative. And I didn't know that she was sick until a couple of hours ago. She stuck a letter in my seabag, and I just got to it." Young's wide, dark eyes were moist. "She told me not to worry." He laughed. "Now that's a crock. I didn't know what to do, skipper. You're the only person I could turn to."

"Is she seeing a doctor?"

"At Pearl General's oncology center."

It was the same place that the navy doctors had sent Jill. Cancer sometimes made strange bedfellows. It was even possible that they'd seen each other, spoken.

"We can't turn the boat around, Art."

"I wouldn't want that, sir. I just wanted to share this with somebody. With you, because your wife is sick too. Beth Anne wrote that she saw her at the hospital."

No one else on the crew knew that Jill was sick, not even Charlie Bateman. COs were supposed to be invulnerable; somehow above the problems the rest of the crew might have. The chief's problem was doubly his now.

"I suggest that you figure out how you want to handle this, chief," Dillon said. "When you get that worked out, then come to me and we'll figure out how to get it done when we get home."

Young nodded his appreciation. "Will do, Cap'n," he said. "And thanks."

"Think the *whole* thing out, Master Chief," Dillon cautioned sternly, "That includes what you're going to tell your wife."

"Skipper, conn." It was Bateman.

Young nodded. "Yes, sir," he said, and he left.

Dillon answered the call. "This is the captain."

"When you get a chance, skipper, Marc and Ski would like to run something by you."

Dillon glanced at the television monitor. Jodie Foster was just realizing that the alien signal consisted of prime numbers.

"I'll be right there."

DILLON SPLASHED some cold water on his face in his stateroom, got a cup of coffee from the officers' wardroom and went up to the control room.

His XO was hunched over one of the chart tables with Lt. Jablonski and Chief Sonarman Zimenski. They had a very small-scale western Pacific and eastern Indian Ocean chart spread out. Superimposed was a clear plastic overlay, which showed the ocean bottom details: the sea mounts, ridges, abyssal plains, canyons, and littoral regions around the land masses.

Jablonski and Zimenski had worked out a series of plots on the overlay with a thin-line grease pencil, parallel rules, and dividers. All of the work could have been done on computer-generated charts, but tradition dies hard in the U.S. navy. Most sailors preferred using paper charts at least in the initial chalk-talk phase of a proposed operation.

"What's up?" Dillon asked, joining them. He'd decided to grab the *Contact* DVD later tonight and replay it in his stateroom. Captain's privilege.

Bateman looked up. "Marc and Ski came up with an idea for our mission station approach that looks good to me. Could give us a big advantage going in, especially if they suspect we're on our way."

Dillon put his coffee aside. "Okay, what do you have?"

"I got to thinking about what happens when we show up in the Indian Ocean, Cap'n," Zimenski said. "If it's a Kilo we're looking for, she's bound to be real quiet. Especially if they know we're coming for them like Mr. Bateman says. And especially if they have an idea *when* we're going to get there. So I took a look at the new thermocline predictions we loaded at Pearl just before we sailed."

Zimenski replaced the very small-scale chart with a slightly larger one, that showed only the Indian Ocean east to the Malaysian peninsula and south to the Andaman Islands. He placed a matching overlay showing the bottom features, and a second clear overlay showing ocean currents and thermoclines.

"Once we cross the Andaman Basin and get into the Bay of Bengal we'll have a straight shot to where we think the Kilo should be waiting. About five hundred miles with nothing blocking our sound lines."

Dillon knew exactly what his chief sonarman had come up with, but he just nodded.

"If they're waiting for us it'll be beneath the thermocline where they think they're all but invisible to sonar. Pearl predicts the line will be between eleven hundred seventy feet and twelve-fifty. If we make our initial approach beneath this level, and then stick our bow just into the duct boundary, we should be able to hear them as far as six hundred miles out."

Zimenski looked up. "It's a deep sound channel. The Kilo would be in it, looking toward the east. But there's a secondary thermocline about one hundred feet beneath the main line. That's where we'll come in. Minimum sound resistance. Like a megaphone."

"They wouldn't suspect us to be within range so soon," Bateman said. "They might not be so careful with their noise management."

"It would give us the chance to load and roughly preset a pair of torpedoes without anyone being aware of it," Jablonski suggested.

Dillon tried to find fault with their plan, but he could not. He looked up and grinned. "Okay, gentlemen, good plan. Let's do it."

Jablonski was happy, but Zimenski was flying high. He'd just pulled another Jonesy.

"Might just give *us* the advantage," Dillon said. "Payback time for the crew of the *Eagle Flyer*."

"All right," Bateman said, grinning.

2

Marnie Morgan was bored.

For three days they had come up with nothing. She and her partner, FBI counterintelligence Special Agent Brian Fuller, were parked across the street from the embassy of Pakistan. Traffic on Sheridan Circle was heavy, as usual in the early evening. But here, just off the circle, between R Street and Decatur Place, the neighborhood was relatively quiet.

Cars, SUVs, and minivans lined the curbs. The light blue Ford Windstar van with deeply tinted windows attracted no notice. Marnie sat in the back, a pair of expensive earphones on her head, while Fuller talked to his girlfriend on his cell phone.

Bureau surveillance work—any surveillance work—was 99 percent boredom followed by 1 percent confusion. Only very rarely did the subject of a surveillance operation actually say or do anything usable. Most people in the business of hiding something from law enforcement—at least at the federal level—were too experienced or too smart to be tripped up like Washington mayor Marion Barry or the car guy, DeLorean. They'd gotten lucky a couple of years ago with the traitor Robert Hanssen. But a lot of that success story was, in Marnie's estimation, just dumb bullshit luck.

Marnie was cute and well built, but she was tiny. Her father, a used-car salesman in Madison, Wisconsin, had taught his daughter a no-nonsense approach to life. Ya gotta be tough to survive. Marnie was tough.

And Brian Fuller was soft. He thought that he was God's gift to women, but Marnie had never given him the time of day. In her estimation he was going through life with his head firmly planted up his ass.

A door opened and closed in her headset. She sat up and looked through the camera lens aimed through the van's one-way window to a third-floor window in the embassy. It was the living room of Ambassador Sandar Husain's private quarters.

A low-power blue-white laser beam, invisible under most conditions, was beamed from the tip of what appeared to be a cell phone antenna on the back of the van to the window glass of the ambassador's apartment.

Noises within the apartment caused the window glass to vibrate. Even though the Pakistanis had the ambassador's quarters debugged and filled with subaudible white noise, the new Raytheon 7747 processing computer could separate the random vibrations bathing the windowpanes from the people moving around and speaking inside.

At this moment they were listening to and recording everything said and done within the ambassador's apartment in strict violation of international law and diplomatic practices.

But what the hell, the Pakistanis had supposedly captured some of our guys, and were holding them incommunicado, contrary to international law.

"The last thing I want to do is cause trouble," a woman said. She sounded American.

Marnie caught Fuller's eye and motioned for him to get off the phone.

"What possible trouble could you cause, my dear?" Ambassador Husain asked, laughing. Marnie heard an odd noise. A shoe falling to the floor? Then rustling clothing?

"What's up?" Fuller asked, donning a second set of headphones.

"He's got his bimbo up there," Marnie said. Trouble with Brian was that he was handsome.

"So what? He's getting lucky—"

"Shut the fuck up, Brian, and listen, would you?"

"If you don't want to tell me something, then don't tease me. Just don't start," the girl said. Her voice got husky.

There were other sounds, soft, indistinct. Maybe Husain groaned softly.

Fuller grinned at Marnie. "ISI?"

She nodded. "My guess is that she's the one we got the heads-up on a couple of weeks ago. She works in their signals office. But she's really trying to find out if Husain is loyal or not. They've probably got a leak somewhere on the staff and they're trying to find out how high it goes."

"Right," Fuller said. "He's screwing her and she's trying to screw him."

"What do you mean?" Husain asked.

The woman muttered something that Marnie couldn't make out, and then it sounded as if they moved across the room. Maybe to the couch. The sound of a zipper was very clear.

"Beautiful," Husain said.

"I want to see them," the woman said.

Husain groaned again. "Who?" he mumbled. "Good . . . nice . . ."

"Why are they speaking in English?" Fuller asked.

"She's supposed to be under deep cover here," Marnie told him. "As long as she's on American soil she'll always speak English so that she'll not slip someday when it counts."

"You know, the CIA guys we're holding at—"

"What are you going on about?" Husain asked, his voice suddenly sharp.

"Easy, darling," the girl said. "Let me do this for you."

Husain said something that Marnie couldn't make out.

She got on the tactical radio. "Dispatch, blue bonnet. We're reading a possible red flag."

"Send it," the control officer in the J. Edgar Hoover Building responded immediately.

Marnie patched the laser-intercept channel to the operations center as Husain groaned in pleasure again.

"It's one of my fantasies," the girl said. "To see them being hurt."

"It's none of your business, my dear, but—" Husain cut off in mid-sentence.

"Fine," the girl said. There was a rustling.

"Where are you going?" the ambassador asked, alarmed.

"Obviously nowhere if I can't convince my lover to trust me."

"Why would you want to know?"

"I don't care where your police goons are keeping them," the girl shouted. "That's not important. You don't understand."

"Keep your voice down, you stupid woman," Husain ordered.

"I want you to trust me, that's all," she said petulantly. "Is that so hard to understand?"

There was a long silence in Marnie's earphones. She checked the laser transceiver control panel to make sure that it was still working. But then Husain spoke.

"The ISI has them at Kandrach," he whispered. "And it's the last place any of them will ever see alive. Everything will be different now. In Islamabad. In New Delhi. Especially here in Washington." He laughed.

Marnie held the headset tighter.

"Now come back here and finish what you started," Husain ordered.

3

Navy SEAL Lieutenant Bill "F/X" Jackson stood hidden in the shadows behind a bulkhead beam on the *Vinson*'s hangar deck waiting for the saboteurs.

It was noisy here, although most of the activity just now was taking place at the far end of the cavernous aircraft-filled deck nearly three hundred meters aft. No one was expecting the attack. Except for him.

Eight minutes ago the nose gear on one of the F/A-18 Hornets had collapsed, slowly settling the nose of the fighter-interceptor onto the deck. No damage had been done, but the action had created a diversion.

It was just what Jackson had been expecting.

There was a movement to his left, next to the portside weapons delivery elevator number two. Jackson dropped his night vision goggles over his eyes and peered around the edge of the bulkhead beam. At five-ten he was about average for a SEAL: He was built like a cross between a mean bulldog and a solid fireplug and he was smart. At special warfare ops school he'd earned the nickname Special Effects because of the high-tech battlefield tricks he'd developed. Shortly after he'd been assigned to his unit that name had been shortened to F/X.

A lone figure, dressed all in black, face, neck, and hands blackened had the elevator switch panel open and was doing something to the wiring inside.

Jackson scanned the immediate area; slowly, left to right, to make sure that the saboteur did not have help. He spotted no one.

He slipped his razor-sharp Ka-Bar knife out of its sheath on his right calf, eased around the bulkhead beam, and in four silent steps was behind the slender figure in black.

He grabbed the saboteur's head with his left hand, yanked it back none too gently, and raised the Ka-Bar.

Two dark-clad figures stepped out of the elevator and moved left and right, bracketing Jackson, raising their Heckler & Koch MP5 room broom submachine guns with suppressors directly at his head.

"Bang, bang, you're dead, Lieutenant," Chief Petty Officer Bob Ercoli said.

Jackson released his grip and stepped aside, a stern expression on his broad face. "Wrong answer, Chopper. All three of you are dead."

Ercoli and Chief Dale MacKeever, who'd been hiding in the elevator, lowered their weapons and glanced over their shoulders.

MacKeever spotted the Claymore taped in the corner, its business-end pointed outward. Anyone in its path, right where they'd been standing, would have been cut to ribbons when the mine went off.

Ercoli spotted the LED trigger taped to the doorway. He shook his head. "How'd you know we'd be aboard this elevator?" he asked.

"I didn't," Jackson said. "But you should've checked."

The fourth member of his SEAL team, Ensign Terri Vaughan, who'd been hot-wiring the elevator controls so that it would not work, glanced across the deck at the starboard-side forward weapons delivery elevator. "You rigged them all?" she asked.

"A guy can't be too careful when he associates with women the likes of yourself, Lips," Jackson said.

She grinned. "That's sexual harassment."

"Tell it to the chaplain," he shot back with a chuckle, but then he got serious again. "All right, the diversion was okay, if expected. The problem was your choice of battle dress."

"Nobody could see us," Vaughan countered.

"I did," Jackson said. "But if you'd been dressed in standard navy utilities I might have passed by. As it was, the moment you were spotted you stood out as intruders."

Ercoli shot her a look of "I told you so." He was a raging chauvinist and was just civil to her, even though she outranked him, and could outrun and outshoot him, any time any place. So far Chopper's personal problem had not affected the team, and Jackson meant to keep it that way in any way possible. That included not sleeping with Vaughan, who he thought was one of the most attractive women he'd ever met. He had an idea that the feeling was mutual. Out of thirteen hundred SEALS in the navy only nineteen were women. Everyone watched for them to screw up.

"Lieutenant William Jackson, report to the CIC," the IMC blared across the hangar deck. "Lieutenant William Jackson to the CIC."

Jackson glanced up and frowned, wondering what was up that they needed to see him at this hour of the night. "Okay, Chopper, I want you and Shooter to pull the Claymores and LEDs here and starboard. I only did the two forward elevators."

Ercoli and MacKeever nodded.

"Lips, I want you to get started working up a plan of assault on the reactor itself. We're in a neutral port, your team comes aboard, sabotages the reactor, and gets off with the minimum of casualties."

"What do you want us to do to it, F/X?" Vaughan asked.

"I want it to go critical and melt through the hull."

Her pretty oval face lit up. She'd gotten her handle because she had movie star lips. "Fat," Ercoli called them. Sexy as hell, Jackson thought. "That'd make them sit up and take notice in a place like Kuwait City harbor."

"That's the idea."

THE VINSON'S combat information center was one deck down and just aft of the carrier's bridge. A marine sentry intercepted Jackson in the corridor before he got there.

"Sir, the admiral would like to see you in his quarters," the marine said. "I'll escort you there, sir."

The Vinson's battle group commander, two-star admiral Kenneth Nelson, was waiting in his sitting room with the Vinson's CO, Captain Richard Abrahamson, and his XO, Commander Pat Scofield. They were seated around a big coffee table on which was spread a chart of the Indian subcontinent. The Arabian Sea and Pakistan were to the west, and Myanmar and the Bay of Bengal were to the east.

Jackson knew by the chart and by the expression on their faces that they had received the information they'd been waiting for. The reason he and his SEAL team had been delivered aboard four days ago from Okinawa.

Captain Abrahamson looked up. "Here he is," he said. Abrahamson and the admiral were the new navy. They looked like bankers, or like the CEOs of *Fortune* 500 companies, which in effect was the level of complexity of a nuclear aircraft carrier and its far-reaching multiship battle group. And as regular, black shoe navy, they disliked SEALs and the SBS units that provided their backup. Special warfare operations people were prima donnas.

Jackson came to attention and saluted. The admiral sketched a return salute. "How'd your exercise go, Lieutenant?" he asked cooly. Unlike most admirals, Nelson had perfect-pitch memory. He apparently knew everything going on within his command, down to the last detail.

"They could have done better, Admiral. But in the real world they would have gotten the job done. The *Vinson*'s security people didn't have a clue."

The admiral smiled faintly. The rumor was that he and Captain Abrahamson had a running bet that the SEAL team masquerading as saboteurs wouldn't get past first base. The admiral was winning.

"What's next?" Abrahamson asked.

"We're going to take the reactor tomorrow evening," Jackson said. He nodded toward the chart. "That's if we have the time."

"You have forty-eight hours," Admiral Nelson said. "That's when we rendezvous with your ride. That'll be north of the Maldives."

"Have we found out where the CIA guys are being held?" Jackson asked.

Scofield stabbed a finger at a town one hundred seventy-five klicks west of Karachi on Pakistan's coast. "It's an ISI prison at a place called Kandrach."

"I never heard of it."

"Don't worry, not too many people have. The CIA is sending a briefing package out on a COD from Yokosuka. Won't get here until sometime tomorrow afternoon, so you're not going to have much time to bone up." A COD, or carrier onboard delivery, aircraft was a Grumman C-2A Greyhound; a slow mover used to deliver anything from fresh fruit and mail, to personnel and in this case top secret packages.

"We'll manage, Commander," Jackson said. "This is what we get paid for." He and his people were ready.

"Get some sleep, Lieutenant," Admiral Nelson said.

"Yes, sir," Jackson said. He saluted and started to go, but Captain Abrahamson stopped him.

"Are you going to have time for my reactor, Lieutenant?"

Jackson grinned. "Yes, sir. She'll go critical in—" He looked at his watch. "Twenty-three hours and fifteen minutes. And, sir, it's okay if you tell your security people that we're coming. It won't make any difference."

4

Dillon couldn't sleep. He sat at his desk writing the day's letter to Jill, even though it was very early morning.

The poem for the twelfth day out was something really obscure by Yeats. But bits of it were among his all-time favorite lines. Something about exiles who wandered over the land and sea.

Sometimes he felt just like that, like an exile wandering over the sea; he and the other COs of every submarine that sailed. In some ways they *were* what Yeats called renegades. Planning and plotting for the day when they would launch their nuclear weapons.

He sat back with his cocoa, his eyes closed, listening to the Sade CD that Jill had sent with him, and seeing Yeats's words.

Someone knocked at his door. Dillon opened his eyes. "Come."

A signalman from the radio shack came in. "Sorry to bother you, sir. But we received a four group ELF message for-your-eyes-only."

Dillon took the message flimsy. "Anything else?"

"No, sir."

"Ask Mr. Bateman to join me, would you?"

"Yes, sir."

The first three-letter extremely low frequency code group, SSS, had been decrypted as FOR-YOUR-EYES-ONLY, COMMANDING OFFICER.

Dillon opened the captain's safe and using his code book decrypted the second grouping, LQT, as GROUP SEVEN.

If there was to be an ELF message from COMSUBPAC, he figured it would be something like this. The first group was for the radio shack personnel to decrypt. The second group told Dillon that whatever groups three and four turned out to be would involve either a top secret message of a special nature, or a nuclear command authority authorization to release weapons. In either case it would take two keys, and two code cards—his and his executive officer's—to decrypt.

Bateman showed up a couple of minutes later with a cup of coffee for himself and a cup of hot cocoa for the captain.

"What's up, Frank?"

"A group seven just came in."

Bateman pursed his lips as he put down his cup. "We're less than twenty-four hours from clearing the Andaman Ridge," he said. He took his key from around his neck and inserted it into the left slot of the second, much larger safe in the aft bulkhead.

Dillon inserted his key in the right-hand slot, and they turned them together. "This could be it."

"Yeah."

Dillon took out the first loose-leaf notebook and went through the plastic bound pages until he came to PXY, the third ELF group. A pocket in the page contained a pair of stiff plastic packets. He and Bateman cracked open the packets to reveal two cards on which were printed a series of code groups. Bateman used his and a codebook from the safe to decrypt his part of the message with a letter grouping key that only he knew. Dillon used a page marked ASD, which was the fourth ELF group, to decode his part of the message, again using a letter grouping only he knew.

It took nearly an hour for them to finish. When they were done they combined messages, which gave them the final text. It was a cumbersome system, one that seemed to get worse each year when some Pentagon whiz kid figured out a new layer of confusion. But the system was secure. It helped prevent some CO from running amok and start launching nuclear weapons on Moscow, or even Des Moines.

TOP SECRET
FM: COMSUBPAC
TO: USS SEAWOLF

//MISSION MOD 01//

A. YOUR PRIMARY MISSION HAS BEEN DELAYED.

B. STS140 LAUNCH WILL BE DELAYED TO ACCOMODATE YOUR NEW MISSION.

C. YOU WILL PROCEED AT BEST POSSIBLE SPEED TO RENDEZVOUS WITH CVN CARL VINSON AT 08-00-00 N, 70-00-00 E, WHERE YOU WILL TAKE ON FOUR ADDITIONAL CREW AND MISSION PLANS.

D. DO NOT SURFACE.

//BY SPECIAL ORDER OF: ADM. J. PUCKETT JR.//

EOM

"They must have put this in the safe along with the launch codes for the Tomahawks when we went back to Pearl," Bateman said. He was relieved it wasn't a war order.

"That's what I figure," Dillon agreed, replacing the codebooks in the safes and latching the doors. "They must have been waiting for something to happen. Something they couldn't even tell me about until it did."

"Like what?" Bateman asked. His brain was going just as fast as Dillon's. Out-of-the-box orders got everybody's attention.

"I don't know, but I expect we'll find out when we get there." He and Bateman turned their keys and removed them.

"Now what, skipper?"

"Have Teflon and Ski meet us in the control room. I want to plot a best possible speed course to the *Vinson*, and I want Ski to give his people the heads-up. Wouldn't do to bump into anything. The admiral said the shuttle mission was being *delayed*, not canceled. So we're still going to have to come back and finish the job."

5

Scott Hanson hunched his knees up to his chest as he huddled in the corner of his cell listening to the inhuman shrieks of agony coming from down the corridor.

It was his turn next in "the room." It had been that way since they'd arrived here two—or was it three?—days ago.

As red warren team leader he went last. First was Mike Harvey. Next was Bruce Hauglar with his badly burned back and neck. Then Don Amatozio, and finally himself.

They were allowed little or no sleep, only a thin gruel of rice or wheat paste with a few pieces of rotted fish and a lot of curry powder twice a day, and one cup of dirty, tepid water a few hours after each meal.

Hanson was wearing down. He expected the others were wearing down too, though he couldn't know for sure. They hadn't seen each other since they'd gotten here. The food provided very little in the way of nourishment and it gave him violent diarrhea, which further weakened him.

His only clothing was a filthy pair of cotton shorts, soiled by his own excrement. His body was a mass of cuts, bruises, welts, and large blood blisters from the big pliers they used to pinch his inner thighs, the backs of his arms, and the small of his back on either side of his spine.

His four front teeth had been knocked out in the first interrogation session, and then his nose had been broken, and a couple of ribs cracked. It made it hard to breathe deeply.

Amatozio's screams abruptly stopped, and Hanson looked up. He shivered violently for several seconds before he could bring his body back under control.

The screams were bad enough. But it was the silences afterwards that got to him the most. It meant that Don was unconscious. Or dead. But it also meant that his turn was next.

They had not found out any of their names yet. Or at least their interrogators had shown no special interest in Hanson. It was only a slim hope for now. But sooner or later he figured someone would recognize him. Or one of the team, maybe even himself, might crack and identify him.

Each session was the same. There were three questions, the accusation, and then the torture, which was followed by the same three questions, the same accusation, and then more torture. The only variation was in the torture. Sometimes it was pliers, sometimes rubber hoses, sometimes electrical shocks to the testicles. But always the excruciating pain.

The steel door to Hanson's concrete cubicle banged open. Two ISI guards waited in the corridor for him to struggle to his feet and stagger out to them. The first time they had come for him, he had resisted. That's when they had dragged him out and knocked out his front teeth.

He didn't resist anymore.

The cell was six feet by six feet with a low concrete ceiling in which was set a very strong light that never went out. There were no windows, no bed or mattress, not even a blanket. He had to relieve himself into a small stinking hole in the floor.

In the corridor he automatically turned left and tottered to the open door at the end. The guards did not touch him, nor did they speak.

The small, rat-faced interrogator in an ISI uniform, his collar open, leaned against the bare concrete wall in the room. The only furnishing was a three-legged stool made out of steel.

Hanson sat down, the door behind him was closed, and the two guards took up positions on either side of him.

"Good evening," the interrogator said. He was ISI Captain Javid Amin, although Hanson didn't know his name. "We're finally beginning to make some progress. Really splendid. And in such a short time."

Someone came in the room and handed Amin the satellite comms unit they'd used to contact Kuwait City. Hanson didn't turn so he couldn't see who brought it.

"This is what you call an SSIX mini. A communications unit that not only scrambles the signal, I'm told, but squeezes it into a very tiny burst of static and then bounces it off an orbiting satellite." Amin smiled and shook his head. "The infidel are ingenious. We must give them that," he told the man standing behind Hanson.

He held the mini in front of Hanson's face. "All I am asking is that you verify my information. What did you pass to your handler? Did you tell them our little bomb secret? A simple nod of the head will do. Yes, or no."

Hanson remained stock-still. He wondered which of the other three had given the answer to question number one. Amatozio, maybe. It'd be a living hell to be in this situation *and* blind.

Amin handed the mini back to the one who'd brought it in. "Well, we now know about the communicator. Can you tell me how the weapons and supplies were delivered to your mountain hideout?"

Someone from behind Hanson handed the captain a Sterling submachine gun. Amin cycled the bolt, pointed the weapon at Hanson's head, and pulled the trigger.

The firing pin snapped on an empty chamber, but it felt to Hanson like someone had stabbed a giant needle into his brain. He flinched so hard he almost fell off the stool.

Amin smiled faintly, and handed the gun back. "You came here to spy on us. What message did you send to your control officer?"

Hanson was at his limits. He hung his head. He shouldn't have reacted to someone dry firing a weapon at him. He'd been there, done that, in BUD/S training, basic underwater demolition/SEALS, in San Diego.

He looked up after a moment or two and returned Amin's smile. "Fuck you," he said good-naturedly. The sonofabitch was going to call him a terrorist now, and then the torture would begin. He might as well make it worth their while.

Amin's face turned red. "You are nothing but dogshit!" he screamed. "You are a common criminal! You are an international terrorist!"

"Fuck you *and* your mother," Hanson said.

Someone handed Amin an electric cattle prod. This was something new. Hanson's muscles bunched up.

The steel door opened. "Captain, there is a telephone call."

"Not now," Amin shouted. He was insane with rage.

"Yes, Captain, now."

Amin looked beyond Hanson, and hesitated for a moment. Then he came down, and nodded. "Yes, I understand," he said. He looked at Hanson, then jammed the cattle prod into Hanson's chest.

A bolt of white-hot lightning hammered Hanson's body, careened up his neck, and burst inside his head like a Patriot missile coming out of its box, and he fell off the stool, his head crashing onto the concrete floor.

AMIN HURRIED across the compound to his office in the ranger camp administrative wing. He was still seething. The bastard Americans were all alike. Allah had visited His wrath on them. They were frightened. And it would happen again. Another day of rejoicing would come.

He picked up the telphone. "Captain Amin speaking."

"This is Asif."

Amin stiffened. "Yes, General. Good evening. We are making great progress already." Major General Jamsed Asif was the director of the ISI.

"I am glad to hear that, but you have very little time to finish the job, Captain."

"I understand—"

"You do not understand. The Americans may try to mount a rescue attempt."

"Here, General?"

"Yes. We just learned of the possibility. If you are alerted I want you to be ready to execute the spies, and burn their bodies. Do you understand that, Captain?"

"Yes, of course, General," Amin replied. "But what about the woman?"

"Her as well. They must not be allowed to be taken away by the Americans. At all costs. If you cannot defeat the rescue team, kill the prisoners."

6

Bill Jackson sat on his haunches on the narrow swim platform lowered on the *Vinson*'s starboard stern.

The seas ran to three meters, but in the broad path made by the giant aircraft carrier the ocean was flat. It was overcast tonight. There were no stars and no horizon, only a blackness in every direction. Perfect.

He checked his GPS Plugger handheld navigator and then his watch. It was 2300 hours, local. They were in position and on time.

Jackson looked over at the others, then gave them the *go* signal.

Terri, who was point, slipped into the water first, followed by Mac-Keever and then Chopper. Jackson waited for the interval, then turned and rolled backwards into the water four feet below.

It was like running into a concrete wall. The *Vinson* had reduced speed to thirty-five knots; not so slow as to create any suspicions by some scope dope somewhere, but fast enough to bounce the divers around for the first ten seconds.

Murphy's Law, he thought as he tumbled end-over-end in the *Vinson*'s powerful prop wash: Never forget that your equipment was made by the lowest bidder. After they had knocked off the carrier's reactor with no problems, they had spent the remainder of their time going over the mission details, and then checking their equipment. There would be very few second chances where they were ultimately going.

Gradually they came out of the strongest parts of the *Vinson*'s wake, the seas directly behind the big ship still relatively calm. Chopper and Shooter formed up on Terri, and when Jackson reached them they gave him the thumbs-up sign.

"That was some ride," Terri said.

"Yeah. And our taxi should be along any minute now," Jackson said. In addition to the Draeger closed-circuit rebreathers they wore, each of them carried a thirty-five-kilogram pack with their weapons and other gear. Their loads would be lighter during the feet-dry portion of their mission, but still considerable.

"Right behind you, F/X," MacKeever said.

Jackson turned. The *Seawolf*'s attack periscope head jutted one meter out of the water, the oblong hooded lens aperture pointed at them. A single flash of soft red light came from the periscope, and then it disappeared under the water.

"Claustrophobia city, here we come," MacKeever said. He cleared his mouthpiece and slipped under the water just behind Terri. Chopper followed him, and with one last look toward the *Vinson*'s lights already a very long way off, Jackson compensated his buoyancy-control vest and dove into the blackness.

THE *SEAWOLF* hovered at fifteen meters. The bridge deck atop her sail was only a couple of meters beneath the deepest wave troughs.

Terri on lead followed the aft edge of the sail down to the broad deck that materialized dimly like a ghost ship, then back to the open hatch into the escape trunk.

No lights showed from inside the boat in case a reflection through the water could be spotted from the surface, or from a low-flying aircraft. They were taking no chances.

Everything was by feel. Jackson entered the escape trunk feet first behind the others, and when he was in he reached up and pulled the hatch closed.

When he had it dogged, he fumbled for the flood-control valve, finding it just over Chopper's shoulder. There was a very loud *hiss* of high-pressure air, and a lot of serious bubbles came from the bottom of the chamber as the water began to drop.

As soon as it was chest level they spit out their mouthpieces and breathed the relatively fresh air. A second later a dim red light came on.

"I'm glad that's over with," MacKeever said. Despite their training, some SEALs were claustrophobic locking into and out of submarines. MacKeever was one of them. His therapy was griping. He'd never froze on a mission. Not once. He just bitched a lot.

"You'd think they'd find an easier way," he groused.

"You shoulda joined the army," Ercoli said. "I heard those guys even get breakfast in bed."

The hatch beneath their feet was undogged from below, and was pushed up. An officer with carrot-red hair, whose name tag read *BATEMAN*, grinned up at them. "Welcome aboard the *Seawolf*, gentlemen."

Terri pulled off her hood, and gave him a big smile.

"And lady," Bateman amended without missing a beat.

One by one they climbed down into the stores room just aft of the mess room, where they took off their packs and dive equipment. They were handed towels and then followed Bateman forward a couple of compartments to the officers' wardroom.

Frank Dillon was waiting with Jablonski and Alvarez, whom he introduced. None of them showed the least surprise when they realized that one of the SEALs was a woman, and a good-looking woman at that. Except Alvarez, who grinned.

"Pleased to meet you, ma'am," he said.

"Thanks for the lift, skipper," Jackson said. "Would have been a long swim home if you hadn't been here."

"Happy to oblige, Lieutenant," Dillon said. "But now that you're aboard we'd like to know where we're headed."

"You were told nothing, sir?"

"Just the time and place to rendezvous with the *Vinson* and pick up you and your team."

"We're going to Pakistan," Jackson said. He took out a sketch map and unfolded it on the table. "An ISI prison and interrogation center outside Kandrach. Four CIA guys are being held there and we're going to bring them home before it's too late."

"Too late for what?" Dillon asked.

"One of them is Scott Hanson, the president's brother."

Dillon exchanged a look with his officers. "I wonder whose bright idea it was to send him into harm's way? Did they have anything to do with the nuclear test that Pakistan conducted?"

"They witnessed it, skipper. The ISI is probably going to use them to bargain with, especially if they realize who Hanson is." Jackson shook his head. "I don't know the rest of the story, except that a couple of them might be banged up, and the ISI might have an idea that somebody's coming for them."

"No doubt about it," Dillon said. "Anything else?"

"Yes, sir. I wasn't told the significance, except that this was Mother's plan. And that the shuttle launch stays on hold until you send the mission-accomplished signal."

Bateman's eyebrows rose. "Mother?"

For a couple of moments Dillon had no idea who Jackson was talking about, but then he remembered. He smiled. "Carolyn Tyson."

"The director of the CIA?" Bateman asked.

"I was an engineering officer aboard the *Flying Fish*. She came aboard for two weeks on a mission in China. Bright woman."

"She was a SEAL," Terri said. "Her handle was Mother."

"I never knew how she got that," Dillon said.

Terri grinned. "Tyson chicken. Mother hen. Mother. It works like that sometimes, sir."

"If this is her op, then it'll be a good one," Dillon said. "She's the best."

7

Jackson and his SEAL team stayed out of the way for the night and a day en route. They'd been assigned to hot bunk in the goat locker but ended up in the torpedo room where they had a little more space to lay out their weapons and check them one final time.

There was no sensation of speed inside the *Seawolf*, but Jackson had been briefed that they would be making in excess of forty-five knots. They would cover the two thousand kilometers from their rendezvous with the *Vinson* to a point a few kilometers offshore of Kandrach in a little over twenty-four hours.

No submarine moved as fast underwater, and not many surface ships could outrun them, either. It was like being inside a rocket ship.

Bateman appeared at the hatch. "We're on station. Are you guys ready?" he asked.

Jackson looked up and nodded. They'd consolidated their loads. In addition to carrying knives, 9mm pistols, hand grenades, and one LAW rocket each, they carried their suppressed Colt commandos and two thousand rounds of ammunition each. MacKeever also carried a room broom, and Chopper carried his Peacemaker, a folding stock SPAS 12 Franchi twelve-gauge shotgun that could fire thirty rounds per minute. It was guaranteed, Chopper said, to create peace in small rooms filled with pissed-off enemy soldiers. Nobody felt the need to contradict him.

"How far out are we, XO?" Jackson asked.

"Five miles. But we'll get you a lot closer before you have to start swimming. There're a lot of patrols out there."

Terri grinned viciously. "Finally, some decent odds to play with. Frankly, *guys*, I wasn't looking forward to one-on-one."

MacKeever gave her a high five.

Bateman shook his head. "You folks are nuts," he said good-naturedly. "Lay aft to the escape trunk when you're good to go." He turned and left.

"Okay, no hotdogging on this one," Jackson warned. "They aren't going to be in any kind of mood to take prisoners."

"Neither are we, F/X," Ercoli said.

BATEMAN MET them at the forward escape trunk a few minutes later. He was a little tense.

"When we get the green light we'll be two thousand yards off-shore. That's the best we can do. It's kinda busy up there right now."

Jackson unfolded his waterproof chart, and Bateman pointed to a spot a few kilometers west of Kandrach.

"The skipper's giving you six hours," Bateman said. "We're going to back off and snuggle up next to a wreck in about four hundred feet of water until then. Don't be late."

Jackson folded up the map and put it in a zippered pocket. "They might be in bad shape, commander. Have your pharmacist mate standing by."

Bateman nodded. "You might have to wait in the water at the rendezvous point until it's clear for us to surface and take you aboard. But we'll be there."

MacKeever snapped his fingers. "I almost forgot. You know what we're really going to need, sir?"

Bateman's eyes narrowed. "No. What?"

"A hot bath, a massage, and a cold beer."

A green light next to the hatch flashed twice, then the lights in the compartment went to red.

"I'll see to it personally," Bateman said, opening the hatch.

They climbed up into the escape trunk, Jackson last. When the chamber was sealed they opened the flood controls and donned their masks and mouthpieces.

"There's gotta be a better way," MacKeever griped as the water reached his chest. And then even the red light went out.

It was another starless night when they locked out of the *Seawolf* and made their way fifteen meters to a choppy surface, Terri ascending first as point.

Jackson checked their exact position with his Plugger GPS, and punched it into memory. Now they could come back to within one meter of this spot no matter what the sea state was.

To the east the small city of Kandrach lit the night sky. To the west they could make out the rotating green-and-white beacon of Ormara air force base. But straight north the beach was dark.

The water was filled with rotting garbage and oil slicks that were roiled up and frothy in the short, sharp whitecaps. Behind them, to the east and west, a thousand meters or more out to sea, they could see the lights of perhaps as many as a dozen fast-moving patrol boats. With all the racket they were making, *Seawolf* would be in no real danger of detection unless one of them accidentally ran directly overhead.

Jackson gave Terri the thumbs-up signal, and she immediately headed toward the beach. The others fell in behind her at ten-meter intervals.

It took them almost an hour to reach the beach, where they lay in the surf to watch for patrols.

There were a lot more lights here than they'd been able to pick out from two kilometers offshore. The mouth of the Hab River was between them and Kandrach. A bridge crossed a couple of klicks inshore, and from where they lay they could see some traffic. More lights moved along the river, and farther inland, maybe several kilometers, were lights on a tower or possibly a power plant smokestack. It was not on their charts.

There was more activity here than promised in the briefing package Jackson had read. A lot more activity.

One hundred meters from the water's edge the hardscrabble beach gave way to sand dunes, low scrub grass, some scraggly-looking trees, and three sandbagged gun emplacements.

As they watched, an APC came up the beach, its lights off. They were able to hear it before they saw it, and Jackson motioned for them to stay down and to remain absolutely still until it passed. The spotter standing up in the turret was probably wearing night vision glasses.

It was an old Russian BRDM-1, with a crew of five that mounted a 7.62 mm SGMB machine gun. In a real firefight up against a tank, it wasn't worth much. But against someone crawling up from the beach it would do the job.

It passed slowly east to west, and when they could no longer hear its exhaust, Jackson pointed out the three sandbagged gun emplacements to make sure everyone was clear on exactly where they were.

If anyone spotted them, or if they had to fire a single shot, the game would be up and they would have to hightail it back to the rendezvous and wait for the *Seawolf* to come pick them up. If that happened there was little doubt what the ISI would do to the American prisoners. At the very least they would be tortured and beaten, if that hadn't already occurred.

Jackson motioned for them to move out. This time he took point, the other three at close enough intervals that they could reach out and touch the ankle of the SEAL ahead of them.

As they crawled one meter at a time up the beach from the water, Jackson's every sense was attuned to his environment. He was as aware of his people behind him and the activity out to sea as he was of the lack of activity for the moment on the beach, the gun emplacements they had to slip past, and every square centimeter of scrabble and sand in his path.

If he was expecting an armed party to come ashore, he would have booby-trapped the beach with contact mines or Claymores. Not only would something like that slow down the invaders, it would provide an early warning perimeter.

Fifty meters up from the water, Jackson stopped. A nearly invisible monofiliment line at nose level was just a few centimeters in front of his face. He followed the line out in either direction with his eyes, but he couldn't see where it connected.

He reached back and touched the top of MacKeever's head. Shooter's eyes narrowed behind his camo paint.

Jackson gave hand signals to indicate the line, and that they were to crawl over it without disturbing whatever trigger it might be connected to.

MacKeever nodded his understanding and relayed the instructions.

Jackson probed the sand directly on the other side of the wire to make sure that it was clear. He rose up a little and straddled the line, and then carefully moved completely across, making sure that the toe of his boot cleared.

When he was over he waited for MacKeever to cross, then moved forward a couple of meters to let Ercoli clear the trip wire.

As soon as Terri brought up the rear, Jackson headed for a spot halfway between the two gun emplacements toward the west.

Twenty meters out a red light showed briefly from an open doorway. Jackson froze. The others behind him, realizing that their point man had stopped, did the same.

A Pakistani soldier in night fighter camos appeared in silhouette a couple of meters west of his bunker. He stretched, looked out to sea, then directly at Jackson.

For several seconds the soldier remained staring at Jackson, but then he turned and walked a few meters back toward the sand dunes and brush. He undid his web belt, slid his trousers and underwear down around his ankles, then squatted to pee. It was the Muslim way.

When he was finished he got up, pulled up his pants and donned his web belt and holster, then went directly back to the gun mount.

Jackson waited a few minutes in case the soldier's bunker mate also needed to take a pee. When that didn't happen he moved out.

The beach gave way to a series of low, rounded sand dunes behind which were scrub grass and short, gnarly trees that reminded Jackson of olive trees he'd seen in the south of Spain. He'd been over there a few years ago on a training mission with the Spanish special forces.

Beyond the dunes and trees the coastal highway ran roughly parallel to the beach, crossing the Hab River a couple of kilometers to the east.

Jackson checked his watch. They'd locked out of the submarine one hour and fifty-eight minutes ago. They were due back at the rendezvous with the four American prisoners, who were probably banged up and would not be able to move very fast in four hours.

Time was running short.

There was no traffic for the moment. Jackson turned back and explained what he wanted to do.

"I'll be the hitman," he told them. "Terri will be the decoy."

A big grin spread across her narrow, pretty face. "All's fair in love and war, F/X," she said.

"That's the truth," he replied. "We're looking for a truck. No comms antenna. Wait for my signal."

Terri nodded, and started taking off her equipment pack and unslinging her LAWs rocket.

Keeping low, Jackson darted across the road, taking up position in the opposite water-filled ditch. He took off his equipment pack because he was going to have to move fast. He screwed the silencer on the end of his Sig-Sauer P226 9mm autoloader pistol.

The first two vehicles to pass were automobiles, one a battered Mercedes and the other an old Russian Lada. The third was a tanker heading toward the city, and the fourth was a personnel transport truck, its canvas sides rolled up.

Jackson glassed the truck, which was coming across the bridge from Kandrach, with his low-lux binoculars. He could make out that the driver was alone, but very few other details until the truck got within one hundred meters of his position.

The driver was definitely alone. He was wearing an army cap and there was no communications antenna. There were no soldiers in the back.

Jackson motioned at the oncoming truck. Terri waved back.

When the truck was less than fifty meters away, Terri casually got up and walked out onto the road. She had stripped to her bra and panties, her white skin almost incandescent in the truck's headlights. She had left her boots on, but she had wiped the camo paint off her face.

The truck driver jammed on the brakes.

Jackson checked to make sure that the bridge was still clear and that nothing was coming from the opposite direction. They only needed a couple of minutes for this to work. Considering how long it had taken them to get this far, and how much farther the ISI prison was, they needed transportation even if it meant taking a chance.

Terri smiled and raised a hand as the truck came to a complete halt. She headed over to where it had stopped, the driver's eyes practically popping out of their sockets.

Jackson rose up and crossed the road in a run, keeping an eye on the back of the driver's head.

At the last moment he jumped up on the passenger-side running board. Terri ducked down as the truck driver, sensing someone behind him, started to turn.

Jackson fired three shots into the driver's head, blood and brains splattering out the open window.

They had transportation.

8

The fifth surface target closed in from the southeast.

"Talk to me, Ski," Dillon said calmly. He was at the door to the sonar room. "Can you give me the type?"

"Stand by one, skipper," Zimenski said, fine-tuning his BSY-2 display.

They'd been at it for a couple of hours, ever since they'd settled on the bottom less than thirty yards from the wreck of what was probably an old freighter. It seemed as if half the Pakistani navy had suddenly shown up and started pinging all over the place in a serious effort to find them.

The first question was how did they know that the *Seawolf*, or any other submarine for that matter, was going to be here? The answer was fairly simple in Dillon's mind. They'd been betrayed again by the spy in the Pentagon.

But that brought up a whole host of other problems. Like how the hell did the spy know even before the *Seawolf* knew where they were going? Or, what sort of reception was Jackson and his team getting ashore? Or, when it came time to make their pickup, how was he going to do it without shooting at every ship up there?

No submarine commander enjoyed being caught between shallow water shoreward and the open water seaward by a fleet of hostile ASW surface ships.

"Skipper, sierra five is an Amazon class frigate. Bearing one four zero, range eighteen thousand yards, and closing at twenty-three knots."

"Do they have us?"

Zimenski looked over his shoulder and grinned. He was loving this. "Not a chance, sir. They're making so much noise I don't think they could pick out their own blade counts."

"But they're pinging?"

"Yes, sir."

"Keep on it. We've got a few hours to get through yet," Dillon said. He went back to the control room where Bateman and Alvarez joined him at the forward plotting table. Brown was plotting sierra five's position, bearing, course, and speed.

"It's a British-built Amazon class frigate," Dillon said. "The Pakistani navy has redesignated it the Tariq class. But the point is, she's a strong ASW platform. Carries a Lynx chopper and a good ASW weapons load, including a couple of our CAPTOR mines, and the British Spearhead torpedo that we'd be hard pressed to outrun."

It was clear from the plotted positions of the surface ships, which included two fast patrol vessels, two British-built Leander class ASW frigates, and the Tariq, that the Pakistani navy knew that a submarine was here and that they were attempting to box it in.

"We could get out of here right now," Bateman said. "Come back in a few hours after they'd realized they'd missed us." He was playing devil's advocate and everyone knew it.

"We'd be leaving the SEAL team hanging," Alvarez bridled. In the 'hood you took care of your own. By his reckoning it was no different in the navy.

"Just a suggestion," Bateman said. "I'm talking plain and simple navy math," He looked at Dillon. "It's something we have to consider."

"I'm sorry, sir, but what's navy math?" Ensign Brown asked.

"Four SEALS plus four American prisoners makes eight," Alvarez explained. "We're carrying a crew of one hundred thirty-four. The math says you don't kill one hundred thirty-four people to save eight."

"That sucks," Brown blurted.

"I agree," Alvarez said strongly. They all looked at the CO.

"Relax, we've got a few hours yet," Dillon said. He glanced at the chart, and then looked up again. "We *will* not leave anyone behind."

9

The lights suddenly came on and the charge of quarters was standing in the open doorway shouting something.

Captain Amin came awake slowly, despite the commotion. He was in the president's palace; his wife and and mistress and all their children were with him. His first star was being pinned on his shoulder boards. Afterwards there was to be a lavish party on the grounds, with entertainment, food, drink, even fireworks.

"Captain, there is an urgent call for you from Chaklala. Priority red," the CQ shouted.

Amin opened his eyes, then sat up abruptly. "What are you doing here?" he screamed. He looked at his bedside clock. It was the middle of the night. His rage peaked. He threw back the covers, grabbed the Soviet PSM semiautomatic from beneath his pillow and scrambled out of bed, cocking the pistol as he went.

The CQ stepped back in alarm. "Captain, it is General Asif on the secure line for you, sir!"

Something of what the hapless enlisted man was saying penetrated Amin's fog. "What did you say?"

"General Asif is on the secure line, sir. We are going to come under attack at any moment."

A liter of ice water plugged directly into his brain. "The Americans," he muttered. "Sound the alert!"

"No, sir," the CQ replied, holding his ground now that he realized Amin wasn't going to shoot him. "The general wants to speak to you *before* we do anything."

"At least get the base commander out of bed," Amin said.

He pulled on his trousers and boots, then followed the CQ outside, across the administration complex parade ground and into the communications center.

He couldn't believe what he was witnessing. Nothing was getting done. The four enlisted man and one junior lieutenant were sitting around looking at him as if he was an apparition. They were making no calls. They were warning nobody. Their collars were open. There were teacups and food on the table. Pigs lived here.

He snatched the secure phone and pushed the talk button, but before he spoke to the general he screamed at the slovenly troops in front of him.

"This base is coming under attack and all you can think about are your stomachs? Alert the base, you godless idiots. But do it quietly so we can set the trap I've designed. Now! Or do I have to do everything myself?"

The soldiers scrambled to their feet without a clue what they were supposed to do. The call from Chaklala was for Amin only, and the CQ had been carefully instructed *not* to sound the general alarm. And what was this trap the captain was talking about? He'd not mentioned it before now.

Amin smiled inwardly as he turned back to the phone. "This is Captain Amin. Good morning, General Asif. Are they actually coming here?"

"At any moment," Asif said. "Frankly I'm relieved that you seem to be ready down there. There is a submarine parked just off our coast in a hundred meters of water, and four American SEALs are on their way to you as we speak."

"Pardon me, sir, but why hasn't the beach patrol taken care of them? Only four men?"

"I don't know. But you can expect an attack very soon. I want you to stop them, no matter what it takes. They must not be allowed to get anywhere near the prisoners. Do I make myself perfectly clear?"

"Perfectly, General."

"If you think there's a chance that you can not hold, then kill all five of your prisoners. Is that perfectly clear as well?"

"Perfectly, sir."

"Very well, Captain. Carry on."

"Are reinforcements being sent, General?"

"Do you feel that you need them?" the general demanded.

"Of course not, sir. I merely wished to know if anyone else would be approaching this installation tonight."

10

Jackson crawled through the grass to the edge of the dirt road.

Ercoli was ten meters behind him, just outside the cleared no-man's zone alongside the fence.

Terri had crawled to a position across the road from Jackson. Mac-Keever was ten meters behind her.

The prison was quiet, and mostly in darkness. There didn't seem to be anyone in the guard towers along the razor wire and chain-link fence. Nor was the fence illuminated. Nothing moved inside the compound and only a few lights came from the service doors of what might have been the motor pool to the west, and around what probably was the communications center to the east. A generator chugged softly in the night air behind the building, and there were a lot of wires and antennae atop the low, cement-block structure.

A SAM missile emplacement was hidden beneath camouflage netting just outside the prison fence toward the rear of the camp, but the radar dish was not moving nor did the site seem to be guarded.

Nothing was adding up in Jackson's mind. This was a working installation. There were cars and trucks and a couple of APCs parked here and there. The buildings and fences were in good repair. The generator was operating and there were some lights. But the place *felt* deserted.

Terri raised up and rocked her left hand, palm down, back and forth: *"What's going on?"*

He shook his head and motioned for her to wait one.

They'd gotten rid of the driver's body in a ditch on the way up from the coastal highway about eight klicks south. Then they'd parked the truck at the entrance to a gravel pit. Ercoli had gone under the hood and had removed the coil wire so that no one could come along and take their ride. Then they had made their way the last thousand meters here.

The camp was about one hundred meters on a side. A small, windowless cement-block building directly in the center of the compound was surrounded by a tall chain-link fence of its own, with a serious-looking gate made of interlocking metal tubes. It looked like a vertical Venus's-flytrap. Get caught in there, and you'd never get out.

The inner building had to be the lockup where the four Americans were being held.

The initial plan was for Ercoli and MacKeever to go through the fence on either side of the main gate and assault the camp from two directions, making as much noise and smoke as possible.

In the meantime, Jackson and Terri would take out the main gate and guards, and cross to the lockup, where they would take out the flytrap gate and those guards. Two gates, two LAW rockets.

They would release the prisoners and return the same way they had come. By this time Mac and Chopper would be turning outward, providing cover for Jackson, Terri, and the prisoners, and taking out anything else that caught their attention, including the SAM installation.

Once back at the truck they would beat feet for the beach, take out the three gun crews from behind, and swim out to the rendezvous point. They'd brought life vests for the prisoners.

It was SEAL tactics: lots of noise and movement, a hard shock to the enemy. And the element of surprise. Or at least Jackson thought they had. Now he wasn't so sure.

He waited another few seconds, debating his feelings of unease. But they had come here to do a job that wasn't getting done lying around in a ditch waiting for dawn. One of Murphy's Laws stated that you could get killed by doing nothing just as easily as by doing something.

He motioned for Ercoli and MacKeever to proceed with the plan. He and Terri would wait until the assault began.

Jackson got Terri's attention, pointed two fingers at his eyes, and then pointed toward the guard shack just inside the main gate. She nodded her understanding.

Ercoli and MacKeever moved in toward the fence, almost completely invisible in their camos. Fifteen seconds after Jackson gave the go-ahead signal, twin explosions ripped the night air on either side of the main gate, and very large openings magically appeared in the inner and outer fences.

Two guards scrambled out of the guard shack. Jackson hit both with three-shot bursts from his silenced Colt Commando.

Terri, who had crawled up to the main gate, cracked the acid fuse in the Semtex charge she'd placed, rolled back into the ditch, and a second later another powerful explosion lit up the now not-so-peaceful night, blowing the main gates off their hinges.

A few troops were coming out of the barracks to the left, but Mac-Keever was on them, spraying the outriders with controlled bursts from his Heckler & Koch MP5, driving them back inside. It was exactly what he wanted. He unslung a LAW rocket from his shoulder, extended the tube and placed a round into the front door, bouncing off the dirt before it entered.

The building went up in a bright flash bang and thousands of bits of burning wood and other materials rained down on the camp.

Ercoli swept right, toward the comms center and behind it the generator shed. He fired off a couple of quick rounds with his Commando, then put a LAW rocket into the generator shed, darkening what few lights were on in the camp.

Jackson and Terri raced up from the shattered main gate directly toward the central lockup. But there weren't enough soldiers here for this to be a ranger or ISI base. Especially not one in which four American VIP prisoners were being held.

Goddammit, it didn't add up. Something was way wrong here.

Suddenly it was as if a gallon of liquid nitrogen had been plugged directly into Jackson's veins.

"It's a trap," he shouted.

Terri stopped in her tracks and started to look over her shoulder when a Russian-built BTR-50PK tracked armored personnel carrier roared around from the east side of the lockup, its 7.62 millimeter machine gun swinging around into firing range.

Terri dropped to one knee, unslung the last LAW rocket, removed the end caps, extended the tube and raised the weapon to her shoulder. She switched the arm lever to the *on* position at the same moment a second BTR-50PK came around from the west side of the prison blockhouse.

MacKeever and Ercoli were already falling back to the fence, firing at the BTRs as they went.

Each of the machines carried a crew of two men, but more importantly, each was capable of transporting twenty fully combat armed soldiers.

The first BTR was bearing down on Terri, its machine gun depressing toward her, when she pulled the trigger.

The LAW's minimum range was twenty meters, inside of which the missile would not fire. The BTR driver knew it, and he tried to race directly toward the incoming shell, shortening the range. But he was too late.

Terri jumped up at the same moment the LAW 80 rocket hit just below the gun mount, where the armor was less than ten millimeters thick. Capable of penetrating six hundred millimeters of armor, the rocket blew the top off the machine, sending the flat upper deck straight up into the night sky.

The BTR swerved sharply to the left before coming to a halt as it burned furiously. There were no screams from inside the wreckage. The concussion had instantly killed the crew and passengers, pounding their bodies into hamburger.

The driver of the second armored personnel carrier pulled up short and slammed his machine in reverse to get back into the protection of the lockup building as the gunner laid down a screen of suppressing fire.

Ercoli went down hard, but there was no visible sign of damage to his body. MacKeever reached him at the same time Jackson did, and together they managed to drag him through the main gate and into the ditch on the east side of the road.

Terri was right behind them, covering their retreat from the increasing ground fire coming from the vicinity of a two-story building that could have been admin.

"They knew we were coming," MacKeever said, hurriedly checking Ercoli for wounds.

"It's the spy in Washington," Jackson agreed bitterly. What else had the bastard told them?

"We have to get out of here right now, F/X," Terri warned him urgently.

The second BTR had poked its nose from behind the lockup.

Jackson bobbed up over the edge of the ditch. The BTR cautiously moved across the compound toward them. "It's not going to take them very long to figure out that we don't have any more LAWs."

Ercoli was coming around. He was dazed, but not seriously hurt. He had taken a glancing round off the edge of his flak jacket above his left armpit.

A lot of troops were pouring out of the admin building, and even more from the vicinity of the SAM installation.

They were being boxed in on three sides. Their only option now was the back way that they had come in.

Without the four American prisoners.

It was a bitter pill for all of them to swallow. Especially for Jackson, who'd never once left a friendly behind.

There was no telling what the ISI would do to the prisoners once this fight was over with. But whatever it was, it definitely would not be pleasant. Especially if they recognized Scott Hanson.

"Back to the truck," he said. "We'll try for the sub."

No one argued. Even though they did not want to leave with a mission not completed, they understood the wisdom of the order. Besides, Jackson *was* the boss.

Terri covered their backs as Jackson and MacKeever helped Ercoli to his feet. Keeping low, they ran the hundred meters down the ditch until the camp road turned left toward some woods beyond which was the gravel pit.

The BTR was on the rise of the hill at the open main gates. At least one hundred Pakistani rangers dressed in night fighter camos flanked the tracked carrier. But they were moving slow. Too slow.

"Do you think they'll respect us in the morning, F/X?" MacKeever asked, grinning, as they hurried across the road and into the cover of the woods.

"Could be worse," Jackson said.

"How's that?"

"They might have had someone who wasn't stupid in charge. Then we might have been in trouble."

Jackson looked over his shoulder, but there were no immediate signs that someone was on their tails. If it had been his operation there would have been a lot of troops out here in the woods, way outside the perimeter, and choppers with FLIR pods coming up from the south.

"Arrogant bastards," Terri muttered.

"More of them than us, Lips," MacKeever replied.

No one had discovered the truck. Ercoli had recovered sufficiently to replace the coil wire. He banged the hood shut, then clambered aboard as Jackson cranked up the engine and headed toward the seacoast highway, headlights off.

11

0250 LOCAL
KANDRACH ISI PRISON

Scott Hanson's cell was filled with the haze of diesel exhaust and the sharp odors of discharged munitions.

The firefight had been a short-lived one. Whoever had come to rescue them hadn't come by air, nor had they brought enough firepower.

Hanson knew that the moment he heard the distinctive clatter of the Russian-made BTRs coming from somewhere behind the lockup.

Earlier in the evening he'd heard what sounded like preparations by the rangers, as if they were expecting an attack.

They were ready when it came. And the rescue attempt had failed. Another cock-up, probably, just like in the old days outside Tehran.

Scott slumped to the floor in one corner of his cell and hung his head. Spots of light danced in front of his eyes, and he was struck by a very strong bout of cramps.

For the first time in his life he wasn't so sure that he and his people were going to get out of something they'd gotten into. Sometimes you lose, someone had told him once. He'd laughed in the drill instructor's face, because he was young and arrogant.

He shook his head. He wasn't so young any longer. And he certainly wasn't arrogant.

Someone came to his cell door. The key grated in the lock and Hanson tried to push himself farther back into the shadows.

Captain Amin stood framed in the doorway, a dreamy look of triumph on his narrow rat face.

"Now you are mine," Amin said. "All mine." He started to laugh insanely.

12

The *Seawolf* slowly lifted off the bottom sand.

From the periscope platform Dillon extended the reed-thin WLR-15(V) antenna for the radar and electronic signal receiver. The tip of the mast rose forty-five feet above the top of the fair-weather.

Zimenski had reported that no sonar contact was closer than ten thousand yards. The Pakistani navy search pattern was concentrated for the moment to the west. There were twelve contacts, all of them making a lot of noise.

"Coming to three-five-zero feet," Master Chief Young said from the ballast panel.

Dillon confirmed their slow rise on the multifunction display above his head as he got on the growler phone. "ESMs, this is the captain. We're on the way up. But you'll only have a couple of seconds. It's real busy up there."

"Aye, skipper. We're ready," Chief Petty Officer Donald Ridley responded.

"Sonar, conn."

"Sonar, aye."

"Ski, if our separation from any of the targets drops below five thousand yards, or if any of them makes a sudden turn toward us, let me know."

"I'm on it, Cap'n."

Dillon had built a visual picture of what was happening on the surface. The *Seawolf* was surrounded on three sides by Pakistani warships. The only direction was shoreward. The only direction he could not go.

The Pakistanis were obviously searching for a submarine, but the only way that was possible was if someone in Washington had tipped them off. John Galt. And if he had passed along that information, what had he told them about the SEALs, or the four Americans they had come to rescue? Especially about Scott Hanson, the president's brother.

"Three hundred feet," Young reported.

"Chief of Boat, prepare for an emergency dive to three hundred feet on my mark," Dillon said.

"Aye, skipper," Young called out.

He was not going to leave his people behind, nor was he going to remain boxed in here, so that eventually he would be destroyed or forced to the surface where he would have to surrender.

The Pakistanis, like everyone else in the world, knew that American submarine drivers were ordered not to shoot, no matter how bad the provocation was. It gave the other guys the advantage.

"XO, sound battle stations, torpedo," Dillon ordered. "This is not a drill."

"Aye, Cap'n. Battle stations, torpedo," Bateman replied crisply. He passed the order throughout the boat.

"Two hundred fifty feet," Young said.

"Load tubes one and two with ADCAPs, flood tubes one and two and open the outer doors," Dillon said, calmly. He got back on the growler phone as Bateman acknowledged that order. "Sonar, this is the captain."

"Sonar, aye."

"We may have to fight our way out of here. I want you to keep a close eye on sierra three and nine. I'm starting TMAs on both of them."

"Aye, aye, Cap'n. They're the two most likely to give us trouble. But I suggest that you include sierra five and eleven. They're the next up."

"Good suggestion, Ski," Dillon said. He passed the order to Jablonski, who had already started the targeting program.

"One five zero feet," Young reported.

"Level off at one-zero-zero," Dillon said. At that depth the fully extended ESMs antenna would be out of the water and sampling every kind of electronic emission topsides.

"ESMs, conn. Stand by."

"Aye, skipper."

"Chief of Boat, stand by to initiate your emergency dive," Dillon said.

"Aye, skipper," Young replied. "One hundred feet. Masthead is dry."

Dillon counted backwards, under his breath. "Five . . . four . . . three . . . two . . . one . . . zero."

Chief Young, his hands on the main ballast control levers, was watching him.

"Emergency dive the boat," Dillon ordered. He keyed the phone. "Ski, this is the captain. Any changes?"

"Negative, cap'n."

"ESMs, this is the captain. What'd you get, Ridley?"

"Skipper, everybody's talking to everybody up there. It's a cluster fuck. But no one painted our antenna. They know we're here, they even know our name, but they're stepping all over each other. And that's not all."

The *Seawolf*'s deck canted sharply down as they headed for three hundred feet.

"What else?"

"There was a firefight at the ranger prison. Looks like there's an all-out manhunt going on topsides, for four SEALs. From the *Seawolf*, skipper. They keep saying our name."

"Chief of Boat, belay the dive," Dillon ordered. Ridley spoke Urdu, and right now he was worth his weight in gold. "Make your depth six zero feet, and get me as close to shore as you can."

13

Jackson pulled up short just as another light flashed briefly toward the seacoast highway. Terri studied the scene in her binoculars. All the lights from the bridge west had been turned off.

"Lots of traffic down there, F/X. No headlights," she said. "I'd guess they were looking for someone."

Jackson had been checking in his rearview mirrors all the way down from the ISI prison camp. He'd caught glimpses of lights all the way. But they weren't in a hurry. The traffic on the highway gave him the reason. They had set a trap.

"Okay, we're on foot from here," he said. He shoved open the door and got out of the truck.

Ercoli and MacKeever, who'd ridden in back, jumped down. Terri joined them.

"Looks like they've got us boxed in," Terri told them.

"Not very sporting," Ercoli offered.

"Use the last of the Semtex to wire the truck," Jackson told Ercoli. "Put it right under the driver's seat."

Ercoli unslung his pack, and grinning, scrambled under the truck.

"How many Claymores do we have left?" Jackson asked.

"Two," MacKeever said.

"Set them up at twenty-meter intervals on the east side of the road," Jackson told him.

"But the beach where we came in is on the other side of the road, F/X. West," MacKeever said.

"That's right. So we make 'em think that we're heading east, the Claymores covering our tracks." Jackson glanced up the hill the way they had come from the prison. He could see lights in the distance. "Shake a leg, guys, we're going to have company real soon."

Terri walked a few paces away from the truck and studied the highway through her light-intensifying binoculars. Jackson joined her.

"Are they organized?" he asked.

"Doesn't look like it," she said. "They're just moving back and forth between the bridge and what looks like a fortified checkpoint about five klicks out."

"They're trying to screen the road to keep us on this side."

"But that's dumb," Terri said. "They'd be better off hiding a half-dozen fire teams in the ditch on the other side of the highway—" She caught her own mistake. "Oh," she said.

"Right. Who says they haven't done that too?" Jackson asked.

Ercoli and MacKeever joined them a minute later. "If they get snoopy they're in for a couple of surprises," Ercoli said.

"We're out of here," Jackson told them. "I'll take point, Terri can take up the rear. When we get to the highway we'll cross one at a time. Might be somebody watching from the other side."

They waited for his next order.

"If there is, the rest of us will fan out and hit them with everything we've got. We're not surrendering, and nobody gets left behind."

With one last glance at the slowly advancing BTR and column behind them, Jackson headed west away from the dirt road. He kept low so that they wouldn't stand out to someone who might be scoping the hill through night vision equipment, but he moved fast. Once the ranger force from the prison reached the deserted truck the game would be up.

The Pakistanis had been way too timid with their ambush at the prison. And unless, as Terri had suggested, there were fire teams hunkered down across the road, their attempt at a blockade was crude as well.

The biggest problem, and possibly an advantage, Jackson thought, was in the numbers. The Pakistani rangers weren't up to the standards of the SEALs, or Green Berets, but they were good. They were motivated. And there were a lot of them.

The rangers knew what they were up against, and they knew that the SEAL team would try to make it back to the beach.

But they outnumbered the SEAL team by more than twenty-five to one. Added to that was the rangers' superior firepower. There was one BTR coming down from the prison, at least two on the beach, and possibly more on the highway.

It could tend to make the Pakistanis overconfident, although their noses had been bloodied in the prison yard. And if they weren't careful they would be getting another dose of the same medicine at the truck real soon.

Twenty-five meters from the seacoast highway the terrain dropped into a long, broad drainage ditch. There were times, especially during the monsoon season, when flooding would be a problem. The deep ditches took care of that.

Jackson motioned for them to spread out and take up positions just below the lip of the paved highway.

They waited for a break in what appeared to be a continuously circulating convoy of trucks and beat-up old Fiats, Russian-made Ladas, and American Chevy station wagons, all painted olive drab.

Terri scoped the opposite side of the road, and then gave Jackson the sign for all-clear, with a question mark at the end. She wasn't 100 percent sure.

He nodded his understanding and signaled for MacKeever to go across first.

They had to wait a couple of minutes for the next break in traffic, and then MacKeever scrambled up onto the road and ran across, flat out, throwing himself into the ditch on the other side.

A minute later he popped up and signaled the all-clear.

A canvas truck filled with regular army troops ground past slowly as if the driver and lookout were searching for something. Or somebody.

Jackson motioned for Ercoli to go next. When the truck was clear he jumped up and raced to the other side, dropping over the edge about five meters west of MacKeever.

A few seconds later he signaled the all-clear. Jackson turned to Terri and was about to motion her across when there was a short, sharp explosion from behind them, on the hill. It had the distinct sound of a Claymore mine being tripped, its C4 explosive charge sending out a hail of steel ball bearings.

A moment or two later the second Claymore went off and almost simultaneously the Semtex wired to the truck's electrical system blew with a very impressive bang that lit up the night sky above them.

Jackson looked over his shoulder at the fireball rising straight up into the sky. "Shit." He had hoped that they would all be across the road first.

What little element of surprise they had going for them was gone. It wouldn't take the rangers very long to realize that the booby traps were a diversion.

All traffic on the highway had ground to a halt. The nearest station wagon was about thirty meters to the east.

"All right, Lips, move it out," Jackson called to her.

They scrambled up onto the paved surface together, but Jackson beat her across. He was about to jump down into the ditch when a heavy line of fire walked its way up the highway toward them.

Terri went down hard, her shoulder bouncing on the highway, her feet flying up in the air.

"Sonofabitch." Jackson unslung his Colt Commando, flipped the selector switch to full automatic, and unloaded a fresh box magazine of thirty 5.66mm rounds into the station wagon.

The firing stopped immediately.

MacKeever and Ercoli jumped up and hosed the canvas-covered troop truck fifty meters to the west.

Jackson scooped the stunned Terri up by her web belt, slung her over his shoulder, turned on his heel and disappeared down into the ditch.

MacKeever and Ercoli caught up to him before he scrambled up on the other side. Ercoli took point and MacKeever took rear guard this time.

Without a word they raced as fast as they could through the low scrub brush directly toward the beach five hundred meters down a broad swale and then back up through a series of tall sand dunes that marked the limits of some ancient high tides.

Ercoli slowed down when they reached the trip wire they'd crossed over on the way up. He motioned for them to pay attention and delicately stepped over to the other side. He turned back and helped Jackson and Terri across, and then headed out again.

They held up above the two sandbagged gun emplacements they had passed on the way up. Ercoli and MacKeever took out their suppressed 9mm Sig-Sauer pistols and headed out: MacKeever to the east, Ercoli to the west.

Terri had been hit high in her left hip. She was coming around now, and she helped undo her trousers and pull them down. Jackson got a large pressure bandage from her first aid kit and bound up her wound. When he looked up she was gritting her teeth in pain.

"You're down there to fix my wound, not look at my ass," she croaked with a grin.

He returned her smile. "And a fine ass it is, Lips."

He helped redo her trousers when Ercoli and MacKeever emerged from the gun emplacements and motioned the all-clear.

"You up for a swim?" Jackson asked her.

She groaned softly. "It'll be better than being carried around like a slab of meat, and pawed by a sex maniac."

"Hang on."

Jackson picked her up in his arms and sprinted down to where Ercoli and MacKeever were studying the beach through their low-light binoculars.

But it was Jackson who spotted the BTR one hundred meters to the east and heading their way. Out to sea were the lights of at least a dozen warships, maybe more. Behind the beach, they could hear the sounds of a lot of soldiers bearing their way. And from somewhere inland they could hear the distinctive chop of helicopter rotors. A lot of helicopters.

"F/X?" Ercoli demanded urgently.

"The *Seawolf*," Jackson said.

They sprinted across the beach toward the water's edge fifty meters away. Before they got halfway, the BTR opened fire, bracketing them almost at once.

MacKeever turned, yanked an H&W stun grenade out of his vest, pulled the red ring, and tossed it toward the oncoming BTR. It was like going up against a Bradley with a squirt gun.

The grenade landed well short, but went off with a very impressive bang and a fireball flash that was not intended to kill anything, but merely to stun and distract the target with noise and light.

The BTR stopped firing immediately. Jackson and the others reached the water, pulling out their rebreathers as they ran.

Jackson gave Terri her mouthpiece first, then donned his own and submerged as automatic weapons fire from the beach sprayed the water all around them.

14

The *Seawolf* hovered at sixty feet.

On the periscope platform Dillon waited for word from sonar that they were in the clear before raising the small attack scope for another snapshot of what was happening on the surface.

Sierra five and nine, both fast patrol boats, were excellent ASW platforms. They carried the British Mk 24 Tigerfish Mod 2 antisub torpedoes. So far they had come the nearest in the past forty minutes. Twice Ski had thought the *Seawolf* had been detected, but each time the Pakistani warships had turned away at the last possible moment.

The Tigerfish was loaded with only two hundred pounds of high explosives with a maximum top speed of only thirty-five knots. But she was one of the stealthiest torpedoes in anybody's arsenal. Once she was in the water and running, she was extremely hard to detect and therefore avoid.

"Conn, sonar. We're in the clear, skipper," Zimenski reported.

Dillon glanced at the multifunction display as he raised the Type 3 attack periscope. They were in 175 feet of water under two thousand yards from the beach. The much larger search scope would have given him a better picture, but its radar signature was huge compared to the Type 3.

He did not want to get caught this close to shore. They had absolutely no maneuvering room. If they were detected here they would have a rough time of it. But so were the SEALs having a bad time of it topsides. The nearer to the shore the *Seawolf* could be positioned, the easier it would make the recovery operation.

He stopped the scope's rise when the head was only three feet above the surface. The control room was lit red for action stations, surface, to help preserve their night vision.

"Conn, sonar. Skipper, I'm picking up faint underwater noises less than fifty yards out, bearing three-four-niner. Nonmechanical. Could be our swimmers."

There was a lot of activity on the beach, but nothing in the water yet.

Dillon lowered the attack scope and raised the Type 20 search scope so that its head was still five feet beneath the surface. He dialed in the low-light feature and looked through the eyepieces.

At first he could make out little more than the dark gray of the water, but then he spotted what looked like a slow-moving shark. He increased the magnification, and suddenly he was seeing three, perhaps four, human figures heading in their general direction.

It was their SEAL team.

He sent three red flashes, followed by one, and then three more.

The figures immediately angled directly toward the *Seawolf*'s fairweather.

Dillon looked up at his XO. "Take the medic and four men aft to the escape trunk, Jackson and his people will be knocking on our door momentarily."

"All right," Bateman said, and he left the control room.

"Conn, sonar. They've got us," Zimenski reported. He was excited.

"I need a few minutes, Ski. Our SEALs are on the back porch."

"We're not going to have much leeway, skipper. Sierra nine has us for sure. She turned inboard a half-minute ago, and sierra three and five are doing the same. Sierra nine is now at three-five-zero-zero yards, bearing one-seven-eight degrees at twenty-seven knots."

"Are we clear either to port or starboard?"

"Negative, the other two are bracketing sierra nine."

Dillon worked out the scenario in his head. Because of her jet drive *Seawolf* turned equally well either left or right. But coming in, he'd studied the chart. To starboard the water got deeper much quicker than to port.

"Which one is starboard of nine?"

"Sierra five."

"Okay, stand by, Ski," Dillon said. He glanced through the scope.

The swimmers were below his angle of view. "Marc, I want you to target sierra nine and five," he told his weapons control officer.

"Aye, skipper," Jablonski replied crisply. He was in his element now.

"Chief of Boat, prepare to come to all-ahead flank with a sharp turn to starboard. New course one-eight-zero."

"Aye, skipper," Young repeated the order.

"Teflon, I want a best possible course out of here, considering the elimination of sierra nine and five. I want to hug the bottom all the way until we reach fifteen hundred feet."

"Roger that, Cap'n," Alvarez said. "I concur with an initial course of one-eight-zero."

Dillon got on the growler. "Charlie, how's it coming back there? We've got company."

"The outer hatch is open," Bateman reported.

"Tell me the minute they're aboard and the hatch is secured," Dillon ordered.

"Aye, Cap'n."

"I have a weapons solution on both targets. The A cables are connected, both weapons are warm."

"Firing point procedures," Dillon ordered.

All the relevant data was loaded into the Mark 48 ADCAPs memory systems, the torpedoes were targeted, the tubes were ready in all respects, and they could be launched at any time on the captain's order.

"Sierra nine's speed and bearing are unchanged. Range, two-eight-zero-zero yards," Zimenski reported.

"Conn, this is Bateman. They're aboard, the outer hatch is sealed."

"Hang on, Charlie," Dillon warned. He turned to his crew. "Fire one, fire two."

It was an act of war against a sovereign nation. A sovereign *nuclear* nation. Supposedly an ally.

"Acknowledge," Jablonski responded without hesitation. "Tube one is fired. Tube two is fired."

"Master Chief, get us out of here now," Dillon said.

"Both fish have cleared the outer doors and are running hot and true," Jablonski reported.

"Cut the wires," Dillon said.

Under normal circumstances each torpedo would stay connected to the submarine via a thin, tough data wire. Guidance data could be sent back and forth to the weapon while it was en route to its target.

If the wire had to be cut because the submarine had to make a rapid change in position, the torpedoes automatically switched to internal guidance and targeting systems that at this range couldn't miss.

The *Seawolf* suddenly dug her right shoulder into the sea, her decks canted sharply down and to starboard, and she accelerated like a shell fired from a cannon. Everyone not strapped into a seat or bunk reached out for something to hold on to.

"Conn, sonar. Skipper, sierra nine and five are turning port and starboard. They know that they are under attack."

"How about the other surface targets?"

"They're starting to scatter now, Cap'n. I don't think that they counted on us shooting. It's got to be a mess up there—" Zimenski cut it off. "Stand by. We have one, no, two contacts in the water. Inbound now at twenty-eight knots and accelerating. Bearing one-seven-eight." Jablonski paused for a moment. "The sounds are very faint, but contacts are evaluated as torpedoes. Mark twenty-fours."

Since *Seawolf* was accelerating away from the shore, away from shallow water, they were leaving behind a lot of disturbed water because of echo bounce off the bottom. "Release a bubble maker now," Dillon ordered.

The torpedo-confusing device, which looked like a long, thin artillery shell without a pointed end, was ejected from the three-inch signal launcher forward from what was actually the boat's pharmacy.

"Recommend that we stop our turn on a new course of one-zero-zero degrees," Alvarez suggested.

It would maneuver *Seawolf* into presenting her starboard flank to the incoming torpedoes, but it would leave most of the disturbed water and the bubbles from the decoy well aft.

"Make it so," Dillon ordered.

Seawolf immediately slowed her rate of turn, stopping precisely on the new course while still accelerating like a scalded cat, and diving to follow the bottom contour.

They all heard the distant explosion as the first Mark 48 found sierra nine. No one said anything. Seconds later they heard the second explosion as sierra five was struck.

"That'll get their attention," Jablonski said dryly.

"Talk to me, Ski," Dillon said.

"Both fish are going for the bait."

"Any other threats in the water?"

"Negative, Cap'n. We're clear on one-eight-zero now."

Dillon glanced over at Alvarez who was working out the angles and speeds in his head. "Recommend we remain on course for five seconds longer, then turn to new course one-seven-five."

"Very well," Dillon concurred. He keyed the growler phone. "Sonar, conn. What's happening with sierra nine and five?"

"Both are good hits, Cap'n," Zimenski came back. He was pleased. "Both targets are dead in the water. Sierra nine is sinking rapidly. I'm hearing hull compression and bulkhead failure noises. Sierra five is flooding, but not as fast."

"Does five constitute a further threat?"

"Negative, skipper," Zimenski said.

"Keep a sharp eye, Ski. We're on our way out, I don't want someone coming after us without me knowing about it."

"Suggest we deploy the 'twenty-nine."

The TB29 was a passive tactical sonar system that was towed behind the *Seawolf*. It was very sensitive, especially to long-range targets and to threats coming from their rear.

"Do it," Dillon ordered.

"Skipper, they're heading every which way *except* toward us," Zimenski said. "They're born-again believers."

15

DAWN
KENNEDY SPACE CENTER

"T-minus ten seconds," the voice of KSC blared almost everywhere throughout the space launch complex.

For Thoreau it was the same each time he got to this point in a countdown. There was very little for anyone aboard to do in the last few seconds except pray. And that he did. Silently to himself, thinking about the *Columbia* accident.

"T-minus nine seconds . . ."

As mission commander, Thoreau rode the right seat, while Susan Wright, the STS 140 pilot, rode left. Wirtanen, Conners, and Ellis rode in the seats behind them; at this moment actually below them.

"T-minus eight seconds . . ."

Thoreau glanced across at Susan and grinned. She gave him the thumbs-up, but he could see that she was just as unsettled as he was. It had taken eighteen months for the shuttle fleet to come off its post-accident grounding.

"T-minus seven seconds . . ."

Some missions started out as smooth as glass. Everything from conception to construction and from liftoff to touchdown went without so much as a popped circuit breaker. Others were nothing but trouble from the get-go: computer problems, mechanical and electrical problems and crew problems. It seemed never to end, so that by the time they got to this point on the launchpad everyone aboard was damned glad to finally be getting out of Dodge.

"T-minus six seconds . . ."

A few rare missions, though, were like this one. *Challenger*'s and *Columbia*'s last came to Thoreau's mind, and he shivered. STS 140 had an odd feel to it. Starting with the change in mission orders, to the president's call, to the parameters showing up on the Web, to the almost surly attitude among the crew, Thoreau had the willies.

"T-minus five seconds . . ."

The latest hitch was the six-day launch delay for no apparent reason. Scott Buzby, STS 140 mission director, had finally admitted that nothing was wrong with *Discovery*. The delay had been ordered from Washington.

"T-minus four seconds . . ."

Three times in the last three days Thoreau had almost pulled the plug and quit. But he wasn't built that way. He'd already been told that if he or any of his crew stepped down, someone would take their place. But if one dropped out, *all* of them would be replaced.

"T-minus three seconds," the KSC announcer said. "We have ignition."

Thoreau felt the deep-throated vibration inside his body; from the seat of his pants up into his chest cavity.

"T-minus two seconds, main engines are a go."

Whatever was going to happen, it *was* good to get out of Dodge, Thoreau thought.

"T-minus one second . . . and liftoff on a mission to broaden man's knowledge of medicine in space in which another new frontier of science will be addressed on the international space station for the benefit of all mankind."

16

DAWN
SEAWOLF

I t was local dawn in the Bay of Bengal when Dillon walked into the control room with a cup of coffee.

Ship's time was 0009 GMT, just nine minutes past midnight. But submerged, *Seawolf* never really slept, and neither did the captain. Especially not when they were on a mission with weapons release authorization.

"Captain has the conn," Bateman announced. He'd come up a few hours ago when they were making their final approach to their mission station. It was designated *feather duster* and was at the approximate spot where the *Eagle Flyer* had been sunk by the unknown Kilo sub.

The rest of his prime crew had also left their bunks and drifted back to their duty stations, relieving the junior grades who usually stood the night and early watches. There were no arguments.

Twenty-four hours ago they had come to periscope depth about one hundred miles southeast of Sri Lanka to send their mission report. Dillon detailed everything that he had done, half expecting to be recalled to Pearl; possibly to be replaced by the *Springfield*, which was already in the South Pacific.

The reply had come within ten minutes, and had been as simple as it had been timely.

Z170024ZJUL
TOP SECRET
FM: COMSUBPAC
TO: USS SEAWOLF

A. USS SEAWOLF Z170014ZJUL

B. OPERATIONAL UPDATES

1. MOST URGENT THAT YOU PROCEED TO FEATHER DUSTER AT ALL POS-SIBLE SPEED. DISCOVERY SET FOR LIFT OFF AT 0059Z 25 JUL WITH REN-DEZVOUS NLT 36 HOURS.

2. RENDEZVOUS WITH VINSON NOT POSSIBLE AT THIS TIME. HOLD YOUR SEAL TEAM UNTIL FURTHER NOTICE.

3. UNDERSTAND YOUR DISAPPOINTMENT. A POSSIBLE RETRY IS BEING WORKED OUT. NO WORD FROM PAKI NAVY REF YOUR WAR SHOTS.

4. YOUR PRIMARY MISSION IS GO. YOU ARE AUTHORIZED UNRE-STRICTED OPS 200100Z TO 230001Z. REPORT WHEN POSSIBLE WITHOUT COMPROMISING SECURITY.

GOOD LUCK GOODING SENDS

XXXXX

EOM

190025ZJUL

BREAKBREAK

Dillon glanced up at the multifunction display. They had made their cautious approach at 1,200 feet in a duct between sharp thermo-clines, and they were still at that depth now. Hovering almost eight thousand feet above the sharply sloping bottom.

Seventeen thousand yards northwest was a narrow seamount that rose to within six hundred feet of the surface. If the Kilo was here, they figured that's where it would hang out.

"Sonar, this is the captain. What do we have?"

"Sonar, aye. I have one small vessel, moving slowly, bearing zero-four-three, range twenty-five thousand yards and opening. Designate it sierra one. It's probably a small commercial fishing boat. I'm hear-ing deck sounds, maybe winches, maybe an ice-making machine.

"I have sierra two, range forty thousand yards, bearing one-niner-five, making twenty-three knots on a one-two-zero course. It's definitely a VLCC, probably heading from the Gulf to Japan."

A VLCC was a very large crude carrier. An oil tanker in excess of one thousand feet in length. They made a lot of noise. Everything stayed out of their way.

"Anything submerged showing up at any range, Ski?" Dillon asked.

"I saved the best part for last, Cap'n. I think we've bagged ourselves a Kilo boat. I'm not sure yet, I'm still washing the noises, but I'd bet my Tom Clancy collection I'm hearing the occasional pump noise, and what's probably a motor going south in their air-handling system."

"Range and bearing?"

"About where we figured, Cap'n. She's parked on the seamount, bearing two niner five, range just over seventeen thousand yards. I'll designate the contact as sierra three."

"Okay, good job, Ski. As soon as you have a positive identification I want to hear about it. We have about thirty-six hours before anything happens, but the instant the Kilo heads to the surface I want to know."

"Aye, Cap'n. We're on it."

Dillon thought about the captain of the Kilo submarine. They still had no idea what country the boat belonged to, except that it wasn't Pakistan. But if it was the same submarine and crew that had fired shots at three satellites and the civilian research ship, they were here to do the same thing again. Only this time the crew of *Discovery* would come into harm's way. Recklessly.

But it would take patience to bag them, Dillon thought. For all of them. The slightest noise would give them away.

He looked up and motioned for Bateman and Alvarez to join him at the chart table.

"Ski thinks he's detected something on the seamount," Dillon said. "Could be our Kilo. Which means we're all early to the dance."

"We could back off out of his range for the time being," Bateman said. "*Discovery*'s not due to rendezvous with the *Jupiter* for another thirty-six hours, assuming she got off okay. Might be easier on the crew."

"But he might move," Alvarez pointed out. "And we might not be so lucky finding him the second time around."

"We'll stay here," Dillon said. He'd already made his decision, he just wanted input. "I want no noise."

"She'll have to start for periscope depth sooner or later," Bateman suggested.

"That's right. And when she does we'll use her noise to cover us. We'll load two tubes with ADCAPs, flood them, and open the doors."

"Are we going to follow them up, skipper?" Alvarez asked.

"Absolutely," Dillon said. "That's one show I definitely don't want to miss."

"All right," Bateman murmured.

17

DAWN
THE WHITE HOUSE

President Hanson was an early riser, and he expected key members of his administration and especially his staff to accommodate him. Nevertheless he was surprised to learn that his national security adviser Dennis Nettleton, his chief of staff Brad Stein, and his director of Central Intelligence Carolyn Tyson were waiting for him outside the Oval Office.

The sun was just cracking the horizon on what promised to be a beautiful morning in the nation's capital. His secretary, Mrs. Gladys Anderson, had laid out his schedule on his desk, and had turned the television to CNN, which the president always watched first thing. The sound was down, the remote control lying next to his agenda.

A navy steward brought his coffee, and then left discreetly, closing the door behind him.

CNN was live from Karachi. It was late afternoon there. Bonfires burned in the streets where tens of thousands of people had gathered. Many of them carried signs and banners condemning the U.S. imperialists, Satan's tools, in English. American flags were being burned. And in a dozen spots effigies of President Hanson were going up in flames too.

"It's worse in Islamabad," Carolyn Tyson offered.

"It took them long enough to react to our raid," the president said. "What were they waiting for?"

"They didn't know if we were coming back," Dennis Nettleton suggested. "At least they haven't put our people on display. Yet."

"Where's Howard?" the president asked. Howard McCann was secretary of state.

"He's on his way," Stein said. "But he's going to recommend against recalling Haggman." William F. Haggman was the U.S. ambassador to Pakistan. Our embassy, in what was called the diplomatic enclave in Islamabad, was under siege as were our consulates in Karachi, Lahore, and Peshawar. But McCann was cautioning against any overt reaction.

The situation had gone critical too quickly for any realistic chance of getting Americans out of the country. The State Department could only issue a warning for Americans to stay out of sight as much as possible.

"I'm going to override him," the president said. "General Musharraf is still unavilable to me, as is Ambassador Husain. It's time that they begin to learn the consequences of their reckless actions."

Hanson was angry. He'd given his word to the American public that rogue states like Iraq or Pakistan guilty of terrorism against U.S. interests would not go unpunished. In any event, when presidents got angry, the people around them usually backed off. It was the wisest course.

"What about *Seawolf?*" he asked.

"Dillon is on station, Mr. President," Tyson said. "Pearl hasn't heard from him since he made his report yesterday, but they're certain that he made it okay to the Bay of Bengal."

"*Discovery?*"

"She's twenty-four hours from her first rendezvous with the *Jupiter,*" Tyson said. "They'll be over the Indian Ocean and in range of the Kilo's laser, if the submarine is there, for about five minutes."

"But there'll be other passes?"

"Yes, Mr. President." Tyson handed him a briefing folder that contained the ephemeris for *Discovery-Jupiter*. It was a table showing the exact dates and times that the shuttle-satellite pair would be visible from the Bay of Bengal.

"Presumably the Kilo will have to come to the surface, or at least to periscope depth, to fire its laser," Nettleton said. "When she starts up, *Seawolf* will be there to intercept her."

"That's not the only mission," the president said sternly. "And I want to make that perfectly clear. We're not only going to stop the bastards from harming our satellites, but we're going to find out who is actually doing the shooting." He looked at them. "We're all still agreed that it's not Pakistan's submarine?"

"We have high confidence that it's not," Tyson said. Among the president's administration, she was the one person least intimidated. She was respectful of presidential power, but not fearful of it. "But we don't know whose it is."

"Very well. Now, what's being done to rescue my brother and his team out of Kandrach?"

"A submarine-launched SEAL strike is still our best option," Tyson said.

"It didn't work the first time," Stein pointed out.

"Admiral Puckett believes that the spy the ONI and FBI call John Galt was responsible. He could have tipped off the Pakistani intelligence service that *Seawolf* was on the way."

"What's to stop it from happening again?" Stein asked. They all had enormous respect for Tyson. He was playing devil's advocate.

"In the first place, he's managed to elude capture for two years, which means he's either very bright or very lucky or both. He has to know that the list of people who know *Seawolf*'s orders has to be very small. Each time he blows the whistle he sends up a bright red flare. We *will* home in on him if he keeps it up. And in the second place, I suggest that as soon as *Seawolf* has finished her primary mission, that she be tasked to return to Kandrach to finish the job. This time the list of people who know where she's going will be much smaller than the first time. And I'm sure that Dillon and his SEALs will want a second chance." She grinned viciously. "I would."

"That makes sense," President Hanson said. "Anything else?"

Carolyn Tyson took another folder, this one marked *Top Secret*, out of her attaché case and handed it to the president.

"There's even worse news, I'm afraid, Mr. President."

"Tell me."

"We have confirmation from two independent sources—one in Switzerland and one in Islamabad itself—that Pakistan's air force has five nearly operational long-range missiles. Their three-stage rockets, that they designate TK7s, are French Aérospatiale M4s that are normally launched from a submarine. These have been modified to be ground-launched. From the bed of a semi-truck, or a flatbed railroad car. Each has a range of a little more than four thousand miles."

That got their attention.

"Mr. President, within a very short period, once they fix what we're told are guidance system problems, Pakistan will be able to launch its thermonuclear weapons not only to any spot in India, but just about anywhere in Japan, all of North Africa, Israel, and the Gulf region, which includes all the Arab oil fields. They can reach Moscow and St. Petersburg, as well as Norway, Sweden, and Denmark, and just about all of Europe."

"Sonofabitch," President Hanson said softly.

"Yes, Mr. President," his DCI agreed. "We have a very big problem."

PAYBACK

NOON
CHAKLALA, PAKISTAN

resident and Prime Minister of Islami Jamhuria-e-Pakistan Army General Pervez Musharraf walked into the national command authority chamber at the stroke of noon and took his seat at the head of the long, obsidian table. That fool of an American president Gerald Hanson continued his efforts to make diplomatic contact even though he'd been repeatedly insulted by a low-ranking official at the embassy in Washington. Musharraf almost chuckled aloud, but he restrained himself. Now was no time for levity. The U.S. was still their biggest ally *and* their greatest enemy. The enemy of all Islam.

Present around the table, which was in the Joint Strategic Headquarters compound, were his entire NCA membership: Army Chief of Staff Gen. Karas Phalodi; Navy Chief of Staff Adm. Tajuddin Khan; Air Force Chief of Staff Gen. Naeem Baquar; ISI Director Maj. Gen. Jamsed Asif; Employment Control Committee Director Saiyed Ullah; Development Control Director Dr. Mohammed Malik; and Strategic Plans Division Director Army Gen. Javed Naqoi.

With Musharraf, these seven men were in complete control of Pakistan's immediate future and they all were acutely aware of the fact. They now had five city-busting thermonuclear weapons mated to five long-range guided missiles that would soon be operational.

The question on the table was what should be done next?

Musharraf fixed his gaze on each of them in turn, willing them to understand the gravity of what they would decide here. But he also wanted to instill in them the courage of Allah, because in his estimation they would need that courage and resolve now more than ever before in the history of their nation.

"Gentlemen, thank you for convening on such short notice,"

Musharraf began mildly. "As you are very well aware, our decisions today will be critical to Pakistan's welfare, *In'shah Allah*." God willing.

"*In'shah Allah*," they murmured in unison around the table.

Musharraf settled back in his tall leather chair and turned to his army chief of staff, General Phalodi. "What do you recommend?"

"There is only one course of action open to us that makes any sense, General," Phalodi began forcefully. "We must strike India now, and hard. She is our enemy and nothing will change that. Their bumbling atomic energy commission has not been able to develop a thermonuclear weapon. They've come up with fizzles. But that situation cannot last indefinitely." He looked around the table for support. "I recommend that we strike now."

"Where do we hit them?" Musharraf asked. Phalodi's vehemence was expected. The man wanted to be president. He had to make his mark.

"New Delhi and Calcutta to kill their leadership and as many civilians as possible. Then their nuclear weapons depot at Secunderabad, and finally their Bhabha atomic research center."

"That is only four weapons."

"We keep the fifth in reserve," Phalodi replied without hesitation.

"Attack now and we will be destroyed," ISI General Asif spoke up.

Everyone turned toward him. Musharraf nodded for his intelligence chief to continue. Asif had no ambition to become president or prime minister, so in some respects his opinion was even more valuable than Phalodi's.

"Because we refuse to reopen our dialogue with the Americans they may very well lend their support to India—"

"What else is new," Phalodi interrupted.

Musharraf silenced his army chief of staff with a glance.

"America may give India its intelligence *and* military support," Asif warned. "If that happens we could not win, even with our fine new toys. It would take more than five superbombs to damage India beyond retaliating." Asif looked around the table. "That is, if we were allowed to launch."

Musharraf raised a hand to quell any objections for the moment. "What do you recommend?"

"Our nuclear weapons were meant to be developed but never deployed. The U.S. dropped only two very small nuclear weapons on a nation they'd formally declared war on, and fifty-seven years later they are still being vilified for the act."

"What do you want us to do, turn our weapons over to the Americans?" Phalodi shouted. Spit flew from his mouth.

"Merely having such weapons in our arsenal will be enough to insure that no nation, not India not the U.S., will ever dare attack us." As Phalodi had done, Asif looked around the table for his support. "Having the weapons, but *not* using them, is the key to our survival."

"What do you suggest, specifically, Jamsed?" Musharraf asked. It wasn't clear to anyone around the table whom Musharraf supported the most. It was a dangerous situation for all of them. It wasn't only Pakistan that could be lost here today, there were careers on the line.

"We must make a formal announcement of our capabilities. *All* of our capabilities. That includes our missiles and launch abilities. If need be, we can make the video of our test available to the Western media."

"Madness," Phalodi fumed. His face was red, his fists clenched.

"Not madness, but good sense. We will either be a part of the world community, or we will not. We can either take our place at the table of superpowers, or else those of us who survive will be reduced to picking through the rubble of our cities. After the World Trade Center and the counterstrikes on Afghanistan and Iraq, the Americans are fighting a different war."

Asif's moderate position was something of a surprise to Musharraf and the others around the table. The ISI chief had always been a hawk. "What else?"

"The Americans obviously know that we are holding prisoners at Kandrach. Their rescue attempt proved that much. We must immediately kill the prisoners in such a way that it will appear they lost their lives during the rescue attempt. That will make it possible for us to return their bodies. All their bodies except for the woman's. We can never return her, or even acknowledge that we ever had her."

Musharraf looked at the others. "Have there been any indications that the Americans know we have her?"

"None," Asif said.

"That is all well and good," Phalodi interjected angrily. "But a few prisoners are not our major problem. India is. And India will never attack us with her nuclear weapons."

"Then why must we attack first?" Asif asked.

"To stop their agression in Kashmir once and for all."

Musharraf held up a hand for Phalodi and Asif to stop their bickering. He turned to SPD Director Gen. Naqoi. The strategic plans division was responsible for recommending in broad strokes Pakistan's plans for its strategic nuclear weapons.

Naqoi was another man like Asif who knew his job and who had no political ambitions other than staying alive. He was a true man of God, a true believer in Islam. Pakistan's nuclear weapons were, as far as he was concerned, truly weapons for Allah and all of Islam.

"If we do decide to launch, and I will not argue against such a course of action at this time, then may I suggest an additional six targets?" Naqoi said. "At least six targets, which of course would suppose a further buildup of our weapons stockpile before we act."

Musharraf was fascinated despite himself. "What are these six targets that we should also strike?"

"Why, that's simple, General. Paris, Berlin, Moscow, Tokyo, Tel Aviv, and Riyadh." Naqoi listed the cities without so much as a blink of the eye. No one could tell if he was serious or not.

"Insanity," Phalodi said. "Do you want us at war with the world?"

Naqoi turned to him with a vicious sneer. "There is not much difference hitting those targets versus hitting New Delhi and Calcutta, you utter fool. General Asif is correct for a change. Brandish the sword, but do not swing it until someone else takes the first blow."

Musharraf raised a hand again to cut off the discussion. Dissension tended to dilute power within a committee, concentrating it in the hands of the chairman. It was a situation that Musharraf had worked diligently to foster. It would start to pay off now. He would make the final decisions that the entire National Command Authority would take the blame for should the situation backfire.

"The American prisoners we're holding at Kandrach will be kept alive for now," he said. "That includes the woman. We may use them as tokens of our good faith at some future date. Show our humanitarian goodwill despite their cowardly attack on our naval vessels operating under the law well within our own territorial waters."

No one argued. They were past the discussion phase and they all knew it.

"All five of our thermonuclear weapons will be mated to their missiles, and will be dispersed across the nation, as we have planned. Four of the weapons will be targeted, as General Phalodi so wisely suggested, with the fifth to be held in reserve."

Phalodi looked smug.

"There will be no further tests, of course, but as General Asif so brilliantly suggested, we will not launch our attack on India. Not yet, though it may become necessary very soon."

Asif sat up a little straighter.

They were like children, the thought crossed Musharraf's mind. But very dangerous children.

Air Force Chief of Staff Gen. Baquar looked up from some notes. "There is another problem that we must address here."

"What is it?" Musharraf asked.

"The Americans have launched one of their shuttle spacecraft. They mean to repair their *Jupiter* satellite. If that is allowed to occur, then their intelligence services will have the capability of detecting our deployed missiles on their mobile launch platforms."

"Our asset is in place in the Bay of Bengal," General Phalodi reported. "At least that is what I have been told."

"It is," Asif said. "But the ISI feels that there is a considerable risk in attacking the satellite at this time. If the laser should miss the satellite, the beam could conceivably damage the shuttle, perhaps even injure an American astonaut. The Americans would retaliate."

"Against whom?" Navy Chief of Staff Admiral Khan interjected. "The submarine does not belong to us. All of our boats are tied up alongside their docks. In very plain sight."

"The satellite must not become operational," Musharraf said. There were nods of agreement around the table. Asif and Naqoi were the only dissenters. Since neither of them had any ambitions beyond their present positions, their voices were not so important on this issue. "It will be a statement they won't miss."

"Very well, General," Asif said. "I merely hope that we find our way through this maze."

"We will make it so, Jamsed," Musharraf said. "Pakistan counts on us."

2

Space was silent, which made the slowly unfolding panorama of the blue earth all the more majestic for Paul Thoreau.

Discovery was above and behind the disabled surveillance satellite. Her payload doors were in the open position, the heat reflectors deployed. The open bay was pointed earthward.

Susan Wright had moved them into a matching orbit with controlled burns of the orbital maneuvering system engines, while Wirtanen and Conners waited for the go-ahead to suit up. They would make the EVA for the repair mission, which meant that Dr. Ellis was only a passenger until the repairs were completed and they went on to the space station.

He hung upside down beneath the upper bay port side window in the overhead, while Thoreau watched from the starboard window. Ellis used a Hasselblad camera to take some stunning photographs of the satellite against the backdrop of the mid-Atlantic ocean.

The sky was relatively clear for this time of year, but a dozen jet airliner contrails crisscrossed the ocean between the U.S. and Europe and North Africa.

Each orbit took approximately ninety minutes to complete. In one and a half orbits from now, Conners and Wirtanen would be suited up and outside. They would be two hundred and fifty miles above the Bay of Bengal.

Everyone aboard was tense.

"Can you spot any damage?" Thoreau asked.

Ellis was shooting the slowly tumbling satellite through a 100mm telephoto lens. It was like looking at the wounded bird through a small telescope. "Nothing yet," he said.

"They probably hit one of the guidance modules in the center bay. Just inboard of the solar panels."

Discovery was about two hundred meters out, giving them a perfect view.

He didn't know exactly what he was looking for. Certainly not blast damage. Even accounting for the distance, and the relatively low power of a laser portable enough to be carried aboard a small submarine, the beam would not have been very wide here. The damage would be the size of a pinprick compared to the six-ton satellite that was nearly the length of a school bus and almost as big around.

The *Jupiter* was tumbling at a rate of only a couple of turns per minute. Still, it was hard to brace himself in weightlessness so that he could steady the camera.

Then he had it.

A small blackened spot, maybe a meter or a little less from the junction of one of the solar panel wings that spread thirty meters to either side.

"I see it," Ellis said, firing off photographs as fast as the camera's motorized drive would take them.

"I've got it too," Thoreau said. He used a pair of 10X50 binoculars. "Inboard from the port solar panel."

"Inside the *U*."

"That's it," Thoreau said. He turned around and handed the binoculars to Conners, who gracefully drifted to the window and braced himself for a look.

He had to wait for the *Jupiter* to slowly turn around, and he raised the binoculars to his eyes. "Got it," he said, studying the damage. "They hit the beta package. About what we figured."

"Stand by, I'm going to get us closer," Susan Wright said.

They all reached out and grabbed a handhold.

She alternately hit short bursts on the attitude control thrusters, jockeying the shuttle into a position close enough for the remote manipulator arm to reach.

She took her hands off the controls and looked up. "Zero relative velocity. We're in position."

"Nice touch," Thoreau complimented her.

Susan Wright unbuckled from her seat and pushed herself up next to Ellis so that she could look out the upper window. "Cool," she said. She glanced over at Conners. "Wanna trade jobs, Rod?"

Conners gave her a grin. "Not a chance, Mouse. That's my ride out there."

Dillon got a cup of coffee and went up to the control room after he'd written his daily letter to Jill and read the poem.

This was a short one by A.E. Housman, a poet whom Jill had introduced to him just on this trip. Already he was starting to like the man's vision, especially the part when he said something to the effect that he had sweated hot and cold.

Ice and fire; he liked it because command was like that sometimes. And if truth be told he'd had to contend with a balance between fear and desire on more than one occasion.

He was smiling to himself when he reached the control room. Maybe poetry should be a required subject at the PXO and PCO schools. Vince Howe would probably have a hemorrhage, but that would make it all the more interesting.

"Good evening, gentlemen," he said.

Bateman looked up. "Captain's on the conn," he announced.

"What's the situation, Charlie?" Dillon asked. He glanced at the multifunction display above the periscope platform. They were stationary at a depth of six hundred feet. On his orders Bateman had moved them above the lower thermocline a few feet at a time to minimize their noise. It had taken nearly twelve hours to rise six hundred feet.

"We're on station, skipper. Tubes one and two are loaded, without presets and without flooding."

Dillon glanced at the digital time readout on the display. Local dawn was coming up in less than sixty minutes.

"*Discovery* should be coming up on the horizon from the southwest in fifty-eight minutes," Bateman continued. "That's four minutes before nautical dawn. Just about the same time the *Eagle Flyer* reported the laser strike on the *Jupiter*."

"It's about time we get to work," Dillon said. He took down a growler phone. "Sonar, this is the captain. What's sierra three up to?"

"She's been real quiet, Cap'n," Zimenski said. "That noise I was hearing in the air-handling system suddenly stopped about three hours ago. Someone must've wised up and fixed it. At first I thought that I'd lost her, but then I heard a couple of hull pops. She's still not completely settled down."

"Same range and bearing as before?"

"Yes, sir. I would have heard her moving off if she'd tried to sneak away."

"How long have you been on duty, Ski?" Dillon asked.

"Not too long, Cap'n. Honest." Zimenski said. "Are we going hunting soon, sir?"

"Real soon. You know the drill this time. You know what I'm going to try to pull off, so stay frosty back there."

"Yes, sir," Zimenski came back crisply.

Dillon turned to his XO. "Battle stations, torpedo," he said. "This is not a drill."

"Aye, Skipper," Bateman said. He pulled down a handset and got on the IMC, which transmitted his voice throughout the boat. Under silent running the announcement was muted, impossible to detect outside *Seawolf*'s hull. "All hands, all hands, this is the executive officer. Battle stations torpedo. This is not a drill. Battle stations torpedo."

The on-duty men and officers all sharpened up. Fire details manned their stations. All watertight doors throughout the boat were closed. Even the cooks sprang into action, preparing loads of extra food for what could be a long haul.

Everybody aboard was more than ready for this one. Not only had an innocent American civilian boat been sunk with all hands presumably lost. But the Pakistanis were holding four American prisoners.

"All right," Bateman murmured.

etting ready for their EVA to fix the satellite, Wirtanen and Conners kept their chitchat to a minimum.

Everybody aboard *Discovery* was tense. They'd all attended the military briefing at KSC, and Thoreau had told them what the president had told him. All of it was extraordinary.

As Susan Wright had put it so very well: Spaceflight is dangerous enough as it is without some wacko firing laser beams at us.

She was on the upper deck getting the remote manipulator arm ready to deploy. Wirtanen and Conners would ride the arm across to the satellite.

Conners's first job would be to latch onto the mammoth satellite at the axis of its rotation, where the relative motion was the smallest. From there he would pull himself hand-over-hand to one end of the *Jupiter* where the rotational motion was the greatest. He would position himself so that the jets on his manned maneuvering unit would point in the opposite direction. Anchoring himself, he would touch off short bursts of the nitrogen jets, which would slow and finally stop the satellite's spin, first in one axis, and then in the second.

From there Wirtanen would be brought over at the end of the RMA with the tool kit and the guidance system replacement packages.

They were on the mid-deck, across from the airlock that led out to hard space in the open payload bay.

Conners strapped on his urine collection unit and bag, and then awkwardly pulled on his spandex mesh suit of long johns. Plastic tubing, which carried cooling water, interlaced the suit.

Wirtanen was just ahead of him, sliding into the lower suit and adjusting the thick-soled boots.

When he was finished he helped Conners into his lower suit, and then drifted over to where his upper hard shell aluminum torso was attached to a bulkhead. He ducked under it and slithered into place.

Conners helped him make the electrical and liquid connections mating the two halves of the space suit, and then locked the airtight rings.

Wirtanen in turn helped Conners to this stage.

"How's it going down there, guys?" Ellis called from the upper deck access hatch.

"I'm glad that we're not in a hurry," Conners replied.

They donned their gloves, and then checked each other to make sure that their communication carrier assembly and Snoopy cap were on correctly, and that their display and control module, primary life support subsystems, and secondary oxygen pack all were properly attached and showing normal indicators.

"*Discovery*, EVA one, how do you copy?" Wirtanen said.

"You sound good here, Don," Susan Wright's voice came through his headset. "Rod, do you copy?"

"Five by," Conners said.

"Roger," Susan Wright acknowleged. "Ready to rumble when you guys are."

They donned their helmets, and sealed them. The suits pressured up, all indicators again in the green.

Wirtanen entered the airlock first, and when the inner hatch was confirmed sealed, the air inside was pumped out. He opened the outer door into the payload bay and pulled himself out into space.

He closed and resealed the hatch and gave Conners the okay to repressurize.

The pressure inside the suits was kept at 4.2 pounds per square inch compared to a normal earth sea level pressure of 14.7 psi. For the past twenty-four hours the pressure inside *Discovery* had been lowered to 10.2 psi to help acclimatize Wirtanen and Conners for their EVA. The hour before they locked outside, they had been on pure oxygen. All of that was designed to counteract the possibility of suffering the bends because of the decreased pressure they would be working under.

Except for the fact that the air seemed a bit cool and dry, Wirtanen had never been able to tell any real difference. At least not enough of a difference to affect an astronaut's performance.

A couple of minutes later the outer hatch opened and Conners slid out to join him.

"Ready to get it on?" he asked.

"Let's do it," Wirtanen said,

They looked up at the dark expanse of the earth. They were on the nightside now, just approaching the east coast of South Africa. There were not a lot of city lights, but there was a big lightning storm to the north that was spectacular. Within a half hour they would be coming up on dawn over the Bay of Bengal when the real danger would begin.

"Space," Conners said. "The final frontier—"

"*Discovery*, this is mission control Houston, say again?"

5

Captain Mohammed Zahedi stepped forward to the sonar compartment. He'd been in this situation with this crew and this boat three times before. This time would be better. No complications.

They had rested on the seamount for thirty-six hours to make sure that they were in the clear; that no warships, especially no American warships, were lurking within passive sonar range. So far they'd detected nothing but commercial traffic on the surface.

Zahedi was an Iranian naval officer, though 2606 was not an Iranian submarine. He had been on loan for the past three months. The Iranian Supreme Naval Command Authority had agreed to the transfer because the host nation was a friendly government that had helped with military equipment in the past, and Zahedi needed operational experience. No submariner in Iran's small fleet of four Kilo boats had gone into combat conditions yet. What he had learned in the past ninety days, and what he would learn in the coming months, would be priceless.

"Are we in the clear?" he asked. The tiny sonar compartment contained only two display units: One for the passive/active low frequency sonar unit mounted in the bow, and the second for the array of passive hydrophones mounted along the hull.

Chief Sonar Operator Lt. Lee Samsong looked up and nodded seriously. "I have five targets, Captain, all of which are commercial. The nearest is fifteen thousand meters, bearing zero-eight-zero. The range is increasing."

"No surprises this time, Lieutenant?" Zahedi asked. Samsong had been on duty when they were spotted by the American research vessel. He had not evaluated the target properly. Which could have been a disaster.

"No, sir. Four of the targets are almost certainly longline fishing boats. But we are well outside of their fishing grounds. The fifth is another very large crude carrier, east of us, and on an easterly heading."

When Zahedi had first come aboard 2606 some of the men, including young Lieutenant Samsong, had displayed open arrogance. Iranians were ragheads. The only reason they weren't still driving camels as in the sixteenth century was because of the oil deposits under their deserts and the American and British help they got to retrieve the wealth.

Samsong had been well trained, as were the other fifty-eight officers and men aboard. But none of them had been trained by Dr. Usama Hussain Hassan.

Zahedi smiled inwardly thinking about the absolute hell that man had put him through. There were no failures in Dr. Hassan's elite submariner officer classes. The pool of qualified Iranian naval officers wasn't large enough to allow dropouts. Everyone passed, even if the grueling eleven-month course killed them. Which it nearly had on more than one occasion.

But Dr. Hassan was the only Iranian ever to be trained at the British Royal Navy submarine commander's Perisher school. Every bit as tough as the American PXO and PCO courses, Perisher turned out some of the best submarine drivers in the world. And Dr. Hassan had passed the course third in his class. A fact he never let any of his students forget.

"You may be going head-to-head with the very best submarine officers in the world, aboard the very best boats ever built. American or British, you will consider yourself extraordinarily lucky merely to survive a hostile encouter, unless you know a few skills of your own. Skills that I will teach you."

Hassan's words were etched in the soul of every Iranian submarine officer he taught.

"Learn your lessons well, gentlemen. What you learn here may very well save your life, and the lives of your crew someday."

This operation, *Mission al'gamar,* the moon, was putting those instructions to the test. Zahedi did not mean to lose this crew, even if they weren't his own countrymen, or this boat, even though it wasn't Iranian.

"You have detected no other submarine?" Zahedi asked.

"No, sir," Samsong replied. "Not within the limits of my equipment," he added, to cover himself.

"Very well. Keep a very close watch. We will begin now."

"Yes, sir."

Zahedi stepped back to the control room. His crew was ready. He wished that he had his own people aboard. But it could not be helped. And they were out here helping brothers and friends in a righteous battle.

He glanced at the boat's chronometer and the mission clock on the bulkhead beside it. They were approaching local dawn. The American shuttle would be in orbit beside the damaged *Jupiter* spy satellite. Why he had been ordered to cause even more damage to the satellite before it was repaired and at the same time that *Discovery* and her crew were in such dangerous proximity was completely beyond his comprehension. He was certain that it was a political decision. One that he could not or would not question.

He turned to his short, stocky, flat-faced XO, Lieutenant Commander Yong Ki, and nodded. "It is time to commence operations."

"Yes, Captain," Ki responded crisply. He pulled down a growler phone. "Sonar, conn, are we clear to surface?"

"We are clear," Samsong responded.

Ki switched to the 1MC. "All hands, all hands, man your battle stations, laser. All hands, all hands, man your battle stations, laser. Close all watertight comparments."

A muted bell sounded throughout the boat as the watertight doors were closed and dogged.

Ki switched channels. "Engineering, conn. What is the status of our laser power unit?"

"Eighty percent and climbing," Viktor Stalnov, their chief engineer, replied. "Are we headed up?"

"Momentarily," Ki said. They spoke English aboard.

"You will have one hundred percent by the time we reach transmission depth."

Ki replaced the phone with precision, like everything he did. He considered himself a battle-seasoned submarine veteran by now. It was an illusion that Zahedi meant to disabuse his XO of once they got back to port.

"Diving officer, make your depth one-five meters," Ki ordered.

"Aye, aye, XO, make my depth fifteen meters," the diving officer responded. He began issuing the necessary orders.

"Make your speed all ahead slow, course one-two-five," Ki ordered.

The diving officer repeated the order, and Ki turned next to the weapons officer, Lt. Kim Nam, who happened to be his brother-in-law. "Report when you are at one hundred percent power, and have acquired your target."

"Aye, aye, XO," Nam replied.

Not bad, Zahedi thought, watching and listening from his position beside the periscopes. It was from here that he fought his battles. Maybe this mission *would* go without a hitch, unlike the previous one. He hoped so. Killing innocent civilians or dealing with survivors was distasteful to him. Battles were supposed to be pure. Even if the civilians were American.

The flash traffic they received last week was thankfully wrong. No American warships had shown up, especially not the American submarine that military intelligence had warned him about.

Zahedi smiled. Even the eggheads made mistakes sometime. But then they never had to come out here to do battle in the real world.

6

Don Wirtanen was tethered above the cargo carrier *Leonardo* in the payload bay. The earth was above him. The RMA was 75 percent extended, its end effector within a couple meters of the slowly tumbling satellite.

Jupiter looked immense up close: unapproachable and unstoppable. It seemed to be as big as a small house. Anything tangling with it would definitely get hurt.

"Ready for the first power up," Conners's voice came through Wirtanen's headset.

"Roger, you're go for first power up," Houston concurred.

The nitrogen jet stream from Conners's MMU immediately froze into ice crystals. The satellite's tumble began to slow down.

Conners, braced against the lower bay of the satellite, fired a second short burst of his maneuvering jets. *Jupiter* slowed and came to a complete halt along its lateral axis.

Its rotation end-over-end was very slow.

Conners shifted position, his movements slow and exact. To be thrown off the satellite even with its present very low rotational speed could mean that he might not be able to make it back to the shuttle on his own.

"Ready for horizontal axis power up."

"Roger, you're go for horizontal power up," Houston replied.

It only took one short burst for *Jupiter* to slow and stop.

"The beast is tamed," Conners reported.

"Copy that, Rod," the controller in Houston said. "Good job."

The arm slowly powered back to the payload bay, where Wirtanen maneuvered two file-cabinet–sized guidance packages into place and attached them to the arm. Untethered from *Discovery* he moved into position on the RMA's end strut and slipped his bulky booted feet into the restraints.

"Take me for a ride, Mouse," he radioed.

"Happy to oblige," Susan Wright came back.

The RMA inched its way back to the now-stable satellite. Wirtanen started to sing an off-key rendition of "Daisy Bell" better known as "A Bicycle Built for Two" that had become something of a tradition among American astronauts.

CONNERS HAD already moved to the guidance system bays located amidships between the two flimsy-looking solar arrays. They had to take care not to touch the panels. If they were damaged in any way, the panels would not produce enough electricity to power the satellite's systems. *Jupiter* would end up a very large, very heavy, very expensive piece of orbiting junk that would eventually spiral back into earth's atmosphere and burn up. The only alternative would be another expensive mission to retrieve her and bring her back to earth for repairs.

Ahead, in the distance, a band of reddish-gold light began to encircle the earth from pole to pole, as *Discovery-Jupiter* approached the dawn over the Bay of Bengal.

7

The BSY-2 display came alive.

Zimenski adjusted a few controls, then made a grease pencil mark on the screen. The Kilo was on the move.

"Conn, sonar. Sierra three is on the way up," he reported.

Dillon appeared in the doorway almost instantaneously. He donned a pair of headsets. It took a moment or two until he could distinguish that he was hearing propeller turns and hull decompression noises. "Good job, Ski. Now don't let him go."

"I'm on it, Cap'n."

"Can you confirm that she's a Kilo boat?"

"Yes, sir. I've got that much, but the computer can't ID her yet." Zimenski adjusted filters by hand, washing the sounds electronically, separating the various frequencies and mixes of frequencies that his acoustical equipment was picking up.

"What's her rate of ascent?"

"Fifty feet per minute."

"Gives us twelve minutes," Dillon said. "Soon as you find out who she belongs to let me know. We can't finish this without that."

"She's not Iranian or Pakistani, I can tell you that much," Zimenski said. "She's a newer model, different blade characteristics than their boats."

"Keep on it, Ski," Dillon said. He took off the earphones and went back to the control room. He did not hurry. The crew expected him to remain relaxed no matter what. And he thought better when he was calm. It was a trick that he'd learned hunting squirrels with his dad in Ohio.

"Okay, we're on it," he told his crew.

Master Chief Young as COB was at his position at the ballast panel. Alvarez as diving officer stood directly behind the planesman and helmsman strapped into their seats. Brown was at the nav tables, and his XO Charlie Bateman was overseeing the TMA and weapons control panel that was Jablonski's sanctum sanctorum.

"Sonar, conn," he said into the growler phone. "Is sierra three's rate of ascent holding?"

"Aye, Cap'n. Fifty feet per minute. She's passing five hundred fifty feet. Relative bearing zero-two-zero. She's making turns for two knots, on a course of one-two-five."

"Stand by," Dillon ordered. He looked at the multifunction display. They were dead in the water, hovering at six hundred feet, their bow pointed fifteen degrees west of due north.

Dillon switched channels. "ECMs, are you ready back there?"

"Aye, aye, skipper," the electronic countermeasures operator replied.

"Mr. Alvarez, make your speed two knots, come right to course zero-three-five."

"Aye, make my speed two knots, come right to new course zero-three-five," Alvarez repeated.

Brown plotted their new course and speed.

"Master Chief, bring us up to periscope depth. Make your rate of ascent six zero feet per minute."

"Aye, come to periscope depth, make my ROA six zero feet," the Chief of Boat repeated. *Seawolf* started up.

"Skipper, suggest that we shape a course and rate of ascent to get in behind sierra three," Brown called out. "Once we're in her baffles there's no chance she'd hear us. We could flood our tubes and open the outer doors."

"Thank you, Mr. Brown," Dillon said. He did not give the order. He switched back to sonar. "Any changes, Ski?"

"Sierra three is steady on her course, speed and rate of ascent. But, Cap'n, I'm picking up something weird. It's a high-pitched whine. At first I thought that they were having some sort of a malfunction in their active sonar equipment. But now I don't know."

Dillon had an idea. "Pipe it over to the weaps console," he said. He turned to Jablonski. "Ski's picking up something strange from sierra three. He doesn't know what it is. See if you can make it out."

Jablonski pressed his headset against his ears and listened for several seconds. He looked up, an evil smirk on his face. "It's a charging circuit. But real big. Maybe a giant capacitor."

"A high-energy laser power supply?" Dillon suggested.

"I don't know what else it could be aboard a submarine, skipper."

"Did you catch that, Ski?" Dillon said into the phone.

"Yes, sir. But if that's what it is, then they're about ready to go active. The charger is winding down."

"Do you have an ID on her yet?"

"Negative, Cap'n. She's gotta be a new boat. She's not in my computer."

"Swell," Dillon thought. His job had just been made a hundred times more difficult. Their primary mission goal behind stopping another laser strike was to find out who was behind the attacks.

As his dad used to say: There's more than one way to defur a feline. If they couldn't ID the Kilo here, they would follow it back to the barn. And woe *betide* the sonofabitch who got in their way.

8

Conn, sonar!" an excited Lt. Samsong called.

Zahedi snatched the growler phone. "This is the captain."

"Sir, I have a new target, designated sierra six. I evaluate it as a submarine, but I cannot say the type yet."

Zahedi crashed the phone back in its cradle and stepped around the corner to the sonar compartment.

Samsong was busy at his console, one hand on the controls, the other holding one side of his earphones against his head.

He looked up. His eyes were wide. "It came out of nowhere, Captain," he said. "One minute the sea around us was empty and the next he was there."

Zahedi donned a pair of headphones and listened. He couldn't hear anything that made sense, and he was about to ask the young lieutenant if this was a joke, when Samsong raised his hand.

"There. Very soft. Sounds like a British Trafalgar. A pump jet."

Then Zahedi picked up the low, rythmic pulsing noise from the mush. It was like someone ruffling a bedspread or perhaps fluffing a pillow; but it was more regular than that. Definitely a mechanical noise. The sounds had been described to him by Dr. Hassan. But the British wouldn't be here. That made no sense.

"What are they doing?" he asked.

"He's on his way up," Samsong said. He adjusted a control. "Relative bearing one-zero-zero, just aft of our starboard flank. Rising at about fifteen meters per minute. Just a little faster than us."

"What's her range?"

Samsong adjusted another control. "Nine thousand meters and closing very slowly."

Zahedi took off his headset and laid a hand on Samsong's shoulder. "Good job, Lieutenant. But now the real work begins. Stay alert."

Samsong puffed up with the unexpected praise. "Yes, sir," he said sharply.

Back in the control room, Zahedi looked at his crew. They knew that they had company. Now it was up to this Iranian submarine captain to show his mettle. They waited.

"Mr. Ki, come to battle stations torpedo," he ordered. "It seems as if we have a job of work to do before we surface to make our laser strike."

"Very well, Captain," his XO said. He made the announcement throughout the boat.

Zahedi walked over to the weapons console, where Lieutenant Nam had already started a TMA on sierra six based on the inputs the sonar sensors were supplying him.

"Are we ready to fire?"

"We have a good fix on the target, Captain," Nam assured him.

Lieutenant Samsong had correctly evaluated the strange noise as the sounds of a pump jet drive. But he was mistaken in thinking that it was a British Trafalgar submarine stalking them. On the contrary, it was the American *Seawolf* that he had been warned about. Which was better. The British might fire first and ask questions later. But the Americans would never do such a thing. Even the terrorist attacks in New York and Washington, and the reprisals in nearby Afghanistan and Iraq, had not appreciably loosened their trigger fingers. Americans were basically cowards.

Zahedi smiled inwardly. Well, it was too bad for them, because their submarine school was very good. But this was the moment he had been waiting for.

"Preset torpedoes one and two," Zahedi told his weapons officer. "I want a very tight spread. Put both weapons forward of amidships, in the area of the control room."

"Yes, sir," Lieutenant Nam said. He made the proper inputs to his console, and less than thirty seconds later the line of indicators showing the status of each weapon turned green except for the bottom three lights. The tubes had not been flooded, the outer doors were still closed, and the weapons were still safetied.

"Stand by," Zahedi told his crew. He turned to his XO. "Flood tubes one and two, open the outer doors and report when you're ready to fire. Look smart now."

His XO, working in concert with his weapons control officer, the chief sonar operator, and the torpedo room section chief, did the jobs that Zahedi had trained and retrained them for. Over and over they had practiced the battle stations torpedo and firing point procedures until they got very good.

They were ready to do battle in less than forty seconds. "Tubes one and two ready to fire in all respects, Captain," Ki reported.

"Verify final range and bearing to target," Zahedi said.

"I have a solid solution, Captain," Lieutenant Nam reported.

"Fire one, fire two," Zahedi said.

9

Conn, sonar, we're under attack. I have two high-speed screws incoming. Time to impact just under six minutes. Evaluate the weapons as the Swedish four-three-X-ohs."

"What is our friend doing now?" Dillon asked.

"No changes in her aspect, Cap'n. She's still heading to the surface, same rate of ascent, making two knots."

"Let me know if anything changes, would you, Ski?"

"Ah, yes, sir," Zimenski said.

Brown, who was running the paper plot, looked away in embarrassment. He had warned the captain to come in behind sierra three's baffles.

"Looks as if our Kilo captain is a confident man," Dillon told his crew.

"Captain, we have less than six minutes to do something," Bateman suggested as diplomatically as he could. "Should we flood tubes one and two?"

"We have plenty of time," Dillon said lightly. "Mr. Alvarez, come to all stop. Chief, zero our rise."

His crew gave him a double take, but gave the orders. The multifunction display showed their speed and rate of ascent coming to zero.

"I wonder where they got the Swedish torpedoes," Dillon mused. "They're not very fast, but they're sophisticated." He shrugged. "We'll have to let Pearl figure that one out. Might even bounce it to the Pentagon. It'll end up being a political issue."

By bringing *Seawolf* to a halt they were no longer heading toward the incoming torpedoes, which would give them a few extra seconds before impact. But dead in the water made it next to impossible for the incoming weapons to miss. And the window for Dillon to do something that would work was rapidly narrowing.

The one aspect that bothered him was what sierra three *wasn't* doing. The usual tactic was for the attacking CO to put the pedal to the metal after he launched and dive for the nearest thermocline in anticipation of a counterattack.

But then the Kilo's captain had to be wondering why the submarine that he'd fired on wasn't taking any evasive action of its own, or firing back.

This would probably go down as the most nonchalant attack in the history of the modern warfare, Dillon thought. At least the opening minutes were playing out that way.

"Charlie, flood tubes one and two, and open the outer doors, if you please," he said.

"All right, sir," a much-relieved Bateman said. He passed the order to the torpedo room.

"I want our shots offset, Mr. Jablonski. Two degrees right for the starboard torp, and one degree left for the port weapon."

Jablonski looked up from his console, startled. "Excuse me, skipper, but our starboard torpedo will be a clear miss past sierra three's bows. The port fish will just miss her stern."

"That's the idea," Dillon said. "The bow shot is going to be a dud, and the stern shot will go off just aft of and a bit beyond her prop. I want to damage her, not kill her."

Jablonski turned back to his console and adjusted a series of controls. "The presets are entered, skipper. Tubes one and two are ready to fire in all respects."

Bateman was talking to sonar. "Two minutes to impact," he said.

"Firing point procedures," Dillon ordered.

"Completed," Jablonski reported a moment later.

"Match bearings and shoot one and two."

Jablonski scanned his indicators, then pressed the firing buttons on his console. Within seconds hydraulic rams ejected two Mark 48s into the water. The moment they cleared the bow, they went active and headed for the target.

"ECMs, this is the captain. Deploy the bubble makers and standby the Masker on my order."

"Aye, aye, skipper."

Canisters were ejected from amidships that made huge clouds of bubbles meant to confuse an incoming torpedo. In this case, since *Seawolf* was stationary, the rising bubbles would fool the incoming torpedoes' guidance systems into believing that their target was making a desperate dash for the surface.

"This will be close," Bateman said. He reached up and grabbed a handhold.

Everyone else in the control room not strapped down did the same.

Dillon got on the 1MC. "Attention all hands, this is the captain. Brace yourself for two near-miss warshots."

The first torpedo exploded somewhere aft and slightly above the fairweather, hammering the *Seawolf* so hard that she heeled ten degrees to starboard.

The second five-hundred-pound-high explosive warhead exploded directly forward of amidships in the area of the control room, but fifty feet above. This time the *Seawolf* was skidded sideways on her keel, The lights flickered, shut off, then came back on.

"ECMs, this is the captain. Release the Masker now," he ordered. He turned to Bateman. "Damage reports, please."

10

The Kilo was hard over on her port side, accelerating as she turned and headed for the thermocline two hundred meters below. Zahedi had given the order to bug out when *Seawolf* launched her two fish.

"Our first weapon was a miss, but the second appears to be a solid hit," an excited Samsong reported.

"Give me verification," Zahedi ordered patiently.

"Sir, I am hearing damage noises," the chief sonar operator said. "Some compartments are flooding, and I can hear machinery sounds that mean whatever it is was knocked off its noise suppression mountings. And I think that I'm hearing fire alarms. Maybe even someone shouting."

"Is the boat sinking?" Zahedi demanded.

"No, but she is dead in the water."

"How long before the incoming weapons impact?"

"Two minutes," Samsong replied, his voice rising in pitch.

Zahedi turned to his electronic countermeasures officer. "Release noisemakers."

"Wait, Captain," Samsong came back. "The first torpedo is starting to veer left. He'll pass well in front of our bow. Maybe their weapons console sent a faulty signal after our torpedo hit. But it will be a miss."

"What about the other one?" Zahedi asked. His blood was rising. He'd never been fired at in anger.

"It's veering right, but not so much," Samsong said. "It will be very close, Captain."

"Are the noisemakers deployed?" Zahedi demanded.

"Yes, Captain. They are in the water and functioning normally," his ECMs officer responded.

Zahedi did the geometry in his head. Torpedo two was coming in at an angle aft of 2606's starboard beam. It would either just miss them aft, or just hit in the area of their stern, which could destroy their means of steering and propulsion.

"Come right ninety degrees," he shouted at his XO.

Ki issued the order and they slowly came back to an even keel and then started to list to starboard.

"The first torpedo is past our bows," Samsong called out. "The second . . . this will be close . . . impact now!"

They heard the high-pitched whine of the American torpedo's screw passing to their stern.

Zahedi was about to breathe a sigh of relief when the Mark 48 exploded directly behind them. He was knocked to his knees. His head smashed into the under section of the attack periscope's case. He saw stars. When he reached up to touch his head, his fingers came away bloody.

Ki came over and helped him to his feet.

"Get back to your post," Zahedi snarled. He was embarrassed. He snatched the growler phone. "Engineering, this is the captain. What's your situation?"

"We're taking water around the stuffing box, but it's nothing we can't handle," Stalnov shouted. There was a lot of machinery noise back there. "Our biggest problem is the prop. At least two of the blades are bent. I can't guarantee anything over three or four knots. And even at that we might throw a shaft bearing that will shut us down totally."

"What about some good news?" Zahedi asked.

"Our rudder is intact, but she's going to be a bastard to steer. The rudder shaft is also bent. On top of that I'd guess that the laser's mirror alignments are way out. I suggest that you get us home, Cap'n. If you can."

"Is there no way of fixing the laser?" It was impossible to believe that he had failed.

"Not out here," the chief engineer said.

"Try!" Zahedi screamed.

"No, Captain. It is impossible, I tell you. Get us home, or kill us."

Zahedi closed his eyes for a moment. He was still seeing stars. He switched to sonar. "This is the captain. What's sierra six doing now? Is she sinking?"

"No, sir. She's lying dead in the water. But, Cap'n, it sounds like they're trying to load another torpedo."

"I thought you said that we hit their control room," Zahedi shouted.

"Yes, sir. But maybe they can fire their weapons from the torpedo room. I don't know, sir. All I know is that I'm picking up what sounds like loading noises."

Zahedi hung up the phone. He looked at his XO and shook his head. If he'd had his own crew none of this would have happened. "We're done for now," he said. "We have crippled the American submarine. She's dead in the water, so she can't follow us. But her torpedo crew is trying to launch another attack on us. And our laser is no longer functional." He shook his head in an effort to keep on track, not to go wild. He wanted to hit something. "Mr. Ki, take us home, best possible speed and course."

"But, Captain, shouldn't we stay and fight?" Ki asked. His tone was insinuating. "The American submarine, as you say, is damaged. We still have weapons."

"You don't understand, you idiot! The fact that we hit them, and they missed us, was one chance in a million. Our propeller and rudder are damaged. As it is we will be very lucky to get away with our lives, and only if we leave immediately." He wanted to smash Ki in the face. "Get us out of here. Now!"

"Aye, Captain," Lieutenant Commander Ki said, an expression of contempt on his round features.

11

S ounds like he's got a damaged prop," Dillon said, holding the earphones close.

"Definitely an asymetrical flow," Zimenski concurred. "She'll be lucky to make three knots."

"Is she bugging out?"

"Yes, sir. Range is eleven thousand yards and opening. Course is—" Zimenski adjusted his equipment, then looked up in surprise. "One-five-zero, Cap'n. She's not going to Pakistan or Iran. She's heading south, for the Andaman Sea."

"We're going to follow them, Ski. How far back can I put us and still make it close enough for you to maintain a solid contact?"

"With the noise she's making, forty thousand yards, Cap'n."

"We'll stay here for one hour before we head out," Dillon said. "But once we're in the groove, you *will* take the next two watches off. And that's an order, sailor."

Zimenski was grinning ear to ear. "Aye, aye, skipper."

At the door, Dillon turned back. "Damned fine job, Ski. Even Jonesy couldn't have done it better."

There couldn't have been a greater compliment.

Dillon went back to the control room. "Good job, gentlemen. Sierra three is damaged and presumably heading home. To the southeast."

He let that sink in.

Brown was plotting the Kilo's new course and speed.

"Secure from battle stations, torpedo," Dillon told his XO. "We'll stay right here for the next hour, and then we're going to follow her."

He called ECMs. "Secure from Masker. Good job back there." Masker was a specialized noisemaking program emitted from the bow sonar dome that simulated a submarine in trouble.

"Thank you, skipper."

"They were in the Kilo's baffles so she would be deaf to anything aft. That was made doubly so by all the noise her damaged propeller was making. She would have trouble detecting a freight train roaring in on top of her."

"I want my officers in the wardroom in ten minutes," Dillon told his XO. He got on the 1MC. "All hands, this is the captain. We're in the clear for now. Well done, gentlemen. Tonight is steak night."

He turned back to his XO. "Have Lieutenant Jackson join us in the wardroom."

"Will do," Bateman said.

12

Conners turned the last fastener in place with his power screwdriver, and breathed a sigh of relief.

"The last one is secured," he said. He released his handhold and turned to the right. He was sweating lightly. In near weightlessness the simplest of tasks were often the most physically demanding. Turning a screw, for instance. When force was applied to the screw head, the screw remained in place but the astronaut spun around, unless he hung on.

"Good job, Rod," Houston said. "When you guys get back, how about coming over to my house with your tools. I've got a DVD player that's acting up."

"Tell you what, Houston, we'll make you a deal," Wirtanen said. He hung upside down over Conners's left shoulder, his feet pointed toward the earth.

"What's that?" Houston asked.

"We're taking the rest of the day off. Just send your DVD up here before supper and we'll see what we can do."

"I'll get right on that one," Houston promised.

"Hey, guys, did you happen to notice where we are?" Susan Wright's voice came over their headsets. "That's Australia's north coast down there. We're passing over Darwin."

Conners looked up and realized that she was right. They had been so busy working the *Jupiter* fix that they had not realized that more than six hours had passed. "Bye-bye, Bay of Bengal?"

"Roger that," she replied. "Bye-bye, Bay of Bengal. How about coming inside? I'll buy lunch."

FINAL CONFLICT

1

Marnie Morgan and Brian Fuller were once again parked in front of the Pakistani embassy.

"Same shit, different day," Fuller would say. They had been on this assignment forever, it seemed. And the only nugget they had mined was the one short conversation between Ambassador Husain and his bimbo from the ISI in which the place where they were holding our guys was mentioned.

Since then they'd picked up zip, and Marnie was more than bored. She was actively pissed off at Brian, who did nothing but bitch.

Today they were using the white Toyota Capital City Cleaning Company van. It wasn't as comfortable as the Windstar because it was crammed with more electronic surveillance equipment. "More shit to take care of in a crappy truck," Fuller complained. But it was anonymous.

"Brian, why don't you do something useful, for a change," Marnie suggested. "Why don't you go up front and play with yourself, or something? Maybe it'll make you a happy camper for a little while."

Fuller flashed one of his million-dollar smiles that got to her every time, and shrugged. "But I like to bitch. Maybe if you and I could play together . . ."

"In your dreams—" she said, but Fuller held up a hand, while holding his headset with his other.

"We have an incoming to Husain's cellphone. It's encrypted."

Marnie turned to her decryption panel that would make a preliminary pass. If an encryption algorithm was found, the conversation would come out in the clear. If not, the phone conversation would be simultaneously recorded and patched downtown to the Bureau's powerful decryption computers. If that didn't work, the entire conversation would be routed out to the National Security Agency's main decryption center at Fort Meade just outside the city. It was the most extensive facility of its kind anywhere in the world.

The mobile computer began chewing on the conversation, which to Marnie's ears sounded like nothing more than squeals, groans, pops, and static.

Fuller worked at the trace panel. "Bingo," he said triumphantly. "It's the same number as last week."

Marnie immediately patched the call to the Bureau's XMP Cray decryption system. Ambassador Husain had received a call just like this one, ten days ago. It had been too short for the Bureau or NSA computers to come up with an algorithm, but this conversation now would add to the database, giving them a chance to come up with something.

She looked at Brian. She was hearing the conversation in her left headset as it came out of her decryption equipment, and in her right headset as it was routed back to her after being washed through the Bureau's gear.

At first, both signals sounded exactly the same, except for a two-second delay. But then the right signal started to sound like human conversation.

"Come on," she urged under her breath.

"It's coming from a tower in Georgetown," Fuller said. He pulled up the reverse billing directory on his monitor. It might not show where the conversation was originating from, but it would provide a name and address for the customer.

The sounds in her right earphone were definitely those of someone talking. A few words or snatches of words began coming clear. It was like someone was trying to speak over the roar of machinery in a factory.

". . . committment . . . naval . . . last . . . *Seawolf* . . ."

"That's John Galt," Marnie shouted in amazement.

"Stewart Ellington. It's a P.O. box in the city."

"Get the box holder's physical address. The main branch will have it on file," Marnie told him. She got on the radio. "Dispatch, this is blue bonnet. I have an urgent red flag. We need assistance."

"Go ahead, blue bonnet."

Fuller came up with an address that he pinpointed on a map of

Georgetown. "It's an apartment building. South side of the street. The Winfield Arms. Top floor, four-oh-two."

The cellphone conversation was still going on in her headset, but it was meaningless again.

Marnie repeated the address to the mission dispatcher as Brian climbed up front behind the wheel, started the van, and pulled away from the curb.

"This could be John Galt," she said. "We're rolling." This got the dispatcher's attention.

"Help's on the way. ETA less than fifteen."

"We're monitoring the phone call. If he breaks it off we're going in immediately."

"Watch yourself, Marnie."

"Will do."

THE LIGHTS were with them, and eight minutes later they made a first pass in front of the Winfield Arms. There was a fair amount of traffic, both vehicular and pedestrian, but nothing looked out of the ordinary.

The four-story brownstone apartment building was well maintained and was an expensive address. The cars parked along the curb in front were mostly Mercedes and BMWs. Marnie was monitoring the tone connecting the in-service cellphone that John Galt was using with the cellphone provider through the tower. One moment it was there, and the next it was gone.

Fuller was turning left with the light at the corner. Marnie yanked off her headset and tossed it aside.

"He just pulled the plug," she shouted. "He might have spotted us."

Fuller made a hard-right U-turn, tires squealing, horns blaring as he expertly dodged traffic.

Marnie got on the radio. "Dispatch, this is blue bonnet. We've lost the signal. We're going in."

"You'll have backup in under ten minutes."

"Block the street behind the building. We might flush him toward you."

"Will do," the dispatcher replied tersely. There was no further reason to warn them to be careful. They were trained special agents who knew their jobs.

Marnie pulled on her dark blue windbreaker with *FBI* stenciled in yellow on the back, as Fuller screeched to a halt at an angle in front of the apartment building.

They were out of the van at the same time, pulling their weapons as they ran. Startled pedestrians immediately began to scatter. Marnie carried the Sig-Sauer P226, while Fuller carried the larger, though lighter, Glock 17. Both fired the European 9mm Parabellum round.

A woman in a blue pant suit was just coming out of the apartment building. They brushed past her and into the small lobby. The emergency stairwell was to the right, the elevator straight ahead, and the mailboxes to the left. A short corridor went back to the two apartments on this floor and an emergency exit to a courtyard garden in back.

The only way down from the upper floors was the single stairwell and the one elevator.

The elevator car was on the ground floor. The door was closing. Fuller went across the lobby, blocked the door from closing, then reached inside and shut it off.

Now there was only one way down.

Marnie took point as Fuller, his pistol in both hands, muzzle up, positioned himself to one side of the stairwell door, out of the line of possible fire.

He nodded, and Marnie opened the steel door, ducked inside and swept her pistol left to right up the stairs.

Nothing moved.

She signaled for Fuller with one hand, and scrambled up to the turn of the first landing, holding her gun out in front of her.

Still nothing moved on the stairs above her, nor could she hear anyone coming down.

She stopped at the first floor and peered out the window in the emergency door. The corridor was empty. With Fuller maintaining a half-flight interval below her, she worked her way up to the fourth floor where she paused to catch her breath and look through the window.

The corridor was deserted. The doors to apartments 401 and 402 were closed.

Fuller caught up with his partner and this time he took point, slipping out into the thickly carpeted corridor and silently reaching the door to 402. He flattened himself against the wall beside the door and waved her on.

When she was in place across from him, she tried the doorknob. It turned easily in her hand. She looked up at Fuller who gave her a nod, and then she shoved the door open and fell back.

He entered the apartment in a rush, keeping low, moving fast, sweeping the room with his pistol.

"Clear," he shouted.

Marnie came in as he swept the adjoining kitchenette to the left. She smelled cigarette smoke. An ashtray on the glass and brass coffee table in front of an off-white leather couch held the stub of a still burning cigarette.

There was something about it that was bothersome. But she couldn't quite put her finger on it.

A short hallway led back to the bathroom and bedroom that overlooked the small courtyard.

Marnie backstopped Fuller as he checked it out.

"We just missed him—" Fuller said, when all of a sudden it struck Marnie.

She raced back to the living room. The cigarette's filter tip was smudged with lipstick. Lipstick!

"Goddammit," she shouted in frustration. She turned her lips to her lapel mic. "Dispatch, this is blue bonnet on foot. John Galt is dressed as a woman! Tall, wearing a blue pant suit with long blond hair." She stared at the cigarette. "And bright red lipstick!"

2

ISI Director General Jamsed Asif bit his tongue to hold back a sharp retort. Pakistan's existence teetered on the brink of disaster, and it was up to the ISI to hold it together until their nuclear missiles were ready to fly.

If that meant that he had to continue dealing with lunatics, then so be it. *In'shah Allah.*

He looked across the empty runway and deserted tarmac toward the mountains. Such views always calmed him.

North Korea was essentially a bankrupt nation, with nothing but disintegration in its future. Pakistan, on the other hand, was the real power of the two.

And soon Pakistan would become the seat of power for the entire Indian subcontinent and all the nations surrounding it. The goal was worth his patience.

"My dear General Syng, of course I am certain of my information," Asif said. For the past hour since his plane had set down at this isolated and deserted former DPRK air force installation he'd tried to placate Gen. Sin Syng, director of the Democratic People's Republic of Korea's Central Intelligence Service. "It came from the usual impeccable source."

"Perhaps he made a mistake," Syng shouted. He was an easily agitated man. His position in the government was an extremely tenuous one. They stood just inside the ruins of an old aircraft hangar. Their bodyguards were not in sight.

"He has never been wrong before," Asif tried to assure his North Korean counterpart. "The warship that attacked *Most Revered* two-six-oh-six was the American *Seawolf* submarine. Her captain is Frank Dillon, a highly reliable and resourceful officer." Asif handed a manila envelope to Syng. "That is his dossier. The fact that your submarine survived at all is a miracle."

"Don't talk to me about miracles, Asif," Syng raged. "My government has done yours a very great favor at a very great risk to our own security. It is why we are meeting here, like animals in the wilderness, instead of civilized men in the city."

"It is a job that your government has done admirably well," Asif said. He did not add: And for which your government has been handsomely paid.

"Why weren't we warned of the attack?"

"But you were warned. That is why *Most Revered*'s captain decided to arrive at the firing point early. He expected to detect the arrival of the *Seawolf*. Apparently something went wrong."

"Do not impugn my crew of brave sailors. It was you who insisted that we have an Iranian naval officer in command. Now see where it has gotten us."

"Mohammed Zahedi is the most capable and cunning submarine commander in any navy outside England or the United States."

"Do not mention those warmongering nations to me," Syng screamed.

It was all an act, of course. Asif knew this. And Syng knew that Asif was aware of his reasons for such histrionics. Even the director of DPRK intelligence could not be certain that his conversations were being monitored, even here.

"There will be extra compensation for your government, of course," Asif went on smoothly.

"There better be."

"But the job is not finished. The *Jupiter* satellite was successfully visted by the crew of *Discovery*. We must assume that it has been repaired. It must be taken out of commission again once *Discovery* has landed."

"I'm listening," Syng said.

What Syng had not asked was why the second attack had been planned on the satellite while the American astronauts were working on it. Asif didn't completely understand the logic himself, except that Pakistan was taking its rightful place around the table of nations.

Despite all the international nonproliferation treaties, and satellite protection acts, Pakistan *would* continue to develop thermonuclear weapons and the means to eventually deliver them intercontinentally. And Pakistan *would not* tolerate any nation spying on it by any means.

"I assume that *Most Revered* was damaged," he said.

"Yes, but my people tell me that the damage can be repaired in very short order."

"Good. Then that is what must be done. *Most Revered* must return to the Bay of Bengal as soon as possible. But first you will have to deal with the *Seawolf*."

Syng laughed. "I am listening."

"He'll follow your submarine back to its base," Asif said. "He may even attempt to destroy the boat once he knows its destination. I believe that you should make preparations."

"Thank you for your concern, General Asif, but my staff assures me that a submarine of that size would never enter the Yellow Sea so close to our coast. The water is simply too shallow here in most places. It has been our natural defense."

"Perhaps you are correct. But the Americans seem to be doing the unexpected lately."

"If *Seawolf* shows up in our waters, our glorious navy will overwhelm it. With no room to maneuver, the Americans would have to understand that any attack on us would amount to suicide on their part. We would kill them all, and rightly so."

3

"**G**entlemen, sierra three is a North Korean submarine," Dillon said as he poured a cup of coffee. Eight of his key officers, plus Lt. Bill Jackson, were gathered in the wardroom.

This news did not come as much of a surprise to any of them. *Seawolf* had tracked the Kilo boat for twelve days across the Bay of Bengal, down the Strait of Malacca and back north into the China Sea. Thirty-six hours ago they had crossed the Ryukyu Trench that rose sharply from depths of twenty-five thousand feet onto the Asian continental shelf, through the islands between Japan and Taiwan and up into the Yellow Sea, where the water was less than two hundred feet deep and in some places of open sea less than one hundred fifty feet.

The Kilo did not turn west toward mainland China, but instead angled to the northeast, toward North Korea.

"We hurt her, so she's running back to her home port for repairs," Dillon said. "But I don't think that her captain is a North Korean. And maybe some of her crew are from somewhere else too. Which means that we still have a job to do."

"What's your best guess, Captain?" Bateman asked.

"I don't think her captain is Pakistani either. They just don't have the submarine experience to fight the way sierra three's skipper and crew fought." Dillon shook his head. He had done a lot of thinking about this over the past few days. He had drawn some conclusions. They weren't etched in platinum, but they were better than hunches.

"Russian?" Alvarez asked.

"Maybe," Dillon said. "I think their laser is probably Russian, which means they're carrying at least one Russian techie."

"Pakistan is the only country with a vested interest in knocking out our *Jupiter* system," Bateman suggested. He was playing devil's advocate.

"I think you're right, Charlie," Dillon said. "But our assignment is to not only stop the attacks, but to find out who's doing them." He looked around at his officers. All of them good men, ready to do whatever he asked of them. The *Seawolf* was not a democracy, of course. But a good CO knew how to ask for, listen to, and take good advice.

"Well, we have the advantage, Captain," Jablonski said. "The Kilo boat thinks that they killed us back there. They think we're dead, or at least no danger. They can't know that we've followed them."

"That's a point," Dillon agreed. Twenty-four hours after the fight, *Seawolf* had come to periscope depth, raised their comms mast, and phoned home. Their orders were specific: Follow the Kilo home and find out who's fighting her. The only problem in his mind was John Galt. If the spy were at a high enough level in the Department of Navy he might have seen or perhaps gotten wind of what *Seawolf* was up to.

"If they somehow knew that we were here, we'd be heading into big trouble, sir," Brown said.

"How's that, Mr. Brown?"

"The water's way too shallow for us to maneuver effectively. We'd only be able to develop about seventy-five percent of our top speed."

In waters shallower than the length of the submarine the shock wave of the bow moving through the water echoed back from the bottom *before* the stern of the submarine passed by. It created a powerful drag, almost like suction, that slowed them down.

"We can't dive deep beneath a thermocline, nor can we run away very fast," Dillon summed it up for them. "But we can fight. And if need be that's exactly what we'll do. This mission remains weapons hot."

No one flinched.

"They damaged three of our satellites, and they would have fired a fourth time, while our astronauts were right there. That, according to Washington, was an act of war."

Since Afghanistan and Iraq there was a new world order. Although some countries, evidently North Korea among them, could see what was happening around them, they did not yet understand that Americans were no longer willing to turn the other cheek.

The incident twelve days ago in the Bay of Bengal may have given them the general idea. But the point was going to be driven home for them real soon. In a way that the North Koreans and anyone else doing Pakistan's dirty work would not mistake.

"They're probably heading for Nampo," Bateman said. "Their best repair and retrofit yard is there. But once we're sure, what then, Captain?"

"How much do we know about this repair facility?" Jackson asked before Dillon could answer.

"We have the charts, if that's what you mean," Bateman said. "We also have some satellite photos, and we have the capability of listening to at least some of their military communications."

"Okay. Assuming they do go to Nampo for repairs, we're still not going to know who's conning that boat. Or who's running the laser."

"No, we're not," Bateman said. "What do you have in mind, Lieutenant?"

"I suggest that you settle on the bottom as close in as you can, and let me and my people go ashore and snoop around."

Bateman stared at the SEAL officer for a long moment, then turned to Dillon and raised a questioning eyebrow.

"Do you think that you can pull it off?" Dillon asked.

"Well, Kandrach would have gone okay if they hadn't been tipped off that we were coming," Jackson said. "With the element of surprise on our side . . ." He smiled. "We can do it, skipper."

4

Ma'am, can you hear me?" Scott Hanson called softly. He looked over his shoulder at the door to his prison cell. Sometimes a guard listened from the corridor. If Hanson was quiet he could hear the man shuffling his feet. But there was nothing tonight.

He turned back to the narrow crack that he'd managed to pick in the mortar between a couple of concrete blocks in the corner. "Ma'am, I'm an American. If you can hear me, give me a sign, please."

His tiny cell reeked of human waste and his own filthy body. There'd been no retaliation after the attack nearly two weeks ago. In fact, their torture had even stopped. But Hanson had not been let out of his cell, nor had his food and water rations changed. He didn't know how much longer he could go on. Just the effort of picking the loose bits of mortar from between a couple of concrete blocks near the floor had taken him four days and nights. The opening was only four or five inches long, and not very deep. The mortar joint was smeared with blood from his damaged fingers.

But it was something. He had managed to do at least one thing.

He glanced again at the door. Had he heard something? He held his breath and listened. But the cell block was quiet. Deathly still.

He turned back to the wall. "Ma'am, can you hear me? This isn't a trick. I'm an American just like you. A prisoner."

Hanson had picked up snatches of conversation from the ISI captain and the guards in the torture cell and in the corridor, about a fifth prisoner. An American. A woman whom they had rescued from the ocean. It wasn't clear why she was being held prisoner if she had been rescued, but Hanson was fairly sure that she was still here and that she was in the cell adjacent to his.

Once he began to suspect that there was a woman prisoner here, he had listened even more carefully to the goings-on out in the corridor. He heard the cell door next to his being opened, and then closed just before his own food and water were delivered each day. And once he thought that he'd heard a woman's voice, crying or pleading. But it was cut off, as if a hand had been clamped over her mouth.

It wasn't much to go on, Hanson knew, but he had to do something; anything, rather than simply lie in his cell and wait to die.

Someone whispered something. It was very soft and indistinct, but he was sure that it was a human voice coming from the next cell.

He bent closer to the corner. "Ma'am, if you can hear me, talk a little louder."

"Who are you?" a woman's voice came through.

Hanson's heart leapt into his throat as if he had just won the lottery. "My name is Scott. What's yours?"

"Marcella. My friends call me Marcie. What are you doing here?"

Hanson stopped short. This could be a trap. The comments made by the captain and the guards could have been a setup. They'd gotten nothing from him during their interrogation sessions; maybe this was a new tactic. Maybe the woman worked for Pakistani intelligence. Or maybe their conversation was being recorded.

Maybe, he thought. But he didn't believe it, even though it was very difficult to hold onto even a shred of optimism when you were alone.

"I work for American intelligence," he told her. "The Pakistanis tested another nuclear weapon. We were sent over to see what they were up to."

"There's more than just you?"

"Four of us," Hanson said. "But I haven't seen my people since we were captured. How about you, Marcella? Is there someone with you?"

"No," she said, after a long pause. "At least I don't think so. I was the only one aboard the sub."

"What happened?"

Again there was a long pause before she answered. Hanson could envision her huddled on the floor in the corner of her cell, just like him, wondering if this was some sort of ISI trap.

"We weren't spies or anything like that," she said. "I was the captain of the *Eagle Flyer* out of Sarasota, Florida. We were a research ship studying sharks, mostly. Up in the Bay of Bengal. We spotted a sub on the surface and when Art—my first officer—tried to call a securité the sub fired a torpedo at us and we blew up."

"Do you think that anyone else got out?"

"I don't know," Marcella Wallner said. "I hope so, but I don't think so. I think I was lucky. Until I got here."

"Whose submarine was it?"

"I don't know," she said. "I was pretty well out of it when they pulled me aboard. And when we docked they blindfolded me before I was taken away."

"Are you okay now?" Hanson asked. "Are you injured? Are they feeding you?"

She didn't answer, but he could hear her sobs.

"Marcella, listen to me. We're going to get you out of here. They know back home where we are. They tried once to rescue us, they'll try again. Believe me."

"They keep raping me," she said. "I'm bleeding, sometimes a lot. And I can't pee. I'm scared."

"We're going to get you out of here, I promise you."

There was only silence.

"Can you hear me, Marcella?"

"Yes."

"We're going to get out of here." Hanson laid his forehead against the wall. "Now, tell me what you look like. I have a terrible time matching faces to voices."

5

Dillon raised the search periscope for a snapshot once it was fully dark topsides.

They were above the mud bottom in one hundred fifty feet of water just outside the main shipping lanes, a stone's throw from the Nampo Bay Bridge. They were twenty-five miles as the crow flies from downtown, but less than four miles from Nampo naval repair facility number one.

Coming in last night had been hairy. Like threading a needle. Half the DPRK's Yellow Sea Fleet was guarding the approaches. It made Dillon wonder if John Galt had found out that they were coming and had informed Pyongyang.

But if that were true, one of the ASW ships would have detected *Seawolf,* Dillon thought. They weren't that stupid, were they?

The bridge was poorly lit. There was no traffic, but an army truck was parked on the center span. In the distance to the east, the night sky was aglow from the lights of Nampo, which was a city of about one hundred fifty thousand people. But closer at hand the navy base was very well lit.

Or at least most of the sprawling facility was brightly illuminated. The west side of the base was in darkness, however. All the lights in that part of the base had been switched off for some reason.

Dillon dialed up the scope's low-lux circuitry and looked again at the naval repair facility. The well-lit areas were a blur in the binocular eyepieces. But the dark sections glowed in shades of pale green.

A Kilo boat, with a black unmarked fairwater, was being moved toward the open doors of what appeared to be a roofed-over dry dock. He could make out two men in coveralls on the bridge, and see the four powerful tugs that were maneuvering the damaged warship.

It was no coincidence, Dillon decided. The Kilo boat being maneuvered into the dry dock was the submarine that had fired the laser. *Seawolf* had damaged her, and she had come home for repairs.

But the transfer into the covered repair dock was being done under the cover of darkness. The fact that the Kilo was here, and was going to be repaired, was being kept a secret.

Why?

He stepped back and powered the scope down.

Because they failed to take out the *Jupiter* satellite. They were going to try again ASAP. Which meant that the Pakistanis were probably getting set to test something else that they didn't want the Americans to see. Maybe a long-range missile on which they could mount their thermonuclear weapons. That was no stretch of the imagination.

"Are Jackson and his people ready to go?" Dillon asked his XO.

"They're standing by at the after escape trunk," Bateman said.

"Ask the lieutenant to come here, please. There's something that he has to see first."

Bateman got on the phone and called for Jackson.

Dillon called sonar. "How's it looking, Ski?"

"Nobody's closing in, Cap'n. Still lots of activity seaward. They're obviously running a picket line. But if we've been detected, nobody's letting on."

"How about inside the bay?"

"Some commercial traffic, maybe fishing boats. It's hard to tell, there're a lot of bottom echoes. But something heavy's being moved across the base. I'm hearing the screws of four big tugs."

"They're moving our Kilo into dry dock," Dillon told his chief sonarman. "If anything heads our way, let me know."

"Roger that, Cap'n."

"Our SEALs will be locking out in a few minutes. Follow them in. If anyone takes an interest in them let me know about that right away too."

"Aye, Cap'n."

Dillon was going to ask if Zimenski had gotten enough sleep over the past few days, but it was a useless question. The sonarman either had or had not gotten enough sleep. Nothing could be done about it now. He was needed at his station.

Jackson, his face blackened, dressed in UDT gear minus the mask, fins, and rebreather, came from aft. "We're set to get out of here, skipper. You wanted to see me, first?"

"I want you to take a look at something, but stand by one," Dillon said. He called the radio room. "This is the captain. Are you picking up any traffic about us?"

"Nothing yet, Captain."

An ultrathin radio intercept antenna had been raised eighteen inches out of the water and they were monitoring Nampo military traffic on a wide range of frequencies. Some of it was encrypted. But the DPRK's algorithms were easy to break, even for *Seawolf*'s limited seaborne decryption gear. The computer chewed on the en clair language as well. An alarm was sounded on certain programmed key words, such as: *Seawolf, american submarine, attack, Kilo, laser.*

"Keep your ears open."

"Will do, sir."

Dillon raised the search periscope, did a quick three-sixty and then a second before he turned back to the dark side of the naval repair facility. The Kilo was halfway inside the dry dock. Two of the tugs had backed off, leaving the final push to the stern pair.

"Take a look," Dillon said, stepping aside.

Jackson studied the image for a full minute, then slowly panned the scope to the right and then back again, ending up on the dry dock.

He looked up. "We won't have to go searching for her after all."

"There'll be yard workers crawling all over the place."

"Not until they get the boat chocked and the water pumped out of the pen," Jackson said. "By then we'll be aboard, and maybe even gone."

Bateman joined them. "What about the Kilo's crew?"

"No reason for them to be aboard when their boat's in dry dock for repairs," Jackson said. "If *Seawolf* were in the same situation would the crew stay aboard?"

"A couple of officers, maybe some of the engineering crew," Bateman answered. "But certainly not everybody."

"Then it's still a go."

Dillon nodded. "If you get into a shooting match I'm not going to be able to hang around here for long."

"If we're cut off, we'll try for the border, skipper," Jackson said.

"Just bug out, and see if you can warn our people that we're coming."

"You know the mission," Dillon said. "Good luck." They shook hands.

Jackson grinned. "Payback time," he said. "With interest."

"All right," Bateman murmured.

6

Jackson went back to the aft escape trunk in the engineering spaces. Terri and the others were suited up and waiting for him.

A pharmacist's mate and engineer's mate were there to help the team lock out. Jackson dismissed them.

"Give us a couple minutes, would you?" he asked.

"Sure thing, Lieutenant," one of the mates said, and they left the compartment.

"What's the scoop, F/X?" MacKeever asked.

"I got a look topsides. They're moving the Kilo into a dry dock. Bearing one-seven-three about seven thousand yards out."

"Any radio traffic?" Terri Vaughan asked.

"Nothing about us so far," Jackson told her. "If we can get over there in time, we should be able to get inside the pen before they start pumping."

"I wouldn't want to be caught inside the pen when they do start pumping," MacKeever griped. "Four SEALs, plus a couple of seawater pumps, equals a shitload of hamburger meat."

"Then we'd best hustle," Ercoli said. "The SDVs are already on deck." He picked up Jackson's rebreather and equipment packs and helped him on with them.

"Did you bring the other duffle?" Jackson asked Terri.

She ducked around the corner, took a large, waterproof, buoyancy-compensated duffle bag from a locker and brought it back. MacKeever helped her stuff it up into the escape trunk.

"What's that?" Ercoli asked.

"An extra rebreather in case we bring a prisoner back and don't want to drown him," Terri said.

"And four satchel charges," Jackson told them. "We've chased this

Kilo boat halfway across the Indian Ocean. I don't want to do it again."

Terri grinned sweetly. "It's the only way to make sure, Chopper."

Ercoli couldn't help but laugh. He liked blowing up things. "I hear you, Lips. I surely do."

"CONN, ENGINEERING."

Dillon answered. "This is the captain."

"The team is away, Skipper."

"Thank you," Dillon said. He switched circuits. "Sonar, conn. The team is away."

"I've got 'em, Cap'n," Zimenski said. "They're clean so far. No one's taking an interest in them or us."

"Keep your ears peeled."

"Will do."

"Radio room, this is the captain. Anything from the intercepts yet?"

"Negative, skipper."

"Very well." Dillon glanced at the mission clock that Alvarez had started the moment the SEALs locked out. It was 1352 GMT. The time-elapsed hand showed two minutes since the team was away.

They were using a pair of portable swimmer delivery vehicles, which were small underwater sleds. The SDVs could pull them through the water at five to six knots. It would take them around forty minutes to make it under the bridge and across seven thousand yards to the sub pen. If they were lucky another ten minutes to gain entry and another ten to get aboard.

After that it would be purely a matter of chance how long they would have to remain aboard the sub to accomplish their mission. They might encounter stiff resistance. They might not find what they were looking for: mainly logbooks, written orders, and the hard drives from the Kilo's computer systems. They would also try to get to the laser weapon, to find out who had made it. And, if possible, grab one of the ship's officers to bring back with them.

Anyone else aboard was expendable. The North Koreans had fired the first shot.

But there were a lot of variables in which a dozen things could go wrong.

One of the SEALs' Murphy's Laws of combat that Dillon remembered was that if the enemy is in range, so are you.

He raised the search periscope and deflected the angle of the lens downward. There was nothing to be seen on the surface of the water directly ahead of *Seawolf*. The SEAL team's rebreathers left no trail of bubbles, nor did their SDVs make any kind of a wake.

Nothing was out there.

He raised the lens angle. The Kilo was almost all the way inside the dry dock now. Even if the yard workers were efficient it could take them the better part of an hour to get the submarine's chocks in place so that the pen's doors could be closed and the dry dock could be pumped out.

It was cutting it close for Jackson and his team. But they would make it if they didn't run into trouble.

"Anything wrong, Captain?" Bateman said softly at his shoulder. No one else in the control room could hear him.

"I don't know, Charlie. Just a feeling that they could be heading into another trap."

"We shouldn't have gotten through their picket line so easily."

"That's what I was thinking," Dillon said.

Bateman managed a smile. "I guess that's why they pay us the big bucks: to think and worry."

Dillon nodded. "Come to battle stations torpedo and missile. I want tubes one, two, seven, and eight loaded with Mark forty-eight ADCAPS. Three and four with TLAMs, and five and six with TASMs."

Bateman did not flinch. The captain had ordered up a serious array of firepower. The torpedoes were the best in any navy in the world: extremely long-range, super-accurate, and extremely lethal.

The TLAMS—Tomahawk land attack missiles—could deliver a one-thousand-pound warhead dead on a target out to thirteen-hundred miles.

And the TASMs—Tomahawk antiship missiles—could deliver the same warhead out to nearly three hundred miles with a pinpoint accuracy no matter what maneuver the warship might make.

The nuclear versions of the TLAM missiles that *Seawolf* carried on this mission could deliver the two-hundred-kiloton W-80 nuclear warhead.

In addition to the pair of nukes, *Seawolf*'s loadout on this mission included a mix of forty-eight torpedoes and conventional Tomahawks.

"What are the targets, Captain?" Bateman asked.

"Put the TLAMs on the headquarters building and their intel facility. We'll use the ADCAPs and TASMs to blow a hole through the fleet if need be when it's time to leave."

Bateman smiled faintly. "That *will* get their attention."

"That's the idea, Charlie," Dillon agreed. "I don't want a lot of casualties. I just want them to know that we're here and not very happy."

7

Captain Mohammed Zahedi emerged from the Kilo's forward loading hatch and paused a moment in the darkness. Most of his officers and men were already gone. Stalnov had stayed aboard, however, to start the repairs on his precious laser equipment. Lieutenant Nam and a few engineering staff had also remained to help.

There were some yard workers in the shed, but not as many as there would be once the sub was properly chocked and the water in the dry dock pumped out. Then there would be dozens of workmen crawling all over his boat. Getting her ready to fight again.

From on deck he could not see the damage. But for the past twelve days he'd had plenty of time to think about what happened out there. They'd been very lucky to have survived the encounter with the *Seawolf*. He knew that. But he had begun to wonder if it was luck that had allowed them to survive. Or if it had been an extremely well-planned war shot from the American boat, meant to disable and not to destroy.

But why? What was the point?

The American boat had laid a trap for them in order to protect their spy satellite. And at the proper time they had sprung their trap.

The only reason that Zahedi could think for the American captain to fire a disabling shot was to force 2606 to withdraw and return to her home port for repairs.

Zahedi stared at the still-open dry dock doors. He could see the bridge and beyond it, the open sea at the head of the bay. The *Seawolf* had been destroyed. Or at least so heavily damaged that it should have been impossible to follow 2606 here. Zahedi had listened to the sonar tapes. He had heard the flooding noises with his own ears.

But he had a very odd feeling between his shoulder blades. It was as if a sniper was taking aim at the middle of his back. The thought was unsettling.

He walked aft to the boarding ramp, looked up at the empty bridge atop the fairwater, and went ashore.

With any luck the repairs to his boat would be completed in the forty-eight hours promised so that he could put back to sea. Trying to relax and find a bit of recreation in North Korea was like trying to find safety in the tiger's cage. It was impossible. One wrong move and you could be denounced as a traitor to the Beloved One or Dear Leader, or whatever they were calling Kim Jong II these days, and you could be summarily executed.

The DPRK was politically aligned with Iran, but that's as far as it went. The sooner Zahedi was gone from this place the happier he would be.

A Russian-made Zil limousine and driver were waiting for him outside. When he cleared security he climbed in the back and was driven across base to Yellow Sea Fleet headquarters.

Unlike the dry dock shed, which was in darkness, the three-story brick headquarters building was bathed in lights, though most of the windows were dark at this hour.

The armed guards at the main entrance snapped to attention as Zahedi passed. He signed in at the security desk and was directed to the third-floor conference room of Fleet Adm. Chi Losan.

Off the elevator he turned left, and walked down the deserted corridor to the admiral's conference room. His shoes made no noise on the lush carpet. He'd been here only once before, three months ago, when he'd arrived to take over as commanding officer of 2606. The admiral was a tiny, shriveled monkey of a man with a ridiculous number of ribbons and medals on his white uniform. Five minutes talking with him, however, dispelled any notions that Zahedi had that the man was stupid. The admiral was anything but. And by the end of the brief meeting with him, Zahedi had changed his mind about the medals too. The admiral had most probably earned every one of them.

He girded himself, knocked once, and went inside. The admiral was not there. Only General Syng sat at the long conference table.

The general looked up, studied Zahedi for a long moment, and then shook his head. "So, at last you managed to return our submarine to us without completely destroying it and killing the crew," he said. His tone dripped with sarcasm and anger. He was a very dangerous man to have as an enemy.

"I'm sorry, General, but it was a trap," Zahedi said. Admiral Losan he respected. But this one was like a hooded cobra, coiled and ready to strike.

"You were warned," Syng said. He did not motion for Zahedi to take a seat. "How soon will our submarine be repaired and ready for sea?"

"I am told forty-eight hours, sir."

"You will return to the Bay of Bengal as soon as humanly possible and finish the job that you bungled," Syng ordered. "Is that perfectly clear to you?"

"Yes, it is, sir," Zahedi said. "But may I ask how the general knew what happened? I haven't submitted my full report yet."

Syng studied the Iranian officer again, as if he were looking at an interesting bug through the lens of a microscope. There was a cruel set to his eyes and narrow mouth. "I was informed by a reliable source what your actions were. And were not."

"General, did your source tell you if the American submarine that I fired on was destroyed?"

"It was not," Syng informed him. "It was even suggested that the American warship might come here—"

It was as if a bolt of lightning had struck from a clear sky. "You fool," Zahedi said in wonderment. He suddenly saw everything. The trap, the *Seawolf*'s lucky shot, and the noisemaking program to fool them into thinking they were damaged.

Syng jumped to his feet and fumbled for his pistol. His face was a mask of rage. No one talked to him like that and lived. No one.

"The *Seawolf* is already here," Zahedi said. He turned to leave, but Syng pointed his pistol at him.

"Stop," the North Korean general ordered.

Zahedi turned back. "I'm telling you, General, that *Seawolf* is already here. *Inside* the navy's harbor blockade. He probably followed me in. So I suggest that if you want to keep this facility intact you alert the navy, and get a security team down to the dry dock before it's too late."

"How can you be so sure?" Syng demanded.

"I fought against this man once. That was enough."

Zahedi hesitated for just a moment, then left the conference room and headed in a dead run for the stairs.

8

Jackson and Ercoli scrambled up the side of the submarine with the grappling lines they had tossed on deck.

Terri and MacKeever waited in the water, watching a couple of yard workers doing something on the upper gallery, and three men on the dock near the bow of the Kilo. If the workmen spotted what was going on, she and MacKeever would take them out with their silenced room brooms.

The Kilo's forward loading hatch was open, but no light shone from inside the submarine. The deck was deserted and mostly in darkness too. There were deeper shadows on either side of the fairwater, but all of that would change as soon as the pen's doors were closed and the water pumped out. Then, under the complete safety of cover, the interior of the dry dock would be brilliantly lit, and the engineers and welders would begin repairing the battle damage, working twenty-four hours per day.

Their window of opportunity was right now. And it would not stay open for very long.

Jackson and Ercoli crouched on deck for a couple of seconds, then they tugged on the grappling lines.

They immediately moved to the open hatch a few meters forward of the fairwater's leading edge. Terri and MacKeever scrambled up on deck, crouched a second to gain their bearings, and then joined Jackson and Ercoli.

They were exposed on deck in the open, expecially this close to the bow. Three yard workers were doing something with what looked like a portable welder. If they turned around they would almost certainly spot the intruders and sound the alarm. But there were probably still some crew aboard, and it would be just as foolhardy to blindly barge into an unknown situation.

Jackson cocked an ear to listen. He could hear a voice from inside the sub. Very low and indistinct. Probably one or two compartments either forward or aft from the loading compartment. A very dim red light illuminated the lower rungs of the ladder and the deck grating directly below.

Jackson took out his suppressed Sig P226, cycled the slide, and decocked the hammer. The gun had no conventional safety catch, just like his other favorite weapon, the Steyr GB. For this mission his load was the 9mm copper-jacketed serrated hollow point ammunition that was absolutely deadly over the entire range of the weapon. Whatever he hit *would* go down.

He motioned for the others to hold for one second and then follow him down. They nodded their understanding.

He lowered himself through the hatch and climbed noiselessly down into the submarine. The boat smelled of diesel fuel and something else. Something foreign, odd; maybe something in the galley.

The voice came from somewhere aft. Possibly the control center. Ercoli started down the ladder, MacKeever and Terri right behind him.

Jackson climbed the rest of the way down, and quickly looked both ways along the central passageway that ran for most of the length of the boat. All the hatches were open. It was like looking down a long tunnel lined with a maze of pipes, wires, lights, and valves.

He couldn't see any of the crew, but he could hear one of them talking, possibly on a telephone. Jackson could only hear one side of the conversation. But it was in English. The crewman was asking something about a faulty indicator light. Whoever he was talking to was apparently giving him a hard time, because the crewman kept insisting that the light was red, not green.

It was the same in every navy, Jackson thought. No one listened if they could help it.

The conversation suddenly stopped. A slightly built man in khaki slacks and a dark sweater or jacket came into view. He did something at an electronic panel, shook his head, and then looked up. Directly at Jackson.

Jackson raised his Sig and fired one shot, hitting the man in the forehead and driving him backward off his feet. The noise wasn't very loud, even in such a confined space.

He made his way into what was the control room and swept his pistol in a tight arc to cover the entire compartment. But the now dead crewman had been the only one in the conn.

He turned back to his team. "There's at least one other crewman aboard, and possibly more to help with the repairs," he told them. "But it looks as if most of them jumped ship."

They nodded.

"Okay, you know what to do, people, so let's get it done," Jackson ordered.

No one looked at the dead man, whose blood was splattered along the port bulkhead and the overhead. He wore North Korean navy lieutenant's pips on his shoulder boards.

Terri and MacKeever turned on their heels and headed forward. They would shoot any of the crew they encountered, and set one-third of the satchel charges around the torpedoes in their racks. Then they would work their way aft again, mopping up if need be. They would plant one-third of the charges in the bilge or battery compartments beneath the control room, and the final charges aft in the bilges below the engineering spaces.

When Jackson had outlined the mission parameters for them, which included taking down anyone they encountered, no one had offered the slightest objection. The crew of this boat had killed the innocent scientists aboard the *Eagle Flyer*, and had been willing to place the lives of the vulnerable astronauts in jeopardy.

This was war. It had been since 9–11.

Ercoli carried the suppressed version of the new 10mm Heckler & Koch MP5 room broom, in semiauto mode. The weapon made more noise than the Sig P226 pistol, but it was a lot more effective at taking out the opposition.

Their first sweep through the boat would be for crew, the second for hard drives and information, and the third to get them back into the water.

Jackson pointed out the Kilo's crude version of the American BSY-1 weapons control computer system aft of the periscope platform. On the way out they would retrieve the systems' hard drives, if there was time.

Piggybacking, Jackson taking the port side compartments and Ercoli starboard, they started aft when they heard sirens outside. A lot of sirens.

RIDING IN the Zil all the way across the base, Zahedi kept waiting for the alert to be sounded. He expected a lot of lights and noise; troops pouring out of their barracks, armored personnel carriers and mobile guns all converging on the submarine repair dock.

It wasn't until the Zil pulled up in front of the covered shed where 2606 was tied up that air raid sirens started to sound all over the base.

"Fools!" Zahedi cursed. Everyone here was afraid of making a decision—any decision—for fear it would be the wrong one. Initiative was a notion completely foreign to most North Koreans.

Well, they were going to lose a submarine, if they didn't start very soon. And they might even get their noses well bloodied if the *Seawolf*'s captain decided to lob a couple of land attack missiles on the base.

Zahedi jumped out and ran across to the guardhouse, waving his papers.

One of the guards came out of the hut, his rifle slung over his shoulder. He glanced up at the siren atop the building as if it were a nuisance and nothing more. Then he looked back at Zahedi, mild curiosity on his flat face.

"Open up, you idiot!" Zahedi shouted, in his limited Korean.

It was the same man he'd passed coming out of the shed less than fifteen minutes ago. But the soldier held out his hand for Zahedi's papers.

There were no troops yet. Only sirens. Zahedi handed his ID through the bars.

The guard studied Zahedi's papers for several agonizingly slow seconds, and then turned and went back into the gatehouse. Zahedi could seem him through the window. The man was discussing the situation with another soldier, who finally picked up a field telephone to call for instructions.

Suddenly Zahedi was calm. He almost laughed. So be it, he

thought. His Kilo boat would either survive or it would not. *In'shah Allah*. God willing.

Something was approaching. He looked over his shoulder in time to see a half-dozen loaded troop trucks racing from the barracks. Behind them were a pair of mobile missile launchers.

Maybe there was still time after all.

9

In engineering, Jackson held his pistol on a Russian officer. The two North Korean mates they had encountered lay dead: one of them in the hatch and the other lying half in one of the diesel engine's oil sumps. Ercoli had slung his room broom and was taking photographs of the Russian-made hydrogen-fluoride/deuterium-fluoride (hf/df) laser's power and control sytems.

The actual laser beam was transmitted to the focus head forward via a two-inch-thick fiber optic cable. Jackson recognized the device from a briefing on Russian-made weapons in development that he'd received in San Diego a couple of years ago. He wasn't really surprised to see it here aboard a North Korean warship. Though he was surprised to see a Russian officer aboard, even if Captain Dillon had suggested the possibility.

It had been something under three minutes since the sirens had begun to sound. They were running out of time.

"Chopper, we have to go now," Jackson said urgently.

Ercoli took three more digital images, and then looked up. "Done," he said. "Let's rock."

"Do you speak English?" Jackson asked the Russian officer. The man's name tag read *STALNOV*.

The Russian didn't respond.

"Get the hard drives, I'll be right behind you," Jackson told Ercoli, who immediately left. Jackson told Ercoli, who immediately left. Jackson pointed his pistol at Stalnov's head. "Last chance, pal. If you don't speak English, you're dead."

"I speak English," Stalnov said. He looked like he wanted to rip Jackson's head off. "Where did you come from?"

"My mother," Jackson said. He stepped aside to let the Russian go first. "We're leaving now. If you drag your heels or try anything at all, I'll put a bullet in the back of your head. Do you understand me?"

Stalnov's eyebrows rose, but he nodded. "Yes."

"Move."

In the control room, Ercoli had the front panel of the weapons control computer off. MacKeever and Terri were waiting at the ladder to the forward hatch. "Two bad guys down," MacKeever said.

Jackson handed the Russian over to them. "Get him out of here. If he tries anything, kill him. Chopper and I will be right behind you."

Terri's lips pursed, but she nodded. "Thirty minutes, F/X," she said. She took Stalnov roughly by the arm and pulled him to the ladder. "Don't fuck with me tonight, comrade, I'm not in a particularly charitable mood," she warned.

"Soon as you get the hard disks, get out of here, the satchels are set to go off in thirty minutes," Jackson told Ercoli, and he ducked back along the passageway to the captain's compartment, which was just forward of the officer's wardroom.

The sirens outside were still wailing, but so far there had been no indications that anyone was coming aboard to storm the boat.

The CO's cabin, secured only by a curtain across the doorway, was tiny. A compass, ship's clock, depth gauge, and growler phone were clustered on the bulkhead above the pull-down bunk. A chair sat in front of a small pull-down desk that was open. But the desk's compartments and drawer contained only blank paper and a few books all in English.

In English.

Jackson pondered that for a moment. Was it possible that the North Koreans had gotten a rogue British submarine commander to work for them? It seemed like a very long stretch in Jackson's mind. The Brits he knew were straightforward guys.

Something caught his eye. A bit of color sticking out from the edge of the bunk. He pulled the bunk down. A Muslim prayer rug, cap, and well-worn traveler's copy of the Koran were tucked under the pillow. There was some handwriting on the inside cover of the book.

Arabic script. The skipper was an Iranian. Jackson would have bet almost anything on it. They were the only ones out here that he knew about who had access to the British Perisher's training methods.

He headed forward on the run, stuffing the book into a waterproof pocket in his UDT suit.

Ercoli and the others were already gone by the time he scrambled up on deck.

The interior of the dry dock shed was still in darkness, but he counted at least three yardworkers down in pools of blood.

Then everything happened at once. All the lights came on. The dry dock's doors began to rumble shut with a tremendous din of squealing metal on metal. And someone started shooting in earnest, raking the deck, sparks flying off the steel plating.

Jackson fired three shots in return as he took two steps to starboard and dove into the water.

Something vey hard slammed into his thigh just below his left hip the moment his head hit the water. "Goddammit," he shouted inside. He *hated* to get shot. Just hated it.

2340 LOCAL
YELLOW SEA FLEET HEADQUARTERS

Alone in the conference room, General Syng drummed his fingers on the tabletop as he waited for his call to Qindao to go through. Captain Zahedi's report had not been as surprising as the man's outburst. He was uncultured, as most Iranians were. They were only a generation or two beyond their desert nomad heritage. It had been only political chance that had allowed an Iranian navy officer to attend Perisher. That, and Iran's purchase of four Kilo submarines from the old Soviet Union some years ago, *before* the DPRK could do the same, gave them the advantage in experience. But only a temporary advantage. Admiral Losan reported that his people were learning very fast. They had the proper motivation: Learn or die.

This deal brokered by Pakistan was clearly to North Korea's advantage. Payment was in hard Western currencies— U.S. dollars, British pounds, and Swiss francs—which North Korea desperately needed. And the Yellow Sea Fleet's submariners were gaining much needed experience.

In the meantime, ISI General Asif's warning that the *Seawolf* might follow *Revered Leader* here, of all places, had worried Syng more than he let on to anyone except the Dear Leader himself.

He was given the authorization to approach their allies for help, and Beijing had agreed immediately.

Vice Adm. Wang Jiying, commander of the PRC's North Sea Fleet, had jumped at the chance to corner an American submarine in such shallow waters.

"It will be my pleasure to provide assistance to our friends in the struggle," Jiying had promised.

And he was as good as his promise. Lying just offshore, in ultra-silent mode that no passive sonar in the world could detect, were four PRC Han class nuclear submarines. They were slow and leaked radiation, but they were deadly warships all the same. And four against one were good odds, especially when the American boat would be hampered in her ability to operate in such shallow waters, and hampered in her political will to fight a most-favored-nation trading partner.

The call finally went through and Vice Admiral Jiying came on the line. "You would not be calling at this hour unless your situation has actually developed."

"Yes, thank you, Admiral Jiying, the situation may have developed as we had forseen."

"I know, General Syng. My on-site commander, Captain Chou Hua, informed me two hours ago. I ordered him to stand by until we heard from you."

Syng wanted to leap through the telephone and take the stupid old man by the throat. If the Chinese had called two hours ago the North Korean navy patrols could have been alerted. He calmed himself.

"Yes, thank you, Admiral. Will you be ready to strike once the hare is flushed to your hounds?"

"Send him to us and we will kill him," the admiral said. "I guarantee it."

Syng managed a thin smile. "Then we will bait the trap and you can spring it."

After the connection was broken he sat for a few moments contemplating the ramifications of what they were going to do. Killing an American warship with a large loss of life would have major political ramifications. But the situation could be turned to North Korea's advantage.

Syng got his cap, went downstairs to his car, and ordered his driver to take him to the quarters of Minister Chan Do-Sang, across base. Do-Sang was the civilian political adviser to the fleet. He was a man used to being in complete control, and being informed at all times.

NAMPO DRY DOCK

The shooting had finally stopped and the dry dock's huge doors were safely secured. Now, nothing could get in and wreak more havoc.

Nor, Zahedi thought with pleasure, could anyone caught inside escape. Once the pen was pumped dry he hoped to see the body of at least one American intruder.

The lights inside the pen were on. Zahedi stepped out onto the walkway to which his boat was secured. There were bodies near the bow of 2606, and there was a splash of blood on deck opposite the forward loading hatch.

The lieutenant of the guard unit that had responded to the alert gestured for Zahedi to hold up.

"Pardon me, Captain, but this area is not secured yet," the small, runt-faced officer warned. "I cannot guarantee your safety."

"Whoever was aboard my boat is either dead or already gone. Don't you see the blood on deck?"

"It might be from one of the welders, or one of your crewmen. You said you left crew aboard?"

Zahedi had been so worried about his boat that he had momentarily forgotten about Stalnov and the five others aboard. He brushed the lieutenant aside and made directly for the boarding ramp. He pulled his Russian PSM pistol from inside his tunic, stepped aboard, and went to the open hatch.

At first nothing seemed amiss. His boat was quiet, just as he had left it.

"Captain, please wait, sir—" the lieutenant called from the walkway.

Zahedi blocked the man out. Something small and dark was lying on the passageway grating below. He cocked his head to see it from a different angle. Then he knew. It was a footprint, and Zahedi knew exactly what had been stepped in to make the print.

It was blood. Someone aboard had been injured. And someone had tracked the blood to the escape trunk ladder.

Zahedi hurriedly climbed down into his boat. He held up at the base of the ladder. Lieutenant Nam's body lay in a heap near the laser power transfer panel in the control room. Nothing moved, and there was no noise except for the soft whir of air-circulating fans and the distant sounds of the sirens outside.

He had to assume that whoever had come aboard his boat had gotten what they had wanted, killed his crew aboard, and left. But what exactly was it they wanted to find out?

Zahedi went aft, stopping only long enough to make sure that Lieutenant Nam was dead. He stopped at his compartment and looked inside. His eyes went immediately to his bunk. The pillow had been moved and his Koran was missing.

For a second Zahedi drew a blank, but then his breath caught in his throat as if he had just smelled something disagreeable.

He had been ordered to take nothing on this assignment that would identify him as an Iranian. But inside his Koran he had written notes about the births of his seven children. In Tehran.

It was the Americans. Probably a SEAL team from the *Seawolf.*

He continued aft, finding the bodies of the two engineers mates. The laser had apparently not been touched. At least it did not appear to be damaged. But Stalnov was nowhere to be found.

Zahedi stared at the laser for a long time, trying to imagine what had happened here. Trying to figure out why the Americans had not only taken the huge gamble of bringing their submarine into such shallow waters, but then putting a team aboard.

They had probably kidnapped Stalnov, which was proof that a Russian was helping to destroy American spy satellites. They had stolen his Koran, which proved that an Iranian was the commanding officer.

And what else?

Theft. Kidnapping. Sabotage?

Had they placed explosives aboard that could destroy his boat?

Zahedi raced forward to the control room. He snatched the shore phone from its bracket and got the base operator. He needed to get his crew aboard right now. They had to find and disarm the bombs before it was too late.

11

Jackson felt pretty good, although he had lost a fair amount of blood. But the cold water combined with the tight UDT suit had helped to stanch the blood flow long enough for them to get clear of the dry dock.

They were well out into Nampo Bay, hanging in the pitch dark forty feet beneath the surface. Overhead there was a great deal of traffic: Smaller boats that buzzed like angry power saws, and much larger patrol vessels whose big screws churned up the water enough when they passed directly overhead to toss the SEALs around like salted peanuts in a bottle of Nesbitt's orange soda.

They risked a dim red light so Terri could secure an elastic bandage around the wound in Jackson's thigh.

The Russian had been having problems breathing all the way out. He watched the first aid, but he looked as if he wanted to break free and swim for the surface. The only thing holding him back was the greater fear of the razor-sharp Ka-Bar knife that MacKeever held menacingly. He might drown, but if he tried to get away Shooter would cut his throat. He stayed put.

Finished, Terri looked up and gave Jackson the question sign. He answered with the thumbs-up. He checked hs GPS Plugger navigator, which contained an inertial positioning system as well as a satellite receiver.

They were still twenty-five hundred yards from *Seawolf*. He showed the readout to his team, then signed for them to move out smartly.

North Korea's reaction had occurred so fast that they'd had no time to make an attempt at escaping by land. Their only option at this point was *Seawolf*.

If the CO had bugged out they would be in some deep shit. And they all knew it.

They grabbed handholds on the SDVs and cranked the electric throttles wide open. They had one shot at this, and *only* one shot.

They heard an explosion in the water somewhere behind them. Then a second, and a third, and several more.

They sounded like small depth charges to Jackson. Possibly grenades. The pattern started from the direction of the dry dock, and was working outward into the bay. Right on their heels.

The odds had just changed. For the worse.

1606 GMT
SEAWOLF

Dillon left the conn and stepped smartly around the corner to the sonar compartment.

It seemed as if every warship in the North Korean navy had put the pedal to the metal all over inner and outer Nampo Bay. They were looking for somebody in a big hurry. And there was no question in the mind of anyone aboard *Seawolf* exactly who it was they were looking for.

Nor was there any doubt in Dillon's mind what this was all about. John Galt had betrayed them once again. His jaw tightened just thinking about the bastard. The North Koreans knew that *Seawolf* would be showing up right behind the Kilo, and Galt had somehow known that a SEAL team would be put ashore.

Sonar supervisor Lt. (jg) Chuck Pistole stepped aside for the captain, but neither Zimenski nor the other three operators looked up from their consoles. The screens were alive with multiple contacts, most of them extremely strong. The four technicians were extremely busy.

Jablonski had been listening to some of it on his weapons console headphones in the control room. He'd picked up the small explosions.

"Marc's hearing a series of small underwater explosions, shoreward," Dillon said. "Has it got something to do with our guys?"

"Ski's working on it, skipper," Pistole said, covering his mic. Bateman had the conn, and he and Jablonski were keeping track of the numerous passive contacts that sonar was feeding them.

"Sierra twenty-seven, range eleven thousand yards, bearing three-zero-five and opening," one of sonar operators callled out. "Estimate target speed is one-seven knots on a course of two-five-zero."

Pistole relayed the new target information to the conn. "Can you say the type?" he asked the operator.

"Stand by," the young man said. He adjusted his equipment. "It's coming up now, sir."

Pistole read the line that was just spitting out of one of the printers behind the sonar console operators.

"Sierra twenty-seven is a Six Hainin class large patrol craft," he relayed the information to the XO.

Ski looked over his shoulder at Dillon. "It's our guys, cap'n, coming from the sub pen."

"What are they shooting at?"

"Lieutenant Jackson's people aren't the ones setting off the charges. There's a couple of small patrol boats out looking for them. They're tossing small depth charges into the water. They're trying to force our SEALs to the surface."

"Means our people are trying to make it back," Dillon said. "How tight are they?"

"Right now there's a thousand-yard separation, but the patrol boats *will* catch them," Zimenski said.

"Maybe we'll give the Koreans something else to keep them busy," Dillon said. He patted Zimenski on the shoulder. "We're not leaving without them, Ski."

Dillon went back to the control room. "Our SEALs are on the way back. Soon as we get them aboard we're getting out of here. In the meantime we have some work to do."

His control room crew sharpened up.

"Man the helm and planes. Master Chief, stand by the ballast board," Dillon ordered. He called engineering. "Mario, stand by for all-ahead full. We're getting set to bug out."

"We're ready now, Captain," Battaglia promised.

"Are my TLAMs warm and ready?" Dillon asked his weapons officer.

"Aye, skipper," Jablonski said. "They're spun up and targeting data has been entered."

It meant that the Tomahawks' electronic circuitry had been switched on and diagnostically checked. The gyros and other electromechanical systems had been brought up to speed, and the status of the missiles' fuel, pumping, and ignition systems had been checked out as well. Electronic information targeting the missiles on Yellow Sea Fleet headquarters building and fleet intel HQ had been entered into the missiles' computers.

"Make tubes three and four ready in all respects."

"Aye, making tubes three and four ready in all respects."

Flooding the tubes and opening the outer doors, so that the missiles could be ejected from the boat and then fired, was a noisy procedure. Every North Korean warship with sonar in the bay was going to hear them.

"I want firing solutions on the four targets to seaward that offer us the most threat," Dillon said.

Alvarez was helping process data for Jablonski. He knew exactly what the skipper was going to try. He was grinning.

"I want all tubes ready in all respects for firing. Target the Mark forty-eights in tubes one and eight, along with our TASMs in five and six on the seaward targets. We'll save two and seven for reserve."

"Aye, skipper," Bateman replied, repeating the orders.

Dillon called the torpedo room supervisor. "I want reloads as fast as you guys can hustle back there," he advised.

"You got it, skipper," Lt. (jg) Howard Doolittle replied crisply. This was the kind of a mission they'd trained all their careers for. He was eager.

Dillon switched to sonar. "How's it look, Ski?"

"Cap'n, if you're planning on that diversion you talked about, now would be a good time, sir. The depth charges are coming awful close to our team."

"Stand by."

Dillon looked at his crew. "Gentlemen, it's payback time."

"All right," Bateman said.

"Firing point procedures, tubes three and four."

"Aye, aye," Jablonski shot back.

"Shoot three. Shoot four."

The noise of the hydraulic rams shoving the Tomahawk missiles out into the sea was distinctive. Nobody on the boat could miss it, or fail to understand the consequences. The *Seawolf* had just fired two missiles in anger on a sovereign nation against whom no state of war had been declared.

"That'll get their attention," Bateman said.

"And then some," Master Chief Young mumbled.

12

General Syng was shown into the sitting room of Minister Do-Sang's private quarters. Whatever the disturbance across base he was certain that it was being taken care of by security forces. He had bigger fish to fry this night.

Captain Zahedi's outburst would not go unpunished, but for the moment the submarine commander was needed. No one in North Korea's submarine fleet was as knowledgeable as the Iranian. And the *Revered Leader* would be leaving for patrol within forty-eight hours.

On top of all that, the hard Western currencies that Pakistan was paying were a godsend to Pyongyang. The man who assured the continued flow of cash would rise even higher than Dear Leader's intelligence chief.

If no mistakes were made.

Minister Do-Sang, dressed in a garish red brocade smoking jacket, his whispy, thinning white hair like a cloud around his head, sat across a lacquered coffee table from Fleet Adm. Chi Losan. The pair had evidently been arguing. They both seemed agitated, the admiral more so than the minister.

"Good evening, Minister," Syng said. He came to attention and saluted, then nodded to the admiral.

"What is all the commotion out there?" Admiral Losan demanded. "I'm told that there are intruders."

"They won't get far, I guarantee it, Admiral," Syng promised. He turned his attention back to the minister. "The situation that we discussed has arisen."

"Yes, I know. Admiral Losan and I have been discussing the very issue," Minister Do-Sang said. He looked angry. "Is there confirmation?"

"Yes, Minister. I just spoke with Admiral Jiying, who is in communication with his squadron leader. The *Seawolf* is here, in Nampo Bay."

"What is being done?"

"*Seawolf* will not leave our waters alive," Syng said.

"Monstrous," Admiral Losan shouted. "I am fleet admiral, and I forbid this insanity." He got to his feet and gave both men a withering stare. "If we go head-to-head with a warship of the *Seawolf*'s power it will mean disaster for us. With or without Chinese help. That one vessel could utterly destroy not only this installation, but the entire city of Nampo, if its captain chose to do so."

"The Americans would never fire a shot in anger at us," Minister Do-Sang said, trying to placate the admiral.

"I agree," Syng said. "Despite the terrorist attacks against them by bin Laden and his righteous warriors, the Americans have held back."

"They destroyed the Taliban, you fool," Admiral Losan shouted.

"A renegade government," the minister said. "We are a sovereign nation. We exchange special diplomatic missions with the United States. They will not begin a war with us."

"I will put a stop to this, if you do not desist," Admiral Losan warned.

The minister picked up a telephone, issued an instruction and immediately two armed guards came to the door.

"Admiral Losan is relieved of duty as of this moment," the minister said. "He is to be placed under immediate house arrest. He is to be allowed no telephone calls, or to receive any visitors."

"Yes, Minister," one of the guards said. His hand was on his sidearm. He gave the admiral a polite nod and stepped aside to clear the way.

"You won't get away with this, Chan," Admiral Losan said calmly, once again in control of himself.

The minister waved him away cheerily. "Of course I will." He smiled. "Perhaps you will come to your senses in due time. One can hope."

0008 LOCAL
ABOARD 2606

Zahedi shined the beam of his flashlight on the olive-drab bundle that was just out of his reach in the bilge beneath the torpedo room. He needed something like a boat hook, something to extend his reach.

The package was a bomb. There was no need to open it to find out. The Americans wouldn't have put anything else here.

The only questions left were when was it set to explode, and were there others.

Zahedi heard someone aft. His crew had finally started to arrive to help.

"Up here, on the double," he shouted.

The bomb suddenly fizzed like a sparkler and a split instant later the lights went out for Zahedi.

0009 LOCAL
VIP HOUSING

From a third-floor window General Syng and Minister Do-Sang could see smoke and flames rising into the night sky from the direction of the sub pen. Syng was beside himself with fury.

"It seems as if Admiral Losan might have a point after all," Minister Do-Sang said.

What sounded like a pair of jet fighters *wooshed* very low overhead from the direction of the bay. But they were too low, Syng thought at the same moment two explosions, one immediately after the other, brightened the night sky as if it were day.

Syng had just started to turn toward the minister when the window they stood in front of burst inward in a million shards.

The minister took the full brunt of the flying glass directly in his face, blinding him, and cutting his neck and throat in a dozen places. He staggered backward as he began to rapidly bleed out.

Syng was not blinded, but the side of his face and neck were shredded by flying glass. One piece lodged in his windpipe so that he could not call for help.

He fell back and dropped to his knees as he struggled for a breath of air free of blood.

He was going to die on the stupid floor of a political hack's sitting room. It made no sense to him. What's more, it wasn't fair.

The Americans were supposed to play by the rules. They had always played by the rules. Otherwise the rest of the world didn't stand a chance.

13

Conn, engineering. Our SEAL team is aboard."

"What kind if shape are they in?" Dillon asked. They'd all heard the massive explosion at the sub pen moments before the two Tomahawks hit their targets. The SEALs had sabotaged the Kilo.

"Lieutenant Jackson took a round in the leg, but he says it's not too bad."

"Have the pharmacist's mate look at him, but hang on, we're getting out of here," Dillon said. He replaced the growler phone.

"I have firing solutions on four targets that'll make a hole for us," Jablonski advised from his console.

"Very well. Firing point procedures on tubes one, five, six, and eight," Dillon ordered. "Chief of Boat, get us out of here right now."

"Aye, skipper," Chief Young responded.

"Skipper, recommend course two-seven-five, depth one-four-zero to coordinate with weaps firing solutions," Alvarez said.

"Make it so, chief," Dillon said.

"Aye, skipper, course two-seven-five, depth one-four-zero."

The *Seawolf* turned left, her bows down only a few degrees because they didn't have a lot of depth to work with. As it was, submerging to 140 feet would put their keel ten feet or less from the bottom silt. Wrecks, old piers, or rocks jutting up from the bottom would pose a serious problem, except that Alvarez and Jablonski had shaped a firing solution and course that would bring them back over the same track they'd crept in on. They knew that line was clear.

Targets one and two, on which they would use the Tomahawk anti-ship missiles, were Soho and Najin class frigates. Three and four were a pair of Chong-jin class torpedo patrol boats. The patrol craft were fast and maneuverable, but their sonar equipment wasn't very sensitive and they had relatively small weapons loads.

The frigates were something else. Built in Naijan shipyard, the Soho displaced nearly 1,900 tons, with a crew of 190 men and officers. In the early years the North Koreans had a lot of trouble with the ship. But those problems had been solved. At 246 feet on deck she was a more than adequate platform for ASW helicopter operations.

The Najin at 1,500 tons was a little lighter than the Soho, but she was longer at 334 feet and faster. She was primarily a mine layer and could continue to deliver depth charges for a very long period because of her large weapons load.

Jablonski had targeted the TASMs on the frigates. The Tomahawks might not sink either ship, but they would do a lot of damage. And the strikes would probably discourage all but the most fanatical officers from continuing the fight.

But there was only one shot at breaking out. If they missed, they would find themselves surrounded by half the DPRK navy.

Dillon walked over to the plotting table where Alvarez and Brown laid out the problem on the Nampo Bay chart. The way to the open sea was clear for the moment. But the frigates and patrol boats were rapidly converging on that course in response to the noise *Seawolf* had made firing her missiles.

They would catch up with no problem and block any chance of escape on that course. The patrol boats would lay down a series of torpedoes, while the frigates laid down mines and depth charges as their ASW helicopter hovered dropping buoys directly over *Seawolf*'s position.

It would be like shooting fish in a barrel.

Except that Dillon wasn't going to play by their rules, something the North Koreans should have already figured out. He wasn't going to wait until they shot at him. He was going to shoot first.

"Conn, sonar," an excited Zimenski called.

Dillon snatched the phone. "What do you have, Ski?"

"Cap'n, I have solid returns on four new targets, sierra twenty-eight through thirty-one. Evaulate them as Han class nuclear submarines. Bearings are spread eighty degrees across our bows, ranges between twenty-five thousand and thirty thousand yards."

"Find out what we have in the computer. I want to be real sure about this," Dillon said calmly. It was a trap. Getting past a couple of

North Korean frigates and patrol boats was one thing. But the addition of an outer screen of four nuclear submarines was something else. Something a bit more dicey.

His orders authorized him to go weapons hot, at his discretion, against Pakistan and whoever was helping Pakistan destroy our satellites. That was North Korea.

Adding Communist China into the mix upped the ante. He could not call this one home at the moment. He would have to fight his way out of Nampo or surrender his submarine.

Dillon glanced over at his XO and smiled. "The North Koreans have called in the cavalry," he said. He turned back to the phone. "What do you have, Ski?"

"Definitely Han class, Cap'n. Sierra twenty-nine is sail number four-oh-eight and sierra thirty is sail number four-oh-five. The last built. The computer hasn't come up with the other two yet, but it's chewing the problem. All four boats are showing the same frequency lines. They're Hans. No doubt about it."

"What are they doing?"

"Just sitting there, sir. Waiting for us to try to break out."

"Keep a close eye."

"Will do, Cap'n."

Dillon replaced the growler phone, careful not to move fast. Calmness was his watchword. The the CO's attitude, for good or bad, had a very large effect on his crew.

"We have four Chinese nuclear submarines waiting for us about thirty thousand yards out. I want TMAs started on them now." Dillon glanced over at the rest of his control room crew. "It's going to get a little busy around here. But that's why we came. So, let's get to work, gentlemen."

"All right," Bateman said.

14

O nly the officers aboard Chinese nuclear submarines wore dosimeter badges. Last night Captain Chou Hua's badge was already starting to turn milky, indicating that he was taking too much radiation.

It was why China's submarine commanders, when they did sail, would never hesitate to fight. Do the job, get it over with, and return to base. It was a man's only chance at survival.

Pity his chief engineer, Lt. Cmdr. Xu Yongguo, and the poor bastards back in engineering, right next to the leaking reactor, didn't have the same chance. When they left on a long mission, base records pulled their files and sent them to graves registration just in case. It's one of the reasons most Chinese nuclear submarines spent most of their time tied to the docks. They were death traps.

"Conn, sonar."

Capt. Hua pulled down the growler phone. "Have the Americans started their move?"

"Yes, sir. They closed the two outer doors they used to fire the missiles, and I am detecting reloading sounds."

"Course and speed?"

"One-two-five, accelerating now through twenty knots, captain. I don't know if they've detected us, but I think I know what their captain will attempt to do."

The chief sonarman was Lt. Youan Peng Fei. He was the nephew of Vice Adm. He Peng Fei, a deputy commander in chief of the navy. He was a bright young man, who, because of his position and connections, was not hesitant to use his brain and to express his opinion.

"Stand by," Hua said. He turned to his executive officer, Lt. Cmdr. Shi Tsu-Lin. "Fire tubes one, two, three, and four. *Seawolf* is on the way out."

"Yes, sir," his XO snapped. He turned and issued the firing point procedures and match bearings orders.

"Captain, I think that the Americans plan on shooting their way out of the bay," Sonarman Peng Fei said. "I've worked out their probable firing solutions on the Soho and Najin. If they could take out those two ships, they would be clear."

"Which is why we are here, Lieutenant," Captain Hua said. "Attend to your duties. I want to know the moment *Seawolf* does anything else. Anything at all."

"Fire one," Tsu-Lin ordered.

The first SET-65E was ejected from the 533mm farthermost starboard tube on a blast of compressed air that made the entire hull ring like a bell.

The XO fired tubes two, three, and four at two-second intervals. It was the signal for the other three submarines in the flotilla to each fire four of their fish.

Sixteen torpedoes would soon be heading toward one very good American submarine. But only one submarine for all that.

"Everyone shoots at once and keeps shooting until the American is dead," Hua said.

His XO looked over. "Yes, sir. But first I think that he will kill some of us."

"Yes, he almost certainly will," Hua agreed. "Fate."

15

have three . . . make that four high speed screws in the water."
Zimenski's voice came down the passageway from sonar. He
hadn't bothered with the phone.

Dillon stepped around the corner. "Chinese?"

"From sierra thirty. Sounds like SET-sixty-five Es," Zimenski
adjusted a display. "Time to impact just under four minutes."

"The other three submarines will be firing at any moment. Let me
know when it happens."

"Yes, sir," Zimenski said. He was flying. He was in his element.

Dillon walked back into the control room. "XO, match bearings
and shoot tubes one, five, six, and eight," he ordered.

Bateman repeated the command, and started the firing procedures.

Dillon went to the chart table and glanced at the situation as
Brown was plotting it.

"Chief of Boat, come right to new course zero-zero-five. Move
smartly now."

"Aye, skipper, turning starboard to new course zero-zero-five."

Dillon reached up to brace himself. "Weaps, do you have solutions
on sierra twenty-eight through thirty-one?"

"Yes, sir. Tubes two, three, four, and seven are ready in all respects."

Bateman looked over from the firing console next to Jablonski.
"Tubes one, five, six, and eight have been fired."

"Firing point procedures, please, on tubes two, three, four, and
seven, and then match bearings and shoot," Dillon said. "Cut all
wires."

"Aye, skipper," Bateman responded.

"We won't get them all, Marc, so as soon as we have reloads I want
those four boats retargeted," Dillon ordered.

Zimenski was on the growler. "Cap'n, I have many high speed

screws incoming. I estimate at least twelve, possibly as many as sixteen fish heading for us."

"Keep an eye on sierra twenty-six and twenty-seven. I want those frigates out of action."

"Yes, sir. Time for the first fish from sierra thirty to impact is now three minutes and stretching," Zimenski said.

The rate of closure had been over six thousand yards per minute with the *Seawolf* heading directly for the Chinese submarines at twenty-five knots, into the torpedoes incoming at forty knots. By turning away, the closure rate was decreasing, stretching the time to impact.

The problem was the new course. They were now heading directly toward the Soho that was already starting to drop depth charges.

"Tubes two, three, four, and seven are away," Bateman reported. "Time to impact on our first two fish on sierra twenty-six and twenty-seven is now two minutes thirty seconds."

"Very well," Dillon said. He called sonar. "I'm going to duck in behind Soho just before she's hit, to shield us from the Chinese torpedoes. Let me know when I have the angle."

"Yes, sir. Time to impact now two minutes forty-five seconds."

It would be close. Dillon turned to his COB. "Chief, bring us to periscope depth."

"Raise to periscope depth, aye, skipper," Young responded.

Dillon leaned against the periscope railing and watched his crew doing their jobs. Everything was in place now. His tactics would either work or they wouldn't. With the odds stacked against them they had only this one chance.

16

The American captain was actually fighting his boat rather than running away. Lt. Peng Fei was right. The *Seawolf* meant to get past them all even if it resulted in destroying the ships that were legally correct to be in their home waters.

It was astounding.

"Captain, evaluate the incoming torpedoes as Mark forty-eight ADCAPs," the chief sonarman said. "One of them has locked on us."

"Time to impact?" Hua asked. This had suddenly become anything but the academic exercise in geopolitical realities that he had been told it would be. It was turning into a worse-case scenario. He felt a sense of detachment.

"Two minutes."

Hua held the phone against his ear. He stood at the chart table looking at what he had plotted. *Seawolf* had fired what were probably Tomahawk missiles at the frigates, and two Mark 48s at the nearest pair of North Korean patrol boats.

The American captain was trying to blast his way clear of the harbor. But that would have put him directly in the path of Hua and his flotilla.

Hua shook his head in vexation. He had fired too soon in his eagerness. He had given away his tactical advantage of surprise.

"Captain, suggest we deploy noisemakers," his XO, Tsu-Lin, said.

Hua looked up out of his daze. He wasn't going to simply throw away his command because an American warship had fired at him. "Deploy the noisemakers immediately. Come to all-ahead flank, turn right to a new course of—" He did the rough calculation by sight on the chart. Submarines 404 and 402 were to starboard. But they were just far enough away to give him the needed turning radius. "New course one-nine-zero."

Tsu-Lin gave him a double take, but issued the proper orders. Turning to that course would place them behind 404, which would then become the target for two of the four American torpedoes.

If there was time.

"Firing point procedures for tubes five and six," Hua ordered. His two remaining loaded torpedo tubes were targeted on the *Seawolf.*

"Firing point procedures complete. Tubes five and six are ready in all respects."

"Match bearings and shoot tubes five and six," Hua said triumphantly.

He called the torpedo room commander. "This is the captain, how are the reloads coming?"

"As you would expect, Captain," the lieutenant, whose name Hua could not remember at this moment, shouted. Han class submarines were equipped with poorly engineered reloading equipment.

"Hurry up, you bastard. Our lives depend on it," Hua screamed. He braced himself and looked around.

"Fire five," Tsu-Lin reported. "Fire six." He looked up. "Both torpedoes are running hot and normal, Captain." He glanced at the weapons console display, which showed that they now had no weapons ready to fire.

"Now we shall see," Hua said.

They all heard the distant explosions, four of them in close order, as *Seawolf*'s weapons found their marks against the North Korean navy.

Hua's flotilla was next.

17

We have four solid hits," Zimenski reported. "Sierra twenty-four and twenty-five have been obliterated. Sierra twenty-seven is sinking fast. I'm hearing breakup and compression noises. Sierra twenty-six is also sinking, but slowly."

The depth charge attack had stopped. Sierra 26 was the Soho.

"Do we have the angle yet, Ski?" Dillon asked.

"Cap'n, we have the angle now. Soho is five thousand yards off our portside."

"Chief of Boat, come to all stop. Rig for silent running," Dillon said. He got on the 1MC. "This is the captain. Silent running now."

All noises aboard *Seawolf* ceased. The normally quiet submarine became suddenly very quiet. The only noises they could hear were the crashing sounds of machinery breaking loose aboard the sinking Najin and Soho frigates.

They heard three distinct explosions in the far distance.

"We have three hits. Sierra twenty-seven and sierra twenty-eight," Zimenski called. "Stand by—"

The Mark 48s were considerably faster than the Chinese SET-65Es. They had reached their targets first.

"Sierra thirty turned behind sierra twenty-eight . . . I think. The first and second fish both hit sierra twenty-eight. Number three is a clean hit on sierra twenty-seven. But number four shut down. I've lost contact."

"Two-to-one odds. That's better," Bateman said.

"Stand by . . . stand by . . ." Zimenski called. His voice rose an octave.

The hydraulic shockwaves from six powerful explosions, one almost right on top of the other, hammered the *Seawolf.*

Something broke loose forward, several circuit breakers popped and reset themselves. Chief Young jumped up to shut off a powerful jet of water that suddenly appeared above the ballast control panel. The control room lights flickered a couple of times and then steadied down.

"All hits on sierra twenty-six," Zimenski reported. "There's almost nothing left of her."

"What about the other incoming torpedoes?"

"They've passed us. Three are heading for pieces of sierra twenty-seven, the rest are shutting down."

They heard three distant explosions as the sinking wreckage of the frigate Najin was hit again, and then silence.

Dillon called the torpedo room. "Doolittle, how are my reloads coming?"

"One through six are done, skipper. Give me two minutes and you'll have seven and eight."

"Good job," Dillon said. It was some kind of a record. He switched back to sonar. "Ski, what are the North Koreans doing?"

"Scattering, Cap'n. All of them are heading back into the bay."

"What about the Chinese?"

"Stand by," Zimenski said.

Dillon turned to his crew. "Chief, stand by to get us out of here with as much speed as you can give me on the same course out as before."

"Aye, skipper," Young replied.

"Cap'n, you're not going to believe this," Zimenski came back. "Sierra twenty-nine and thirty are intact. They're turning toward us and making lots of noise. They've put the pedal to the metal. And they're reloading. Sounds like they're in a big hurry."

"Are there any other threats?" Dillon asked.

"Negative, Cap'n, just sierra twenty-nine and thirty."

"Marc, I want TMAs on sierra twenty-nine and thirty. Make tubes one through four ready in all respects, two torpedoes on each target. I'm going to fire one and three first."

"Aye, Captain." Jablonski repeated his orders and set to his task.

"Get us out of here, Chief," Dillon ordered.

Chief Young turned *Seawolf* to starboard, the long way back to their original course in order to avoid the debris from the destroyed Soho frigate. Her right shoulder dropped as she accelerated.

Dillon reached up and braced himself.

Winning this fight—and he felt that a win was now a foregone conclusion because the Chinese Han class submarines simply could not match the *Seawolf*'s speed of reload—gave him no satisfaction. A lot of good men, ordinary sailors and officers simply doing the jobs their bosses had ordered them to do, had lost their lives tonight.

More were going to die in the next few minutes.

It was a waste. Because of what? he asked himself. Arrogance? Stupidity? Or, simply a blind hatred of America's success as a nation and as a people?

Lo! Death has reared herself a throne
In a strange city lying alone
Far down within the dim West,
Where the good and the bad and the worst and the best
Have gone to their eternal rest.

It was Poe, the one poet who Dillon had introduced to his wife. Poe's mood was dark, just like Dillon's mood at this moment.

18

We missed," Peng Fei shouted.

Hua stepped around the corner to the sonar compartment. "What are you talking about?" he screamed.

The chief sonarman was frantically adjusting his controls. But the solid white line had shifted again to a course of one-two-five. There was no mistaking what it was.

"He's accelerating through twenty knots, captain," Peng Fei said. "He's sierra eighteen, the American submarine."

"They were solid hits. We all heard them."

"Yes, sir. Our torpedoes hit the remains of the North Korean vessels the *Seawolf* hit. The rest ran out of fuel."

"No damage?" Hua asked. "Nothing?" He was scarcely able to believe that eighteen torpedoes had missed their mark. He and 403 were supposed to be heading into the bay to administer the insurance shots on the wreckage of the American warship.

But it was true. He could read the display on the sonar screen.

He stepped back into the control room, his eyes going to the six red indicator lights on the weapons console. He called the torpedo room.

"This is the captain. How are my reloads coming?"

"Five minutes," Lieutenant Linshong shouted. "But tube four is out of commission. The bastard seal is damaged."

Hua replaced the growler phone. "Five minutes," he told his crew.

"Perhaps we should turn around and head for the surface," his executive officer Tsu-Lin suggested. "He won't fire at our back."

Hua shook his head. "If we die it will not be like cowards. Think of our families if we returned home in disgrace."

"Think of our families if we *don't* return home," Tsu-Lin said.

19

I have solutions on sierra twenty-nine and thirty," Jablonski said.

"Make tubes one and three ready in all respects," Dillon ordered.

"Captain, those tubes are ready in all respects," Bateman responded immediately.

"Firing point procedures, then match bearings and shoot."

"Aye, Captain," Bateman said.

Twelve seconds later both torpedoes were ejected into the water, their motors kicked off, and they accelerated away from *Seawolf* like scalded wildcats.

"Tubes one and three are fired. The weapons are running hot and normal," Bateman reported.

Dillon called the sonar room. "What are the Chinese doing?"

"Still trying to reload, Cap'n," Zimenski said. "But it sounds like they might be having trouble with one of their tubes. It's not been flooded. Same speed and bearing as before. Range is three thousand yards and closing fast."

"Time to impact?"

"Eighty-five seconds."

"How deep are they, Ski?" Dillon asked.

"One hundred forty feet."

"Let me know if they turn away," Dillon said. He turned back to his COB. "Bring us back to periscope depth."

"Aye, skipper, rising to periscope depth," Young replied crisply. Everyone was hyper-charged.

The Chinese submarine captains only had a couple of choices now. They could turn tail and make for the surface, in which case Dillon would abort his two torpedoes. Or they could deploy noisemakers and take evasive action in order to confuse the incoming weapons, giving themselves time to launch their own counterattack.

The latter action would be suicide. The Chinese SET-65Es were no match for the Mark 48s, nor were the Chinese countermeasures.

"Ski?" Dillon prompted.

"Same bearing. The rate of closure is increasing now," Zimenski said. "Neither target has deployed noisemakers, nor has either target changed course. Cap'n, they're heading right at us."

"Are they rising to match our depth?"

"Negative. They'll pass under us, or whatever's left of them will," Zimenski said. "Time to impact nine seconds."

Dillon reached up and grabbed a handhold. This would be close. The stupid bastards, he thought. They might not have tactics, but he couldn't fault their courage.

Both torpedoes hit solidly. Because of the proximity to the targets, *Seawolf* was hammered by the shockwaves.

They passed over the fatally damaged Han 405, *Seawolf* buffeted in the roiled water. The Chinese submarine's compartments were flooding, machinery was crashing all over the place, and secondary explosions popped off here and there through the flooded sections of the hull.

Sierra twenty-nine was one thousand yards to port, and had suffered the same fate. Her hull was scattering in pieces on the bottom of the bay.

There would be no survivors, Dillon thought. It was a waste that the politicians in Washington and Beijing would have to somehow work out. Whatever the North Koreans had to say would be mostly ignored. But the Chinese were a most-favored-nation trading partner. They were an economic giant that would not be ignored.

He called sonar. "How's it look, Ski?"

"We're clear, Cap'n."

Dillon put the phone back. His crew were watching him. Waiting for his next order. He managed a faint smile. "Good job, gentlemen."

"Thank you, sir," Bateman said. "Where now, skipper?"

There really wasn't any other choice. He glanced at Alvarez and Brown at the chart table. At *Seawolf*'s next refit the chart tables would be removed. The navy was finally doing away with everything except electronic charts. Too bad, he thought.

"Mr. Alvarez, shape us a best possible course back to Kandrach. We have a job to finish."

"All right," Bateman said.

20

The CQ came to Captain Amin's open door in the bachelor officers quarters and knocked on the frame.

He was respectful tonight. After the attack a couple of weeks ago everyone in the ranger camp was being extra careful. No one wanted the blame for being so unprepared.

Amin sat at his desk in front of the window. He glanced up at the CQ's reflection in the dark glass. "Yes?" he asked softly.

"It's General Asif for you, sir. He is on the telephone from Chaklala in the adjutant's office."

Amin shivered inside his chest, but he forced a look of mild indifference on his features. "Very well," he said. He put down the pen he'd been using to write a letter to his mistress, straightened his jacket, and followed the CQ across the parade ground to the administration building.

The guards in front snapped crisply to attention. Amin saw with satisfaction that the entire course of the electrified fence around the camp was well lit, as were the guard towers. The SAM radar dish was turning, and the damage that the American attack force had caused had been repaired.

This time they were prepared for anything that the Americans might throw at them.

Amin returned the salutes, and inside the CQ left him in the adjutant's office.

"Good evening, General Asif," Amin said into the phone. He did not sit down. "Do you have some instructions for me?"

"Yes, I do, Captain. I want you to listen very carefully, because there must be no misunderstandings, no mistakes. Am I clear to this point?"

"Yes, sir. Very clear."

"The four men you are holding as prisoners have more value to us than we first realized. The American attack showed us this."

"Yes, sir." Amin had a sick feeling that he knew what was coming next. He had developed a hatred for the Americans in the cells. They were defiant, Godless bastards. Scum. Dogshit underfoot.

"They are to be cleaned up, their wounds tended to, and given proper food and clothing. A doctor will arrive tomorrow to help you with this task."

"We should move them to another . . ."

"There will not be another attack," Asif shot back. "You are to do as you're told. Do you understand?"

"Yes, sir," Amin replied, though he did not understand. But someone else would have to do the job. He would not personally touch them, or even oversee their rehabilitation.

"When they are fit enough to move under their own power, they are to be allowed outside in the fresh air where they can exercise."

"Yes, sir, I understand," Amin said. But another thought struck him. "What about the woman?"

"Do what you want with her. I don't care. Officially she's missing at sea. Nobody knows that she is there, nor will she ever leave alive. My recommendation is that she be disposed of immediately. But I will leave that up to you, Captain."

"Yes, sir. I will attend to everything, General," Amin said. "How soon must they be ready?"

"Very soon," General Asif said. "Within the week."

"It will be as you have ordered, sir."

After the call Amin remained in the adjutant's office for a long time thinking about his orders. He wanted revenge for the trouble the prisoners had given him, and for the attack on this camp. They were blemishes on his record.

And he would get his revenge. He smiled. There were many gates to paradise for the man whose eyes were truly open.

21

Dillon stood at the hatch to the goat locker, chief's territory, where Jackson and his SEALs were bunking. It was getting late and he was tired. But first he wanted to see about his people.

The pharmacist's mate, PO Jack McGovern, had just finished giving Jackson a tetanus injection. "Good shooting, skipper," he said on the way out.

"How's your patient?"

"He'll be walking with a limp for a couple of weeks. But he'll be okay, sir," McGovern shrugged. "They're pretty tough."

"I wouldn't want to arm wrestle one of them," Dillon said.

"No, sir," McGovern agreed, and Dillon stepped aside to let him pass.

Terri Vaughan stood in the passageway just outside Jackson's compartment. A few of the bunks were occupied and the lights were low, so they kept their voices down. Aboard a submarine there was almost always someone sleeping.

"How's the lieutenant?" Dillon asked, coming down the passageway.

"Good evening, Captain," Vaughan said. "Aside from the fact that he's his ornery self, he's just fine."

Dillon looked around the corner into the compartment that three engineering chiefs had vacated for the three male SEALs. Terri slept in a bunk rigged for her in a corner of the sonar equipment room where she could have a little privacy. Jackson was perched on the edge of his cot. He was alone.

"How are you doing?" Dillon asked.

Jackson smiled tiredly. It had been a long day. "I guess I'll live, skipper. I understand that you bagged some bad guys."

"A couple. It sounded like you did a number on the Kilo."

"She won't sail again. And I think it'll probably be quite a while before they clean up their dry dock."

Dillon had already read Jackson's brief preliminary report. And he had looked in on their Russian prisoner who had been put in a dry stores locker for safekeeping. The Russian refused to answer any of their questions, or even give his name, rank, and serial number. It didn't matter. They got that much from the papers he carried. That and the submarine commander's Koran proved that the North Koreans had help from a lot of sources. All of it designed to aid Pakistan.

Once they had cleared North Korean waters, he had raised a communications mast and sent a brief message via SSIX to Pearl. He would follow up with a more lengthy patrol and mission report in the morning after he got some sleep.

"We're heading back to Kandrach unless my boss tells me otherwise," Dillon said.

Jackson's tired smile broadened. "I was going to ask you about that, skipper." He glanced at Vaughan. "None of us liked the way it worked out the first time." His expression darkened. "I just hope the brass understands what went wrong."

"Because of the spy?"

Jackson nodded.

"They do now," Dillon said. "If it's going to be a problem, we'll scrub the mission."

Jackson thought about that for a moment. "It probably got pretty bad for them after we left."

"That's why we're going back," Dillon said. "So you have a little time to get strong."

"I'll make sure he takes his vitamins and does his rehab exercises, Captain," Vaughan said with a vicious grin. "We've both got practically the same wound."

"Where are MacKecver and Ercoli?"

"In the crew's mess. They get the munchies after every mission," Jackson said.

Dillon was about to leave, but he turned back. "Does it hurt?" he asked.

Jackson rubbed his leg. "A little."

"No, I mean getting shot."

Jackson shook his head. "Not at all. It just makes you feel stupid that you didn't duck when you should have."

22

0300 LOCAL
KANDRACH ISI PRISON

Amin stopped at the door to the woman's cell.

There'd been a lot of activity here so far tonight. The prisoners and their cells had been hosed down. Portable toilets and water supplies had been brought in, along with cots and blankets. The prisoners had been given freshly laundered clothing and had been fed rice with lamb and vegetables, as well as plenty of hot tea.

Already the cell bay smelled a lot better than it had. For at least that much Amin was grateful.

A guard came to unlock the cell door, a knowing smirk on his face. Ordinarily Amin would have called the stupid bastard on such an attitude, but he didn't feel like it tonight.

"No matter what you hear, don't come in," he told the guard.

"Sir?" the man asked, not sure he'd heard correctly.

"It may get a little noisy tonight, you know. Just ignore it. I'll let you know when to let me out." Amin forced himself to smile. "You understand, don't you?"

The slovenly guard returned the grin, and nodded. "Of course, captain. Whatever you say, sir."

A small wattage lightbulb had been put into the fixture embedded in the concrete ceiling. The cell was only dimly illuminated.

Amin's heart skipped a beat when the lock snapped home behind him. He put out a hand as if to ward off an attack, but then he chuckled to himself. He was being foolish.

The woman, her back to him, lay huddled on the cot. The blanket was pulled up around her shoulders. She had a lot of dark frizzy hair that spilled over her pillow. She was a small woman, with tiny, delicate features.

She could have been an Iranian, Amin thought. Iranian women

were dark, delicate, and very beautiful. A lot like his mistress in Chaklala.

But this was a different situation for him. Here and now he had the power of life or death over this woman. He could do anything . . . anything at all to her and it would be perfectly legal. Anything that he could imagine.

And, Amin decided, he could imagine a lot of interesting things.

He started across the room, unbuttoning his jacket. At the cot he gently pulled the blanket away from her shoulders. She wore what looked like a man's work shirt, which was a little disappointing. He'd imagined pulling the blanket back and finding that she was naked.

He eased her over onto her back. Her eyes remained closed and she didn't resist, even when he pulled her shirt apart, ripping the buttons.

Her breasts were small, but fantastic. Amin's breath caught in his throat as he caressed first one nipple and then the other.

Her skin was bruised, but it didn't matter to him. This was going to be very good.

He started to pull the blanket farther down, when Marcella's eyes came slowly open. She smiled at him, then reached up to draw him down to her.

She *wanted* him to kiss her breasts. It was better than fantastic. Maybe he would keep her around much longer than just tonight.

He got down on one knee and her hand came to the back of his head to guide his lips to her breasts.

She suddenly grabbed a handful of his hair and pulled his head back. Her left hand came up, and something very hard and jagged slashed across his exposed neck.

It hurt more than anything he could imagine. He cried out and reared back, but she followed him up, slashing at his throat with whatever jagged thing she held in her hand.

Blood sprayed all over her bare breasts as he continued to fall backwards. It was his blood, he realized with a growing horror. He squealed like a pig and tried to push her away. But she was incredibly strong. She kept slashing at his throat, making it impossible to fight back or even to catch his breath.

The back of his head hit the concrete floor with a dull smack. He could do nothing now but cough and gasp for air. He was drowning, and still the woman slashed and hacked at his neck with what looked like a jagged piece of rock, or maybe a piece of concrete block.

He looked up at her in amazement as the lights began to grow dim. Her face was totally devoid of any emotion, and she made no sound.

Help, Amin screamed in his head. But he could not make his lips work, and the lights continued to darken.

23

LOCAL DAWN THE NEXT DAY
SEAWOLF

Seawolf ran at periscope depth, connected by an electronic umbilical cord via downlink to a Milstar satellite in geosynchronous orbit 22,300 miles above earth. Somewhere over the horizon to the east was the jumble of islands off the southern tip of the Korean peninsula.

Shipping traffic was heavy, but no warships were looking for *Seawolf*. She was like a well-fed predator moving silently amidst the sheep. No one knew that she was here, not even Pacific Fleet headquarters in Pearl Harbor with whom she was communicating.

Dillon sat alone sipping his coffee in the officers' wardroom as he waited for Pearl's response. He'd sent his lengthy mission message four hours ago, and then had ducked back deep, beneath the local thermocline to wait.

A half hour ago they'd received the one-letter ELF message advising them to surface to receive instructions.

A four-hour turnaround time was like the speed of light for Pearl. Especially in a case like this in which the international political ramifications were so great.

Seawolf's mission report and request had probably been bounced all the way to the White House. Hopefully they had taken his warning to keep the need-to-know list to the absolute minimum seriously.

Bateman appeared in the doorway, a message flimsy in his hand. His expression was unreadable, except that he seemed like a big golden lab about ready to leap into the water to retrieve a downed duck.

"We're going to Kandrach, officially. Unrestricted ops," Bateman said. He handed the message across the table. "They went out on a limb, but it was because Admiral Puckett trusts you."

Dillon had to smile thinking about Vince Howe. Bateman laughed, reading Dillon's mind.

"Yeah, it would frost Vince's ass if you could tell him about it."

Z012106Z AUG
TOP SECRET
FM: SOMSUBPAC
TO: USS SEAWOLF

A. USS SEAWOLF Z011717ZAUG

B. JOINT CHIEFS ADVISORY 0108A

1. BEIJING REPORTS ACCIDENT WITH FOUR OF ITS NUCLEAR SUB-MARINES IN YELLOW SEA. ALREADY INCIDENT IS BEING CALLED GREAT-EST SEA DISASTER IN CHINESE HISTORY.

2. PYONGYANG IS SCREAMING INVASION. KH11 PASS SHOWED EXTEN-SIVE DAMAGE TO DRY DOCK, YELLOW SEA FLT HQ, AND INTEL HQ AT NAMPO NAVY BASE. YOUR ASSESSMENT CORRECT. BECAUSE OF THE TIME OF NIGHT CASUALTIES WERE MINIMAL.

C. JOINT CHIEFS ADVISORY 0108B

1. PAKISTAN HAS ADMITTED THEY HAVE FOUR U.S. DETAINEES. THEY ARE OFFERING TO HAND THEM OVER FOR U.S. TAKING A NEUTRAL STANCE ON PAKISTAN'S NUCLEAR DEVELOPMENTS.

2. YOUR REQUEST REF A IS GRANTED. UNRESTRICTED OPS IS AUTHORIZED.

3. CVN CARL VINSON WILL STANDBY AT AREA BRAVO 378 TANGO 555 TO RENDER ASSISTANCE.

4. REPORT AS NECESSARY.

GOOD HUNTINGXXX ADM PUCKETT SENDS

EOM

Dillon looked up from his reading. "I think maybe one of these days Vince might see the light. Maybe he'll pick up a rumor or two."

Bateman shook his head in innocence. He was going next to PCO school, which was one of the navy's biggest gossip and rumor mills. "I can't imagine who'd do something like that."

"Steak tonight, Charlie. And the chocolate ice cream somebody brought aboard without telling me."

24

FOUR DAYS LATER
KANDRACH ISI PRISON

Three Alouette assault helicopters with Pakistani ranger markings touched down in the prison parade ground just before sunset.

Even before the rotors ground to a halt, a Russian jeep and a pair of troop transport trucks made their way across the camp and pulled up.

A young ranger lieutenant jumped out of the jeep and waited as Maj. Khalid Zafar dismounted from the lead helicopter.

The lieutenant saluted. "Welcome to Kandrach, major. I'm Lieutenant Ali Hamid."

Zafar glanced at the jeep and trucks. "Are you going somewhere?"

"Yes, sir. I have orders to withdraw the moment you arrive."

"I see." Coming in, Zafar had seen that the SAM targeting radar antenna was not rotating. Nor had he and his squadron been challenged. "Have you left the cooks and maintenance people? Or are we expected to guard the prisoners, defend the camp, *and* wash our own dishes?"

Hamid managed a weak smile. "No, sir. The usual camp support staff will remain. Your specific orders from Chaklala are in the camp commandant's office."

"Is he, whoever he is, here?"

"No, sir. That is to be your position."

"Very well, Lieutenant, have a good trip," Zafar said dismissing him. He sketched a salute then turned to his men who had dismounted from the helicopters. "I want the perimeter secured at once. I want the SAM equipment up and running within fifteen minutes. I want the prisoners checked. And find the mess sergeant. I'm hungry, and I expect that you are hungry as well."

Zafar headed over to what he assumed was the administration building as Lieutenant Hamid and his people left the camp, and Zafar's rangers secured the gates.

His orders from General Asif, director of the ISI, were contained on one page sealed in an envelope lying on the commandant's desk.

Zafar and his rangers were to secure the camp, make sure that the American prisoners were well fed, that their medical needs were met, and that they be prepared at some date in the very near future to participate in a prisoner handover.

Under no circumstance, the general wrote, was Major Zafar to expect a second attack from U.S. forces, nor was he to maintain an openly defensive posture.

Zafar's number two, Lt. Abdul Shabud, came in a half hour later to report that the SAM installation was up and running.

Zafar handed him the orders. "What do you think, Abdul? We're to defend this camp without looking like we're defending it."

Shabud looked up. "Should we shut down the missile launcher?"

"No, leave it up and running. We will defend this camp with what we have." Zafar shook his head. No good would come of this. But, orders were orders. "Let's go meet our prisoners again."

"We have a problem, sir," Shabud said. "In fact we have at least two very big problems."

"Tell me," Zafar said, steeling himself.

"One of the prisoners we brought down from the mountains is dead. Sergeant Dahani thinks he's been dead for at least two days. His body was placed in a bag, but it's still on his bunk." Syed Dahani was their medic.

"Which one was he?"

"The one named Bruce Hauglar."

Zafar remembered all their names. He'd thought that they'd fought bravely up there, especially considering their injuries. "He's the man with all the burns."

"Yes, sir."

"What is our second problem?"

"There is a fifth American prisoner. A woman."

"Where did she come from?" Zafar asked. He was sick at his stomach thinking how she must have been treated here. Some ISI troops were little more than animals.

"She says that she was the captain of a civilian research ship that was torpedoed by a submarine in the Bay of Bengal. She was the only survivor. They brought her here."

"Incredible," Zafar said.

"There's more, Major." Shabud said. "The reason we were sent down here. We got it from one of the guys manning the comms truck. The woman evidently killed the captain who was in charge of the prisoners. He was trying to rape her and she cut his throat open with a piece of concrete that she chipped from her wall."

Zafar thought that he was beyond surprise now. "Who was this unfortunate captain who couldn't keep his trousers buttoned?"

"It was Captain Amin," Shabud said.

"*Our* Captain Amin, from the depot?"

Shabud nodded. "One and the same."

"Well," Zafar said. He sat down. "Well now, how about that." He looked up and managed a very slight smile. "Just between us, Abdul, I think that there is some justice in the world after all."

Shabud nodded. It was obvious that he agreed, but he didn't want to voice his opinion out loud. "What do we do now, Major?"

"Secure the camp, guard the prisoners, and have something to eat," Zafar said. "What else is there for us to do?"

"I meant about the SAM radar, sir?"

Zafar thought about it for a moment, then nodded. "I think that General Asif is correct after all. Shut it down, Abdul."

25

CVN70 *Carl Vinson*, her battle group arrayed around her, cruised one hundred miles off the coast of Pakistan. There had been no reconn flights to test her defensive perimeter, nor any radio challenges from the Pakistani navy.

The massive carrier was turned into the wind for air operations. Her flight deck was alight, and busy with activity.

Bill Jackson, in full night-operations battle gear, hesitated at the boarding hatch of the lead AH-1W Super Cobra marine ground attack helicopter, and looked up toward the bridge. He couldn't make out anyone because of the glare, but he straightened up and saluted anyway.

He clambered aboard and strapped in beside Terri Vaughan. She gave him the thumbs-up as did Ercoli and MacKeever. The four marines with them nodded respectfully.

The gunner said something into his helmet mike, and moments later the helicopter lifted off the deck, pointed its nose sharply down and to the left, and headed toward Pakistan's coast like an angry wasp. Three other Super Cobras, each carrying eight marines, lifted off and slid into formation beside the squadron leader.

Somewhere to the north, within a mile or two of Kandrach, *Seawolf* waited at periscope depth as a safety net in case something went wrong.

"It's the least I can do since we've come this far," Dillon told Jackson two days ago.

"I'm glad that you won't miss out on all the fun, sir," Jackson said, shaking his hand.

He and his team plus the Russian prisoner had transferred over to the *Vinson* on Washington's orders. *Seawolf* had done more than her share. The *Vinson*'s marines, plus Jackson's SEAL team, would mount the rescue operation using assault helicopters with F/A-18 Hornet fighter cover it necessary.

Jackson smiled, and his people returned the smile, knowing exactly what he was thinking. It was finally payback time.

"Conn, radio room. Skipper, the choppers are feet dry."

"Any reaction from the opposition?" Dillon asked.

"Nothing yet. The *Vinson* says their guys are being illuminated by a lot of radars, but no threats."

"Stay with it."

"Yes, sir."

Dillon looked through the search periscope again. He did a three-sixty sweep, the third in as many minutes, but there wasn't another surface ship in sight on sonar in any direction.

Picking out the low-moving helicopters would be impossible, so he didn't bother to try. They ran without lights and even the flash of their exhaust was suppressed.

Somebody at the prison was in for a very nasty surprise within the next few minutes.

"Battle stations, missile," Dillon told his XO. "Just in case."

"Aye, Captain. Battle stations, missile, just in case," Bateman responded.

26

The prison seemed deserted, although it was lit up like day.

Jackson's helicopter suddenly banked very hard to the left and the gunner opened fire on one of the guard towers. From his vantage point near the open hatch, Jackson could see 20mm Gatling gunfire from the other three choppers concentrated first on the four guard towers, next on three Alouette helicopters parked on the parade ground, and then on the Venus's-flytrap gate into the prison lockup, a truck sporting a dish antenna and a lot of VHF whips, and finally the SAM installation.

There was some sporadic incoming fire that died down when the first Alouette ignited in a huge ball of flame.

Several other explosions extinguished the camp's lights, the night illuminated now only by the fierce fires burning all over the place.

The four Super Cobras touched down hard in front of the prison lockup, and disgorged their twenty-eight Marines plus Jackson and his SEAL team.

Twenty marines set up a defensive perimeter while Jackson, his three people, and four marines scrambled over the blasted remains of the lockup gate.

Ercoli went first, and within fifteen seconds had attached a small charge of plastique with a quick fire acid fuse to the steel door.

He backed off ten feet, turning his head just as it went off with a dull bang, and the steel door fell off its hinges.

Jackson all of a sudden had the same premonition he'd had the first time they were here. It was Murphy's Law of combat: If your attack is going well, you've walked into an ambush.

He called out to the two marines who were already at the doorway, when they went down under a lot of gunfire from inside the cell bay.

Jackson and Ercoli reached them first and pulled them out of the line of fire. One of the marines had taken a round in the face, and he was dead. The other one had taken a couple of rounds in the middle of his Kevlar vest. He would be bruised but he was coming around already.

More gunfire erupted from all over the camp, concentrating on the marines defending their perimeter.

"F/X, this is Lancer," the marine team leader's voice came over Jackson's helmet comms unit. "We can't hold on for long. Hustle it up."

"Will do," Jackson radioed back.

He and Ercoli tossed flash-bang grenades through the open door. Seconds later they went off with big magnesium flashes and very loud explosions.

On the count of two, they rolled through the door into a long, narrow corridor, spraying MP-5 fire left to right. Bullets ricocheted all over the place.

They sprinted down the corridor as MacKeever and Vaughan came right behind them.

Jackson pulled up short and signaled for the cease-fire. There were four Pakistani rangers down. Two dead for sure, one breathing through a chest wound, which according to SEAL lore was nature's way of telling you to slow down, and the fourth sitting on the floor propped up against the wall in a pool of blood. He wore major's pips on his shoulder boards, and he was trying to raise his pistol. He had a wound in his face and at least one in his gut.

"The prisoners," Jackson motioned for his people and the marines to find them, as he approached the downed officer.

Major Zafar wanted to bring his pistol up and fire at least one round into the bastard American, but he had trouble controlling his arm. He couldn't see very well either. But his mind was still alert. He knew that he had lost, and he knew that part of the reason was because his own ISI had gotten in over its head with the Americans and would not support him here. This had been a suicide mission, and they'd known it all along.

"It's all over, Major," Jackson said. "I don't know if you can understand me, but we just want to get our people and then we'll leave."

"Bastard," Zafar mumbled. With a supreme last effort he raised his pistol at the American and began to squeeze the trigger when a thunderclap exploded in his head.

* * *

"F/X, WE'VE got one of the good guys in a body bag in here," Ercoli reported from one of the cell doors.

"Bring him, we're leaving no one behind," Jackson said.

Ercoli and one of the marines brought the body bag out while Terri, Shooter, and the other marine helped the three CIA agents and a woman out of their cells. She came as a complete surprise.

"Who's that?" Jackson demanded.

"She's an American," one of the prisoners said. "She's coming with us."

"Right," Jackson said. They looked gaunt and beat up, but seemed able to move okay.

"Lancer, F/X, we're on our way out," Jackson radioed. "One of your guys is down, and another hurt by the front door. We need help right now getting them back to the choppers."

"We're on it," the marine team leader responded. "Shake a leg."

"Time to go home," Jackson told his people.

The gunfire had all but stopped. Four marines hustled through the ruined gate. One of them slung the dead marine over his shoulder and headed immediately back to the helicopters. The other marines helped with Hauglar's body and the rest of the prisoners.

In minutes they were all back aboard the Super Cobras, and lifting off. They turned south, directly toward the sea and the *Vinson* battle group waiting offshore with enough firepower to start and finish a war with just about any nation on earth—Pakistan included.

NOON LOCAL
OMAHA, NEBRASKA

L adies and gentlemen, the president of the United States," Nebraska state VFW Commander Paul Olsen announced. He stepped away from the podium as the audience filling the auditorium at the VA hospital got to their feet and applauded.

The VFW's annual meeting and dinner was scheduled for this evening at eight. But the president had to be back in Washington. The final push for votes on the extension of the ABM treaty was coming up in the Senate. He couldn't miss it. The VFW had met him halfway by hastily organizing this lunch for him. Hanson was a very popular president, especially among veterans.

Brad Stein had been on his cellphone for the past fifteen minutes at the side of the stage. As Hanson walked to the podium and shook Olsen's hand, Stein handed the president a note.

Without missing a beat, Hanson glanced at the note, and then stepped to the microphone. When the applause died down he gave the audience of four hundred the famous Hanson smile.

"I'm truly sorry that I won't be able to stay for the banquet tonight. I understand that you'll be served chicken à la king. It's one of my personal favorites, and I'm sure yours."

The audience howled with laughter. In fact, they would be served corn-fed Nebraska filet mignons.

When the audience was quiet again, Hanson allowed his smile to fade. "Several weeks ago the government of Pakistan conducted an aboveground test of what we evaluated as a thermonuclear device in the three-megaton range. A city buster. This act flew directly in the face of every nuclear nonproliferation and test ban treaty in effect around the world. Treaties that the government of Pakistan signed."

A sober mood came over the audience. The president was telling them old news. But something big was coming. They could feel it.

"Under my orders, a team of four specialists were sent to Pakistan to monitor the test. They were arrested and taken to a secret prison where they were starved, beaten, and tortured almost continually around the clock for all this time.

"For national security reasons I cannot tell you how we found out where they were being held. But we did."

Hanson let his eyes sweep the audience. It was another of his old campaign tricks. He could make it seem that he was looking directly at each individual.

"I directed our armed forces to mount a rescue operation. Just one hour ago, units of the navy's Seventh Fleet conducted that operation with only minimal casualties."

Hanson smiled and nodded confidently. "I just received word that the rescue mission was a complete success."

The applause this time was thunderous. Most of the men here had been on the battlefield. Some of them had been POWs in Vietnam and North Korea.

"I want no one hearing my voice today to make the mistake of believing that the United States will tolerate any threat—and I emphasize *any* threat—to the security of this great nation or to its citizens whether they be civilians or in uniform."

The applause was huge. The television and radio networks scrambled to break into their regularly scheduled programs to broadcast the bulletin.

Hanson caught Brad Stein's eye across the room and he nodded. The fat was in the fire now because the United States had attacked Pakistan, which only last year had helped round up the Al Qaeda terrorists. Most of the world press was ignoring North Korea, and China continued its silence about the incident in the Yellow Sea.

But the real brouhaha wouldn't start until the media found out that among the prisoners rescued from Pakistan was the president's brother.

Hanson let the applause wash over him like a soothing salve. There was an ancient Chinese curse that came to his mind: May you live in interesting times.

Well, the president thought. They certainly were living in interesting times.

ENDINGS

ow about a beer, Mr. Hanson?" Frank Dillon said as the president's brother came over with the woman the navy had rescued. They'd accepted Dillon's invitation to the *Seawolf*'s post cruise blowout.

"The name's Scott, if you don't mind, Captain. I've had my fill of the 'Mr. Hanson' bit. And a beer would do just fine, thank you."

On these picnics the officers wore striped aprons and stupid hats, and did all the cooking and serving not only for the enlisted crew but for all the wives, sweethearts, parents, and kids of anyone connected with the boat.

Dillon, wearing a German jaeger hat with brush, manned the beer and wine table along with his XO Charlie Bateman.

"I'll have a white wine, please," Marcella Wallner said.

Dillon poured her wine first, and then Hanson's beer. "You came as something of a surprise to Lieutenant Jackson."

She smiled and glanced at Hanson. "I've had a habit of doing that most of my life. I was born a tomboy. The only girl on the block who liked pulling the legs off spiders."

"She came as a surprise to me too," Hanson said.

There were more than three hundred people here. They had taken over the park on the island's west coast. They were only twenty miles from Pearl Harbor, yet they could have been on a jungle planet, or in another age in history. The scenery was lush.

A boy of about ten came rushing up to them. "Dad, Dad, you oughta see the waves. They're humongous."

"My son, Logan," Hanson said. "Everything is humongous to him lately."

An attractive, plainly built woman followed with a wispy long-haired blond girl of about thirteen.

"Captain, I'd like you to meet my wife, Gina, and our daughter, Ashley," Hanson said.

"No rank here. The name is Frank," Dillon said. "I'm pleased to meet you, Gina. Ashley. My wife, Jill, is around here somewhere."

"We've already met, and she introduced me to some of the other wives as well," Gina Hanson said. Her smile was radiant. "I wanted to thank you for taking part in rescuing my husband and his team." She glanced at Marcella. "And Marcie."

"It's part of my job."

Gina Hanson nodded. "I know. But I just wanted you to know how grateful we are." She held his eye for a moment.

Dillon nodded. "May I give you a glass of wine?"

"Red, please," Gina said. "Children, go play." They took off like they were shot out of a cannon. "Scott, take your beer and mingle." She accepted her glass of wine. "Thank you, Frank." She turned to Marcella. "Now, Marcie, let's you and I have a chat, and then we'll introduce ourselves around."

They headed down the broad path to the beach, leaving Dillon and Bateman alone for a moment.

"So, congratulations are in order," Dillon said.

Bateman grinned. "I found out this morning, when did you hear about it?"

"Five days ago when they took my boat away from me."

"Being SUBRON CO isn't a shabby exchange, Frank," Bateman said. SUBRON was a submarine squadron. It was the next big step up the chain of command from being the boss of a boat. Bateman had been relieved of duty aboard the *Seawolf* and ordered to the prospective commanding officer's course at New London.

Dillon nodded, but his heart would always be aboard a submarine at sea. "With any luck you'll be assigned back here."

"I don't want a shore job."

"Not at first, Charlie. And that's a promise," Dillon said. "You're going to make one hell of a submarine captain."

Dillon's wife, Jill, came over, and Bateman excused himself to pour more beer. She was lean from her bout with cancer, which at this point was in remission. Her face was round, her eyes green and her blond hair short. She looked like everybody's idea of a Junior Leaguer, or the subservient navy wife. She was anything but. She gave her husband a peck on the cheek.

She nodded over her shoulder at the unruly softball game in progress. The crew was blowing off a lot of steam, Jackson and his SEALs with them. "Tough patrol?"

"Fair to middlin'," Dillon admitted.

"I talked to Suzanne. She said she knew about Art's mistress almost from the beginning. Did he talk to you?"

"Not until this time out. Said she had cancer and didn't know what to do."

"Pleasant woman," Jill said. "Suzanne came to the hospital every day to be with her until the end."

Dillon opened his mouth and started to say something, but Jill stopped him.

"Don't try to understand women, Frank. You can't. Suzanne accepted three things about her husband. His first mistress was the sea. His second mistress was Beth Anne. And his third love was his wife."

"Thou wast all that to me, love, for which my soul did pine," Dillon said. *"A green isle in the sea, love. A fountain and a shrine. All wreathed with fairy fruits and flowers. And all the flowers were mine."*

It was Poe. "To One In Paradise."

Jill smiled warmly. "You're learning, darling. You really are." She turned and looked toward the beach path. "Did I see Gina Hanson and Ms. Wallner heading that way?"

"Yes," Dillon said, and his wife smiled at him again and headed to the beach. She stopped and looked back. "It'll be good to have you home on a regular basis, you know."

Dillon nodded, though he wasn't all that certain his career would turn out exactly like that so soon.

SENATE HEARING CHAMBER
WASHINGTON

Adm. Joseph Puckett Jr.'s diminutive figure seemed lost behind the large oak table facing the six senators on the raised arch. The hearing was in camera so the media were not allowed. The senators had brought some of their aides and several attorneys. Puckett had come alone from the Pentagon with only his briefcase, which was open on the chair beside him.

Chief among Puckett's detractors was Senator Thomas Lerner, the ranking Democrat from Minnesota, who thought that the navy was first among the services for wasting money. He glared down at the admiral.

"That sub driver of yours damned near started World War III," Lerner said as an aside, and then he leaned over to say something to Senator Walter Wasserman on his left.

"He accomplished his mission," Puckett responded.

Lerner hadn't expected an answer, and he looked at the admiral in surprise.

"Our *Jupiter* satellite is back in service, which means that Pakistan and India can no longer hide their actions from us. With the destruction of the Kilo submarine and its Russian-built laser, North Korea will think twice about doing something like that again. And the Chinese have not brought up the destruction of their four submarines, which tells us that they knew they were in the wrong. They took a gamble and they lost. It is a gamble they will not take again soon."

Lerner and the other senators were looking at Puckett as if he were a bug under a microscope.

"I would say that if anything, Captain Dillon did a fine job of *preventing* World War III."

"Do you know how much his cowboy tactics cost the American taxpayer?" Lerner demanded angrily. He was a heavyset man with deep jowls and stern eyes.

Puckett took a bound report out of his briefcase and handed it to an aide to pass up to the senator.

"The cost analysis is there," Puckett said. "The dollar amount is quite high. In the tens of millions. I think actually two-hundred-eighty-seven million, and change."

"And change," Lerner said in amazement. "How do you justify that?" he demanded. "Can you tell us that much?" He looked at the others. "We'd at the very least like to get our money's worth."

Puckett took a second, much thicker, bound report out of his brief-case and handed it to the same aide who brought it to Lerner.

"The CATO Institute along with our own analysts and those from the State Department and the Central Intelligence Agency came up with another cost analysis."

"What's this now?"

"This second estimate is in the tens of *billions* of dollars. It's what we estimate the damage would have cost the American taxpayer if we had done nothing."

DULLES INTERNATIONAL AIRPORT

Two black Ford Explorer SUVs with government plates pulled up to the Air France entry at Dulles.

FBI Special Agents Edward Matthais and John Harwig got out of the lead SUV. A third agent handed Lt. Cmdr. Viktor Stalnov out to them. The Russian's hands were handcuffed in front of him, and he looked subdued. His future back in Moscow was bleak.

Special Agents Marnie Morgan and Brian Fuller helped the Pakistani ISI internal affairs investigator, Sardi Lenihar, out of the second SUV. She too was handcuffed, but unlike Stalnov she was imperious.

She was tall, dark, and beautiful. Ambassador Husain knew it when he'd taken her to his bed. And she was sure that everyone else around her knew it as well.

Also unlike Stalnov, who was returning to Moscow via Paris to face trial for treason, Lenihar was returning to Islamabad to a heroine's welcome.

A blow had been struck against Pakistan. But it was not a mortal blow. There was more work to be done, and she would be at the fore-front of the effort. She was too outstanding an intelligence asset to toss aside.

"Unlock my handcuffs," she demanded, holding her hands out.

Marnie laughed at her. "Yeah, right."

The woman turned to Fuller, but Marnie took her by the arm and led her across the sidewalk to the federal marshals waiting at the doors. They would escort the prisoners to Paris.

Back at the car, Fuller stopped Marnie. "How about a drink after we ditch the wheels?"

"Yeah, right," Marnie said. But then she bit her lip. "Okay," she said. "But only if we have dinner afterwards."

Fuller winked at her. "I knew that even the ice maiden couldn't resist my charms forever."

She took a swipe at him. "Ice maiden?" she demanded.

NORTHWEST TERRITORIES
CANADA

The black sail of an unidentified nuclear submarine broke through the pack ice of Lancaster Sound between Baffin Island to the south and the exceedingly bleak Devon Island, home of the north magnetic pole, to the north.

This was at nearly 75° north latitude. The only living souls were the few dozen people in the town of Resolute on Cornwallis Island one hundred and fifty miles to the west.

Under a leaden sky, a team of six men clad in white arctic gear clambered up on deck of the submarine and wrestled several heavy cases onto the ice pack.

They were sweating from exertion when they were finished setting up their equipment two hours later.

One of the men aimed a small dish antenna toward the south as a second took off his heavy gloves and, working bare-handed in the sub-zero cold, entered a series of commands on the laptop computer.

When the proper display came up on the screen he nodded to the one at the dish antenna who stepped aside, and hit *enter*.

All of them instinctively looked toward the south. Some of them shuddered. But it wasn't because of the cold. It was because they knew that nothing in the world would ever be the same again. Not after what they had just done.